David de Wolf

Ephraim's Bones

– A Novel –

Mazo Publishers

It is not incumbent upon you to finish the task, but neither are you free to absolve yourself from it.

(Avot 3, 21)

•••

Ephraim's Bones

ISBN 978-1-956381-238
Copyright © 2022 by David de Wolf
Email: wolf.david.de@gmail.com

Published by
Mazo Publishers
Website: www.mazopublishers.com
Email: info@mazopublishers.com

The front cover artwork is adapted from an original lithograph by David Roberts: *Jaffa, Looking North* (1839), Cleveland Museum of Art.

CONTENTS

Part 3

INCARCERATION

The nauseous sensation urged him to open his eyes, but he managed to postpone the inevitable. It came from the utmost depths. As rusty screws thrusting into a flaccid mass. A distorted premonition of misery and devastation. The agitation grew into an overwhelming distress that took possession of his brain and seemed to burst inside his skull. The desire for light fought with his need to shut himself off from certain doom.

He became aware of a dead smell. A stench that was familiar, as if he had not smelled anything else for days, but now it was stronger. Unbearably penetrating. Still, fetid water. Overpowering vapors of rotting algae and spoiled fish.

Hollow sounds. Echoes of hell. The grunting of locks, the abrasive noise of iron bars as they crashed into place. Gulls screaming, or was it people? Dull thumps, as if someone were slamming his fists against the wall.

With aversion he finally opened his eyes. He stared at a weathered, solid wooden door with its closed hatch and rusted bars. Two large iron hooks beaten into the wood indicated the location of the bolts. He slowly turned his head. Doing so caused a stabbing pain.

Large, hewn blocks of stone. Moist. Unwavering. In a few places the remains of yellowed plaster could still be seen. The walls merged seamlessly into a stone barrel vault which only emphasized the seclusion. On the wall opposite the door was a large hole with a woven network of iron wires and bars, through which a weak light scarcely found its way. But even light was dark here. Against this harshness all light irrevocably evaporated. On the ground he saw a beetle scuttling into a corner. Apparently there was an exit for insects.

The feverish observations only briefly delayed the dawning of rational awareness. A prison cell. He was locked up. How could this be possible? A feeling of repulsion and horror washed over him.

His bed was no more than a stone elevation of the floor, with a gunnysack for bedding. There was an iron table with a wooden chair. In the other corner he saw a large jug. Slowly he got up. He looked through the opening from which the powerless light wavered. It was evening. Despite the pain in his whole body, he lifted himself up onto the stones that formed the windowsill. Looking out, he saw the Gothic forms of a Venetian palazzo about ten yards away. He was unable to see below the window, but he knew what was there. Water. The smelly canal, rats. Above him there was only dark sky. He shivered in the cold and sank back on his bed. Gradually images from the previous evening began to flash through his brain.

He was standing on a bridge. Where? Somewhere near the Rialto? He had drunk a lot. Someone was waving a stick. Was he hit? He heard police whistles. The gas lamps swayed before his eyes. The top hat and the long coat of an Austrian policeman who wanted to grab him, sprang to mind vividly. The policeman had a ludicrous curly mustache. He ran away from him. Panic. Had he stumbled? Or had he fled the scene? He didn't know anymore. At some point he had lost consciousness, he concluded.

The details he could remember were razor-sharp, but there were absolutely no connecting elements, nor did he succeed in bringing any order to it all. No matter how hard he tried, he had no way to explain his presence here. He gazed again at the walls that held him. He concentrated on things he had to know. Who he was. Why he was in Venice. Joseph Socher. No, Johann Lichtman. Journalist, writer. Anton Pennekamp, the director of the newspaper in Cologne for which he wrote. Max! He knew that he had come to Venice on Max's advice. After the disappointment and the problems in Paris. Rivka his sister. His family. What would his father think of this? If he ever found out. Frankfurt was far away.

But what on earth was he doing in a dungeon? He had simply come to Venice to find some peace of mind.

Footsteps echoed in the corridor outside his cell. They startled him from his thoughts. The peephole in the door opened and Joseph sensed cold eyes looking into the cell, searching for him. Someone unbolted the heavy door and, crackling, it swung open. A guard appeared in the doorway.

With his boot he pushed a tin container of food and a jar of water forward, then slammed the door closed again.

"Wait!" Joseph shouted, but his request was lost in the noise of the locks. He looked at the tray and saw a bowl of green goo with a spoon in it. On its edge sat a piece of bread. The jar contained brown water. He drank it at a draught. He didn't touch the soup. Despite his misery he smiled at the thought that he would later tell his father that it was not kosher.

Alone again, he tried once more to reconstruct how he had ended up here, in this forsaken place. He assumed that everything would soon be put right. Nothing could explain his presence here. In the few weeks he had been in the lagoon city, he hadn't done much, and certainly nothing illegal. He had met a number of people. He had written something for himself. No wild things. Or?

After being left to his fate for a few hours, Joseph heard footsteps again. It sounded like two men this time. The ritual with the latch repeated itself and the door opened.

"*Mitkommen*," ordered one of them. Joseph got up and the other man grabbed him harshly and tied his hands behind his back.

"What is going on? Why am I here?"

"*Maul halten*."

They pulled him through narrow corridors with cell doors on both sides, then pushed him roughly up some stairs and into an office at the end of a long corridor where they shoved him into a chair. His hands remained tied. Opposite him, behind a large writing table, sat a man who stared at him in silence. Joseph deduced from the many decorations and the exuberant uniform that this was a high-ranking officer. A few times Joseph tried to say something, but each attempt brought a blow on his back with the baton as a sign that he had to keep silent.

"Name," the man said after a few minutes.

He didn't feel like pretending to be a great freedom fighter. Cooperation would probably yield more. "Lichtman. Johann Lichtman."

The man nodded. "That's on your papers, indeed. Is that your real name? All revolutionaries use different names."

Joseph indicated that it really was his name.

"Where and when were you born?"

"Frankfurt. 20 October 1834."

"Where do you live now?"

"Cologne. *Holzmarkt*."

Again the man nodded. "Twenty-five and already done for." He made a note and sat down comfortably. "Right. Lichtman. Just tell me. What do you know about the attack the day before yesterday? You were there, weren't you? You do not deny you were there, do you?" He smirked, as if he had already won the game.

"I don't know anything about an attack. That's the truth. You can't hold me. I am innocent."

"You are certainly not innocent. It's about whether you were the instigator."

"What are you talking about?" Joseph began to despair. His

interrogator now stood up and walked around the room.

"Tell us about that night. In detail. We have all the time in the world," the voice came from behind.

Everything around him went dark. How could he tell the truth when he himself no longer knew exactly what had happened. "I had a drink with some friends. And then we went home. On a bridge... I don't really know exactly where."

"I'll help you. The *Ponte de la Fava*," the policeman said softly, only to continue at full volume: "On the way to the prosecutor's house, right?"

"I don't know any prosecutor. I've only been here for a few weeks. I only know some writers."

"And some people from the old Manin club. Isn't that the truth?"

"Manin? Excuse me. I don't know what Manin is."

"Who Manin is. You think you are smart by feigning stupidity." He nodded at the guards. "Take him away. Eventually he will talk."

"Where are my belongings? My papers, my money. I want to talk to someone. I want a counselor," he tried desperately when the strong arms grabbed him again.

"You don't need documents here. And your money pays well for your accommodation here."

"I want to speak to a counselor," Joseph repeated.

The man now beckoned a guard to indicate that the interrogation was over. They took Joseph away, but they did not bring him directly to his cell. After they had descended the stairs again, they went into a dark corridor and ended up in what looked like a clothes warehouse.

"Strip, Lichtman."

In the meantime, two more guards had arrived and apparently it all didn't go fast enough.

"Come on. We don't have the whole day. Take off your clothes," growled a tall man, one of the new ones.

Joseph looked around but there was no help anywhere, so he started taking off his socks and shoes. While he unbuttoned his vest, one of the guards grabbed Joseph's glasses. "You don't need them here." Joseph knew that objecting would make things worse. He took off his trousers, struggling to keep his balance, with the four men laughing around him. He stood in his underwear now. One of the guards took a hold of his underwear.

"Need some help, little man? Everything. Understood?"

Joseph took off his underwear and stood naked in front of the four men.

One of them chortled and said to another. "You owe me hundred francs, Sührstein. I told you he was a Jew."

Sührstein walked towards Joseph and spit in his face: "Bah. You scum. Typical, I lose my money to the Jews again."

The leader of the group pushed everyone aside. "Come along. Cleaning time."

Two of the guards took him to a small side room where he saw some buckets of water. Water taken straight out of the canal, to judge by the stench.

"Against the wall." A bucket of cold foul-smelling water splashed over him.

"Turn around." A second bucket followed. Joseph thought that the horrible cold would give him a heart attack.

One of the men threw a cloth at him. "Dry yourself."

Joseph huddled and shivered. He saw from the corner of his eye that the other two guards were leaving and that they were taking his clothes with them.

Before he could say anything, another snarl thundered through the hollow space: "Here. Put on." He got blue trousers with black stripes that were far too big for him and a shirt of the same material. Half of its buttons were missing. He quickly put the clothes on, hoping that they would warm him. Without further ado, the guards pushed him out of the room and brought him back to the cell, where they threw him roughly to the ground. The now-familiar sound of the lock followed.

Joseph fell back onto his prison bed. He just wanted to sink into sleep and oblivion.

A conversation from a few days earlier came to mind. Joseph had talked about Rabbi Elisha ben Abuyah and his pupil, Rabbi Meir. Elisha was called *Acher*, the Other, because he was considered a heretic. The Talmud told how the two went for a walk and had walked as far as was permissible on Shabbat. *Acher* said, "Go back." The heretic felt responsible for keeping Meir on the right path. Meir replied, "Please, you should come back as well." *Acher* did not go back.

Proudly Joseph had proclaimed that he felt like *Acher*. Sometimes someone has to go beyond what was allowed, to get things done, to make progress. Now, here in his cell, he wondered where all this courage and desire for freedom had brought him. Shouldn't he just have remained a pious Jew in the *Judengasse*? There, at least, there was an exit, albeit a narrow one.

Part 1

1

(1852)

BEHIND THE SPLENDID VIEW

There seemed no way out. The curvature of the alley made any prospect of an exit impossible. A deliberate plan to keep someone in place. The forward-leaning houses seemed to participate by obstructing the view upwards. No green, no air or birds, no wind, just a gray stripe that only intensified the suffocation in the *Judengasse,* the center of Frankfurt's Jewish ghetto.

Joseph did not allow himself to be dispirited, not even by the drizzly rain that miraculously found its way down through the narrow crevice between the houses. He maneuvered resolutely between the chickens running loose over the slick, bumpy cobblestones, deep mire filling the spaces between them. To prevent himself from slipping, he had to slow his pace every now and then. They should level the whole alley and pave it properly. What, they should demolish the entire area and make it into a decent neighborhood.

It was still early, but already quite busy. Children were playing on the streets and here and there women had started to display their merchandise on plain shelves supported by ramshackle struts, the cackling poultry drowned out their chattering and squabbling. A single man strode home from morning services.

Joseph had already completed this obligation, and during the part of the prayer where one asks for forgiveness, he thought he might as well confess his sins for this whole day. Would that be worse than waiting until he had actually done them? But then again, what he had planned wasn't that terrible. Or was it? He did not know. He just didn't know that much anymore.

From behind the houses came the yells of the battalion that was quartered in the Dominican monastery just on the edge of the Jewish quarter. Despite all the battles, revolutions, and treaties of the past decades, Frankfurt was still a proud, independent city-state with its own army. Unfortunately, because of this independence, the laws for Jews in Frankfurt were more stringent than in the rest of Germany, where the liberal Napoleonic spirit had gained more support, even after the failed revolution of 1848, four years ago now.

At the end of the *Gasse*, where the fence used to be, he traversed the *Judenplatz*. He did not want to take the shortcut near the cathedral, but rather, the lively route along the river. The rain was stopping and it was getting lighter. At the edge of the Jewish quarter, renovations had started. In several places, the run-down buildings had even been torn down to make room for new, large, and more comfortable houses. Building materials blocked the street and signs indicated the route to the quay. Against his better judgment, he decided to go straight ahead over a pile of construction rubble several meters high. Almost on top, he stepped on a slippery wooden plate and lost his balance. He looked around to see if anyone had seen him bumbling, but nobody paid attention. To his dismay, he saw that his trousers were stained with mud. On all fours he climbed back down. Via the detour he now reached the hustle and bustle of the quay. Workers drove heavily loaded carts towards the bridge over the Main, fishermen dragged their nets. Everywhere on the quay were barrels, ropes, and piles of merchandise. A colorful spectacle of masts, trusses, sails, and cranes danced on the water. Gulls skimmed the river, flew towards the slaughterhouse, or came to rest on the mooring posts. A group of people stood at the jetty where the steamboat with a long, dull thrust announced that it was going to moor. At the railing, a few cheerful women surveyed the quay for possible lovers.

Past the slaughterhouse, Joseph walked to the *Rententhurm*. Here it was quieter. Now, he took his time. Sitting down on one of the poles by the quay, he let his gaze go over the river. The low spring sun broke through and watching its reflective glare stretch toward him on the water, Joseph felt as if it were shining just for him. He pulled his beret a little further over his forehead. The light radiated hope and the water was luring. It flowed away from here. The Main joined the Rhine and from there, ran into unknown territories. Joseph had never been outside Frankfurt. Until a few years ago, he had never even been outside the Jewish quarter. Although the French had demolished the walls of the ghetto* decades earlier and officially there were no more restrictions, Joseph's family still lived in the same house in the *Judengasse*. Not much had changed in the mentality on both sides: the Orthodox Jews showed little inclination to look outside their own world and the citizens of Frankfurt would never be used to Jews in their neighborhoods. The taunts were still frequent. Those who had adapted – the less strictly Orthodox and those who had assimilated – moved to the new neighborhoods of *Ostend* and *Fischerfeld*, to spacious houses with all the new facilities. Some of the buildings there even had gas lighting. Away from the memory of oppression that screamed from the old walls. And most of all away from the stench.

In front of him was the most beautiful part of the bank where the more expensive residences sat. Where distinguished people with carriages were picked up. Where neatly dressed men with high hats paraded, arm in arm with elegant women. Where the wealthy went through the stock exchange notes and the latest news. At the end was one of the residences of the Rothschilds. For a long time, they had kept their house in the *Judengasse*, not far from where Joseph's parents lived. When Joseph was a little boy, his father had often pointed it out to him: "That is where the Rothschilds live. Our own kings. The richest family in Europe and yet one of the most pious families in Frankfurt. The city wanted him to keep his bank open on Shabbat, but he just refused. Ha!" he said proudly as if that refusal by the Rothschilds made him a hero.

Joseph startled when a rattling carriage drove by. He was not looking for the upper classes; different, higher aspirations drove him. *Buchladen* Holstein was his goal. The small bookstore was one of the last businesses to survive in the old city. Sometimes, when Joseph had some money, he would buy a book there, which he then would smuggle into their house and hide behind his schoolbooks in the room he shared with his older brother, Aron. At first, he had considered keeping them behind the beautiful volumes of the Talmud he had received at his *Bar Mitzvah*, but something prevented him from doing so. It did not feel right to use the pearls of Jewish thought as a cover for his private affairs. In addition, his father would discover the truth if he took down one of the volumes. God forbid that his parents would find out what he was reading. He would probably be able to explain it to his mother, but his father would downright condemn him. Joseph assumed that righteous Aron knew about his secret treasure, but was still benevolent enough not to compromise him. Yet he didn't feel completely safe and somehow, he had the idea that his brother was keeping the knowledge as collateral against a future occasion. And so, he had built up his own library behind the books he was supposed to study in school. Controversial Jewish books by Spinoza and Mendelssohn, which he did not fully understand, but above all, non-religious, romantic literature. Goethe's *Werther* had touched his soul. Byron, Schiller, Hugo. And Heinrich Heine, his hero.

Holstein was located at the *Tuchladen*, an alleyway between the cathedral and the *Frisch*, the market, where they sold everything that lived and was edible. The street was accessible via a low wooden underpass, similar to those in the ghetto, but for Joseph there was a big difference. The houses here were straight, allowing the light to fall on the street. The walls were mostly of stone with large rectangular windows, so the sun could shine into the rooms. The straight lines created order.

Joseph loved this order. It paved the way for clear rational thinking. Germans knew what order was, in contrast to the Jews muddling along in the *Gasse*. Planters hung under the windowsills, giving the exteriors a friendly appearance. He imagined that inside it would be pleasant and cozy. Best of all, the street was clean. He wiped the dried mud from his trousers and opened the door of the bookshop.

Holstein was his *Gan Eden,** his paradise. Fruits everywhere, but Joseph was especially interested in one forbidden fruit. He enjoyed the serene tranquility after the noise of the street. The owner, Günther Holstein, a good-natured, well-read man, gave Joseph a friendly nod when the sharp doorbell made him look up from his papers. Everywhere the bookshelves reached the ceiling. Joseph could hardly read the book titles high above him. In front of the bookcases were long tables with more books. He grabbed one with poems by Heine and started to read, although this was not really the purpose of his visit.

After a while he strolled further to the back of the shop, occasionally taking a book and browsing through. The bookseller looked mirthful over his glasses, thinking his thoughts about this adolescent boy. At the back of the shop under the tables were drawers, with golden rings around the finely finished wood. Joseph opened the middle one; the drawer creaking over the wood. Always an unpleasant moment in which he looked up to see whether the owner was keeping an eye on him. His treasures lay in these drawers. Apparently, the stack had been untouched since the last time. On top lay one of the many prints of the Rhine Valley. In the foreground a mysterious ruin in shadows, behind it the landscape opened up with the river disappearing in the hazy distance between the mountains. Fairy-tale moonlight reflected on the water on which a lonesome boat sailed away. Joseph's imagination could fill in everything he was yearning for. This was even better than the real river. He put down the book he had previously picked up and searched deeper in the pile.

At the very bottom of the stack was a print that did not belong to this series. Joseph had taken it out of another drawer and put it underneath, for safekeeping. In a corner of the paper on which it was glued, was written in large red letters "sold". Joseph suspected that Holstein had done this for him, as in a silent agreement. But he thought it was too dangerous to buy the print and keep it at home.

He looked at the print, which he could dream. A beautiful, half-dressed girl, her breasts uncovered, played on a lute with in the background the beguiling mystery of the Rhine Valley. She sat like an unreachable nymph on the rock, haughty, but with a breathtaking beauty. The devilish seduction of the Lorelei. A fantasy with fatal powers. Joseph could look at this erotic glory for hours. Not only because of the excitement but also because of the desire to break loose. The desire to experience beauty, to travel, to discover the world.

An unexpected movement startled him. A girl his age passed by, smiling. He clumsily tucked the print beneath the others. The girl pointed to the book that Joseph had put on top of the drawers. "You're better off reading than looking at pictures," she laughed. Struck dumb, he closed the drawer, took the book, and rushed out of the shop, sliding on the wet paving. To collect himself, he sat down on a bench in the street. His breathing slowed and inadvertently he started to walk back home. He heard the bells of the cathedral. Stupid. Completely forgotten. His lesson with Rabbi Eliezer. That other world of books. He quickened his steps and reached the house of the rabbi on time, sweaty despite the cold. In his hand he still held the book, which, in his excitement, he had forgotten to return to the shelf: *Jenny* by Fanny Lewald, he read. Apparently a female writer, but he had never heard of her. Probably one of those stories that the bourgeois ladies dreamed of; he had even caught his mother reading dime novels of this sort. For a moment he considered bringing it back immediately – with apologies. He didn't want to keep the book, but now that he had it, he might as well read it. He put the book under a few stones next to Rabbi Eliezer's door.

After Joseph had completed the college, he started going to Rabbi Eliezer for Talmud lessons every Monday and Thursday. At school he had often been bored. After the endless hours of Torah study, he had been taught German and English, but these lessons had not brought him the wider window on the world he had hoped for. And his father had forbidden him to go out with the Christian boys in his class.

Rabbi Eliezer's lessons weren't much better. The rabbi lived in one of the better houses on the square. He smoked heavy cigars and the smoke overwhelmed Joseph as soon as he entered the small study. At first glance, the room did not differ much from the bookshop. It was smaller, but it also had bookcases on all walls. Two desks with chairs were the only furniture. Hardly any light came from outside, the candles on the tables fought against the weak half-dark of the room.

On the bookshelves the complete rabbinical literature had been assembled. Hundreds of brown leather volumes stood between hundreds of black leather volumes, *Talmud* Bavli, Talmud Yerushalmi, Mishna,* Midrashim,* Tosafot,* Responsa,* Shulchan Aruch,** comments from *Rashi, Rambam, Ramban, Abarbanel*. The comments of the *Acharonim** on the *Geonim** and the comments of the *Rishonim** on the *Tanaim*. Books about the path that should be followed and books about the prayers to be said. While in the bookstore the books changed place, new books were added and old ones disappeared, everything here seemed to be stuck on these shelves for all time.

Joseph sat opposite the rabbi and opened the book.

The rabbi coughed and said: "Today we will continue with *Masechet Ma'aser Sheni.*" He looked over the book. "Last time we discussed that ten percent of the harvest should be given to the Levites. Can you tell me exactly how this worked? Where should it be brought to?"

"Jerusalem."

"Very good. And why isn't that mentioned in the *Talmud Bavli?*"

Joseph wanted to say that it didn't matter at all because the temple had not existed for over a thousand years and, to his knowledge, Jerusalem was now an Ottoman city where nobody wanted to live.

"Because Babylon has nothing to do with the land of Israel," he said.

"Now tell me something about *Neta Revai.*"

Joseph did his best to explain it and the rabbi nodded. For three quarters of an hour, their eyes remained glued to the books through the darkness and the cigar vapor. The rabbi read the sentences about the money that could be used to buy off the tenth part, but that must not be badly minted, nor out of circulation, nor belong to anyone else. And if the tenth part was then bought free and redeemed, the money must not be spent inappropriately, and all this time Joseph thought of nothing but the nude beauty in the print and the girl in the bookshop.

"*Gut yom tiv*, that you may have a happy and kosher Passover," Joseph said politely when the lesson was over.

He didn't really feel like going straight home. There, he was supposed to help with the annual Pesach cleaning. Pesach, *chag cheruteinu*, the holiday of our freedom, he scoffed to himself. If there were a festival with more restrictions and less freedom, it was Pesach. The celebration of the exodus from Egypt but also of what was not allowed. And of the cleaning madness. Weeks in advance the stress seized his mother and after a while he couldn't bear to be at home anymore. He didn't feel free at all.

Nevertheless, every year he welcomed the festive evening itself when it finally came. It was the announcement of spring and that meant, above all, that another terrible winter was over and that they would no longer have to sleep together in that one stifling but warm room where the stove was.

There were two ways to enter the house. The front door gave access to his father's shop. Coats, hats, trousers, all clothes imaginable. The *schmatte* trade. Second-hand sales and repairs. The whole shop was full of fabrics that had to be treated very carefully. The family lived on the first floor and to get there one had to go up the stairs in the back of the shop, which were completely barricaded with towering stacks of clothes. If someone came to visit them via the front door, the family first had to remove the stacks in order to clear the way. Afterwards, they returned everything to exactly the same spots at the stairs, locking the family in by clothes again. They themselves always entered and left through the back door. The first floor consisted of three bedrooms, a living room divided in two and a kitchen. Above them were two more floors where the Kleinblatts lived, even more pious than the Sochers, if possible.

"You are late. Where have you been?" his mother shouted from above the stairs. She wore a brown towel as headscarf, covering her curly brown hair. In a strange manner it made her gentle face unnecessarily sharp. The color of the scarf was a mismatch with her blue eyes.

"Rabbi Eliezer," Joseph shouted in return.

"I've already started cleaning your room, but I expect you do the rest. Your room should be ready by this evening."

Joseph stormed to his room. Pesach cleaning meant taking everything from its place, the books as well. Aron, sitting behind his table studying, looked up smiling. "She didn't do the books. She left them for you. Rest assured," he said.

In the days that followed he had no time to go back to the bookstore to return the book and even perhaps see the girl again. In the days he hadn't seen her, she had grown in his imagination; she had become his personal Lorelei. Pesach preparations filled every moment – cleaning, searching for *chametz*, shopping, fitting new clothes, and studying a lot. But he had started reading the book he had taken with him. The story of a Jewish woman who wanted to free herself to live as a writer, grabbed him. It seemed as if it were about him; as if he had written it himself. He read how miserable Jews were in nineteenth-century Germany. However, he should not read, he should act. Time for deeds. He put the book away and thought of Heine: "*Denke ich an Deutschland in der Nacht, dann bin ich um den Schlaf gebracht.*" [1] With ever-greater conviction he felt that he also had to detach himself to follow his great calling. Until now it had been just playing around, but now it was for real. He was a writer. He felt it in every fiber of his body.

"*B'chol dor vador chayav adam lirot et atzmo, kilu hu yatzah miMitzrayim.*" [2]

He heard his father proclaim the sentence with vigor, but the words reached Joseph more gently. The glass of wine he had drunk in one sip made him look at his second glass with blurry eyes. But he was enjoying the *Seder*: the wine and the whole evening. It was unlike every other evening of the year and stood separate from the tedium of religious practice.

His family around him felt close as they hadn't been for a long time. His father at the head of the table, his mother opposite, near the kitchen. To the right of his father were Aron, two years older than he, and Nathan, his brother of twelve. On the other long side his sister, Rivka, who was three years his younger, sat next to him. The table shone with festivity. All the special Pesach china and cutlery that came out of the cupboards just once a year. Just seeing the half-forgotten objects was like meeting long lost friends again. The polished silver gleamed, the glasses full of wine shone. Everyone had a beautiful edition of the *Hagaddah** in front of him. The *matzahs** were hidden in beautiful, multi-colored napkins.

To Joseph, the essential question of what this evening meant suddenly seemed too absurd to ask. He wanted to question everything, but the evening of the *seder* was outside and above all reality. In the past few weeks he had often found excuses to stay away from the preparations, because he was lazy and because he was not convinced of the holiday's fundamental meaning. But when his father pronounced the *kiddush* at the beginning, everything was in order – the six of them in their best clothes, the promise of delicious food, and above all, the warmth and unity of the family. The notion that all his co-religionists were now doing the same thing at the same time, made it impossible to resist the timeless grandeur. All evil would pass their house. He always got the second question, the question of the wicked child, but that didn't bother him. Throughout the evening, his father always managed to make them feel as if they had left Egypt themselves.

The next day Aron said, "On *Shabbat chol hamo'ed*,* Papa is planning to go to the shul of the new rabbi again. In the temporary synagogue. Nathan and I are also going. Papa insists that you join us. Rabbi Hirsch is really fantastic. A smart and honest man."

"Isn't that what all rabbis are supposed to be?"

"Oh, you, always those foolish jokes."

"I have heard that the Rothschilds bought him."

"What slander. And what if they gave money to have a good rabbi here? Better than spending it on a new carriage or expensive paintings or such like."

Joseph thought he had been negative enough. Aron couldn't follow his humor anyway. "I will come too. Don't worry."

"And the Rothschilds have the best intentions," Aron concluded.

"You can take it from me that nobody has the best intentions with us. For the Liberals we are old stupid Orthodox people. For the stupid Orthodox we are too worldly. For the Liberals we are too reserved, for the conservatives we go too far."

"All sentences you have read somewhere. You copy your life from a book."

"Look who is talking. All you do is learn the Talmud by heart and have superfluous discussions about it."

"You are still so young. I also wanted to be different when I was your age."

"Ah, my wise, old brother. All day long busy being different and then you get angry when others say you are different."

Going upstairs, he sat down at the small table in his room. In his juvenile hubris he decided to write a letter to Heine asking him whether he was still planning to finish the *Rabbi of Bacharach*. If not, Joseph could do it.

After the service on Shabbat the rabbi spoke a few words in German, which Joseph thought was a good sign. His words had power. He spoke of the dry bones of Ezekiel, referring to the text in the *haftara*.* Afterwards they didn't head directly home. His father made a detour towards Ostend, one of the new neighborhoods. Maybe he started to see the advantages of moving?

"This is really a very good development," his father said. "Rabbi Hirsch has rekindled hope among the people, after all the hassle we have been through with those reformers. I can tell by the way people are acting."

A few weeks later, after the service, Joseph found himself walking next to Rabbi Hirsch. He gathered all his courage and asked him straight if he could visit him because he had some urgent questions. The next day the rabbi himself showed Joseph into his new house.

"Come inside. Joseph Socher, isn't it?" the rabbi asked kindly.

The windows were open and the light flowed in. Between the buildings, Joseph saw the green banks of the Main.

"The view is beautiful, rabbi."

"Yes, although the street is called *Hinter der schönen Aussicht.* (3) We can ask ourselves what the real beautiful view would look like."

Joseph laughed. He felt even more comfortable when the maid brought coffee and cake.

"Have you heard the joyful news? We are going to build a new synagogue. Not before long the first stone will be laid."

Joseph confirmed that he had heard this from his father.

"What can I do for you," the rabbi asked.

"I want to study, rabbi. In Bonn. Perhaps you can help me to convince my father."

The rabbi nodded thoughtfully. "I also studied in Bonn."

Joseph told of his fear that his parents would not allow it and of his big plans to be a writer. "But it all seems so difficult."

"Thoughtful questions and I wish I had the right answers. I do have answers but I don't know if they are the right ones."

Joseph looked at him wondering, afraid that the rabbi would not answer out of modesty, or perhaps out of fear of putting his cards on the table.

"A person is respected when he is strong. I think the Germans don't like our weakness at all. The Liberals have a Judaism without Jewish content. That makes them weak. We should not tackle the problem by adapting to others. That is death. From within and from our own strength we must change, although without being blind to the world, and then we will live." The rabbi stood up and walked to the bookcase. "Normally I don't parade with my own work, but perhaps this could help." He took a thin book and gave it to Joseph. "Read this, if you want."

Nineteen Letters on Judaism by Ben Uziel, Joseph read. "Thank you, rabbi. Did you write this?"

The rabbi nodded. He did not sit down again, from which Joseph gathered that the conversation was over. The warmth of the man touched him, but still, Joseph wondered why he should walk in public with this man's book, while the rabbi himself did not dare to put his name on it.

As soon as he got home Joseph started to read. The text was astounding. The first of the nineteen letters contained everything he thought. Maybe in the form of questions, but still. The unhappy, self-chosen isolation, the inability of self-determination, always at the mercy of the whims of other people, the poverty and Judaism's inability to let people blossom, the narrow-mindedness of the meticulous hair-splitting in the Talmud, and the duty to occupy oneself with prayers and rituals all day long. The book clearly described the reality of this ridiculous situation.

This would be his safeguard. He could use this against his parents. If the rabbi had brought it up, why should he have to keep his mouth shut? In his arrogance and excitement, Joseph decided that he had read enough. The questions in the first chapter of the book made the answers superfluous. It was all so clear. He had more important things to arrange.

After Pesach Joseph had apologized to Holstein. "I had not even noticed," he responded with a generous smile. Completely reassured, Joseph now walked through the bookstore. He roamed past the shelves and, as always, picked up a book now and then. Slowly but surely he came to the rear of the shop. He searched in the pile, but he didn't see the print. He started looking in other drawers, but the thing was nowhere to be found. Did he dare to ask Holstein where it had gone? A little further on, the shopkeeper was sorting out a pile of recently purchased volumes. Joseph saw him look up, perceptive, it seemed.

"Sold," said the man.

"But the stamp said sold." It didn't bother Joseph that they didn't need to mention the subject of their conversation.

Holstein shrugged his shoulders.

Exuding self-confidence, a skinny, pale young man entered the shop. He was exuberantly dressed with a beret aslant on his tangled hair. A well-groomed moustache and a small beard accentuated the open face. His bright eyes sparkled as he confidently looked around. Joseph stood a few meters away, listening attentively.

"I have to tell you Holstein, your bookshop is better than the best in Cologne," he heard the young man say.

"Thank you, *Herr* Löwe. It is good to see you here again. How are things in Cologne? How is your father doing?"

"Nothing special." The young man turned his gaze to Joseph: "Are you staring at me? What's eating you?"

Joseph stuttered some inaudible words and wanted to leave, but something forced him to stay. He turned to the shelves as if searching for a specific book, and continued to listen in on the conversation. Did he have the nerve to address this Löwe?

"Are you studying in Cologne?" he asked clumsily.

Löwe looked up, slightly disturbed but mostly amused. "Studying in Cologne? That's not even possible. For that you have to be in Bonn. You go to Cologne for business." He stretched out his hand. "Werner Löwe."

Joseph excitedly shook his hand. "Joseph. Joseph Socher. I want to study in Bonn."

"There is not much else to experience in Bonn," said Werner with conviction. "For real life you have to be in Cologne. Frankfurt is nothing compared to Cologne."

"Maybe I will see you there?" he said in a whim before he realized it.

"Yes. Come and visit us. We live in the city center. You will enjoy Cologne."

"Deal. I'll stop by." Joseph cheerfully took leave of Werner. He had found an opening. He would start with Cologne. This friendly Werner would certainly help him there.

Joseph now went regularly to Rabbi Hirsch's service. He still needed a yes from his father and he knew that the synagogue visits made his father happy. One of these times they left the building with Baruch Mandelbaum, an acquaintance of his father who nodded friendly, "Good evening, *Herr* Mandelbaum, how are you doing? How is the leg?"

"Good, God is blessed, thank you." The man stopped for a moment as if he was considering something. "I don't know if I can ask you this, but my son has gone away this summer and he was responsible for the distribution of our *shul** magazine. I really can't do it myself anymore with my leg. Do you know anyone?" He looked at Joseph meaningfully. "Would you like to have something to do? You could start this week already."

With his father's eyes fixed on him, Joseph could not refuse. He promised to distribute the magazine with the latest news, the Shabbat times, and the weekly Torah thoughts every Thursday. At first, he was not very enthusiastic about the idea. Everyone would see him as a representative of what he was carrying around. What did he know about the contrary assumptions or provocative statements in the magazine? He decided to share it with his little brother, both to create some time to chat, and, even more to remove the psychic weight of the task. Distributing a bulletin with a nine-year-old boy was not a statement, but just some extra work outside the house. No risk that he would be seen as a disciple. Every Thursday throughout the summer he delivered the publication with Nathan. A nice side effect was that he earned some money. They often went to *café Levy* for a drink.

One day, toward the end of their rounds, Joseph suggested going somewhere else than Levy. "Some place really chic. On the *Rossplatz*. We have money now." Nathan first looked excited but the smile disappeared straightaway: "I don't think Papa would allow that."

"Come on. It's not that bad. It could be nice."

"We can't eat and drink with the *goyim*.*"

"The *goyim* don't drop dead after they've eaten. Let's have a look. It's close by. We can always leave. And we only will have a drink." They walked through the major streets of the new city lined with monumental, stately buildings. They came to a vast square where Joseph saw a coffee house, *Der Englischer Hof*. "That looks good," he said. He approached the door, with Nathan following nervously. "Be a good boy. Behave well." Nathan nodded and they entered.

The long room had large windows facing the street. Between enormous mirrors, huge columns reached up to a gracefully decorated ceiling. At least ten waiters staffed the high buffet. Huge chandeliers with yellow gas lamps hung above green upholstered chairs and tables draped with white lace tablecloths. People were eating, conversing, and reading. Joseph and Nathan timidly looked for a spot. "Here by the window," whispered Joseph. They took seats opposite each other. Behind Joseph a group of men made noisy jokes, while behind Nathan a man sat alone at a table full of delightful dishes of meat and cheese with a variety of sauces. The lower half of his head was bald and on both sides above that two bunches of wavy white hair sprang out. Two large, white sideburns ran like scouring brushes to the sharp corners of the mouth. Joseph nodded at Nathan to draw his attention to the man. Together they giggled softly.

"Looks good, don't you think," Joseph remarked, while making himself comfortable. "Something different than that chaos at Levy." Nathan nodded, still dazed. Joseph ordered coffee, tea, and cake.

While waiting for their order to arrive, Joseph tried to reassure his little brother, but to no avail. The boy kept on fidgeting in his chair and had already gotten up a few times to the annoyance of the man with the devilish hair.

"Let's leave," Nathan urged. "Shouldn't we be bringing the rest of the bulletins? Or...?" He giggled nervously, "do we just put them somewhere behind a tree or something?"

"But, Nathan, shame on you. Aren't we getting paid for the job? We just have to finish it. Otherwise, it is theft."

"I thought you had become a bit more lenient these days."

Joseph wanted to answer that he hadn't at all, but then the waiter arrived with their cake and drinks. Moving his chair to make room for him, Nathan lightly bumped into the other man's table. The man looked up again, irritated.

Nathan reached for a cake, but Joseph held him back. "You have to say the *bracha** first." Nathan did, but then Joseph grabbed his arm again. "Maybe this is not such a good idea after all. Forget about it. Let's go. Don't forget the magazines."

Joseph put some money on the table and they got up. Nathan started to shoulder the sack of literature but it slipped and with a thud it hit the glass of the grumpy man. Wine flowed over his newspaper. The man jumped up, trying to save the newspaper. At least his clothes had been spared.

"Look out, you little rascal," the man shouted in anger. "Is there no more order in this world?" Everyone in the cafe stared. Immediately a waiter rushed over and apologized to the man. The waiter then turned to Nathan and said with restrained anger: "Get out of here. What are you Jews doing here, anyway? Go back to the rat hole you have crawled out from."

As quickly as they could, they hurried to the door, bumping into a well-dressed man on his way in. Joseph recognized him from a meeting of the board to which he had gone with his father. David Salomons, the chairman of the Liberal group. With his top hat in his hand, Salomons waved toward the interior of the cafe. "Not too successful, your entrance into this mundane world," he said sarcastically.

"It's nothing, sir. We wanted to leave anyway."

"I didn't know that you Orthodox people came here. You're from Hirsch's synagogue, aren't you?" He spoke the words with contempt. "I dare say this is not the most appropriate venue for you."

"If you want to know, sir, they don't want Jews here," replied Joseph.

"That's not true. Take me, for example. They treat me with the greatest respect. But then again, I am first and foremost a German." He laughed. "Come on, don't let it bother you. If you want to visit such establishments, you should also visit our temple. Then you can broaden your horizon and get the respect you deserve."

"I don't know, sir. I will think about it. Goodbye."

Nathan stood outside drying his tears.

"What a bully," Nathan wept. "How did the waiter know that we were Jewish? Do we smell? Do we have crooked noses?"

"Or did he just see that we were carrying bulletins with Hebrew texts in large letters?" Joseph suggested light-heartedly. Nathan looked a bit dumbfounded and then they both burst out laughing. Nathan promised not to tell Papa. But Joseph decided that he certainly would not share these endeavors with his brother again.

The next Shabbat he decided that he would visit the Liberal synagogue. It was crowded and he had trouble following the service; all prayers were in German and large parts of the text were unfamiliar. What especially stuck in his mind was the small whining organ that accompanied the singing. Overall, he found the experience disappointing. He had hoped to find something to his liking here, but apparently when they had thrown the Talmud and twenty centuries of tradition out of the window, they had also lost everything that made the experience beautiful. This was half-hearted.

Salomons came to him after the service: "Well? Better than that old jumble of yours, isn't it? We maintain spirituality, we just dispose of the superfluous bombast."

"It is indeed different here, sir," said Joseph diplomatically.

"Someone who has been here once, comes back. You will see. The people are with us. We also intend to hold the Sabbath on Sunday in the future. Nobody wants to be in that disorganized chaos of Orthodoxy anymore. Screaming barbarians, gibbering rabbis; just look what kind of clothes they wear. What nonsense they spout." He set up a low hollow voice in an attempt to imitate a cantor: *"A new light will shine on Zion."* As if we were going back to that wilderness. To Jerusalem! Preposterous. No, Orthodoxy is moribund. And that is a blessing, because otherwise there would be no future for our faith. Wake up, we live in modern times. All that medieval drivel in the Talmud... We have to get rid of the idea that we are a special people. No wonder the Germans avoid us when the Orthodox represent us. We are just Germans with a different religion. That is all. That is why we do everything in German. We have to make it understandable. Ezra also used the vernacular when he taught the people."

Joseph wanted to point out that the Talmud did not originate in the Middle Ages, but he didn't see any point in doing so. For a moment he considered telling this man with a lot of bravura that he too was done with the old way. That he aspired to other things. Study. Secular topics. Bonn. Did the anonymity of this encounter open the door to saying these things? Joseph kept his mouth shut.

"They say we are destroying the faith," Salomons continued. "That we destroy Judaism. That we are the first step toward leaving the faith. But the truth is exactly the opposite. We are the saviors. We will ensure that the faith continues. Mind you, the faith, not the ridiculous assumption that we are a separate people. The collapse of faith lies with the Orthodox. Because of them, people give up. We are the consequence, not the cause." He waited a while, but Joseph did not respond. Salomons continued with great conviction: "Here you can anticipate new light. We are a light for the nations. You know that, don't you? That is exactly what we do. We associate with others so that we can pass on our values and norms. For the illumination of the world. Sitting in a ghetto or shtetl does not bring light. A new light will indeed shine, but not as the the old believers assume. There it will always remain dark." He held back for a moment, as if he had been too fierce. "I hope we will see you more often."

The man walked away, leaving Joseph feeling even more unsure of what he wanted. He was angry with himself for not finding the right responses to Salomons' statements. His thoughts were chaotic. As far as he could tell, this form of Jewish practice resembled Christianity.

And people left that in droves as well. Why try to be like something that seemed doomed to perish? He would need to read more about this because as a writer it would be imperative to order his thoughts and analyze everything scrupulously; Not to impress with witticism, bluff, or nice anecdotes.

By distributing the magazine, Joseph slowly became a well-known member of Rabbi Hirsch's congregation. During the services people smiled at him and many stopped for a chat. At times, this kindness made Joseph feel like a traitor. The people and the whole faith seemed to be more friendly, more approachable than ever. As if the faith was making one last attempt to win him over. But he knew that it was easier to see the positive side, now that he had taken a big step away from it in his mind. In the end, it was not about finding a way that would be more flexible. That would just lead to another *Judengasse*. He had to break away. It would hurt and there would be tears. But eventually it would be clear to everyone that this was the right move. He would do it after the summer.

Joseph found his father's trunk in the small box room and put it on top of the pile. Nobody would notice the difference. In his room he inspected everything he would take, arranging it in a way that it would be easy to pack without making a conspicuous pile that would stand out. He thought himself an organizational success.

Yom Kippur* was a torment. Normally the synagogue offered enough distraction against hunger and thirst, but this time it seemed that the service would never end. Joseph had a headache from fasting and praying was the only antidote that Yom Kippur offered. "*Chatanu.* We have sinned. Forgive us." He tried to divert his thoughts from his plans but couldn't manage it. Again, he wondered whether he would be acquitted if he confessed his future sins now.

After the evening meal, Joseph joined his father and brothers in collecting the parts of the *sukkah** that had to be built immediately after the fast. Aron had already stacked the planks neatly on top of the trunk. Slowly but surely, with every load that went down, the trunk became more visible and signaled to him: "didn't we have an appointment, you and I?"

They built the *sukkah* in the usual place in their yard against the walls and the dilapidated fence that separated them from the old cemetery. Joseph did not want to reveal his true colors, so he pretended to be more passionate than ever. Weakness was not an option. Several times after his father indicated that it was fine, Joseph tied extra knots, hammered unnecessary nails in the wall, wound ropes around pieces of wood that didn't support anything. His father frowned but did not interfere.

"Joseph, where are you? I have great news." His father's voice came from the bottom of the stairs. Under his heavy beard, he was gleaming. "I got you the sixth *aliyah** for next Shabbos. Incredible that I succeeded, isn't it? The sixth!"

Joseph's birthday would be next week and his father was giving him the most wanted gift, to be called to the highest honor in the service, reading the Torah. On his thirteenth birthday, at his *Bar Mitzvah,** Joseph had read the Torah text of the week and because every year the same *parasha** fell out on his birthday, he felt that this text, the story of *Lech Lecha,** had become his. The story of Avram whom God commanded to leave his father's house: *"Go for yourself! Leave everything you love and start something new."* At thirteen, he had learned the text by heart. Every year since, his father had tried to buy him an *aliyah* but every year to no avail. Apparently, his father did not have enough influence or money. This time he had succeeded. The sixth of the seven parts of the weekly text. Which part was it again?

"Fantastic, Papa. I will do my best." He hugged his father and started to go up the stairs.

"You're really happy, aren't you?"

Joseph turned around and stretched every muscle in his face to make sure there was no hint of disappointment: "Of course. I am very grateful. I'm going to start practicing right now."

The synagogue was crowded. Sure, not all of them came because of me, Joseph thought, but soon the excited whisper made clear that the Rothschild branch from Paris was visiting. After the first part of the service, the Torah was removed from the ark. While waiting his turn, Joseph reviewed his text just to be sure. Before him, as number five, James Baron de Rothschild was called up. Accompanied by one of his children, the banker from Paris walked to the *bima,** the raised dais. So, this was the nobility of Frankfurt, our nobility. At first sight, nothing pointed to his exceptional status; perhaps his clothes were of slightly better quality, but for the rest, he looked like the usual bourgeois. He had dark hair with a part on one side. A round, delicate face, not at all puffy. A confident and pleasing appearance. Only his posture and his way of walking made one suspect a man of power. Joseph placed him in his late fifties. Suddenly Joseph realized that he would have to shake his hand after the reading. That was the custom. It made him nervous. James de Rothschild, son of the greatest banker ever. The richest man in Europe.

"*Ya'amod, Yosef ben Ephraim, shishi,*" [4] came the call. Uptight,

Joseph put on a *tallit** and walked to the *bima*. Because of his nerves, he forgot the usual practices and immediately started with the blessings that accompanied the *aliyah*. He opened the scroll and looked for the beginning of his text. With a steady voice he started reading. He made a mistake and immediately he corrected himself, but the mistake made him aware that he was reading; he heard himself reading. He bolstered his confidence: "Don't worry, Joseph, you know the text by heart. The baron is just another person." He read on, but someone corrected him, well meant, because every word had to be properly pronounced. He could not immediately find what the improvement was about. He had not noticed the mistake himself. A little confused, he repeated the whole sentence just to be sure and continued. Concentrate, Joseph, concentrate. The only thing he could think of now was how he stood there. Another slip of the tongue, one he noticed himself. He looked up, exactly in the gentle eyes of James de Rothschild, who kindly smiling encouraged him. Next to him stood his son, about ten years old. A cute child. Distracted Joseph murmured the sentence again, only the last word was audible. Would they correct him again? He got away with it. How much further did he have to go? Desperately he continued. Another correction. A slight panic attacked him. *L'zaracha natati et ha'aretz hazot.* He stopped, closed his eyes and thought. He did not know how to concentrate. He opened his eyes, saw a window and the air. Bare branches of a tree against a gray sky. He wanted to run away, outside, but somehow he managed to look at the text again and complete his section. When he had finished reading, the baron shook his hand with a charming smile. His son was still standing next to him and his father pointed to Joseph. "Edmond," he said, "shake his hand." Normally this would have been the most spectacular event in his life, but now Joseph felt like a convict, put on display on the market square. He wanted to crawl away in a corner, but he had to stand there, waiting for the axe to fall, until the next man had read his part. His own eyes closed, Joseph sensed the eyes of the entire municipality focused on him. He hated the synagogue, he hated himself, he hated everything.

His father shook his hand when he sat down. "You should have prepared better."

"I did, Papa," Joseph replied.

"Oh well. Everyone makes a mistake once in a while. That doesn't diminish the splendor. You got a handshake from the baron."

After the service, he collapsed into his bed. What a failure. Anger and shame competed for dominance. He tried over and over again to reconstruct where and why things had gone wrong. Had it been disinterest? Nerves because of the Rothschilds? Overconfidence?

Unconscious rebellion? Whatever, he thought, he had no answer, but one thing he knew for sure: if at all possible, he would never show his face there again.

He walked to the box room and told the trunk: "It won't be long now."

His father wanted to see him. In the living room. Joseph feared the worst. They rarely used the living room, only when there were important guests, or on Shabbat and the holidays. The windows to the street were always hidden behind heavy curtains, and anyone who ventured in during the week took a candle. The furniture was heavy and old. Sometimes, late at night, his father sat at the table studying by the light of a single candle. As a child, Joseph had loved to be with his father while he was immersed in the books. His father didn't actually have time for him, but he felt very much wanted. In those hours, the pile of books grew higher and higher and Joseph wondered how his father could still see the forest through the trees. Every now and again his father looked up and smiled at him, without speaking a word. As he grew older, Joseph came to hate the room. He considered it the epicenter of rigid dogmatism, the ultimate proof that there was no light within Orthodox teaching. He could feel the tension as soon as he entered the room. He felt extremely unwelcome.

His father looked up. "Aron told us that you have plans to study in Bonn. Forget them," he said briefly, after which he read on, as if that were the end of the matter.

Aron, the wretch. Could he never keep his mouth shut? For a moment Joseph doubted. Accept the decree for the time being or fight it with reason? "I discussed it with Rabbi Hirsch. He also studied in Bonn."

His father had no need of rationality. "It's better to do something with which you can earn money. Not something that costs money," he said, and he continued with voice raised: "It is a disgrace. You put us all to shame." He looked at his books from which he seemed to draw inspiration. "Shame," he repeated. And softer he said: "And we always thought that Rivka would be the problem."

His mother entered, asking what was going on. Joseph looked to her for support, but there was none there. In the presence of her husband, her desire for freedom and independence quickly faded. Joseph felt more pity for her than for himself. She would never dare to choose his side or her own for that matter, when his father was around. The latter shook his head and made a gesture that she should leave. She quietly closed the door behind her.

"I'm going to Bonn, whether you like it or not. To study. I want to become a writer. You are living in the Middle Ages," Joseph said desperately.

His father hit the table with his flat hand: "You are not going anywhere. You are not going to study with the *Goyim*. You will stay here and you will behave. You start working in the business. Period. And as for your future: We already have an arrangement with the Kleinblatts. And if Batia Kleinblatt is not good enough, there are plenty of pious candidates in the neighborhood." As if his father realized that he had lost his normal calm, he added in a more controlled voice: "We have to start soon because the municipality of Frankfurt strictly limits the number of approved marriages."

Batia Kleinblatt, the girl from upstairs! Joseph did not know whether he should cry or laugh. This was absurd. He ran out of the room. In the hallway Aron and Rivka sat on their knees, clearly eavesdropping.

"Dirty traitor," Joseph hissed in passing. Rivka wanted to follow him upstairs.

"Joseph, I support you," she whispered.

"You go and tell him that. He has probably already mapped out everything for you too." With a heavy bang he slammed the door of his room. His plan was ready. He would give in to his father, satisfy him, tell him he wasn't going. And then, in a few weeks, he would just leave without informing anyone. Certainly not Aron, perhaps Rivka. He trusted her, but he wasn't sure if she could keep silent under their father's pressure. He would just leave a letter and go.

A little later there was a knock on the door. It was his mother.

"Joseph, Joseph," it sounded softly. "Please, may I come in? We have to talk." Joseph reluctantly opened the door. His mother reached out and stroked his hair. "I do understand. But your father is so afraid that..." she didn't finish the sentence. "Wouldn't you first, before the big step, stay at home for a year and help papa in the shop? Then you can study at the same time to get higher. And besides that, you can continue to learn with Rabbi Eliezer. Wouldn't it be better to stay together as a family? It might be good for someone like Rabbi Hirsch, but for simple souls like us...?" His mother waited a moment. "I think that we all have to trust *Ha Kadosh Baruch Hu** and just be ourselves."

"Here? In this smelly street where you stumble over the chickens? Sorry, mama. If I want to achieve something in the world, I have to leave. Here in Frankfurt, I can't get any further. I am locked up here." He waved with a vague gesture around him, wiping away his tears with his sleeve. "Rabbi Eliezer's room doesn't even have windows."

"Poor Joseph," his mother said softly as she left the room.

Incarceration

A resonant pounding woke him. The walls vibrated and surprisingly the noise seemed to come from above. He had gotten used to the sounds around him and although they remained horrifying, he could now place most of them. But this sound was different. After a while it stopped. Just a part of the inferno, he concluded.

How long had he been here now? After some hard thinking he figured it out – this was his fourth day in the cell. He had decided not to be the clichéd prisoner, putting lines on the wall to count the days, pacing up and down to keep the body and mind active, thinking of freedom while standing in front of what tried to be a window, envying birds because they can fly anywhere and are free. That wouldn't help him, it was nonsense. Above all, he did not want to let those thoughts absorb him. He did not want to adapt. Conformation was the worst option. That was to accept defeat. No, he would not revolt, but silent resistance was also worth something.

He had better things to do. Thinking. He had to start thinking again systematically, analytically. Until now his thoughts had been flashes, disordered and illogical. He envisioned all kinds of scenarios, but they had no basis beyond the false assumptions in his head. From there they became reality and were always terrifying. Writing would have helped, but without pen and paper he would just have to remember it all.

Freedom, he now realized, was a strange phenomenon. He would have expected physical confinement to be the most disturbing aspect, yet this turned out not to be the essence of incarceration. Of course, it would be nice if he could just walk out of the door and he never again wanted to see a door without a handle. The prison itself was a physical trial, the material manifestation of depravity. That was probably why prisoners who had forgotten the outside world could survive. They only had to worry about the dullness, the harassment, and the discomfort. They had already left behind the real evil and the real power. For Joseph, the greatest misery was the struggle with those who had him under their control, for one was doomed to lose. Thus the crux of the matter turned out to be his thoughts. They were not free. They were subject to the power that controlled him. That was what made his life hell here.

2

GRAY LAND OF LONELINESS

There was no straight path. Like the *Judengasse* itself, his life so far had been a long series of twists and compromises. But one could only bend so far before something broke. Joseph knew that it would heal, and even that it was not that dramatic; hundreds of young people left home at his age. He was just doing it somewhat differently. He told himself this to make it easier, trying to ignore the indistinct pain in his heart. Trying to convince himself that he was just leaving for a few days.

Silently he slipped out of bed. Aron was asleep. He looked through the tilted window and listened to the pelting rain. With violent gusts the wind warned him to stay inside. This was November. Looking down at an angle, he could see the laundry he had hung up with his mother that afternoon. Apparently, she had forgotten to bring it in. The wind tried with all its might to blow away the white sheets and like wild ghosts they spun over the line. But his mother had probably foreseen this and she had fastened them thoroughly. His mother could defeat the wind.

Standing on his toes, he could see the cemetery in the distance between a few messy building expansions. Criss-cross stones overgrown with wet, muddy grass. This was not a resting place. How could one find peace in this drenched soil? Even stone got soggy in this climate.

He walked out of the bedroom to the box room, returning with his trunk. Quickly he packed some last things from the bedside table, then placed the carefully prepared letter where no one would miss it. Three o'clock, the middle of the night. He looked through the skylight of the living room door, to be sure that no one was there, but also, in a way, to say goodbye. Inadvertently his eyes fell on the box on top of the cupboard. The family piggy bank. Scraped together from hard work. The previous day he had climbed on a chair and had opened the box. At least a hundred *thaler*. Now that he left, his parents wouldn't have any more expenses for him. Was it not reasonable to take an advance on his allowance? But he didn't take it. He could always call on his parents later, after the storm had blown over. He wouldn't disappear from their lives for good. Only now, for a little while, to take the first steps. As soon as he had more solid ground under his feet, he would visit them.

With a soft, definitive click of the back door, he closed his old future.

He tightened his cape around him against the cold and the rain. The desolate streets appeared strange to him in the middle of the night. Hugging his trunk, he hurried over the wet paving stones. Here and there a single gas lantern was still burning, the flickering light reflecting in the rain puddles.

As planned, the carriage was ready at the station, and as agreed, he would ride on the coach box.

"It won't be a picnic," the coachman predicted. The coachman asked him about his papers, and for a moment, it seemed that the whole adventure would stop before it had even started. Of course, he did not have them, but the papers were essential if he wanted the ride. After much discussion, the man eventually agreed that Joseph could come along on the condition that he got off the coach before they entered the city.

"I don't want any trickery," the driver said.

The trip was bumpy and terrible. Although there was a canopy above him, the westerly wind and rain hurtled straight into his face. When it got lighter in the east, the coachman told him they were at the relay stop in Mainz to change horses.

"If you want, you can look around for half an hour."

The last thing Joseph wanted, however, was to wander around in a strange city, with the risk of getting lost and missing the carriage's departure. He hoped they would continue the journey as soon as possible. The other passengers were all in high spirits and cheerfully took advantage of this delay. They hardly heeded the pale skinny boy sitting under the lee of the carriage.

The day brought scarcely any light; the shadowy dark slowly turned into nothing more than a gray haze. As Joseph looked at the dripping branches overhead, he thought his parents had probably read the letter by now. His friends and family in Frankfurt were about to start the *Shacharit*. The last time he missed them was five years ago when he was ill in bed. His father had ordered him to stay in bed and he had done the standing prayer, the *Amidah*,* lying down.

Softly, he started to recite the *Sh'ma*,* mumbling the first sentences with growing conviction. There was no one around. When he finished a few minutes later, he looked around with relief, because no one had noticed him, but also because he had done it. It was one thing to renounce the external features, but he didn't want to lose his belief in the greater good. God would understand that he had prayed without *tefillin*.*

The passengers returned and when the coachman had taken his place again, the journey continued, now along the western bank of the Rhine. The road that followed the winding river was at times little more than a path and was in terrible condition. As they jolted over yet another big bump in the road, Joseph was afraid that the carriage would tumble over. How devastating would it be if they had an accident now. It was not the thought of the injuries and pain that made him shudder, but the thought of enduring that pain in the cold and the rain. The river was deserted and the hills were languid dark lumps. Joseph crept sideways and curled up against the coachman. The latter growled a little, but allowed Joseph to stay there and doze off.

A bump startled him from an indistinct dream. He did not know whether he had slept for minutes or hours.

"Where are we, sir?"

"Just past Bacharach," the coachman replied with a yawn. "We're going to make a short stop. And boy, did you get some sleep?"

"What a pity. I would have liked to have seen the village."

"Nothing missed, boy. Nothing going on in Bacharach."

Joseph wrapped himself deeper in the blankets that the coachman had given him and decided to stay awake. Not seeing Bacharach was one thing, but he certainly didn't want to miss the rock of his nymph. He asked the coachman to wake him up when they got to it.

A few hours later the man poked Joseph. "There lies the Lorelei. But you have bad luck, boy. Nothing to be seen. The fog's too thick."

The carriage rushed along the road that once again ran close to the river. Joseph looked, but the coachman was right. He could hardly see the far bank.

Perhaps feeling sorry for him, the coachman tried to start a conversation: "The Lorelei is really beautiful. So German. You can't have anything more German than that."

Joseph replied, happy that the man was in a good mood: "*Ich weiß nicht was soll es bedeuten, das ich so traurig bin.*" [5]

"Wasn't it a Jew who wrote that?"

"Heine. Heinrich Heine."

"But he was a Jew, wasn't he? That Heine."

"But German Jews are also Germans, aren't they?"

The coachman made a strange sound, suggesting that he wasn't so sure about that. Joseph deemed it preferable not to invite him to expand upon his thoughts. He was pretty sure he knew where that would lead. At the same time, however, he was very pleased with himself that he had passed this first test; the man apparently considered him an ordinary German. It softened the disappointment of the Lorelei. He could always come back.

"I'll drop you off here then, lad," the coachman told him, as the afternoon was ending. The rain had stopped. "We are about five kilometers from Cologne, but I don't dare to take you any further."

Joseph climbed off the coach box and unloaded his trunk. "Thank you, sir."

He looked around in the fading light. He was at the crossing point of the cobblestone road and a sandy path. To his left, the path led through a rolling meadow. To the right, it took a sharp, steep turn up and cut through the edge of what looked like an immense forest. The road ahead descended slightly into a hollow. A large wooden cross superfluously indicated that this was an intersection. In the distance, Joseph discerned the new railway track. "Which direction shall I take, sir?"

"The shortest way is the path to the west." The coachman pointed vaguely with his hand. "It heads directly to Cologne, but it is all up and down. It will be tough with your trunk. This road first descends to the Rhine and then follows it. With all the curves it is much longer, but it's an easier walk, I guess. Whichever you want. The long easy road or the short, more difficult one."

Joseph nodded and the coachman ordered the horses to continue. With a rattling noise the carriage headed off, and soon nothing more could be heard than an indistinct thudding that finally dissolved in the evening sky. Strange that he hadn't even asked the coachman for his name. Joseph decided not to give in to the feeling of loneliness that slowly crept over him. He had made the right choice and this was just a less pleasant experience.

The sky had now completely cleared up. There were only a few thin clouds around the sun, which shone with a weak light. The crystal clear air seemed to predict frost. Crows soared low over the deserted fields. The pervasive smell of the ground mixed with that of fallen leaves and moist vegetation. The aroma was not unpleasant. To Joseph, it offered the fundamental promise of growth and new life.

He heaved the trunk with its long handles onto his shoulder and in good spirits he decided on the short route, the path that descended to the west. He had at least another hour of daylight and five kilometers would be easy to do. Joseph silently recited the prayer for the traveler: *May it be Your will to lead us to peace and to let us reach the desired goals – life, happiness, and peace.*

After half an hour of brisk walking, the handles of the trunk were cutting painfully into his back. He stopped for a brief rest, then continued, now carrying the trunk in his hands. In front of him was a gentle ridge.

Joseph hoped that beyond it he would finally see the city. The light had weakened considerably and the sun set in the clean autumn air with formidable beauty. The hill was steeper than he thought. Joseph was exhausted when he reached the top. The trunk was heavier than ever. His breath formed small damp clouds.

To Joseph's delight he indeed saw his goal in the distance. What stood out was not the city itself but one building. It dominated the view like a giant insect above a field. It was the cathedral, impressive, even from this distance. It had to be immense. On the west side there was only a blunt tower topped with a crane, ominous, like a gallows. In the middle was a void. As if a giant had stood on top of the church and had crushed the center with his gigantic foot.

He resumed his path. The cold made grasping the trunk even more painful. In front of him was another slope and the cathedral slowly sank into the field. Joseph assumed that it would not be far now and that he would see the whole city from the next hill. But when he got to the top, the image did not seem to have changed much. It was hardly any closer. And in the twilight, the contours were no longer clearly visible.

At his wit's end, Joseph lowered the trunk to the ground. He really couldn't manage anymore. Could he leave the thing here and pick it up later? The plan had its advantages. He would reach the city faster and would be less conspicuous. Maybe it would look suspicious to drag a trunk through the streets after sunset. The more he thought about it, the better the idea seemed. All he needed was a good place to hide it, dry and sheltered, and out of sight. He left the path and soon found a small open shed in the fields, actually no more than a sloping roof. Apparently, the farmer who tilled these lands was using it for storage. Joseph sat down for a moment to reflect on the decision. Did he urgently need anything in particular? He took out his provisions -- a piece of bread and a chunk of cheese. The rest he could do without for one day. He hid his trunk under a pile of bags as best he could. Over the pile he draped a piece of leather and with a vague blessing, he left his belongings behind. Back on the path he got cracking, happy to walk normally again, and about half an hour later, as the landscape became more cultivated, Joseph saw the lights of the first buildings. A group of farmers passed him, talking animatedly. They did not pay any attention to him. Perfect, he thought, I don't stand out.

The gate was already closed. Cologne wouldn't let him in. He may not have been a criminal, but a foreign boy – not to mention Jewish, without any documents – was probably not the kind of guest they wanted to shelter.

Fool he was. He hadn't had to leave his trunk behind. For a moment he considered going back and picking it up, but he was too tired. The journey and the walk had exhausted him and he had to sleep. Tomorrow, in the new light, it would all be so easy. A little further in the field he saw a small bush, some trees and shrubs. A sheltered place among those bushes suddenly seemed very attractive. He glanced around to make sure that no one noticed him and dived quickly between the shrubs. He nestled between the bare branches, wrapped himself in his thick coat, and before he could think about saying the *Sh'ma*, he fell asleep.

Deep voices that seemed a part of his dream woke him. They frightened him. It was almost full moon and a light fog spread over the fields. It was freezing cold. He heard men talking further down the path. They were unintelligible, but still very close. The voices were rough and unpleasant, and in his fear, Joseph remembered stories from his father about Germans bullying Jews. Not so long ago, there had been the *hep-hep* riots in which the Germans took to the streets and randomly molested Jews and destroyed their property. His father had seen it all and had stopped believing in reconciliation. It had made him disapprove of any kind of rapprochement. Here, in the field, at night, it all suddenly seemed very real. Joseph shivered and shrank into the shelter. Had his family set up a search for him by now? But despite his fears, the men continued down the path and their voices grew fainter. Relieved, Joseph drifted back to sleep.

It was still dark when he awoke again. It was too cold to sleep. In the east the sky was getting a little lighter and now and then a bird made itself heard. Joseph stretched his sore muscles after the uncomfortable night. A little later, when morning had broken, he entered the city through the gate without any trouble.

The buildings made it look very much like Frankfurt; straight, spacious houses with large windows, clear lines. Wide lanes, park-like avenues with large patrician houses for people who were wealthy enough to escape the stifling center of the city. Joseph headed on for that center, orienting himself by the cathedral in the distance. The streets grew narrower and the houses higher. At the end of an alley with numerous signboards he came to the cathedral square, and on the west side he could discern the block with the silhouette of the gallows on the roof. He shivered.

To his amazement, he easily found an inn where they didn't ask any questions. After a little rest, he went back to pick up his trunk. With some difficulty he found the shed where he had hidden it, but as he came closer, he saw that everything looked quite different from yesterday. Between the bags and pieces of leather he saw a strap of his *tefillin*. He rummaged through the pile and suddenly he saw his trunk a few meters away. Open, upside down. He turned it around and saw that it was empty. In a frenzy, he went back to the shed and started to ransack the place. The only things he could find were his *tefillin* and his *tallit*. The rest of his belongings were gone.

"Everything is gone," he said out loud with tears in his eyes. His books. His papers, everything he had ever written. His clothes. Wherever he looked, he found nothing. He sank to the ground and sat there for a long while. Only when it started to get late did he get up and head back. He could probably buy some clothes tomorrow. He put his prayer shawl and his *tefillin* back in the trunk. They had left exactly the things he needed least. Perhaps they didn't dare to touch these. Probably contaminated.

In bed, he went over the items he had put in the trunk. He was most heartbroken about a sketched pen drawing of his family that his father had commissioned when Nathan was born. His father enthroned in his lavish armchair, untouchable; his mother holding the baby, standing behind him with a melancholic look in her eyes; the children on the floor at their father's feet. They had given it to Joseph on his sixteenth birthday and since then it had always stood on his bedside table. The night of his departure he had taken it on the spur of the moment. Would Nathan miss him?

He had no idea where the Löwes lived. At a loss, he asked the shopkeeper from whom he bought some new clothing, and fortunately, the man was able to give him the address. At the *Heumarkt*. The house of the Löwes was situated between an inn and the underpass of the alley leading to the cathedral. Quiet, stately residences surrounded the square, all neatly in line. Bare trees stood as guardians in the middle of the square. The Löwes' house was smoothly plastered, with a grand entrance on the ground floor and large windows on both sides. A metal plate proudly adorned the facade, indicating that this was the residence of notary Löwe. Joseph knocked carefully and waited. When there was no reaction, he knocked again, harder. He now heard a stumble. Carefully the hatch was opened in the door. Two piercing eyes became visible.

"*Wer da?*"

"Joseph Socher. I was looking for Werner Löwe."

"He's not here. He is in Berlin this week," was the surly answer after which the hatch was resolutely closed.

Disillusioned Joseph returned to the inn. Something had to happen.

He had to act. His money was running out and going back to Frankfurt, with hat in hand, was the last thing he wanted. He asked the innkeeper if there was work somewhere and the man told him to go to the construction site of the cathedral. "They always need workers there," he said.

The next morning at the break of dawn Joseph walked to the building site. It was foggy and the few people who passed him this early hour seemed shadows to Joseph. The cathedral was not far away, at most five hundred meters and from this side, the east side, the narrow alleys almost ran up to the huge building. Some houses even shared a wall with the cathedral. Joseph had never looked closely at a church before, but what he saw now was impressive. Colossal, meter-wide buttresses went up and up effortlessly and clamped narrow, elongated stained glass windows. They seemed to have lost any relation to the human scale. High above, the church continued in a fragmented and transparent maze of arches, spirals, and spire-projecting towers on top of towers with an abundance of fantastic sculpture and filigree. It dizzied him, this work of an awkward giant with the finesse of a goldsmith. At the other end of the cathedral, he saw the monumental front where the two towers of the Westwork aimed at the sky. On top of that stood the crane. The thing still frightened him.

Joseph found the supervisor of the building site in a small temporary structure on the southern transept. There, the demolition of the medieval houses had freed up a larger square. He hesitated for a moment. Occasionally a carriage passed by and at the sides were small stalls where women were doing the laundry in large bins that resembled feeding troughs. What puzzled Joseph was the large number of respectable men around, recognizable by their top hats. The reason became clear to him a little later when one of the laundresses addressed him and asked him how much money he wished to spend for an intimate quarter of an hour with her. She laid her hand around his shoulder. Joseph pushed the woman away and for a moment he was afraid that he caused a riot, when she, loudly cursing, complained to her colleagues.

"What are you doing?" sounded a boorish voice.

"Pardon me, I'm looking for Franz, the supervisor. I have heard that he needs workers."

"I am master builder Franz." The man came closer. Joseph saw a rude man with small eyes in a large head. He had an irregular stubble and greasy, spiky hair. "Let me see you," Franz said. "Who are you?"

"Jo... Johann is my name, sir."

"And why do you think I would have w...w...work for you, Jo... hann," Franz replied mocking.

"A friend brought it to my attention, sir."

"To your attention, ain't it? Hmm, can you work? Hauling stones?" The man pondered Joseph from head to toe. "You don't look like a worker. You talk strange. Where are you from?"

"I will do my very best, sir."

The man examined him once more and came to a conclusion: "All right. You can start. Supplying stones. Report to Braunberger, he will explain it to you. He is somewhere inside. Two thaler at the end of each day. You have to take care of food and drink yourself. Another piece of advice: listen to what your mates tell you and never stand under the hoists, you understand. Falling stones. Poefff." He chuckled. "Flat Jo... ho...hann..." He laughed out loud now.

"Yes, sir. I'll start right away."

Joseph wanted to shake his hand, but the man had already turned around and while spitting on the ground, he walked away, still roaring with laughter.

Joseph walked across the grounds and entered the house of worship itself. It was one big building site, all around were stones, slats, beams, and ropes, and here and there were large ponds of water. Narrow ladders reached the scaffolding on the upper floor. In the vague light of dawn Joseph saw that the building was barred to the east side. Here and there enormous canvases hung from great height to the floor. The rattling sound of the cloths in the wind was frightening. Above this noise he heard the sound of metal on stone. He looked up and saw the men working on the scaffolding. It was cold and he felt smaller than ever, but he did not want to give up now. He decided to put on a hood against the cold and the noise tomorrow.

"Is anyone there? Braunberger?" A man with a large beard emerged from the shadows. He was heavily dressed and he had a large woolen hat over his head so that his face was barely visible.

"I am Christian Braunberger. Please to meet you," he said with a friendly voice.

Joseph told him that foreman Franz had sent him. Christian took off his hat. A sympathetic face with watchful eyes appeared. A relief after Franz.

"All right, Johann. You can join my team. Bringing in stones. You can start right away." He looked at Joseph critically. "Wouldn't you wear something else? And gloves? You look much too delicate to do this kind of work. Your hands will be blistered within a few hours. Here, take these. He took off his gloves and gave them to Joseph. At least that's something. Bring a hat tomorrow."

Joseph thanked him profusely and Braunberger looked at him again:

"You're not from here, are you? Where are you from?"

"Frankfurt."

It looked as if Braunberger wanted to make a comment, but he only pointed at a large pile of stones. "Get to work. Start with the pile there and bring the stones to that hoist there. The men above will pull them up themselves."

Joseph thanked him again and started to work. The stones were heavier than he thought and he had trouble getting them into the wheelbarrow. He wondered how he possibly could endure this all day long. Each time he faltered, Joseph bit his lip and grabbed another one. Franz came by regularly to command everyone to work faster. Finally at eleven there was a lunch break. Joseph sat apart on a pile of stones. He silently stared in front of him, exhausted but glad that his arms could rest for a while. Braunberger came to sit with him, but he was not very talkative. After ten minutes they got to work again. It started to rain and Joseph got soaked. The rest of the day was a nightmare of stones, rain, and the cursing supervisor. Joseph had only one thought: to make it to the end of the day. The other workmen noticed how he was suffering and now and then they jeered at him.

At five o'clock Franz yelled that the day was over. Joseph tried to say goodbye with a cheerful "see you tomorrow." Then, wet and shivering, he walked to the inn. Joseph took off his dripping clothes and dove into bed. How long could he carry on like this? In any case, he had to bring a hat and thicker clothes tomorrow. He wondered whether he would have the energy to go back to the construction site tomorrow. He fell asleep, restless with terrifying dreams of slaves carrying stones.

The next day was easier. In the morning he had resolved to stop if he really could not go on anymore. Furthermore, he was pleased that he had developed a smarter way to load the stones into the wheelbarrow. The only real nuisance was Franz, the supervisor, who deemed that it was all going too slowly. Joseph wondered whether he had ever hated anyone so much in his life. "I'm finally going to write tonight," he told himself as he loaded another stone onto the wheelbarrow. Maybe he would use this miserable experience as the basis for a story. With effort, he pushed the wheelbarrow forward, but after just a few feet it toppled over and he had to start stacking its stones all over again.

"Not like that. You have to steer in the proper direction, with strength, not just push," he heard Braunberger saying.

At the end of the afternoon Franz noticed one of the workmen who was not feeling well, sitting in a corner. The bully hit the man and when he didn't get up, he hit him again, this time with a piece of wood. The man lay there, wounded. Joseph wanted to intervene. He looked around, but no one seemed to care. He retreated until he found Braunberger. "What a beast. I'd hate that to happen to me. I'd like to think I would hit back." Braunberger just responded that it was happening more often. They watched the beaten man stumble to a safe place, away from the construction site. "I ought to have done something," said Joseph, more to himself than to Braunberger. "Apparently I am no Moses," he thought.

The next day Franz was not there. Braunberger asked Joseph during the lunch break if he felt like walking over the jetties in the choir to have a look. Joseph saw no reason to say no. A little later they walked on the outside of the choir between the spires, towers, and flying buttresses.

"Quite a development project," said Joseph ironically.

"It's a grand journey for the German people," Braunberger answered in all seriousness, "and it's a miracle that after three centuries we continue this work and finish this place of God."

Joseph had no answer. Fumbling in his pockets he felt the little booklet of psalms* that had been too dear to him to leave behind. As they walked on, he held it in his hands. Like a talisman? Just as they decided to turn around, Joseph slipped on a wet board and had to grab the scaffolding for balance. The book slipped from his hand and he saw it fall through one of the holes in the roof onto the floor in the choir.

"Did I see something fall?" Braunberger asked.

"It's nothing. A scrapbook. Not worth the trouble."

"If you want, we can pick it up. Not now, but tonight, when no one is here. It's fantastic to walk there in the evening."

"Are we allowed to enter the building site at night?"

"No, but Franz won't be there."

Braunberger had brought a torch and in the flickering light they stealthily found their way through the gloomy cathedral. It was damp and cold.

"This is awesome," said Joseph and he meant it. He accidentally stepped on a piece of wood that fell into a pit, causing a dull clatter in the silence. Immediately dozens of birds flew up. Black crows.

"Shush. Here we have to climb up," Braunberger whispered when they reached the closed fence of the choir. He handed Joseph the torch and quickly climbed up the stairs. Joseph followed him. They were now above the part that was used for the daily Mass.

"Here we can go down again." After some scrambling they reached the floor inside the choir. Joseph looked up; immeasurable windows soaring upwards.

"What we are creating here is for eternity. It will endure forever,"

Braunberger said. "The heavenly Jerusalem on earth."

"Overwhelming, indeed. It is strange. Like being locked up in endless space."

"If you want to understand anything about Germany, look carefully. This cathedral is the symbol of our unification and our strength. This is our art, our soul, our unity. This is the nation we will become. The Lord be praised. Come, I will show you around."

Joseph wanted to say that he also thought it was a bit megalomaniac, but he kept silent. The moonlight that passed through the stained-glass windows, creating a range of colors on the massive, black stones, fascinated him.

They walked silently through the aisle surrounding the choir and here and there Braunberger drew Joseph's attention to a statue or a painting, mostly Christian subjects. Joseph had never been in a church and he did not feel comfortable. The images of crucifixions – how many were there? – were repulsive. He was impressed by Braunberger's knowledge. Why was someone like him a construction worker? Or did all Christians possess this knowledge? Occasionally he wanted to say something about a biblical scene he recognised, but the fear of discovery held him back.

They went under the central large cross and were now, according to Braunberger, about where the booklet should be. With the torch in his hand, he started systematically examining the pavement. Joseph looked for it as well, hoping to find it first. A little later Braunberger shouted: "Here it is!" He stooped and picked up something. He studied the cover with the Hebrew letters on it and then looked at Joseph with a smile. "I had a hunch all the time. Don't be afraid. I won't give you away." He handed it to Joseph. He sounded trustworthy and reliable. "Your secret is safe with me."

"I wanted to..."

"Calm down. I have many Jewish friends. Don't worry. You can't help it, can you?" He laughed. "I'll tell you something. I am convinced that you are the pioneers for the Savior. Come on. Let's continue."

Suddenly Joseph saw a scene on a sculpture he knew. A wood carving in one of the benches on the side. He bent down to take a better look at it. The *Judensau*. His father had described the appalling scene often. It had been on display in Frankfurt at the main bridge. Fortunately, it had already been removed before Joseph's birth; a picture of Jews suckling on a pig. Joseph felt sick. He wanted to leave this sublime monument for the German people as soon as possible. This was Church institutionalized hatred of the Jews.

"Apparently this is also Germany," he said. "Please, let's leave," he insisted, looking around anxiously.

Braunberger shrugged his shoulders. "Everyone has something he is not overtly proud of."

Joseph wanted to reply when he heard a sound close by. They quickly dived into the shade. Now they clearly heard someone approaching. Braunberger extinguished the light.

"Someone there?" they heard a familiar voice calling.

"Be still. It's Franz," Braunberger hissed. He brusquely pulled Joseph further into the shadows, but as a result Joseph lost his balance and crashed into a scaffolding pole. The scaffolding remained standing, but above him he heard an ominous cracking and then a thundering sound. Just as Franz came into their sight and saw them, an immense pile of stones fell with deafening force. They heard a cry of pain above the grinding sound of stone and grit, and then suddenly all became dead quiet. A large cloud of dust obscured their view. Cautiously, they inched forward. As the dust settled, they saw one arm sticking out of the mass of rough, broken stones. Joseph frantically started to remove the stones, but Braunberger yanked him back. "Stop. We have to get out of here. He is dead for sure. Nothing can be done about it anymore. I don't want to be seen here." He started to run, Joseph close on his heels. When they finally stopped, he gasped, "Are you sure he is dead? He saw us."

"Must be." Braunberger stopped for a moment now. "We have to leave here immediately and not speak with anyone about what happened. In the end, they will only wonder why Franz was lurking here in the dark. They will have no reason to suspect us. They will think it was an accident. It was an accident. But we must not be seen. Curse him. That he had to come here just this evening." He panted. Braunberger peeped outside and said it was safe. They climbed over the fence with caution. "Remember, we do not talk about this with anyone. Do you understand, with no one! Ever." He turned around. He was calmer now. "He got what he deserved. I was more than fed up with him. I detested him." He smiled. "Try to forget it. Do not be afraid; I will not betray you if you will also keep your mouth shut." As he walked away, he said: "Tomorrow you must certainly show up, otherwise you will look suspicious." He disappeared into the mist.

Joseph shivered. Braunberger was right. He couldn't mention this to anyone. He looked to the right and to the left and then quickly walked away from the cathedral. When he came home he had a glass of wine to relax. The dreadful sculpture, the ghostly atmosphere of the church, the hatred he had seen, and the inconceivable accident continued to spook him. A second glass made him a little calmer, but nonetheless he was cold. Still dressed, Joseph crawled under the blankets.

Of course, the next day Franz's accident was all anyone talked about. The greatest cowards suddenly unleashed the extent of their disgust for him, how obnoxious he had been, and how they had always stood up to him. Far off in the choir, they could all see the undertaker, busy with his men. During the break, the police officers leading the investigation came to question everyone. Joseph insisted that he knew nothing and that he had been home all night. He worried they might ask him about his papers, but that fear proved unfounded. They fully accepted his story and after the break everyone went back to work.

After work Braunberger interrogated him about what he had told the police. To Joseph, it felt like the man had become a policeman himself. When Joseph had finished his account, Braunberger only said, "Let's keep each other posted."

Braunberger's mere presence was enough to remind Joseph of the incident – as he now called it – and he retained a vague guilty feeling. The man had become synonymous with the whole tragedy. Joseph thought it preferable not to have business with him anymore. He decided to stop dragging stones for majestic Germany; he had to go after his original goals. Something had to happen. This was not what he had planned. He had to find Werner Löwe.

He spent his last money on another set of clothing, then sought out the Löwes again. This time he was more successful.

"Joseph. From Frankfurt. Joseph Socher. Is that you Werner?"

"Joseph? Ah, yes. Wait I will open the door."

"You said I could look you up," Joseph said before Werner could express any sign of rejection.

He told of his departure from Frankfurt. "I am still looking for a place to live," he confessed.

"I have to go to work now," Werner replied. "I'll be back around noon, we can chat then. Let's meet up in cafe *Zum Turm*." He added as an afterthought, "Maybe my father can help. He is a notary. He knows everyone." He laughed and closed the door.

When they met later at the coffee house, Werner spoke a mile a minute about the status of the Löwes in Cologne and how great their influence was.

"Our family can arrange things," he said with bravura. "I will help you. Let me take care of things. You will see what I can pull off." He sat back with a huge grin on his face.

Joseph supposed that he would become some kind of pet project for Werner but he didn't mind. As long as things were going in the right direction, he would gladly play his part.

A few meetings later, Werner said: "I have found a room for you, in an attic nearby. We can go and see it right away. It belongs to a family friend, so they won't ask any questions."

They walked to a house on nearby *Martinstrasse*, a stately four-story building. Joseph looked up.

"Tall," was all he said when Werner knocked on the door. A sturdy man opened it.

"Ha. The new tenant." The man surveyed Joseph and apparently decided that he was acceptable. He led them up the monumental stairs to the third floor, then down the corridor to a small corner where there was a ladder. "Up here," said the man. "Go and have a look. Here is the key. It is the door on the right. I don't feel so sure on this staircase." He laughed, merrily patting his bulky belly. Joseph went up the stairs ahead of Werner. They came to a dark corridor with the door that the man had indicated. Joseph turned the key but could not get the door to move. He looked at Werner.

"Let me see." Werner now tried to force the door with his body, but it still would not budge. "Wait a moment." He grabbed a slat of wood from the floor and levered it into the narrow gap between the door and the frame. He wiggled the slat back and forth and suddenly the door gave way.

Werner was taken aback by his own brute force. "In any case, it's open. Be careful not to close it completely or you'll never get out. Well, take care. I have to go now."

"Thanks, Werner. You are my crowbar. You unlock all doors for me," Joseph thanked him.

He entered the room. It was dark and small, three by two meters, with a sloping ceiling so low that on one side there was hardly any place to stand. There was a bed, with a neat bedspread. Across the room was a desk with a wicker chair in front of it. The shelves above were half filled with books. Here and there, Joseph recognized someone's attempts to make the space more home-like – a small brown carpet, a mirror by the side of the bed, and hanging on the brown walls, two small landscape paintings. It all looked neat and welcoming, and Joseph could picture himself living there.

He opened the thin blue curtains that pretended to cover the window. Weak light lit the floor. He opened the window, which resisted with dramatic cracking and squeaking noises, and looked out to the northeast. Gray, low-hanging clouds hurrying through the sky. It could start raining at any second. On his toes, Joseph could just look over the roofs to the old center of Cologne. Very close, as if you could jump to it, the cathedral with the threatening gallows loomed. This would be his view on the world for the time being, he concluded.

He looked around again and nodded. "This is perfect." He sat down at the desk and promoted it to his writing desk by putting his new pen and paper on it. He felt overjoyed. What to do now? Write his magnum opus? Discover the world? For now, he wanted only to savor the possibilities. Here he was. Independent, free. Here he could write whatever he wanted and put the books he wanted to read on the shelves. Everything he had dreamed of. His parents had been wrong.

He lit the lamp. In the dim light, he wrote the sentence he had been pondering since a morning last April in Frankfurt. "See, this light is my light." Enjoying the hidden paradox, he read the sentence a few times out loud.

Werner told Joseph that his parents wanted to invite him for Sunday dinner. "This is very important to me, so be on your best. Don't talk too much in riddles," he warned with a smile. "And don't worry. My parents are very modern. My father is really an enlightened man."

On the appointed day, Joseph found himself at the Lowe's grand house. There was hardly any goings-on at the *Heumarkt*. A servant led Joseph into a surprisingly small dining room. He noticed a stale smell. Joseph could not imagine why the family crammed itself into this room; the house had to have larger and brighter ones. The heavy green velour curtains were drawn, creating an oppressive atmosphere. They may have been closed to avoid curious glances, but Joseph suspected that opening them would not help. The darkness seemed to have become an integral part of the room and of its inhabitants. How could an enlightened spirit endure here? On the wall hung Christian paintings and other objects unfamiliar to Joseph. All the furniture was made of monumental oak. In a corner, a large solemn clock ticked away the seconds loudly through the overwhelming silence, although its hands never seemed to move. The contrast meant that no one could forget for even a moment that time was passing, but yet simultaneously, everything was standing still.

The table was set for five, but no one was at it yet. Werner's father Eberhard rose from his chair by the fire. "Welcome. Friends of Werner are our friends. We have never had a Jew over for our Sunday dinner before."

Joseph heard women's voices in the kitchen and suddenly a girl appeared in the doorway. The clock seemed to stop ticking. The girl carried a dish and gave Joseph a friendly nod. She seemed to float. Her whole appearance was radiant. She was by far the most delightful creature Joseph had ever seen. All he wanted was to take her in his arms. Forever. That would be enough. Joseph had no experience at all with the opposite sex. The women he knew were either mothers who spent the whole day in the house or girls who completely covered themselves in the black clothing of the ghetto, robbing themselves of any possible physical appeal. His entire fantasy life had consisted of a print of the Lorelei. Now suddenly this dazzling angel stood before him. Were angels female?

"Here. Let me take that," he stuttered, reaching toward the dish. "I'll put it on the table." As he neared her, Joseph smelled her hair. After the first confusion of her appearance, he was now completely lost.

The girl looked at him and laughed: "Don't worry. Sit down. You are our guest."

"This is Maria, my sister," said Werner. "Come, make yourself comfortable. Sit down," he said. He offered a chair and Joseph plunged in, afraid that someone might have read his thoughts.

Mrs. Löwe now also came out of the kitchen and stretched out her hand to him. "Gretchen Löwe," she spoke kindly. Joseph shook her hand. If he wanted the girl, he had to behave impeccably toward her mother, he realized, aware of the madness of that scenario. But it had been thought. During the rest of the dinner, he kept forcing himself – without success – not to look at her.

Werner opened a bottle of wine and filled the glasses.

"Cheers," they all said as they toasted.

"You are Jewish?" *Herr* Löwe stated, as if the observation required justification.

"Yes, sir. But hardly practicing. I am not religious anymore. So that is probably the end of it."

Löwe nodded a little. "I have nothing against Jews. One of my best friends is a Jew. But I assume it's not that easy to give up."

This was heading toward a hazardous path. "Well, we should not be too preoccupied with it," Joseph tried lightly, hoping that with these words they could wrap up the subject, but Löwe continued, unmindful: "They should not have crucified Jesus. Then nothing would have happened."

"Were they not the Romans?"

Mister Löwe almost choked. "You still have a lot to learn, young man. As I said I have nothing against you or the Jews. You can't help it either, but falsification of history is not right."

Joseph wanted to respond, but decided that it would be better just to change the subject. He looked with interest at a painting that hung right in front of him. The representation of a skull and a candle that had just expired, a weak plume of smoke still clearly visible. However, it was more real than real. Löwe explained, "A memento mori. A remembrance of dying. *Vanitas*. The painting reminds us of our mortality."

"*Hakol Hevel*,"* Joseph said softly.

Herr Löwe looked at him, puzzled. Joseph remembered Werner's advice. Would it be wise to demonstrate his knowledge of the Bible here? He had just decided that he had better keep his mouth shut when he heard himself say: "*Kohelet*.* The wise words of *Shlomo*, sorry, Solomon. It is a line from *Ecclesiastes*. Vanity of vanities. Everything is vanity." Everything worse than to be seen as a complete empty featherbrain. Was Maria causing this? "It is also a reference to the story of Cain and Abel."

Mister Löwe nodded, amused. "Cain and Abel? Now you really make me curious."

"Abel's Hebrew name is *Hevel*. The same word. It means something like transience, but also breath. He is murdered by his brother, even though he was a pretty good boy." He stammered: "It's complicated."

"Interesting. People then wonder why he had to die. That pretty good boy." Joseph heard the mild derision. He blushed. If he continued, he would get completely tangled in his words. He would end up elaborating to such an extent on all the writings that it would be completely impossible for these people to follow. Why hadn't he kept his big mouth shut?

Mister Löwe did not want to drop the subject immediately: "So God let the poor fellow be killed. But then again, the mercy of Jesus is quite different from the callous god in your Old Testament."

"As I said, I'm no longer so involved with it all. That is also the reason why I left Frankfurt." He left it to *Herr* Löwe to determine exactly what he meant, the harsh god or not being involved. He prayed to any god for another topic of conversation. "Our rabbis have written a lot about Cain and Abel. It is all very theoretical," he tried to get out of it.

Mister Löwe laughed. It was the first time. At first Joseph was not even sure whether it was laughter or whether his face was twisted with pain. Joseph laughed along.

"Theoretical, yes," Mister Löwe said when he calmed down again. He turned around to take a closer look at the painting. "In any case, it is a masterpiece. Perhaps we Catholics could learn something from these Lutheran heretics."

Joseph did not understand, but nodded vehemently. He assumed that it was something like the Orthodox and the Liberals. In one corner of his eye he also saw Werner nodding in agreement; it seems that he was pleased with the development of the conversation. Maria looked at him with interest. Apparently, he was someone who could talk to her father. It paid off to open one's mouth.

Herr Löwe asked: "Can you read Hebrew? I have a text here that you perhaps could translate for me. It is a piece of paper from someone's legacy. I don't know what it is. Maybe it is totally useless."

"Of course, with pleasure." He was glad that he could do something in return.

Löwe continued: "Perfect. As you can see, we are doing our best to make you feel at home here. We are not narrow-minded." And proudly he added: "We also believe in the prophet Moses." He examined Joseph with an investigative eye: "Be honest: you may practice your religion, you have equal rights. Or almost, it's a matter of time. What more could you want?"

"Indeed," said Joseph, at the same time realizing that he did not want to be too much in this patriarch's debt.

Every now and then he looked at Maria and he imagined that she was looking back. *Frau* Löwe came in with the potatoes and the beef. "Especially for you. We know you can't eat pork," she said. She was friendly but she said little during the meal. Joseph was glad that he was no longer so careful about kashrut, because rejecting the meat would be an insult that he was happy to avoid. The focus on the meal gave him time to regroup his thoughts.

Strangely enough, it seemed lighter inside now. The room no longer stood apart, it had become one with the world. Maria was the only point of light in this dim environment, but without help, she would lose the fight. Joseph saw himself as the savior on a horse who would take her away to a sun-drenched land. Joseph's thoughts wandered off to Moshe who grew up in the court of Pharaoh. Maybe Maria had arrived here in a basket. She didn't belong here. A stranger in a strange land.

It seemed as if Mister Löwe had guessed his thoughts. Or had he betrayed himself with his stare? "Maria has great plans for the future. Tell it yourself, girl."

Maria said nothing, as if she did not want to destroy Joseph's dream herself. "You tell, father."

"Maria is going to Berlin to marry Gustav Görlitz. An honorable man, religious and wealthy. He might be offered a post as papal ambassador. The young couple would then settle in Rome."

That night he could not fall asleep. He could not put her out of his mind for a second. She made him crazy. The idea that she was destined to marry one Gustav. Leaving for Rome. How should he approach her? Could he change her future? She would probably not be at all interested in an uncouth Jew from Frankfurt. Thinking about her aroused desire.

Or was it lust? What was the difference? How could he channel this feeling? Should he be ruined by bad, impossible thoughts? Let her go away. Should he become a Christian hermit? Or, like Shimon bar Yochai, spending twelve years in a cave far away from the world? Ignore it? Live with it? Escape? He did not know. Nothing made sense. But of course, he knew the answer. Forget about her. How, he didn't know yet, but he had to. Just the name. Maria. Joseph and Maria. What if they had a child? Despite his misery, he laughed.

"I must forget her. She is beyond my reach." He kept repeating it until he had churned himself in a restless, agitated sleep.

Incarceration

"Lichtman, mitkommen," barked the voice for the umpteenth time and again he was brought before the inquisitor. The interrogation was a series of repetitions.

"You have to let me go. You have nothing on me," he said before the officer could start.

"Shut up," said the man without looking up from his documents. "Still not in a mood to talk?"

"I know nothing. You have to release me," repeated Joseph, more mildly.

"We made some inquiries about you, Lichtman. Our colleagues in Prussia sent a telegram. According to them, you were involved, indirectly or directly, in a murder case in Cologne." He looked up now. Joseph tried to keep his face from showing any of his feelings. "Your story is getting weaker and weaker, boy. Release? Don't make me laugh? The only question is for how long you will be locked up."

He waited to let the words sink in properly. "What do you know about it?" he then asked.

"About what?"

"The brawl at the bridge. There was a fight. Tell me."

"Something may have happened. I don't know, but what I do know is that I did nothing wrong. I didn't hit anyone."

"Who were they? Names!" The interviewer changed tone now. The expression on his face became honeyed and he spoke softly, as if it should not be heard by the other guards at the door. "I'll tell you something, Johann. If you help us a little, we will help you a lot. You can leave here tomorrow. What, maybe tonight. What do you care if we pick up a bunch of murderers?"

"Really. I don't remember. Things may have happened, but I don't know."

The interrogator dropped the friendly tone: "I'll tell you what happened, although I think you know because you're part of that group of instigators."

"I met a few people in the trattoria. I am in no way connected to them."

"All the easier to give their names."

"I don't know them."

"Do you know the attorney general? Do you know where he lives?"

Joseph let his head hang and said he didn't know him.

"Procuratore Zorzi."

"I don't know him."

"His house has been set on fire."

Joseph shook his head again.

"Signora Zorzi died in the fire. Murder. With premeditation. The death penalty."

"Forgive me. I don't know them."

The officer whistled to one of the guards. "Take him back to his cell." He made the familiar sign that Joseph could be taken away again. For a moment Joseph had felt some hope. Now everything was back to square one. Hope was the worst thing you could have. If there was no hope, there was no disillusionment.

Back in the cell he lay again on his bed, despairing. When had it gone wrong? When he left his parents' home? When he had chosen for himself? Those choices had only been for himself, not for others. Was he more important than the others? He had not expected his choices to have consequences for others.

Why had he not remained an imperceptive Jew? Why did he have to acquire knowledge? To try to know more. Was it not easier to be ignorant? Where had all this gathering of knowledge led?

He heard Max's answer: "I wouldn't call the Jews of the ghetto ignorant or quixotic. They live in another world, but they are certainly not stupid."

Moonlight fell on the hard stones. Joseph turned around despite his alleged disinterest and looked at the hole in the wall. Because he could not see much, he stood up and looked through the barred window. High in the sky was a full moon. What was it? March? April! Then it was Pesach, the festival of our freedom. What wouldn't he do to join any Seder and hear the stories of the Hagaddah? He yearned for the four glasses of wine. He shivered, not from the cold, but from the sudden onset of withdrawal symptoms. The prison provided compulsory abstinence. He desperately tried not to think of liquor. A glass of wine was as unattainable as the moon that did not care about anything.

3

HOUSE OF STRANGERS

Several times in the days after the dinner, Joseph tried inconspicuously to get near Maria. Just being close to her would be enough. And at the same time, he was hesitant, thinking that might be better to adore her from afar than to fail. Once, he saw her when he came to discuss his papers with *Herr* Löwe. The notary had promised to see whether he could help Joseph to legalize his situation. While talking to Werner and his father, he looked at the daughter, hoping to impress her.

"I can provide papers stating that you are a resident of Cologne, but what exactly is your family name?"

"Socher."

"Joseph Socher is going to be difficult. That has the ghetto written all over it. It will cause problems. Only a few Jews are allowed to settle in Cologne each year, only those with the right documents. And you don't even have documents." He laughed. "Take something German."

Werner spoke up. "What do you think of Lichtman?" Joseph let the name resound in his head. "Lichtman. Fantastic," And to the others: "It will be Lichtman. Johann Lichtman. Thank you, Werner. Exactly what I was looking for."

"Johann Lichtman," said Löwe. "Well, that's better. Much better. And there's something else. Our neighbor is a fellow believer of yours. Converted to Christianity, but still… Anyway, I happen to know that she is looking for a writer or an editor for her memoirs. Maybe it's something for you. You claim to be a writer, don't you?"

That neighbor was Mrs. Elsa Blumenreich but her real name was Esther. Werner told Joseph that she had been baptized more than thirty years earlier, in order to get married. That was when she had adopted the name Elsa. She lived alone. Her daughter had died in childbirth, as had the baby, and the son-in-law had moved away. He was somewhere in the Far East, immeasurably rich. A few years ago, her beloved husband had passed away.

A maid opened the door and Joseph cautiously entered a light, very orderly hall, with little furniture. On the left, a straight staircase led to the first floor. There were paintings everywhere; presumably portraits of prominent people. Joseph felt their gazes fixed on him, as he climbed the steps. He gently knocked on the door on the top.

"Please, come in," a deep woman's voice responded.

Joseph entered the room, which was a more luxurious continuation of the hall, but even more sparsely furnished. A small empty table with simple upholstered chairs, a desk with some papers on it, a piano, and a few high bookcases. Order and symmetry. Again, many paintings, but these were all landscapes, except one: facing him, across the room, hung a monumental portrait that immediately captured Joseph's attention. The young woman it depicted was beautiful, even seductive. Self-confident. Worldly and wise. One hand lightly touched her hair. In the other she held a book. Then Joseph saw the woman in the chair underneath, a lonely queen in an empty palace. The same person, without doubt, only much older. Her posture and clothing were more modest than in the painting, but she had the same worldly look. This was not a woman to be trifled with. She might no longer be the enchanting young woman in the portrait, but the years had given her more authority. She was robust and full of strength.

Her gaze went towards Joseph. "And with whom do I have the pleasure?"

"Johann Lichtman, ma'am."

She squinted her eyes as if she were trying to see him in sharper focus. "You are not from here."

"I am from Frankfurt, ma'am."

"Frankfurt? From where in Frankfurt?"

"My parents live near the cathedral."

"That's vague enough," she said dryly. "How is your Talmud knowledge?" Joseph wanted to pretend that he didn't understand, but she gave him no opportunity. "Oh, don't be stupid. You know I know that you are Jewish."

There was no point in further denying it, so, undaunted, Joseph asked, "What gave me away, ma'am?"

"Your language, your clothes, your posture, your nose, in fact everything that has just entered the room. But you probably know that I am also one of the children of Israel. Or was. No, am; I think you can never change that status. In fact, I am still proud of it. For me at least it is not a problem." She laughed to herself and then looked sharply at him again: "But apparently it is for you. Or else you wouldn't want to keep it a secret."

Joseph stammered something inaudible.

"Why are you fleeing your nest? Because you don't like the nest or because you smell so much of it that you have to go diving into a bath of denial because everyone else turns up his nose at you?"

"I want to make my own choices," he said. Elsa stopped for a second, arranged her clothes and then asked: "So you want to climb from the basement to the first floor, don't you? Not afraid that it's just as annoying to be on the first floor when there are seven more floors above you? And worse, that you're going to distance yourself from the people who remained in the cellar?"

Joseph recognized the metaphor and was pleased with his own erudition. It was written by Ludwig Boerne, a close friend of Heine. He responded in kind, "I will build myself a house, based on freedom, for everyone, for all people, Jewish or not."

Elsa Blumenreich smiled. "Nice answer, my boy. Come on, I won't eat you. I have been around." The assuring tone with which she spoke encouraged Joseph to reveal more of his story. Openly, he admitted that he came from a Jewish family. He spoke about his father and his father's business and his piety, his caring mother, and his brothers and sister. "My family is really very kind and good, but they don't allow me any room for myself." He noticed that Elsa looked amused and he continued, "Truly, they don't take me seriously, maybe only my sister Rivka. I want to write and the only thing they say is: "Go work in your father's business and marry the girl from upstairs.""

"And you don't want to do that?"

"No, really, I want to write. Telling about what I know or think I know, about my doubts. About the promise and potential of life. I don't want to ruminate on Talmud texts from fifteen centuries ago. I am not a cow." As he said it, he was himself shocked by the blunt comparison. He blushed and hoped she could laugh at it.

"So you fled."

Joseph found courage: "Not fled. That is too negative. I escaped. I have broken out. Positive freedom, ma'am." He was quite certain that "escaped" sounded better than "fled."

Elsa looked thoughtful. "Positive freedom, indeed. Before 1814, everyone thought that Napoleon would not only liberate us but also would announce the beginning of our great century." For a moment, her eyes glazed with memory. Then her gaze grew alert again, even animated. "I probably have a better understanding of what you want than most people. I felt it too, at a time when it was even more difficult than it is now. My parents were strict Orthodox Jews, also from Frankfurt. Do you know that as a child I saw Napoleon? It was tremendous. What a promise. All the girls were in love with the French as they marched in. The Germans with their short-sightedness and their old feudal structures didn't stand a chance. Liberty, equality, fraternity. The genie was out of the bottle. But after Waterloo it had to be reinserted. For me it all lost meaning. I left politics for what it was. I sided with myself, against my parents. Christianity didn't appeal to me. I hated crosses. It was a practical necessity. Isn't it written, "You'll choose life"? For me, paradoxically, life was a marriage to a Christian man. And I have not regretted it for a single moment," she added.

The story moved Joseph. He reviewed the images in his mind: Napoleon's troops marching through the streets. An unhappy girl whose parents denounced her because she desired to follow her great love. The sadness with which it all ended. The loss of the man for whom she had made the most difficult choice of her life. The deaths of her daughter and grandchild.

Elsa poured tea. This allowed Joseph time to pull his thoughts together. He now examined the room more carefully. The paintings were especially impressive. Elsa noticed his interest. "Do you like art?"

"I hardly know anything about it."

"But you can say whether you like something or not, right? What do you think is the best here? Tell me. It interests me."

It would not do to choose the portrait of *Frau* Elsa herself. Looking around, Joseph noticed a large landscape painting. Viewed from behind, a lonely man, a hunter, slogged on a steep path through a dark spruce forest. It reminded Joseph of the last part of his journey to Cologne. That seemed centuries ago.

Joseph pointed to the painting. "I think he is also looking for freedom, but it doesn't look good for him."

"Casper David Friedrich. Nice choice. I am very attached to it." Again, she seemed to go back in time. "That is a French soldier, defeated by the Germans." She looked again at the painting and laughed: "We Germans love loneliness and the woods. We even have a word for it: *Waldeinsamkeit*." [6]

"To be honest, I don't know much about all that. I often don't see the wood for the trees anymore."

They laughed and Joseph began to enjoy the conversation.

Elsa shrugged. "You just don't want to deal with being Jewish?" A soft smile touched her face. "Redemption. That's what you want. Were it not that our faith is already so full of it." Joseph noticed that she said "our."

"Exactly, ma'am." He appreciated her stating it so directly.

"Very well then." Her voice became solemn again: "I want to give you a chance." Her expression softened as she continued: "Don't smile too soon." She made herself comfortable. "I have lived through a lot in my life. Too much to mention. Still, I'm going to tell it all and you're going to write it down. I'm going to pay you for that. You'll make some good money. Agreed?"

Joseph did not know what to say. He murmured something that Elsa saw as a confirmation.

"So, when will we start? Next Sunday?"

Joseph smiled. "Of course. I'm going to make it the most beautiful story ever written."

"Beauty is not the most important thing, it has to be good. And the truth? Oh, the truth. I will determine that myself." She looked amused and softly repeated as if spoken to herself: "I will decide for myself." Louder she asked: "Don't you wonder why I choose you?"

"I have a hunch."

"Tell me."

"If I dare say it, I am Jewish and you think I will understand your background."

"Very well, my boy. That's part of it. But honestly, you are also much cheaper than an established, professional writer."

"I won't disappoint you, ma'am." Joseph's words came from the bottom of his heart.

"Tonight my good friend Max will dine here. Would you be so kind as to join us?"

Joseph gratefully accepted the invitation, picked up his hat and got to his feet.

"I really will do my best."

"Very well, young man. The best is all we can do. The rest is in the hands of you know who."

When Joseph returned that evening, Elsa was sitting in the same spot, deep in conversation with a well-dressed, small but sturdy man in his forties. He had a round face, small glasses, dark curly hair, and he was balding at the temples. Elsa pointed to Joseph. "Max, this is Johann Lichtman. An ex-*frum* Jew from Frankfurt who is trying to make his fortune in Cologne. He is our guest tonight." She turned to Joseph. "Max Bentoff is a very good friend of mine, and unless something extraordinary has happened since yesterday, still Jewish. Max is the best journalist in Cologne and has perhaps experienced even more in his life than I have." She smiled at Max, "Come, let's eat."

The table was set festively. Elsa sat at the head and Max and Joseph sat opposite each other on the long sides. The large candlesticks between them meant that Joseph had to shift a little when he wanted to see Max, but they also gave him a way to hide, if necessary. At first, they left him alone. The food was delicious and the wine excellent. In the beginning he sat, sidelined, while Max and Elsa discussed politics. It didn't mean much to him.

Max predicted that a great war between Russia and the West was imminent. "There is a power vacuum. The Ottomans are on the verge of collapse, the Habsburgs are centuries behind, the French are still recuperating. It will be between the British and the Russians, I suspect. And it will not be gentle. They all want their own state – Italy, Greece, Romania. And then us, ourselves. Prussia. Haha."

"Yet it may be the only future Germany has."

"I'm afraid you're right, Elsa. But about the Prussians I also have my reservations. It is a strange time. For centuries, hardly anything has happened and now suddenly, in the last forty or fifty years, everything seems to be gaining momentum. Revolutions, civil rights. Our children will never understand how we lived without factories, gas light, telegraph, trains, steamships, you name it. This is really the most dynamic time ever. I am glad to be alive now so that I can experience it all."

Joseph's attention had wandered, but he was immediately alert when Max turned to him. "Have you published anything?" Joseph reluctantly confessed that regrettably, he had not.

"Written anything?" asked Max. With sadness Joseph mentioned the writings that had been lost when his trunk was ransacked. "But I am working very hard."

"I'm a journalist and I know a lot of publishers. If you have anything, I would be willing to look at it." In a jovial tone he added: "And don't be afraid, lad. You can stay Jewish. Nobody cares about that anymore. Everyone is free to choose his god. And me? I have none. Jews, Protestants, Catholics, Mussulmen, whatever. Do you know when the problem starts for the Jews? When they see themselves as a separate people. And then they're surprised to be treated differently. There are even some Jews who want their own country. Now that's just looking for trouble."

"But you are Jewish yourself, sir."

"Yes. Only, I don't care about it. I don't believe, therefore I am. Nor am I going to convert to Christianity or anything else. I am not Heine. Whether they kneel before a cross, bind leather straps around their arms, or lie barefoot on a mat, or as far as I'm concerned, throw a bucket of water over their heads and then begin to dance, they have my blessing. As long as they leave me alone. Nor do I see why the state should bother about it; why some people should have fewer rights than others. It doesn't make sense." He added just to make sure: "Although apparently it does."

"It's not fair that Jews don't have the same rights."

"No, of course it isn't. Let me tell you a secret. The world is not fair. Let that be lesson one. Second, I think that within ten years the Jews will have exactly the same rights as everyone else. Make it twenty years. Just like that. The Jewish problem solved."

"So you are in favor of assimilation?"

"I have faith in people and their religion doesn't concern me. But all people should have the same rights. I even think that women should have the same rights. Is that assimilation? I don't know; men and women will always be different. Take the three of us for example. A so-called convert to Christianity, a completely assimilated unbeliever, and one who wants to break with his faith. What kind of future can Judaism have?"

"I never said I wanted to break."

"I am afraid that you will have to bend very far, my boy." Max took on the role of a wise father dispensing advice. "Very far. I don't know if that is possible. You know what is interesting? The simple fact that the Jews have isolated themselves from the world has ensured that they still exist. That is the point of all of *halacha.** I do think, however, that Orthodoxy has a better chance of succeeding than that Liberal stuff. That is just Luther in Jewish garb. As I said, I think that the problem will solve itself. We will be the last remnants who can talk about it." He added mysteriously: "But I do think an intellectual reservoir is going to burst."

"I don't understand, sir," Joseph said.

"The Talmud sharpens your mind. For generations the Jews have been splitting hairs in the Talmud. So far, they have used it for things that make little sense, excuse my presumption. Now thousands of Jews urgently want to bring this perspicacity to the rest of the world. People will be stupefied. Mark my words."

Joseph liked the idea. Somehow he ascribed this to himself.

"Since we are talking about Jews," said Elsa laughing, "Friday next week is Christmas Eve. I have organized a soiree and I want both of you to come." Joseph had no opportunity to say no. Apparently the invitation was beyond confirmation or rejection.

After dinner they went to the living room where a piano stood. Elsa opened a small cabinet and conjured up a few bottles of alcoholic drinks.

"Whisky. The best there is. Come Joseph, join us. This broadens your mind."

Joseph mannerly accepted a glass and tasted it. It was strong, but after a while his head felt delightfully light.

"Elsa, please play for us," Max said as he pulled a thick cigar from his breast pocket and lit it with great pleasure. He gestured to offer Joseph one, but Joseph declined with a laugh.

"I will play Beethoven for you," said Elsa. "The Tempest Sonata."

Joseph had never heard any Beethoven before. The sounds were so rich and full of passion that he completely forgot where he was. When Elsa had finished the sonata, he could not remember anything for a moment. He had tears in his eyes. Almost beyond word, he stammered, "That was unbelievable. How beautiful you played."

Later, when he walked back to his room, he decided to write a story about a man who falls into a trance while listening to Beethoven and does not remember anything after the final chord.

The weather was exceptionally mild for December. The low sun shone brightly in the light blue sky and Joseph, out for a pleasant walk, was more aware than the past Saturdays that it was the Sabbath. Suddenly, he realized that he had just passed a synagogue.

He had always known exactly what day of the Jewish month it was, but since coming to Cologne, he had lost track. The first few weeks he often had prayed in the morning, but gradually the need had diminished or he had simply forgotten about it. He had also become less careful about his diet. He had resolved to remain kosher in principle, but necessity knows no law, he told himself when sometimes he went to the cheapest restaurant to satisfy his hunger. Pork, however, remained off limits. "I am not that bad," he told himself.

Unobtrusively, he watched the people going inside. He heard singing and he immediately recognized *Hallel*,* the special psalms of thanksgiving. Of course, it was *Chanuka*.* That meant that this Sabbath was also *Rosh Chodesh*,* the first day of the month. Joseph had always loved *Hallel* – so much joy. He knew that soon the congregation would read from three Torah* scrolls. He could picture the *bima* with men around it, wrapped in their *tallitot*. It was so familiar and at the same time so far away.

The building beckoned. Should he enter? They certainly didn't need him as tenth man. If he went in, would he be betraying his rebellion? They wouldn't leave him alone and would want to include him in their community. He wanted to be pious on his own terms, not on theirs. No, it was too late. One could not return to port after sailing and celebrating the departure as a great achievement. Although it was a tempting, safe haven and heavy weather was imminent, he would neither look back nor be afraid. He would make it.

As he walked on, he came to a wide, gracious avenue. Between the trees Joseph found a bench in the sun. It was a December morning like few others. In the sun, it was even pleasant. With his eyes closed, he sensed the source of the light. "Bless my soul," he started to mutter. He knew the psalm for *Rosh Chodesh* by heart. *Otef ohr ka'salma* – Who wraps himself in light as in a garment. Wasn't the intention more important than all else? He had never said the psalm with so much passion and conviction. Hashem would understand him. In any case, for Joseph, the light was there.

Reassured in his decisions and full of hope for the future, Joseph walked back to the shop in the city center. With the money he had received from Elsa, he bought a new hat.

Joseph had asked Werner whether they could attend a Beethoven concert somewhere. After some inquiries, Werner had discovered that the Seventh Symphony would be performed in Bonn that Sunday. Maria would also come.

Excited, Joseph walked with Werner to the train station on the outskirts of the city where they would meet Maria. Joseph worried. What if she were late? He recognized the place. *Sankt Pantaleon*. This was where he had entered the city. In the distance he saw her blue hat. "There she is," he shouted. If possible, Maria was more gorgeous than ever and Joseph tried to find a balance between his shyness and too informal a pose.

"I am delighted that you could join us today. It promises to be a glorious outing."

"Indeed," she said merrily and nodded toward the station. "Hurry up or we'll miss the train."

If at first Maria had been a wonderful, if distant, fantasy, now, going on this trip, she became real. A woman of flesh and blood. As if a simple drawing of a summer landscape, beautiful but sketchy, had turned into a glorious painting, with full colors, with depth, with a story into which one could utterly disappear.

"Have you even traveled by train?" When Joseph admitted that he hadn't, Werner continued. "It's an astonishing experience. Wait, here it comes." Squeaking and grinding, the vehicle on the rails came to a standstill in front of them. A bit shaky, Joseph climbed the steps to the wagon and while holding Maria's hand – with the excuse that he wanted to help her – they looked for a place to sit. It took a while before the train left, and Joseph realized that every fiber in his body was tense. Not afraid, but rather, prepared for something spectacular. His mind was completely alert.

The train sluggishly started to move, then soon accelerated. They shot through the gate making Joseph think of a bullet, fired right through the medieval *Pantaleonstor*, leaving the ponderous structure in shreds and giving way to this lightning bolt of the future. Once outside the city, the train gained momentum and at an enormous speed the colossus rushed through space, in a straight line instead of following the whims of nature. Joseph was a new man in a new age. Time and place became unconnected. Joseph suddenly understood the unlimited possibilities. The challenge of mastering nature evidently had an adventurous, even existential side, with all the dangers that it entailed. One could only surrender to its power. Nothing could stop this train. It was out of his control and this sensation was thrilling. It was absurd to deny that a new era had arrived. This was nothing for old rabbis with long white beards, this was for youth, those young in spirit and open to progress. Long live the future. Science and technology improved life. He would be in the vanguard.

He looked for a moment at Maria who was sitting across from him. She smiled. Was it out of kindness or was she amused at his awkwardness? He looked outside again as the train repetitively shot past the poles beside the rails. In the distance he thought he recognized the crossroads where he had gotten off the coach. That had been a false start. The picture was completely different now. In front of him, the sun was shining in the same spot, invariably. On the horizon the view had hardly changed, but the closer the view, the more fleeting it became. And close to him, every object seemed transient; before you could focus on it, it had already disappeared. Again, Joseph sensed that only he could experience this phenomenon here and now. He decided to use it in one of his future books. But while he was trying to put it into words, an opposite feeling came over him. Now he felt that he himself was part of the growing impermanence and that, completely outside of him, far away yet connected, was a great realm of tranquility.

In the middle of the large town square, Werner pointed to a statue. "That's him."

"Who?"

"Just look." As they approached, Joseph could see that the statue was larger than life. High up on a pedestal stood a looming figure with one foot slightly forward. One hand held a pile of papers. A stern head with a large mop of hair inspired awe. This man was not of this world. The corners of his mouth turned down to indicate that he did not have time to occupy himself with the plebs below. His gaze was towards the distance, towards infinity, where ordinary mortals could not go. But despite the severity, Joseph also saw a boyish kindness shining through.

A giant, but gentle.

He heard Maria speaking next to him: "The Beethoven monument. It was erected a few years ago. The festivities lasted three days. All the famous composers were there: Liszt, Schumann. I have heard that Liszt himself paid about half of the costs. Impressive, isn't it?"

"If I had to portray God, he would look like this," Joseph said with a laugh. "But according to my faith, worshiping statues is completely wrong. And I understand why they forbid it."

"Come, let's have a drink there." They entered a cafe and Werner continued about Beethoven; how he was always looking for his immortal beloved. "They think it was one Josephine, whom he couldn't marry because of the class distinction." Was this a casual remark? In any case Joseph decided not to react.

"Do you know *Romeo and Juliet*?" asked Werner. "Already then and still today. Nothing new under the sun."

"That one I know," said Joseph.

"It is one of my favorites," said Maria.

"I meant 'nothing new under the sun.' "

Werner laughed. "You really live in a different world. Don't you know Shakespeare?"

"I was talking about Shlomo, King Solomon."

"I was talking about a play by Shakespeare."

"I've heard of him, but never read anything."

"You really have to catch up."

"I will, I promise."

When they arrived at the theater later that afternoon, the opulence and splendor of the concert hall dazzled him, but Joseph tried not to show that this world was completely alien. Werner and Maria guided him through the space and soon they were sitting in one of the front rows.

The concert shook Joseph loose from the world. Like the statue, he felt elevated, and he hovered above everything he had ever thought and felt. He got shivers and goose bumps at the same time. His eyes filled with tears of emotion. It seemed too much. After the final chord had sounded, he clapped his hands until they turned red and shouted along with the rest of the audience. "Bravo, bravo…!"

Still stunned by the magnificence of the music, he left the hall with the rest of the audience. Then he turned to Werner and Maria, "That was incredible, unbelievable." No words could convey the depth of his reaction. "It starts off beautifully and then something else comes and that is more beautiful and then it becomes even more beautiful and that goes on and on."

Maria smiled. "Particularly the second part, don't you think?"

"Yes, indeed. It goes on and then those other instruments join and then they go on together and then it gets even more beautiful."

"For a writer, you are driveling pretty seriously," said Werner.

"Good point. I'm going to write about this. It was so incredible ... beautiful. I've never heard anything like it before. So beautiful!"

"Don't start again."

"But do you understand what I'm saying? I feel my soul. This is divine. This is life."

Back in Cologne they parted. Joseph watched with regret as Maria's blue hat slowly disappeared in the crowd, but consoled himself that there would be more opportunities.

The next day he worked up the courage to ask Werner, "Has she ever asked anything about me?" Werner looked at him with a grin. "What have we here? You're interested in my sister? Sorry, but to be honest, I don't think you'd stand a chance with father. You know she is already engaged. His name is Gustav Görlitz. He is from Berlin, a banking acquaintance of father's. Everything's arranged. Rich family. No, Johann, no chance. But we are good, aren't we?"

The following Frid was *Frau* Elsa's soiree. When Joseph entered the room his senses were immediately put on edge. It was as if he were suddenly standing in a pine forest. Everywhere Joseph looked, he saw green, with an occasional flash of gold. In every corner stood a table with a large, ornate candlestick, each with as many as ten arms raised in whimsical shapes. The candles provided a soft, dreamy light. Where Elsa's chair had been now rose a large Christmas tree decorated with colorful balls and candles at the ends of its branches. The grand piano, bearing a large bouquet of flowers, now commanded the center of the room. Somehow the ambience inspired both serenity and merriness.

"Welcome. You're exactly on time," said Elsa as she walked towards him. "The most important guests always come too late, but I'm glad you're here. Take a drink. I will introduce you to some people. First, Anton Pennekamp. He owns a good local newspaper and is a renowned publisher. He could be very important to you. And to me!"

She walked to a group of people near the piano and one of them looked up. It was a tall, older man with heavy sideburns, a bald forehead, deep-set eyes, and a smile that gave him a slightly satanic appearance. Next to him stood a slender woman. Black hair and a narrow face, with close-set eyes and a pointed nose. Despite her mousy appearance she radiated elegance, helped in part by her expensive clothing, *haute couture* from Paris.

"Anton, this is the young man I mentioned, Johann Lichtman," said Elsa. "I would like you to get to know each other." She drifted away, leaving Joseph standing in front of the group.

"Pleased to meet you," said the man, "I am Anton Pennekamp. This is my wife, Odette. She is French, but not all the time. She speaks German better than either of us."

The woman smiled as she stretched out her hand.

"Those are our children, Horst and Hilde. They are your age, I think. It might be nice for you to get acquainted."

Pennekamp looked at Joseph for a while as if assessing him. "So, Mister Lichtman, do tell me, what is going on in and around Cologne?" The voice sounded mocking, but his face was friendly. Joseph awkwardly managed some vague remarks, but he nevertheless found the man rather sympathetic.

They continued to make small talk until Max's flamboyant entry interrupted them. Joseph was relieved to see him. It was like running into a good old friend, although he had only met him once. However, he could not go over to him right away because Elsa had taken the floor.

"Good evening, dear friends. I think we should first honor tonight's occasion. Whom can I ask to sing?" She surveyed the room. Probably by arrangement a boy of about ten came forward timidly. The music's first notes seemed vaguely familiar to Joseph, but when the boy started singing, he knew precisely what it was. *Silent Night, Holy Night*. Joseph felt embarrassed. It was one thing not to keep Shabbat anymore, but it was entirely different to hear a song about the child Jesus next to the Christmas tree. On Friday evening, of all times. Joseph slipped out of the room and went down the hall to the kitchen. If anyone asked, he could always say that he was looking for a drink.

He returned a few moments later, bearing a glass of water, and was just in time to hear Elsa announce the next part of the program: Horst Pennekamp, Anton's son, would play pieces from Beethoven's fifth symphony in a transcription by Franz Liszt.

"Hello, and with whom do I have the pleasure?" asked a hoarse female voice next to him. Joseph had taken the first seat he could find, without paying any attention to his neighbors. It turned out to be Hilde Pennekamp, the publisher's daughter. Joseph was slightly disturbed when he looked at her. She had gray blond, almost white, hair and her penetrating eyes were deep red. Joseph had heard of the phenomenon, but had never met anyone with them before.

"Johann," he said quickly, as he wanted to focus on the music.

"I hope he will play Wagner as well. He plays *Lohengrin* exquisitely."

"*Lohengrin*, yes," he said distantly, hoping the conversation was over.

He took a sip of water to ensure this and tried to pick up the thread of the music again, but he didn't really succeed. When Horst had finished, Hilde got up and with the words "see you," walked over to her mother.

After the applause Max came to find him. Max addressed him informally for the first time. "I see that you don't fully appreciate the Germanic culture. Holy infant so tender and mild?"

Joseph shook his head, puzzled.

"Silent night? Doesn't that ring a bell?" Max laughed. "Come on, don't get angry. I was only joking. I also had a hard time with it at first. I can assure you that you get used to it. Would be a nice song for the Pesach night, ha!" He turned around and walked to Pennekamp, beckoning Joseph to follow him. Joseph was worried. "Do you think that anyone else noticed?"

"It doesn't matter. Even if they did, what do you care? Either, you still believe in your one God and you just toss off a few prayers to yourself in situations like these. Or maybe you really don't give a hoot anymore, and then..." He seemed to be trying to find a fitting expression, "well, then you don't give a hoot anymore. Come, let's have a chat with good old Anton. Always refreshing to hear his insights."

Again, he was introduced and soon Max and the publisher were engaged in a heated discussion about the problems surrounding the financing of the new railway lines, something that did not interest Joseph at all. Anton Pennekamp noticed it and now addressed him.

"Cigar?"

Before Joseph knew what was happening, Pennekamp stuck a big corona between his lips and lit it. The first puff was horrible. Joseph gagged and his head began to spin. Everyone laughed and Joseph sheepishly joined them.

"You'll get used to it," said Max. "Here, a good sip of this brandy will make you feel better." Joseph took the glass, and not wanting to exhibit his lack of experience once again, knocked it back in one draught. It worked indeed. The physical discomfort evaporated and his head felt light. Apparently liquor gave strength.

"Well lad. I heard that you want to become a writer. Can you write?" Pennekamp asked.

"I think so." Joseph coughed the words along with the smoke.

"That's not enough. Most people at a newspaper think they can write."

The brandy had its effect and Joseph felt more confident. He glanced through the smoke at Max for support, then tried again with more assurance: "Let me say that I know I can write. I'm just waiting for the right chance to prove it."

The man thoughtfully puffed his cigar until he was enshrouded by blue vapor. "Max told me you come from a Jewish nest. Have you considered baptism?"

"No, absolutely not."

"That's fierce," said Pennekamp to Max. "It's not that bad. I think the only difference is that instead of not going to the synagogue, you don't go to church." They both laughed so loudly that the other guests looked up.

"What do you think of my chances of publishing something?" Joseph tried when they were quiet again.

"First, I would start writing, lad. But I have no prophetic skills," said the publisher and again blew a big cloud of smoke toward Joseph. "I'm not the oracle of Delphi."

"Looks like it with all that smoke," commented Max.

"I'd rather not write about Jewish affairs, to be honest. I'm looking ahead." Joseph tried to come up with something quickly. "I could start with a piece about the completion of the cathedral?"

The publisher laughed. "Completion! You are an optimist. But do. Just amaze us. You know what? Come to the office on Monday. We'll see whether we can find some kind of editorial job for you."

Joseph thanked him profusely.

"Please, please. I knew you were looking for work. Dragging stones is not a task we should burden the Jews with for too long. It ends up bad for everyone. But Jews make good scapegoats in case of accidents."

That comment startled Joseph. Was he referring to the accident in the cathedral? But how could he know about that? He had given Elsa and Max nothing more than a description of his work there. But he had no chance to react, because Pennekamp continued, more seriously. "What I do recommend is that you broaden your horizons. Go to concerts, exhibitions. Read books about history, philosophy, literature, art. Learn languages, French, English, Latin, and improve your German. *Bildung!*[7] Your motto should no longer be "forget the past," but "forget the old future.""

Joseph promised to do so, and to show that he had already taken steps in this direction, he added: "Last week I went to a Beethoven concert in Bonn. The seventh symphony. It was grandiose. Beethoven is divine."

"Then we have something in common," smiled Pennekamp.

"The most beautiful I've ever heard." He hesitated for a moment, unsure whether it was wise to continue, then ventured, "Do you know the *Sh'ma*? The Jewish creed, so to speak. Those are just words. As if you are in a cave and see the reflection of the sun. Beethoven is the true light, not a reflection."

Pennekamp looked amused. "Have you read Plato?"

"I beg your pardon. Who?"

Pennekamp looked at Max and they both nodded. "Classy, my boy," he now said to Joseph. "I'll give you some books on Monday. I think you have it in you. Listen to Wagner, I advise you."

"I have heard of him. *Lohengrin* seems to be very good," Joseph dared, like a real connoisseur.

Anton Pennekamp's publishing house was located in a stately building on *Wallrafsplatz*, in the center of the city. The publisher was busy and had little time, so Joseph's conversation with him was short, but pleasant. Pennekamp took him to the basement that housed the archive. He took a stack of files from a shelf. "Start by looking at this. These are articles and longer editorial essays that I wrote myself. Not that this is the best we have here, but we need to begin somewhere. Make good use of it."

For the rest of the day Joseph buried himself in the articles. They were certainly interesting, but he did not know exactly what to make of it all. He was sitting in a secluded space underground, reading old texts, but he had a strong premonition that all this was the beginning of something good. He now worked for a newspaper. It would not be long before his own texts would be published. And it was thousands of times better than dragging stones.

A few weeks later Joseph asked Max why he deserved so much attention. Max was silent for a long time. Then he said: "Maybe I always wanted someone to teach." Lightly, he added, "Actually, I missed my vocation. I wanted to become a professor."

Max told him about his experiences as a student in the post-Napoleonic era. He had studied law but, in the end, it was of no use to him. He was refused a position as professor at the university and even forbidden to practice law if he remained Jewish. He definitely didn't want to be baptized, so he went into journalism. "It didn't turn out badly, but it wasn't what I had in mind. If I were young now, it might be different."

"And you really don't have any connection to the faith anymore," Joseph asked.

Max paused, as if checking the past before answering. "No, nothing but old memories. But I have a brother who is still very pious. I respect him and he respects me. Why do you ask?"

"I was thinking of home."

"In the last years I have been to synagogue on Yom Kippur once or twice but it didn't mean much to me. Beautiful memories should not be weakened by a quest to relive them."

Joseph nodded.

"Do you feel guilty because you abandoned your faith," asked Max.

"At times. But it is probably more a feeling of guilt towards my parents."

Max rubbed his forehead, but kept silent.

"I don't know where I belong," Joseph continued. "All the worlds stand completely apart. The world of you and Elsa and then the Löwes. And my family of *Altglaubigen** in Frankfurt." He laughed despite himself.

"Until you claim your own space, you'll probably continue to feel pulled back and forth. And perhaps all those worlds are separate. The Löwes are a very prominent family. I was astonished that they took you in like that." He sighed. "I think you are a good boy and I would like to help you in your journey into the big world. As a friend. Let's leave it at that."

Joseph nodded again, grateful that this man called him his friend.

"Listen," said Elsa, "don't write anything down yet. You probably won't be able to process everything right away. That will come in time."

He was sitting next to her under the immense portrait and she had started to tell her story. Like him, she had been born in the *Judengasse* in Frankfurt. She told him details about her life there and Joseph caught a glimpse of his parents' youth. But Elsa's story was not a happy one. Her family had moved from the ghetto to a nearby neighborhood in the hope that the optimism of the era would persist, but they were disappointed. Napoleon was defeated and Frankfurt became more reactionary than ever. After the Vienna Congress of 1814, Elsa had decided not to be involved with the world anymore. Its outcome and everything Metternich and the rest had decided was a major step backward for the Jews. She was determined that the only thing that would interest her from then on was her own happiness. She had been baptized so that she could marry her great love, a rich industrialist. They had built a house in the new garden district outside the walls of Frankfurt. Slowly but surely, she had begun to believe in progress again, but she wanted only to be a spectator. When Frankfurt remained too narrow-minded, they moved to Cologne. Her husband had a financial interest in the development of the railways. She started to organize salons. "I'll tell you more about that later. Especially who was present. Jews and non-Jews. Industrialists and government officials. Everyone of importance in Cologne. That was when I got to know Max, and Anton Pennekamp."

She poured them both some tea, and sat back comfortably in her familiar chair.

"Do you know when I was born? Please note, I'm not asking you about my age. Beware." She laughed. Joseph shook his head. "In the last decade of the previous century. Does that time period mean anything to you?"

"Of course, the revolution. The French." He stuttered, afraid that his ignorance would be revealed.

"I'm as old as the revolution and look at me now. Derevolutionized. Or how would you verbalize that? Just like the rest of them. All as meek as lambs, writing their memoirs or deciding from their safe places what the world should look like."

She told him about people, known and unknown. All yearning, in their own way, and waiting for the moment when they would be free. Her thoughts wandered and she spoke as if she had gone forty years back in time. Suddenly she became lucid again and returned to the here and now. "And here I am, talking with this boy who wants exactly the same thing." She laughed loudly. "Wasn't it Hegel who said history repeats itself?"

Joseph did not understand. Was Napoleon good or not? His parents had rarely spoken about that time, in 1796. Surely they had been frightened when the French had broken open the ghetto. Afraid of freedom. But he had heard more about the siege that had happened then. His grandfather Shlomo had often spoken about it. Joseph's great-grandparents, Abraham Socher and Fruma Goldblatt, had died during it. Shlomo had never forgiven the French emperor and therefore could not appreciate the personal freedom he had gained. He probably could not have appreciated any freedom, but the story was dramatic, Joseph had to admit. The French troops were besieging the city and had been shelling the Austrian troops for days. The guns stationed on the north side of the city roared continuously. In his unstoppable urge to grant freedom to everyone, Napoleon paid little attention to actual people, living or dead. It was the middle of a hot summer and one just couldn't stay inside, despite the danger and continuous rumbling of the French guns. Everywhere houses were on fire. Large clouds of smoke hung over the city. The nights were especially frightening, with the light of the homes, burning like torches, and the heavy clouds of smoke. In the end, the entire northern part of the *Judengasse* was burned down. The gate was razed, the wall became a ruin. His great-grandparents' house had been pulverized and they themselves had been killed by a collapsing wall on the very last day, after the Austrians had already capitulated. But the ghetto was now open for the Jews to move out, to flee from misery and entrapment. His grandfather Shlomo had not seized the opportunity. He had moved to a building in the even narrower and more depressing part near the south side of the *Gasse*, which had been spared. Joseph's parents had stayed in that same house, maintaining the business of clothes and fabrics.

"*Frau* Elsa, may I ask you something? Did you participate in the revolution of forty-eight? When they wanted to try again?"

"If I had, I wouldn't be sitting here now," she responded bitterly. "Everyone who did is now dead or in exile. Switzerland, France, England. Some left on their own account. And no one is interested in them anymore. You won't hear a word of resistance. Everything is back to the way it was. Back to where it all started." She fell into a fatalistic mood: "Do you know what Heine said? 'Nothing but misfortune has happened to me since I was baptized.' He is an old whiner, but still… It keeps dragging me down." Without saying what she was referring to, she got up. "Today it is exactly eight years since my husband died. His *yahrzeit*, although he was not Jewish." She looked at Joseph. "Do you want to say *Kaddish** with me? It's not allowed perhaps, without minyan and a woman and a man together but it doesn't matter to me. You know the text, right?"

Joseph looked down. "I'll start," he said softly.

When they had finished, he asked: "Are you disappointed in life?"

She laughed, but her face was far from cheerful. "A direct question and I will give you an indirect answer. What do you think? What would you be?"

"Whatever the answer, I think you still have a lot of strength."

Back in his room, Joseph stared at the sentence he had written a while ago. "See, this light is my light." He made himself comfortable at the desk, planning to work on this all night, write a beautiful story around it, polish it, and make it the jewel it deserved to be.

After having gazed at the page for a while, he got up and walked to the little cabinet where he kept his documents. Next to the box with his *tallit* and *tefillin*, lay a small pile of paper. It was a collection of some loose sheets with his illegible handwriting. Unprocessed ideas, raw brainstorms, beginnings. He had already looked through the collection a number of times and, since it was not useful, had put it back. He was convinced that he had already written the right brilliant sentences and he was therefore afraid to throw anything away. He grabbed one and for a moment felt excited because he could not decipher his own handwriting. He had probably written it weeks earlier, otherwise he would have recognized it. He made out the words. "Lying in bed; inventing shapes: filling them with content." Disappointed, he put the sheet back in the cabinet, where it would probably remain until he next sought inspiration, and looked in the cabinet for as yet undiscovered gems.

Incarceration

While lying on his cot with his eyes closed, he spent several hours trying to think about anything but his misery. He kept himself busy reciting things he knew by heart. This soon brought him to the texts from the siddur. The prayers. He began to say the morning prayer no matter how difficult it was. He pulled himself to a sitting position. Lying down would not have been respectable and standing up was too much for him. Didn't the Rambam say that the golden mean was the best? The words reminded him of Frankfurt and his family with painful, nostalgic longing. He saw himself and his father going to the morning service in the old building on the Gasse. Suddenly he saw a vivid image of his mother standing before him.

He continued. The text that came most easily was the prayer to root out the bad and arrogant people and the traitors, to destroy them, immediately. One specific text was much more difficult for him. The prayer of thanking. But he couldn't bear to skip it. In fact, just out of habit, he was already halfway through it before he realized what he was saying. Yet he drew strength from the prayers.

It surprised him that he was not that disturbed about being physically locked up. Usually he was very claustrophobic, but the open window helped. Sometime during the fourth day he had decided not to walk around anymore, but to stay on his cot. It was the sole place in the cell where he could feel the wind from the outside. On that square meter he felt somewhat safe.

Why did he have to be in prison here in Venice? Because of that boy who had been kidnapped to Rome? To enable the liberation and unification of Italy? Lunacy. What purpose did his imprisonment serve in the greater picture? It was all utterly pointless. He would never become a martyr for the Italians. He would certainly not take the lead in demonstrations. He had learned his lesson.

He could die here and no one would ever talk about him again. That was the most likely, and at the same time the saddest, scenario. Or he would be acquitted and would leave the country immediately. He didn't want to stand up for anything anymore. Not for socialist freedom, nor for equality and justice for the people. For nothing. In the future, he would choose his goals and his opponents more carefully. If there had to be suffering, then at least it should be for a really good cause, a noble cause. But for the time being he saw no higher goals in life. Liberation of these people, justice? Who cared? Even Germany wasn't worth it, let alone Italy. He could not come up with anything that could make his sacrifice meaningful.

Was God punishing him now because he had acted selfishly? Did he feel guilt towards his little brother? Was it about the anger when Aron had come to visit? About the irreconcilable views? He imagined his mother crying in bed. Or was it because he had run from the crime scene? Which was not a crime, but still... Cologne came to mind. The huge threatening cathedral. He hardly thought of Maria. She reminded him too much of who he had been not so long ago.

As days went by, a goal started to take shape. If he ever came out of this hell house, he would find Rivka. He didn't want to see anyone else. Not even Max, for that matter. Max had his own free, liberal world in which he had imprisoned himself. Rivka was different. Rivka was the only one who would understand Joseph. He promised himself not to stop looking for her until he found her.

4

(1853)

OLD BELIEVERS

Joseph was sitting at his desk, staring at an empty sheet of paper. A knock on the door made him look up. He couldn't imagine who would visit him so early. He should have stopped before that last glass of wine yesterday. His mouth was dry and when the knock came again, he replied in a crackling voice: "Yes, who is there."

"Aron, your brother. I'm here with Rivka."

This was the last thing Joseph had expected. He got up and looked at the mess in his room. Couldn't they have announced their visit? Had something happened? With mama? He had written to them once he was settled, but their only contact had been by letters. About once every two weeks he received a letter from his parents. Always written by his mother. Usually light-hearted, without any demands. They contained no mention of his little brother or Aron and Rivka, nor did she write about what his father thought. He always wrote back, in the same tone. Mapping out his successes, never confrontational. Above all, they had to think, no, realize that he was doing well. He was living high and dry in Cologne, supporting himself with respectable work. To give it all more weight, he had also mentioned the publisher, Pennekamp.

He slowly opened the door. Aron hadn't changed at all, his curly dark hair hidden under the large skull cap, but at first Joseph hardly recognized Rivka. Her black hair had been cut fashionably and she wore colorful clothes instead of the gray and black in which he had always seen her.

"So, here he is. Our man of the world," Aron started.

Rivka said cheerfully: "Hello Joseph, we wanted to see how our brother is doing. That's okay, isn't it?" She looked around. "Cozy, this room."

"Sure, but it would have been more convenient if you had announced it." As he said it, he kicked some things under the bed and tidied up the room a little.

"Just sit on the bed," he invited, but then he came up with something better. "Let's have coffee outdoors. There is more room there." He looked at Aron and scoffed, "We have kosher places here."

"I don't doubt it."

Joseph led them down the shaky stairs and racked his brains about where to take them. All the coffee houses he knew were not kosher. But there had to be a place nearby where they could have a drink. Without saying anything, he led them to the Jewish quarter where he saw a café on the corner, *Bloch*, a small establishment. He entered and as if he was a regular, he said, "Good morning. Can we get some coffee?" Those present looked up, startled, and the host gave him a look as if he were wondering who the arrogant goy could be. His face grew a bit friendlier when he saw Aron's *tzitzit*.*

Joseph looked around. The place was simple and tidy. There were a few tables and chairs around a large fireplace. They sat down at a table, the host brought coffee, and then it was quiet for a while.

"You don't have to put on a show for us," Aron finally said. "You have never been here before, haven't you? We really can guess what your life is like here."

"And so what? I am happy. I don't eat pork, if that's what you think."

Rivka intervened: "Come on, you two. We can do better as siblings than scoring off one another." She addressed her words mainly to Aron. In a friendly voice she asked, "Joseph, how are you? I've really missed you. Have you published a book yet?"

"I am busy," he replied gratefully. "It's going well. I meet a lot of interesting and influential people here. They help me. In the meantime, I work at a publishing house as a corrector. I might be moving to a better apartment soon."

"Maybe I'll come and stay for a night," said Rivka laughing.

"But of course, you're always welcome. Also at my friends."

"Let's leave the future plans for what they are," Aron said with emphasis. "There are still some things we need to discuss about the past, I think."

"And what would that be?"

"You'd do well to come to Frankfurt one day."

Joseph took a deep breath. "Listen. I didn't have an easy start here. I struggled to achieve something. In the beginning I didn't even have a roof over my head. I dragged stones in a church. I worked myself up. All on my own. So I refuse to let anyone dictate to me now." He immediately regretted having mentioned his work in the cathedral.

"Dragging stones in a church? What, did you build an altar for Joshke? You are really doing well."

Again, Rivka called them to order.

"All right," said Aron, "let's forget about that. But still mama and papa would appreciate it if you came with us to Frankfurt."

"Do you want to kidnap me? That's why you came by instead of sending a letter?"

"Mama is not feeling well. Her heart condition has gotten a lot worse."

"I will visit them, on my own terms. I will let you know."

Aron drank his coffee and said he was ready to leave. "I have said everything I wanted to say." He looked at Rivka. "Shall we go?"

"Already?" Joseph asked. "You came all the way here for a ten-minute conversation?"

"We are also visiting papa's family here. Cousins. They live nearby."

"Aron, I want to stay for a while," Rivka said. "You go see them. I don't know them anyway. I want to talk to Joseph. I'll meet you at the station. At two o'clock, right?"

Aron hesitated, as if afraid he might endanger his mission. "Well... Two o'clock. But don't be late. Trains don't wait like carriages." He shook Joseph's hand and left the café.

Joseph thoughtfully puffed clouds of smoke from his newly acquired pipe. He had decided that he should smoke something and cigars were too intense. A pipe was just right, distinctive and physically bearable.

"Shall we take a stroll?"

"Yes, nice."

"You look pretty. Less, how shall I put it? Less *Judengasse*."

"Yes, I got tired of wearing only boring clothing. You see, I am not narrow-minded."

"I didn't think you were."

"I would also like to leave Frankfurt," she said. "It's too difficult now, with mama's illness. But I support you, really. I fully understand. I'll soon be going my own way, too."

"If you need help, you can always rely on me."

"I want to call myself Renata. I hate Rivka."

"Renata, I have to tell you something," said Joseph, "my name is Johann." As he said it, he burst out laughing. She joined and while roaring with laughter, they walked to the park. It was good to have support.

"You have to tell me everything about life here."

The walk was pleasant. Rivka was very understanding and while they were strolling, with an occasional rest on a bench, they talked nineteen to the dozen about home, about Rivka's dreams and plans, about Joseph's departure, about trains and about his success. When Nathan was brought up, Joseph felt a sting in his heart.

Finally, he asked the question that had been on his mind for a long time: "Has papa forgiven me?"

Rivka shook her head. "I don't know. It's hard to tell. Probably he will say other things when you actually are there."

"Meaning that for now he still scolds me."

Rivka smiled at him. "Come and things will be better."

Joseph let it rest. "Nearby is a shop where they have fun things for children. Let's buy something for Nathan." They bought a large, colorful top and Joseph wrote a nice note to go with the wrapped gift. Then they walked to the station.

"I don't feel like seeing Aron again, so if you don't mind, I won't go in with you."

"I don't mind, brother Johann!"

He kissed her and said softly: "Success with everything, Renata. I'll come to Frankfurt soon and then we'll talk more. Give my love to Nathan. And wish mama a speedy recovery. I will pray for her. I mean it."

Pesach's* approach prompted Joseph to consider the situation. How hard it would be for his parents if his chair remained empty. The whole evening there would be a chilly corner on one side of the table. What would they do with the four questions? Which child would get which question? He thought about his mother. Pesach was a family celebration par excellence. But visiting Frankfurt and pretending would be too difficult. Ignoring the holiday completely was the other extreme, but Joseph feared that there was nothing in between. It would be better to skip this year. He made the decision with pain in his heart but he knew that otherwise there would be much more pain, and not only for him. He decided that he would visit Frankfurt soon after Pesach.

A few days before Pesach, he walked to the small bookshop in the Jewish quarter. He had met the owner before. Chaim Wolf. The man nodded at him as he entered the shop. He already saw a stack of the book he was looking for on a table.

"Ah, the *Hagaddah shel Pesach*. I didn't know you were Jewish."

Joseph ignored the remark. "How much is it?"

He paid and left the shop ashamed. Now that he had started, he decided to go all the way. He bought some *matzah* and a jar of *maror** at grocery Steinmetz.

On Pesach eve, as it grew dark, he realized that all Jewish families were doing the same thing now. They were standing around the table for the *kiddush*.* Pesach meant freedom. Now for the first time, he could really celebrate his freedom. Not a slave anymore, not of his parents, not of his faith, of no one. He was lord and master of his life.

When it got dark, he sat down at his desk. He had emptied it completely for the occasion. He was alone, but that did not matter. He poured wine into a glass, said the blessing, and drank the wine in a gulp. The pace at which he told the story of the exodus was much faster than that of his parents. When he reached the questions of the four children, he got inspired. He would be all four of them at once – the wise, the bad, the simple, and the completely ignorant. His voice rose with the ten plagues. At the song *Dayeinu,* he started humming to himself. *B'chol dor vador* he heard his father roar. The second glass of wine followed. He ate the *matzah* and the *maror* with all of the right *brachot* and texts. A very meager meal followed.

He had just finished the third cup and was considering whether he would recite *Hallel* or just go to bed, when the landlord called from downstairs. There was someone at the door for him. Joseph didn't feel like seeing anyone, especially not tonight. It was nobody's concern what he did here.

"It's the police. They're asking about a certain Lichtman, that's you, isn't it?"

The visit had to be related to the incident in the cathedral. What else could it be? For a moment he wanted to hide, but that would not be smart. He had given them this address himself. They would find him anyway.

"I'll come downstairs." But two policemen had already come up to his room.

"Lichtman?" one of them asked, a slim, tall guy with a heavy moustache, a bit ridiculous with his heavy uniform.

Joseph nodded.

"Do you have papers?" Joseph gave them his documents.

"All right, Johann Lichtman. Can you answer some questions? It is only a formality."

"What is going on?"

"We ask the questions," the other policeman said, a small, sturdy guy with huge hands, not to be meddled with.

"Just a couple of questions," the first officer said. "Do you know someone called Braunberger?"

"Yes, he worked with me at the construction site of the cathedral. But I stopped working there a long time ago. I'm a journalist. I work for Anton Pennekamp, the publisher."

"What do you know about Braunberger?" the other agent now asked. Joseph wanted to say that he knew nothing about him, but the other man interrupted, "Are you Jewish by chance?"

"No," Joseph said perplexed.

"What do you know about that Braunberger?" the other policeman asked again.

"Nothing. I don't even know where he lives. I once had a chat with him at the construction site. But that's long ago. That's the truth. Why do you ask me all this?"

"Do you know Franz Stuck?"

"No, who is he? Or wait, I remember. Wasn't he the foreman of the site? I only knew his first name. He's dead, isn't he?"

The officers came to a decision. "Very well. We will keep your name in the file, Lichtman."

Joseph closed the door. Why had his *Seder** evening suddenly taken this turn?

In the rain, Joseph walked from the newly built Taunus station to his parents' house, following the road along the Main. Frankfurt was as it always had been, as if everything else had been a dream. So familiar and yet so far away. As if he had been put in a different time, placed in a parallel life. He knew everything and he could pick up his old life again as if Cologne had never existed.

Before his departure he had sought Max's opinion and Max had advised him to go. "Make it your own Canossa," he had said. At home Joseph immediately opened his history books and read about Henry the Fourth's journey through the Alps, his strategic move to obtain absolution from the supreme power of the Catholic Church. For three days the emperor had waited in the snow to be allowed to meet with the Pope. Would Joseph have to wait three days to be admitted? Was it worth it?

There was no snow on the streets in Frankfurt, but it was cold and the gray clouds were hanging low over the river. The water was dark. The far bank was barely visible. The traffic on the river was as busy as ever and further on he saw that the new buildings were starting to take shape. He turned away from the quay and walked towards the ghetto. In the *Judengasse* he tried not to meet the curious looks of the people. Did they recognize him? He held his head down, pulled his beret almost over his eyes and only looked up when he arrived at his parents' house. Was this not his home as well? Nothing had changed on the outside, so he assumed that the inside had also retained its suffocating atmosphere. For a while he stood there, ambivalent. He had long been deliberating about literally the right entrance. Knocking on the front door or slipping in by the back door. Eventually he chose the middle way. He knocked at the back door.

"Yosef! You don't have to knock," his father said kindly, calling him by his Jewish name. No trace of surprise. He was wearing the same clothes as the day Joseph had left the house. His face looked tired.

He had more wrinkles than he had half a year ago, but his eyes were clear. He led Joseph to the living room and invited him to sit down. He nodded again and said, "So."

"So," replied Joseph as he shifted in his seat.

His father finally asked him: "What is it like in Cologne?"

"Fine. Lots of work. Things are going well."

"*Gut. Gut.*"

"Where are the others?"

"Away. At school, at work."

"Good."

Should he inquire about the health of his mother or was it better to let his father start about it? His father got up and Joseph wondered if this was the end of their conversation, but he walked to the drinks cabinet and took out the bottle of brandy that would normally only be served on Shabbat. "Fancy a *schnapps*?"

Joseph nodded. His father thoughtfully poured in two glasses and gave Joseph one.

"*L'chaim.*" Joseph returned the toast and put the glass to his lips. He tossed it down and immediately felt the beneficial effect.

"How is mama?"

"She is upstairs, lying in bed. It's all right. I think she shouldn't be aggravated too much. No surprises."

"Like me?"

His father laughed without joy. "Joseph should certainly visit her, but you? I don't know. You are another person." He looked at Joseph with penetrating eyes, "You even have taken a different name. So you are giving up your family. You are also no longer a member of our people, I understand."

No reconciliation seemed possible. No Canossa. But Joseph could still defend his honor.

"Papa, I am as Jewish as you are. But I am also a German. You all should be smarter too. Why can't you respect my choice? Maybe I do go to the synagogue. Do you know? I am free. I can live very well without a synagogue and be a righteous person."

"What arrogance to call yourself a righteous person. It is not up to us to judge that."

Joseph shrugged his shoulders.

"I heard you worked in a church." His father stated it as if it hardly had any meaning.

"Ah, Aron has become a detective. What a cheap wretch he is." He understood that cursing was useless, so he continued in a controlled way. "I had to eat, so for a while I took a job at a construction site.

Is that so bad? Am I suddenly the best friends with the Pope? I am working for one of the more respected newspapers in Cologne now."

His father gave him a sad look.

"If I had known that it would be like this," Joseph continued, "I would not have come at all. I had hoped that we would be able to talk to each other, but all I get is reproaches." He held back for a moment. Then he got up, picked up his coat and turned to his father again. "I find the Christian faith loathsome, so rest assured. I'm not going to be baptized." There was so much he wanted to say. "I will tell you something, papa. It is not always about what other people think or do. Not what is good for the Jews. It's not about you, nor about the community here. It is about me. At last it is about me. I had to leave. I had to go. Because of me. And so far, it turns out that I was right."

"If you say so."

He walked to the door. He could not resist having the last word: "Doesn't Hillel say, "If I am not for myself, who will be for me?" I don't need to find enlightened thinkers who concur. Even in those petty dark times it was already clear."

"It is only half the truth. Hillel goes on. "And if I am only for myself, what am I?"

"And if not now, when?" Joseph riposted, reaching for the doorknob.

"Wait, my boy." His father spoke with a soft but steady voice. Joseph paused.

"I know that I am being hard on you. But don't you think you deserve that a bit? Nathan doesn't even want to see you anymore." He helplessly shrugged his shoulders. "But I don't want us to part with a quarrel. You are my son whether I like your choices or not." Joseph saw him standing and, for the first time in his life, was touched by his vulnerability. Could his father help how and who he was?

Joseph walked back and embraced him. His father had moist eyes. "Come on, papa. It will be all right. I will visit more often and we can all be family again. I promise."

"Go to mama, son. She loves you. You have always been her darling. You were Joseph among the other children. Please." It was the first time his father had begged him this way.

Joseph nodded and as he walked to his parents' bedroom, he wiped the tears out of his eyes. The room was dark. The only light came from a candle in the hallway. He saw the bed and a pile of blankets, but could not see his mother, only hear her long deep breaths followed by short gasps. She was asleep and he didn't want to wake her up. Between the white sheets he thought he saw her face as an even whiter spot. He came a little closer and saw that she was sleeping with her eyes open.

She stared at him without seeing him. Joseph took her hand. He stood there for a while, then placed it gently on the bed and slipped out of the room.

"Tell her I was here, all right?" he said to his father. "That's better than waking her up now."

"I will. Come back." His father smiled as he sat down unsteadily in his chair. He grabbed his glass and lifted it up to Joseph. "*L'chaim*, Yossi."

"*L'chaim*, papa. I will come back."

"Mr. Lichtman, I really would appreciate it if you would accompany our family to the Holy Mass on Sunday." Eberhard Löwe made the announcement without much fuss, as if it was not important, more a courtesy that obviously had to be honored. What could be more German than attending the high mass in the holiest German monument, the cathedral, the highlight of the people?

He felt all eyes staring at him. *Frau* Gretchen Löwe, Werner. And Maria. Was her look begging or did he himself put it in her expression? Would it matter to her if he came? "I will be pleased to attend."

Later that day, when he was alone with Werner, he explained that he really couldn't do it. "It is one thing not to go to the synagogue, another thing to go to church."

"My father would see it as an insult. And you've already said yes. I understand it might be a bit strange, but in the end we all talk to the same one, don't we? God is God. And Jesus was also a Jew. It doesn't have to be such a big problem."

"Your father is supposed to be so liberal. He will certainly understand."

"Listen, Joseph, sorry, Johann. Try to be a little compliant. Comfort yourself with the thought that it has nothing to do with religion or even politics. It is how you deal with each other. Respect, friendship, things like that. Think about what he has done for you. Our family has reserved seats. It should really be an honor for you. By the way, do you think I'm praying in church? If my attention can wander, yours can do the same, right?"

"And you know for sure that the whole family will come?" Had he put too much emphasis on 'whole'?

"Of course. It is important for father. He busted himself for the completion of that church."

Joseph imagined being near Maria during the mass. He would let himself be baptized for her. "I will come. But only once. It won't be a habit."

"We will find you a nice spot. Where you can look around. There are a lot of paintings and beautiful objects." Werner laughed and without meaning it Joseph joined in.

The whole week it gnawed at him. Did he really have to do this? Maybe he was moving away from his faith but wasn't attending church a step too far? That Thursday he decided that a bit more knowledge might illuminate him in this dilemma. In the afternoon he went to visit Max and asked bluntly: "Max, do you happen to have the Talmud?"

Max looked bewildered. "What? No. Why?"

Joseph now told of his awkward situation.

"A new Bible story. *Joseph in the Löwe-den*." [8] Max laughed, annoying Joseph.

"Don't ridicule me."

"Sorry. I hadn't seen this coming. With the Löwes to church! You reap what you sow. Or to remain in our faith, doesn't *Pirke Avot** say that you shouldn't be too intimate with government people? But seriously, what do you think you will gain by studying the Talmud? I don't think you get any other answer than *avoda zara*, that it is idolatry. Not allowed. Period. That wouldn't help you. But, it's about you. Either you are religious or you don't care."

"I just doubt. I don't do a lot of what I am supposed to do. But the other way around it is different. What I'm not allowed to do, I better not do, maybe."

"Good. I shall pay my brother a visit. He has his whole house stuffed with *Gemara** and *Mishna*. I've told you about Avraham, my pious brother, haven't I? Can I explain the situation or should I just bring a wheelbarrow of books?"

"Make it the wheelbarrow," said Joseph.

Max kept his word and in the evening they both sat in Max's study room, plowing through the books.

"Avraham couldn't believe it. He already thought I was doing repentance," he said laughing. He looked at the piles in front of him on the table. "I must say I am almost becoming nostalgic." Joseph also remembered with pleasure the smell of the books of the past.

"Here, I've found something," Max said after a while. "It might have some significance for you. Listen. From the *Mishna*. A Jew is not allowed to enter a city of idolatry, unless there is another way out. I think you could interpret this as: You can enter a church as long as you make sure that you come out intact. In plain language it could signify, "fine, you can do it, but make sure you don't become a Christian.""

A little later Joseph pointed to a page in the book he had in front of him. "Here. I've also found something. The *Rambam* says Christianity is idolatry, but another rabbi...," he looked again. "Rabbi Meiri believes that Christians do worship only one god and that they do not engage in idolatry. I can live with that, combined with what you have found."

"Conclusion: Let's all go to church!" said Max.

For a while they continued looking, but Joseph had found what he needed. He closed his book. Max filled their glasses one more time. "You know that your intended visit to the church caused the two of us to study Talmud all evening. Talking about religious paradox."

"In any case," Joseph said, "I'm not going to be baptized. The Church is completely alien to me. I don't have to worry."

In the end, it was much more frightening and threatening to go to a Liberal synagogue. A deviation from the known was much more disturbing than phantoms from far away.

For a day he felt strengthened by the knowledge he had found, but on Saturday evening he was once again overcome by an indeterminate feeling of guilt. This time it was not faith that interfered, but the memory of Franz, buried under the stones. Images of the evening with Braunberger haunted him. The *Judensau*. Should he return to the scene of the crime; wasn't that the cliché of all criminals? Correction. He was not a criminal, he had just run away.

In bed, he decided definitely not to go to church, regardless of the consequences. He would come up with an excuse in the morning. And he could meet Maria at so many other places. Places that befitted him much better, concerts, exhibitions. With the dream that he was accompanying Maria to another Beethoven concert, he fell into an anxious sleep.

Werner picked him up around ten o'clock. Meekly he walked with him to the home of the Löwe family. They would all leave at the same time. He looked for Maria, but did not see her. All the fears and uncertainties of the past week disappeared into thin air with the terrible thought that she might not even be there. Then it would all be futile.

"Maria," shouted father Löwe. "We are leaving. You can catch up on us."

"We still have time," said Werner.

They were standing in the hallway looking up when Maria appeared at the top of the stairs. For Joseph, she seemed to emerge from a dream. She was wearing a white dress trimmed with blue plaid. Her hair was piled high on her head. She seemed to glide down the stairs, greeting Joseph with a friendly "good morning," as she passed. By the door, she wrapped a pink cloak around herself.

Her soft eyes paralyzed him. He was glad that he did not have to say anything; he only nodded. With Werner, he led the way through the quiet streets. Behind him came Eberhard Löwe with Maria and her mother. He heard her heels on the stones and he had to restrain himself from looking back. As they entered the cathedral, he stopped, as if waiting, uncertain where to go. Maria slipped past him and he was beguiled by the scent of her hair.

They proceeded to the chapel of the holy cross where the service would be held. In the middle row he saw Anton Pennekamp, who looked up surprised and amused as Joseph passed by. Was that Braunberger there? He could not tell. In the chapel stood a prominent cross. Joseph remembered it. It had frightened him when he had come with Braunberger. A larger than life-sized statue of Christ hung from the cross, his nailed arms outstretched, suffering from his wounds. It was probably intended to evoke compassion, Joseph thought, but for him it suggested merely fear and horror. He tried to find something similar in the Jewish scriptures and only Job came to mind. But who would ever think to portray Job in this way? Joseph could not find any beauty in the sculpture. He wanted to turn his head away but the repugnance was so fascinating that he had to keep looking.

"Here are our places," he heard Werner say. He drew Joseph's attention to a man sitting in front of them. "That is Grossman," whispered Werner. "He was Jewish, he converted. He is now the most pious of us all. Quiet now, it is about to begin." The Church ministers came in and walked the length of the aisle, swinging incense pots on long chains. Mass began. Joseph had expected something in the spirit of the synagogue, but what unfolded before him was completely unfamiliar. Even the Liberal service he had attended in Frankfurt did not offer any help. There were no books, only a priest who unilaterally chanted the texts. On the ground in front of the altar knelt a few boys in white robes. High above him a choir began to sing. The stench of the incense nauseated him. I am a fool, he thought. Was this the price he had to pay? He looked up again and saw the man on the cross. Nailed; how lifelike were the sculpted streams of blood. This man was the embodiment of all misery. The expression on his face was lifelike, or deathlike. Someone who had perished in pain and despair. This was a culture of death. I place before you life and death and what do you do? You choose death!

But suddenly he thought they might be right, those Christians. Life was misery and destitution. Could you live with grace if you didn't believe in an afterlife? No wonder they needed a savior. He chuckled at his own thoughts. Werner looked disturbed and motioned him to be calm and serious. In an attempt to avoid seeing the terrible cross, he looked at the other side, where a row of sculptures seemed to standing guard. Inquisitors who would snatch him at the right moment. He had heard the stories about the Inquisition in class.

The choir started again. What surprised Joseph the most was the orderliness and silence in which all this happened. Everyone stayed quiet and still. No Shlomo Levi and Yaakov Goldstein arguing in front of the *bima*. No latecomers praying at their own pace. Here everything was orderly and neat. Was it German or Christian? He couldn't understand the priest's texts. Everything was in Latin. Occasionally the congregation replied in unison and then fell silent again, staring at the man on the cross. Perhaps he should have studied the liturgy a little; now he sat there like an ignorant dunce. At regular intervals people knelt down. In an attempt to blend in, he joined them. He felt ridiculous and increasingly, a traitor. He decided to say the *Amidah* quietly. Or was it too late for the morning prayer? Perhaps he should say *Mincha* instead? This was absurd. Here he was in a church, wondering whether it was time for the afternoon prayers.

He had to concentrate in order to make it to the end. Maria. He saw her sitting diagonally in front of him on the other side of the aisle. He tried to remember her perfume, but immediately the real smell of incense penetrated his nose. He saw her neck. Her high collar of finely embroidered lace. Her body wrapped in the pink cloak. Suddenly she turned her head in his direction. She saw him. In any case, she smiled. He looked away, straight at father Löwe, who was sitting a little further on the same pew. For a moment they looked each other straight in the eyes. The man gave him a friendly smile too. Joseph grimaced back. Were they keeping an eye on him?

He closed his eyes. Franz, the foreman, stood clearly in front of him. The images changed and last night's nightmare returned. It became hallucinatory. Franz hung on the cross. Dust clouds were raging and made Joseph's eyes water. He blinked, wondering whether anyone was watching him. He felt eyes piercing the back of his head, but he did not dare to turn around, afraid to draw attention to himself. He looked again at Maria. But she offered no hope. In effect she had already left and gone to her Gustav. What was he thinking? Maria was beyond his reach. She had reverted to the image he had of her at the beginning, that vague sketch which contained a promise; now only an illusion.

The priest held up the wafers and the chalice. Joseph knew enough to understand what this was. The body and blood of Christ. He had to get out of here. As the whole family moved forward in an orderly manner to take Holy Communion, Joseph turned around and tried to slip out of the church, unnoticed. It was dizzying. He had to persevere, and certainly not stand out now. He staggered but stayed upright by holding on to something. He looked down, and saw to his horror that he had grabbed a stone statue. It was impossible to give this exit any dignity.

Outside, he sat down against the immense buttresses, hoping to pull himself together while waiting for the Löwes.

Incarceration

"Who joined you to Zorzi's house? Elia Banco? Do you know him?"

"I don't know."

"A man called Giuseppe?"

"Could be. Maybe he came to Da Gino for a bite."

"For a bite." The interrogator laughed loudly. "Agitators. All of them. Antonio Moresi. Piero Arnolfini. These names mean anything to you, Lichtman?"

Suddenly he took a newspaper from the drawer of his desk. Joseph recognized it immediately. It was the newspaper in which an article on the famous Mortara case had been published. "Do you recognize this? Or have you lost your memory completely?"

Joseph had to think fast. And the ability to be alert was one of the first things that he lost during his imprisonment. "It has an article I wrote. They made me write it."

"They? Who are they?"

Joseph could not see any way to save himself. He stammered without strength. "They made me write it."

"No will of your own, Lichtman. Such a weakling. And they all see you as a hero because you wrote this. The hero who expresses everyone else's opinion. What the scum thinks is desirable. That's why you went to Zorzi's that evening, of course."

Images flashed through his head again. Giuseppe attacking the officers with a big bat. Elia running away, while shouting at him to get the hell out of there. But he still couldn't finish the story. However much he focused, the ending still refused to come back to him.

"Lichtman, are you there? Revolt, Incitement. Do you know how long you will be in prison for that? At least ten years. Ha. You will have to live on water and bread here just to protect a gang of cowards. I wouldn't think twice. You really can't give me any names?"

"I don't remember," he whispered. He was exhausted. "Please, I can't think anymore. I really don't know. I don't know Zorzi. I don't know where he lives.

Let me go. I am innocent." He fell forward from his chair.

The superintendent addressed one of the prison guards. "Take him away; maybe he will know more tomorrow. But I wonder if anything good will ever come from that boy."

And again, he was dragged through the corridors of the dungeons and thrown into his cell. He had not lied. He couldn't think anymore. To a certain extent he had to comply to survive. To put on a big mouth or show subversive behavior was exactly what the hell watchers were looking for. Then they could really abuse their power. Compliance was conditional, but to what extent? Should he accept that he was locked up? That there was no decent food? That he had to do his needs in the same cell where he slept and lived? That he had not washed himself even once? That at least at the moment, he was nobody, only a number with no rights? That was a lot to ask. That no one would tell him why he was here? That thought required too much strength, and mainly caused him anger, which in its turn was totally useless. But he could not help himself. The question was essential and he knew that there was no reason; he knew that something unjust was happening. He could not accept that. He could only force himself trying to disengage from the thoughts.

"No good will ever come from you." His father's words had resonated and continued to haunt him. They were still pounding after all these years. Even louder than the bluster of his guards and interrogators.

5

(1854)

ASCENDING – DESCENDING

A year passed by. It had been a very busy year for Joseph. He had climbed up the editorial board of Pennekamp's newspaper and continued to work on the memoirs of *Frau* Elsa, whom he visited almost weekly. He also saw Max regularly. Max insisted that he should educate himself further. "Learn. *Bildung*. If you want to write, you have to know much more." He had studied politics, philosophy, art, architecture, music, and literature. He had visited theaters and museums, read books, and taken part in discussions. In addition, he had been doing his best to master some languages – English, French, and even a little Latin. He had moved from the small room on the top floor of *Martinstrasse* to the one below it, not much bigger but a lot more comfortable.

Maria had left. To Berlin, to her Gustav. Joseph's unhappiness lingered for a few months, but eventually he healed.

"She left, so she is no longer here, not even for you," Werner philosophically stated.

"I know. She had to marry."

"She wanted to get married. Forget her."

One afternoon he saw someone standing in front of the house. It was Rivka. She wore black, completely at odds with the cheerful colors that she had been wearing the last time.

"Rivka, what are you doing here? Come in. You must be freezing." It was April and still cold. Inside she warmed herself by the stove, while Joseph waited patiently for her to get comfortable.

"Mama is doing very badly. She is really much worse. I think you have to come. I want you to be with us so much." She gazed at him for a long time. "Also for me. It hasn't been very joyful at home lately. Papa stares at the walls all day, Aron snarls at everyone, and Nathan is getting lost in between. We have moved. You know that, right? To *Ostend*.

"Yes, you wrote me about it. You look very different than last time. What has happened to Renata? You're all Rivka again."

"That's only temporary, for the sake of peace at home. I have serious plans to leave, but I have postponed them for now. I met a very nice man. We are going to get married and live in Paris."

"Chic, madame!"

"He is so charming." She smiled. "He reminds me of you."

"Then I don't know if he's so nice. But *mazal tov* and that there should only be good news."

After looking dully out of the window for a while, she turned around to Joseph and straightened her back, as if she had an important announcement to make. "I have to tell you something." She waited a long time until she was sure she had his total attention. "I'm going to be baptized." Joseph looked at her, without expression.

"Why don't you say something?" she asked.

"What do you want me to say? That I give you my blessing? I don't think there is a *bracha* for this."

"Keep your humor to yourself," she said fiercely. "I'm already preparing. I visit a priest once a week to learn. It will probably happen very soon. I have waited because of mama."

"Why baptism?"

"Because of him, my future husband. Rainer."

"Do I know him?"

She shook her head.

"I was in mass once. I thought it was awful," he said. Afraid that he was too hard and rejecting, he stood up and embraced her. "I understand," he said with a soft voice. "But I'll be honest with you. I am ambivalent. Love might not the best reason for converting. I don't see myself becoming a Christian any time soon." He forced her to look at him. "But I will support you."

She dried her tears. "Will you come home with me now?"

"Of course I will. Tell me about mama."

While they were walking past the *Judengasse*, he got a glimpse of the old house that from now on only would exist in his memory. They hurried on and a few hundred meters further, at a new three-story building, Rivka knocked on the door. Their father opened the door. He looked as if he hadn't slept in days.

"*Shalom Aleichem*. Yossi!"

"*Shalom*, papa. How are you?" He spoke German. His father glanced at him with a serious look. In Yiddish he replied: "Come in, you shouldn't be out on the street in this weather. As you can see, Yossi, we are not so backward anymore." Joseph said: "It's beautiful, papa. The street is very clean."

He entered. It seemed that the odor of their old home had moved with them. Inside, his parents had succeeded in recreating the identical interior as in the old house, the old furniture standing in almost the same arrangement.

"How is mama?"

"She is resting in the salon. You can go in."

Joseph opened the sliding doors to the front room. Because the curtains were completely closed, it was almost completely dark. There was a smell that Joseph did not recognize, a mixture of strange ointments and medicine, unwashed clothes and unclean body parts. It brought death to mind.

She had her eyes open as he approached. Yet he stayed at a considerable distance from the bed, incapable of touching her physically, afraid of decay and death.

"Come near, my boy," she said with a weak voice. "My Joseph."

He came closer. With an effort that he tried not to show, he took her hand and she brought it to her mouth.

"Hello mama." He had no idea what to say. That she looked good was a *chutspah* and he couldn't think of anything else hopeful to say. "How are you?"

She coughed for a long time. "It's almost over, son. I feel it. *Ha Kadosh Baruch Hu* calls me." She looked him straight in the eyes now, but her gaze did not reach him. Her eyes were dull. He had to make an effort to recognize his mother in the sunken face. The yellowish skin was full of spots. "I am so happy that you are here. That you made up with papa."

Joseph did not contradict her. "We are family, mama."

"You are my son, Joseph. I know you are going to do great things. It is predestined."

"We shall see, mama." Shame came upon him. The apostate who was chosen to do great things.

"Come closer." Her look was clearer now. And suddenly she was his mother and not some sick woman in a bed. She took his head in both hands and brought it closer, placing a barely perceptible kiss on his hair.

"Marry a good girl, Joseph. Then everything will be all right."

"I'll go and look for her, mama. I promise."

Rivka's knock on the door interrupted their time together. Joseph remained standing for a while, but when he noticed that his mother had closed her eyes and receded into a restless sleep, he quickly returned to the main room where his father was sitting in his regular chair.

"Is Aron not here? And where is Nathan?"

"Aron is in the school. He'll be coming home for dinner soon. Nathan is outside, playing."

Joseph took a chair and wondered how long he would have to sit there before he could excuse himself with proper decency and go to his room to unpack his suitcase.

"We don't speak the same language anymore, I notice," his father said.

"I am not used to anything else, but if you want, I can also speak your language."

"No, never mind. I want you to feel at ease."

To his delight, his father poured them each some *schnapps*. Joseph desperately tried to evoke images that would chase away the coldness. Images of the past, of the family together, of his mother who lovingly cared for him flooded over him but the memories of his father remained cold. Shouldn't he honor his father? Synagogue visits from long ago came to his mind. Because of the cold, he had tucked himself away in the warmth of his father's thick black coat. The Ten Commandments* were embroidered on the curtain of the *Aron HaKodesh*,* and from the corner where he sat, Joseph could just see the bottom of the right row, the fifth commandment. He had to lean out of the shelter of the coat to see the other ones. Most of the time he remained safely shielded, staring at *Kabed Et* – Honor your father and your mother. Even as a child he had dreamed those letters.

His father had been talking softly all the time and looked at him now.

"Sorry," Joseph said, "I wandered for a moment. What was it like to leave the *Judengasse*?"

"The *Judengasse* is holy ground. Built on the tears of our forefathers. But I stand by the decision I made. Sometimes you have to make strong decisions." Joseph waited as if he wasn't sure whether to react.

"I do understand a bit why you wanted to leave," his father said.

"Thank you, papa. I really didn't want to cause you grief."

"All is well, Yossi."

He got up, kissed his father and said he was going to unpack his suitcase. He sat motionless for a while in the room that was made up for him. This was too much. Too much reconciliation.

At ten o'clock in the morning, 26 April 1854, 28 *Nisan** 5614, Bathsheba Socher, born Samur, passed away. The whole family was at her bedside. When the doctor confirmed that she was dead, Joseph slipped out of the room and sat down on the floor of the main room. He tried to feel sad, but didn't succeed immediately. Desperately he began to ferret through his memory. There had to be a catalyst that would start the grief. Somewhere in all her sacrifices, there had to be an event that would bring tears.

The tour to the other side of the city. He was seven and his father was out of town for two days on a buying trip. An important customer had come into the shop and bought a lot. A couple of boxes with fabrics. He wanted it delivered and his mother decided to bring it herself, so as not to incur any extra costs. To celebrate the successful sale, they had eaten a Steinmetz cheese cake with tea that afternoon. The next day Joseph and his mother dragged the boxes for an hour to the other side of the city. Joseph could barely help, he was so small, but as the oldest, Aron had to stay at home to look after Rivka. When they rang the doorbell, the man opened and told them he didn't need the stuff after all. He also wanted his payment refunded. His mother argued. The man interrupted her immediately, "Get out of here, you Jewish witch." Quietly she had started to count out the money, but she didn't have enough. Joseph remembered heading back home with her. She had walked straight next to him, the boxes heavy in her arms, without a word Joseph's heart had cried. Once he tried, "Mama, it's not fair." She glanced at him lovingly, recognizing his effort, and said, "I know dear. Let's forget about it quickly. Papa will come back tomorrow and we don't want to give him bad news, do we?" They had been silent for the rest of the trip. Mama had borne the humiliation with pride and that evening had gone back with her savings to settle the last of the debt.

He did not know the mourning customs exactly as his mother was the first death in the immediate family. People would come soon who knew them all. Rivka came to sit next to him. Joseph gently touched her arm. They didn't speak. For the time being he didn't want anything. A little later his father also joined them briefly. Joseph also stroked him lightly over his arm. He saw his father's tears and noticed that his own eyes were also moist. There would be no consolation until the funeral, he remembered that much. It was pointless to try to comfort someone at such a moment of total distress.

Now Nathan also joined them. The boy looked at him with a mixture of hatred and distrust. Joseph got up and sat down next to him and tried to take him in his arms. At first Nathan pushed him away, but Joseph persevered until the boy allowed it, burying his head in Joseph's lap and sobbing. His outburst was heartbreaking. Joseph stroked the younger boy's hair and spoke softly to him. How could he not try to comfort him; surely children had their own laws? He looked up and saw his father encouraging him.

He had always feared his mother's death as the worst moment in his life. Although she had never actually given him any reason, she had always aroused Joseph's pity. He had seen her as weak and needy, probably unjustly so. Perhaps it was her coughing, to which they had all become so accustomed that no one even noticed anymore. Sometimes he had been sad and afraid, just looking at her and knowing that one day she wouldn't be there anymore. And now she was gone. It was a reality. Death was here. But this was not a spiritual sensation. It brought about a very earthly feeling. He had never felt so attached to life. It was not fair. His mother was a better person than he was. Why should she have been taken from life? Should not her sacrifice, her virtue, her helpfulness, her contentment have sufficed to grant her a longer life?

Someone had to stay with the body all the time, and Joseph was prepared to take his shift, but Aron stopped him, saying that only people who follow *halacha* are entitled to do this *mitzvah*. Their father, however, shook his head and let Joseph go. A linen cloth was draped over her skinny body. He saw in the canvas the shape of her bones. No more flesh would come to this. Ezekiel could claim the lot. He sat down next to the bed and waited. Not much later the people of the *chevra kadisha** came and they took care of everything – the washing of the body, the funeral preparations and many practical things.

He wrote all night long, inspired, almost obsessed. His mother deserved a statue as a saint. And because the Jewish faith forbade this, he had to erect another monument for her. His eulogy would bestow on her the greatest glory and honor of all. Her name praised, blessed, exalted, celebrated. Her sacrifice, her warmth, her joy for others, her contentment in her simplicity. After a few hours, he read it and he thought it adequate. He would read it tomorrow at the funeral.

They had to walk a long way to the new cemetery north of the city, outside the old walls. A cold wind blew right through Joseph's body. Almost instinctively, Joseph classified the building at the entrance of the cemetery according to the books on architecture he had studied. This was strict Classicism. Something useful from my *Bildung*, he thought. Like a dark gray caterpillar, the unfolded umbrellas moved in a long procession between the large, rounded grave stones that stood out as warning signs in the grass; the dead Jews of Frankfurt. A new stone, engraved with the name Gutle Rothschild, larger than the others, caught his attention. Wasn't everyone equal in death? His mother's resting place would be at the end of a damp gravel path. Four strong men held the two ropes that were stretched under the white coffin. Slowly his mother's body descended into the pit. His father said *Kaddish*. With his umbrella, Aron tried to protect his father from the wind and the rain, but didn't have much luck. In turns, the men took the shovel, and the clods of earth thudded onto the coffin. Now it was Joseph's turn. He stood at the edge of the hole in the ground and plunged the spade deep into the heap of soil next to the pit. He had trouble keeping the shovel straight and most of the sand ended up on the sides of the coffin. He saw how the dirty, muddy earth dripped off along the edges. When they put me in the ground, please let it be dry, he prayed, seriously considering that even in death he would feel better if the sun were shining. The absurd thought reminded him of the trip on the carriage to Cologne. How bad an accident in the rain and cold would have been. Had he sinned by abandoning his mother in that way? Without looking any further, he gave the shovel to Aron. When everybody had his turn, his father and Aron began reciting *Kaddish* and his father looked inviting to Joseph to join. He didn't know this *Kaddish* by heart. Numb, he said what he could, "*Y'hei sh'mei raba...*"

His gaze went around the circle. His father aroused pity; Aron, haughty as ever, beside him. Rivka, unfathomable; and Nathan, who evoked unconditional love. Was Joseph an outsider? Did he not belong here? His eyes went down again, to the coffin. He stumbled through the next *Kaddish*. What could Joseph give her? No more consolation, words also fell short. He wanted to shout, unconstrained, letting go of all control.

When he came home, he tucked the sheet with the carefully chiseled and polished words away with the rest of his belongings.

The eulogy had remained unrevealed in his pocket.

The *shiva** started immediately. The whole family sat on low chairs in the warm living room. Several people came, bringing food. Joseph knew most of them, even if only by face, but they left him alone, aside from an occasional questioning glance that usually ended in a sigh of sympathy. The family immersed themselves in stories from the past. Aron and Rivka were animated, his father remained absentminded. At the end of the afternoon more people came. Aron led the *Mincha* service.

Until the funeral, the reason to be here had been self-evident. Now it became more difficult. Joseph prepared himself for the inevitable battles with his father and Aron. Yet the day turned out to be less arduous than he had expected. Aron behaved normally in every way. The circumstances ensured that the children would not allow their disagreements to surface.

Most of Joseph's worries were about the Shabbat. Shabbat even negated death; all mourning had to be interrupted. How would he survive that day? He was stuck here and had to abide by all the rules. But to his surprise, as Shabbat came in, he felt no resistance at all.

The *kiddush* was like it used to be. The cup with wine glowed in the candlelight as never before and the breads were gleaming. Just being there with his siblings and his father was enough.

The day passed more quickly than expected. He reminisced with Rivka. During lunch, everyone told stories about how righteous their mother had been. How God-fearing, and how she had always effaced herself for the happiness of the family. In a miraculous, outside worldly way, the Sabbath had managed to banish death and bereavement. Somewhere in the afternoon the absurd thought came to him that he would never again be afraid of his mother's death. That involuntary dread would never come knocking again.

On Sunday, Joseph could no longer endure the despondency at home. The power of the family being together stopped working for him. Aron was annoying and at best Joseph was just bored. He walked to the back room where his little brother was reading.

"Do you want to have a coffee with me somewhere? We are already in the fifth day of the shiva. Life goes on. What do you think?"

They decided to have a drink at Levy's and for the first time in two years Joseph had the feeling that they could be friends again. After half an hour, Nathan said he wanted to go home, but Joseph wanted to go for a walk.

"Tell papa that I will be back in time for the afternoon service."

"Will you go back to that scary coffee house that kicked us out?"

Joseph laughed. "It was not that scary. But now that you mention it, why not? I have something to rectify there. I am a few years older and times have also changed."

Without a real goal, he ambled around a bit, and after a while he noticed that he was indeed near the *Englischer Hof.*

To his surprise and joy, he saw Max at a table, engaged in a lively conversation with a young girl. He walked up to their table but the two did not at first notice Joseph was smiling at Max.

"Joseph! What are you doing here?" He got up and shook his hands. "But of course, you could ask me the same question. I am visiting my parents. With my brother. Bonding. This is his daughter, Miriam. My niece."

Joseph greeted her. He estimated the girl to be about twelve years old. She had the same deep and smart eyes as Max. Her sombre clothes and her braided hair intimated that she was religious.

"Pleased to meet you," he said kindly. He wanted to say that Uncle Max was leading her astray already, but he turned to Max: "I'm sitting *shiva* for my mother. Until Tuesday. I managed to escape today."

After Max had consoled Joseph for the loss and asked about the family, he said, "And then you run into me. There is no escaping from me. Come and have a seat." He turned to his niece. "You don't mind Joseph joining us for a moment? He also lives in Cologne and he is a promising journalist."

He beckoned a waiter and ordered for Joseph.

"I didn't even know you had parents," Joseph said.

"Even me, Joseph, even me. In Frankfurt, of all places. So you escaped the *shiva*. And then, of course, you head to the place where it all happens. Where the champs are." He laughed. Joseph seemed lost.

"The *Englischer Hof* is the place to meet celebrities. I don't mean myself. But look there. Don't you recognize him?" He nodded to a table near the window where, with a shock, Joseph saw the grumpy man of two years ago.

"Who is that?"

"Schopenhauer, my boy. Arthur Schopenhauer, the great philosopher. I thought you knew him."

Joseph was appalled. They had had a run in with Schopenhauer!

"I've read him. At least substantial parts. He is a bit of a pessimist, isn't he?"

"The greatest pessimist in Western Europe and its surroundings," Max said laughing. "But that shouldn't spoil the fun. Shall we?"

"What?"

"Have a chat with him. Why not? Barking dogs don't bite."

"He certainly barks." He decided to keep the incident of two years ago to himself.

"Ah what, come on." He turned to his niece. "We won't be long."

They walked to the table at the window and overheard the philosopher talking to a few people further down the long table.

"*Mein Lieber*, I insist that I will bear the expense," they heard him say.

One of the people to whom this was addressed looked cheerfully and said with a loud voice: "Yes, but only for the thing-in-itself." He burst into a guffaw, but apparently Schopenhauer regarded the words with contempt: "What are you driveling? How do you dare to use those words? Those words have tremendous meaning. Written from the deepest insights. You should feel ashamed?" And with this he got up and sat down angrily at another table.

"Come," said Max, "our chance."

Without waiting for Joseph's approval, he went to the philosopher and patted him jovially on the shoulder. "*Herr* Schopenhauer, it's good to see each other again. How is life? Let me introduce someone who has the will to represent your world. Joseph Lichtman, I mean Johann, of course. A fine writer."

Joseph understood how daring the remark was after the quip about Kant, but apparently the philosopher took it well. Maybe he had fewer problems when someone was making light of his own work rather than that of his great predecessor.

He had just taken a huge bite of his cake, so could not reply immediately. Max took advantage of this and continued merrily. "Are you also going tonight. The maestro himself is not there, but as you know, his work is drenched with your ideas. As a matter of fact, I believe that you are obliged to come."

The philosopher remained focused on his food, shifting his attention briefly to give a piece of meat to his dog, lying on the floor next to him: "No. I'm not going. It is one thing to use ideas, another to make music out of them. I'll stick to Rossini."

He turned to Joseph. "You are a writer? Romances for the ladies?" He chuckled.

Joseph realized that this was an important moment and he did not want to make an amateur's impression. He started with ample pretension: "Art reviews. Literature. Philosophy. I write about things that are worthwhile. About freedom and people. Maybe later a major novel."

"Freedom, ha! The magic word of the new generation that is already lost. Freedom, my boy, does not exist. At least not as we think it does. There is only will. A deep, uncontrollable will that steers us."

"Freedom is a difficult idea indeed, sir. Maybe too abstract. Maybe it is better to deal with real things in these modern times?"

"Hmm, in these modern times? Real things? Is freedom not a real thing, don't you think? What is real? Is a people real?"

"In so far as they influence reality, certainly yes. I..." Max interrupted them. "Come, people, these clever exchanges are way too difficult before supper." He looked at the philosopher. "We will not disturb you any further, *Herr* Schopenhauer. But, it would truly be nice to continue this conversation one day."

"Certainly, certainly. I would like to exchange thoughts with this boy, what was your name again. Lichtman. All the best. I am looking forward to it."

As they walked back, Max whispered in Joseph's ear, "Did I do a brilliant job, or not? You should be eternally thankful to me." Joseph now understood Max's intention and laughed. It had indeed worked out well. Without Joseph's really saying anything, the most famous philosopher in Germany had said that he was curious about Joseph's opinions.

"And of course, I saved you," said Max as they had joined his niece at their own table. "I think you would have worked yourself completely into a corner. Next time you had better think twice before saying anything. All the more so when conversing with the greatest thinker of our time."

"And who says I would not have prevailed," Joseph said, a little peeved.

"Come on, boy. Do not deceive yourself. He is a giant and you are a dwarf. But I am as well, perhaps even a tiny gnome, so we don't have to be ashamed. Now, something different. Will you be attending tonight's premiere of *Lohengrin*? Then you will really have had a day. First the most important meeting of your life, and then an opera by Wagner. That's what I call everything coming up German roses."

"I do not know anything about it," replied Joseph. "*Lohengrin*? Tonight?"

"The premiere in Frankfurt of Wagner's opera. I simply assumed you would go. A performance not to be missed."

Twilight was already coming on when he arrived home, just in time for *Mincha*. Again Aron led the service. Through the open door Joseph saw Rabbi Hirsch enter. His father invited the rabbi to say a few words of Torah from which they could all learn. Joseph heard him tell about Japhet and Shem, the sons of Noah, and discuss the connection between the aesthetic world of the Greeks and the ethics of Jewish revelation. When the speech was over, Joseph looked for a place next to the rabbi who kindly addressed him: "I remember you visiting me. Have you read my book?"

"Not yet. I have been learning and reading a lot lately, though. Also Greek philosophers," he added in the hope that this would strike a chord.

Hirsch nodded. "Fantastic, but never forget our sources."

"The Talmud? May I confess something to you," he said in an impulse of sincerity. "You talk about our sources and the Torah is indeed good, but centuries of Talmud study in the spirit of the ghetto have tarnished it in my opinion. And for the rabbis it seems as if the whole Torah only serves the Talmud."

"Ah, I have heard this before. A friend, or rather a former friend of mine from Bonn, Abraham Geiger. He is now the great champion of the Liberals, of reform."

"I don't know him. I came up with it myself. I went to the Liberals once. It was dreadful."

The rabbi nodded thoughtfully. The conversation came to a standstill.

Joseph looked at the clock.

"I have to go." He didn't have the courage to say where. He got up and took his coat.

His father looked up. "Where are you going?"

"I have an appointment."

"We're *davening Maariv* in a minute."

Joseph peeked at the window and saw that it still was not dark. The half-light of dusk lasted hopelessly long. He sat down again and for a while gazed quietly at the floor in front of him. The rabbi looked at him and Joseph felt compelled to say something. "Rabbi, every time I am in my own environment, my life accelerates, and every time I deal with Jewish affairs everything comes to a standstill. This afternoon I spoke with Schopenhauer, for that matter."

"I know him. Dangerous for a layman. He lives only a few hundred meters away from me. He has the really beautiful view. But we could not be further apart in our ideas."

"Tonight, I'm going to the opera. I'm writing for a newspaper in Cologne. I can't occupy myself with petty things anymore."

"I would not call your mother's *shiva* petty."

Joseph blushed to the tip of his ears: "Of course not. I don't mean it that way. I have other needs. The comfort of an evening out with friends, to see light, to experience art. I need that comfort more than sitting on the floor in the twilight. Art makes you realize you are alive. Doesn't the Torah say explicitly, "I place before you today life and death. And you shall choose life." The old ghetto and actually everything here is dead. It is death."

"I understand what you mean, Joseph. But I don't think you do justice to the lines." He slowly stroked his beard as if he wanted to increase tension. It is "today I place before you life and good and death and evil." A slight difference but not insignificant." He smiled. "Don't be afraid of me. I am not your enemy. I am all for a combination of Torah with the modern world." He laughed anew but quickly became serious again. "I hope you will land safely on your feet. You are a good boy, who is just searching. Can I tell you something?"

Joseph looked outside again and nodded. He still had a few minutes.

"Two weeks ago, it was Pesach. Of course, you know the story of the exodus from Egypt. We were slaves. And suddenly we had our freedom. We didn't have to worry about anything. Eating the *manna*, water was the miracle of Miriam, the protection we got from the cloud and the fire. No responsibility. A deceptive freedom." He stopped for a second, but then continued so that Joseph had no time to interrupt. "But you see, the strange thing is that we were afraid to be free. We were all too eager to believe the spies, as long as we kept our so-called freedom in the desert. No choices to make, no temptations. Slaves have a hard time when they are given freedom. In fact, slaves often become the worst slave drivers. Is enlightenment our liberation? Who is actually free?" With a gentle look in his eyes, he turned directly to Joseph. "You don't have to react now. I see that you are on pins and needles. But think about it. All right?"

"All right, rabbi. I really wish I had more time. I hope we will talk again."

"If God wants."

Joseph rose again. But now he was more ashamed in front of the rabbi than his father.

"Boy, dear boy..." was all his father said.

"Papa, please don't make a big deal of this. I will miss only one service and there is already a *minyan*."*

"A great example for your little brother. You've already turned Rivka from the straight path. I wonder if anything good will ever come from you."

Without another word, Joseph left the house. The twilight had finally passed and a promising evening could begin.

The sounds seemed to come from nowhere, straight from heaven to his soul. The music grew more powerful and the strings ever more ethereal. The themes sought each other in a desperate fusion of beauty. From the height, thin sounds kept descending. And then suddenly one jumped up, and another one, seeking freedom. Slowly but surely, a foundation was established, but the movements continued. Connections between heaven and earth. Jacob's dream, in which the angels ascend and descend the ladder, came to his mind.

The prelude of *Lohengrin* was genius and the music was beautiful. But during the rest of the performance Joseph could not stay focused. He found that he could not agree with the underlying ideas. This was narcissism. Here was the ultimate search for salvation, but only personal salvation. He struggled with his statement from a few hours ago. Was the Jewish life of his parents death? Was it really all about him? Wasn't he merely just concerned with his own salvation? Wagner did not provide an answer.

After the opera he sought the company of Max, who was talking to a group of people Joseph did not know, but who clearly belonged to the better circles of Frankfurt. They were evaluating the opera and Joseph joined in with ease. Before he knew it, one of them had invited him for an evening at the *Rothschild Palais an der Grüneburg* the next day.

"*Grüneburgpark*; do you know where that is," Max asked him when they were on their own.

"Yes, it's a long walk."

"Sometimes you really astound me. One moment you are entirely in your role as Johann, the educated cosmopolitan, the next you are just the simple Joseph from the ghetto. Walking? Who is talking about walking? The Rothschilds ensure that their guests are picked up in a carriage. It will be a very special evening. The French branch is there. Jacob and his sons, haha. Make sure that you are at my hotel tomorrow evening at eight o'clock."

It started to snow a little as Joseph left the building. He could not wait to get home and proudly announce that he had been invited to the Rothschilds, but suddenly Joseph recognized the route that he had followed to the cemetery of last Tuesday. Without planning, he found himself headed in that direction and half an hour later he arrived at the cemetery gate. Classicism! Was education the answer? The fence was ajar and he slipped inside. The snowfall became heavier.

The earth was still in a heap on top of his mother's grave. He looked for a few stones and put them on the clods. He gently started to mumble: "*Yit'gadal v'yit'kadash.*" He looked around. No one. Certainly not the nine other men necessary for saying *Kaddish*. He started again. His low voice came from deep in his chest and with every word his voice became louder and more truthful. "*Oseh shalom bimromav, Hu ya'aseh shalom aleinu, v'al kol Israel. V'imru amen.*" He turned around and followed his own footsteps back to the gate. At this late hour there were no coaches available and he prepared himself for a long cold walk back to his parents' home.

Incarceration

The fears of the night were the worst. Sounds he could not place. The moans and groans of prisoners from other cells. Sometimes he thought he heard the noise of torture. Did they still use practices from the Middle Ages here? When he thought about it, he shivered and felt tears rising. Or maybe they were digging a passage. A tunnel to escape? Exhausted, he finally fell asleep, just before dawn. Shortly thereafter, the guards who brought his daily ration roughly shook him awake again. Returning to consciousness after being unaware of the prison for a while was terrible. It made him wonder whether he shouldn't just try to stay awake all the time and suffer gradually, just to avoid the daily shock. He didn't know which would be more horrible.

His thoughts turned to the Biblical story of Jacob waking up after his dream of the ladder. Jacob only had stones for a pillow and he was afraid. The last time Joseph had thought about that text was at the premiere of Lohengrin in Frankfurt. The ascending and descending lines in the music. Was not that the same day he had seen Max and his niece. And had met Schopenhauer? What solution would the philosopher have for his imprisonment? An irrepressible will had little influence when the walls were made of massive blocks of stone.

He tried to remember the music of Lohengrin, but failed. Maybe Beethoven? The Sturmsonate? Could he dream to the music? Allow it to remove him from this place and time. Like a rider on horseback, he skimmed past cities and fields with an unstoppable urge to always keep on rushing. A train journey to Bonn came to his mind. Maria did not exist anymore, hadn't for a long time already.

Who would he miss the most if he never got out of here? His mother. Motherly love was supreme, but she had already definitely said goodbye. Rivka. What were the chances that he would ever see her again? His brothers then? Shouldn't he miss Nathan the most? He could imagine them all vividly, but as soon as his mother appeared, he became weak and it was impossible to think any further.

Should he ask his little brother for forgiveness? In his thoughts he wrote Nathan a letter. How good things can result from bad things. The Torah was full of examples of this –Jacob's lie about being the firstborn, King David's disputable ancestry, and of course, the brothers' sale of Joseph. He was working on the last sentence of the imaginary letter when he realized that since leaving home, he hadn't amounted to much, and decided that his brother probably didn't care about it at all anyway. He tried to tear up his letter in his mind but he couldn't get rid of it.

6

LIVING PICTURES

A carriage brought them to the *Grüneburgpark*. As they rode, Max told Joseph about the background of the family. How the old Mayer Amschel had started his coin business from the *Judengasse* in Frankfurt, had become rich in banking, and had sent his five sons out to Europe to establish the empire. When Joseph asked how they had become so rich, Max shrugged his shoulders. "A combination of being fast and smart, I suspect. Let there be no misunderstanding. They earned a lot from the wars of Napoleon and after. But does that make them complicit? Do we even know what that means? Eventually no one will care about where it all started. Don't think that there was a dispute about how Europe started its colonies in America, Africa, or Asia. It is what it is." He straightened his glasses. "You know, Joseph, most people hate the Rothschilds – the Liberal Jews because they are against fancy rich barons, the Orthodox because the Rothschilds deal with the gentiles, and the gentiles because the Rothschilds are Jews. But it is all probably mere envy." As they arrived, Max quietly gave him instructions on how to behave.

To reach the entrance, they first had to drive along the entire enclosure of the park. Now and then Joseph caught a glimpse of the main building in the middle of lush vegetation. As they passed through the gate into the park, the lanterns along the paths completed the feeling that he had stepped into a fairy tale.

At the top of the stately stairs, a servant collected their cloaks and hats, then led them to the large hall where the festive evening was starting. Every story he had ever heard about the rich flashed into his mind as he walked through the halls. Joseph feasted his eyes on a degree of pomp and splendor that he could never have imagined. Bright white marble walls, columns with beautifully carved capitals, gold decorations, elegant candlesticks, colorful tapestries and Gobelins, heavy velour curtains, stucco work in the most complex patterns, monumental paintings. The wooden parquet floor was laid in an intricate motif. The arrangement of the classic furniture appeared casual, but Joseph suspected that someone had spent a lot of time and energy to make it look so. Even the children's highchairs were meticulously carved in wood and covered with the most expensive plush. It was overwhelming.

"Close your mouth, you look like a monkey," he heard Max whisper next to him. "Now, behave. There, you see Jacob de Rothschild, of the French branch." He held back as they approached the group. "Do you know what? You go. Join them unnoticed. But wait until he speaks to you. Don't start to orate yourself, all right?"

"Are you leaving me?!"

"You should do this on your own."

Max walked on and Joseph stopped nervously a fair distance from the group of four. A large man, dressed in a blue-gray uniform dripping with decorations dominated the conversation. Rothschild stood with two other men, a spindly type, with blond hair, pointed nose, and small eyes – more like a newspaper man, thought Joseph – and a stout, well-dressed businessman, who seemed to be trying to keep the conversation bright and light. Joseph noticed that Rothschild himself kept silent most of the time. It took Joseph a while to understand what they were talking about.

"After Sinop, the major powers have to do something," said the man in uniform.

The spindly one chipped in, "For Russia, it is about the Bulgarians and Hungarians. In order to detach themselves from the Ottoman Empire. Mark my words."

"I thought they wanted Jerusalem?" asked the businessman, almost timid because he apparently didn't know a lot.

The military man shook his head and replied: "Trivial. While the Russians attack the Turks on the flank, they have already won half. And they have already crossed the Danube. Don't forget that Silistra is in Bulgaria."

"The Ottoman Empire is the sick man of Europe," said the spindly man.

Joseph now understood that the subject was the Crimean War, but he did not understand much about the details. He had no idea about the rights of this conflict. The businessman found his courage again and said with conviction, "It is the technical changes that will determine the outcome. New weapons, railways, telegraph. It is a modern war."

The army man agreed and added, "Therefore the Russians will lose, no matter how many men they have. The Russian army is technically inadequate. Very poorly equipped and ill organized."

The third man nodded fiercely. "And it's fantastic that all those reports and photos let us follow it all as if we're there. The newspapers keep us immediately in the know about the daily reality of the war."

Joseph nodded occasionally, hoping that they would not regard him as stupid. He had a vague idea of what they were talking about, but to be exposed was not an option. Max looked at him from the other side of the room and smiled encouragingly, but perhaps also a bit mockingly. Max seemed a safe haven, but something told him to stay with this conversation.

Again, he tried to pick up on the discussion, bearing in mind that someone might ask him a question. Actually, he felt terribly redundant and also a little ashamed. He hated these receptions. Should he learn to appreciate this? Could this be one of those decisive moments? Was that the lesson Max wanted to teach him? The conversation suddenly fell silent and James de Rothschild's gaze fell on Joseph.

"Pardon me, but I do not believe that we have been introduced."

He spoke French with a heavy German accent, but Joseph indicated that German was easier for him. Without any problems Rothschild switched to German.

"Who are you and where do you come from?" It was spoken with a tone that did not tolerate any opposition and required an immediate response. In a fraction of a second Joseph decided that for once it might be useful to tell his true name. "I was born in the same street as you, sir. We were almost neighbors. Maybe you know the name, Socher?"

"Socher? From the *Gasse*? I have to admit that I hardly go there anymore."

Now the ice was broken, Joseph decided to carry on. "We've met before. On the *bima* in the synagogue, here in Frankfurt. *Parashat Lech Lecha*. One and a half years ago. I had the *aliyah* after you."

"Ah. I remember now." Joseph wondered whether that were true, but it didn't matter. The baron now inspected Joseph more closely, and with a somewhat contemptuous look. "You dress like one of those free-spirited artists. Are you going to pose for a painting or suchlike? Do you paint yourself, perhaps?"

Joseph felt a blush of shame, but did not want to reveal his true colors. "No, I write. Also, about paintings." He remembered what Max had told him about the Rothschilds. "Usually from a traditional Jewish perspective," he added. He could not immediately assess whether this was an effective ply, so he continued: "I live in Cologne now. I write for a newspaper. About art, literature, and philosophy. More opportunities in Cologne than here."

"Is that so? You don't enjoy Frankfurt?" The tone was sharp again. Joseph was still thinking what to answer when James de Rothschild continued: "If you're talking about art, you should come to Paris. When our new chateau is ready, you should come and have a look."

"I would be honored." Joseph did not know what to say.

A man who had just entered caught the baron's attention.

"Fine, if you will excuse me now. Duty calls. I hope you will have a pleasant evening. *Enchanté.*"

Joseph sneaked back to Max.

"And did you catch up? Get some interesting investment advice?"

Joseph got past Max's sarcasm. "Pfhh. Don't ever leave me alone in a situation like that again. I barely survived." He wiped the sweat from his forehead. "But then again, he invited me to Paris. I need something to drink," he said while looking around. With perfect timing, a servant came by and offered him a glass of red wine. More at ease, Joseph continued, "We talked about the Crimean War. At least, they did. I had no clue, so I said nothing and that saved me."

"What do you want to know? Shall I explain it to you?"

"Can it be explained? What on earth has Jerusalem to do with the Crimean War?"

"Everything. It is complicated, but let me try. Officially, Napoleon III, the new French emperor, wants to be in charge of the holy places in Jerusalem, the Catholic ones of course. These are now under control of the Turkish sultan. But, it is actually a matter of economic interests, even more so now, with the construction of the Suez Canal. France and England are afraid of the Russians, everyone is afraid of the Russians. Imagine them becoming the rulers in the Levant. See, the Turks don't amount to much anymore and everyone can deal with that, but not with the Russians." He took a break to see whether Joseph was still following. The latter nodded thoughtfully and Max continued. "As for Jerusalem, there are Orthodox Christians there and Tsar Nicholas proclaims himself the great patron of faith. A kind of crusade *après la lettre*, but the other way around, if you get my drift. But as I said, in the end, for the Tsar, it is all about power, land, and possessions – territorial expansion and the conquest of Constantinople."

Joseph had lost track.

Max took a deep breath. "I'll try again. The Ottoman Empire is on its last legs. The Turks are weak and need England and France to protect them against the Russians. If you ever wanted to conquer Jerusalem, now is the time. Who knows how long it will take before a new opportunity presents itself."

"I have no interest at all in Jerusalem."

"Perhaps Jerusalem ought to interest you."

"Why? I can imagine that Jerusalem is important for some very religious people, but besides that? Nobody talks about it. It is also packed with Turks and Arabs."

"And Jews," Max laughed. "You really are still very naive sometimes.

Let me tell you this: For a lot of people, the city is the center of the world. Especially when it comes to religion. Christians, Jews, Muslims – they are all full of Jerusalem. From German emperors to English dukes, and from French despots to Russian tyrants. They are knocking at her door. This century is the century of nations and they all want to be important, pretending to have a higher religious cause on their agenda. And that's where Jerusalem comes in. And behind the religious front, you can deal with your enemies and protect your economic interests. In the Holy Land everything has changed. The Turks have to comply with the dictates of the European superpowers."

"Now you are talking like an oracle again. I thought it was only important to us and then only as an idea; something we sing about on Pesach. Next year in Jerusalem."

"It has become more than just a song. Someone recently told me that thousands of Jews, *Ostjuden** mostly, *chassidim** and followers of the Gaon of Vilna, have already settled there. As far as I'm concerned, they can continue their quarrels there. On a more serious note, many go there to die and to be buried." With great concentration he took a puff of his cigar and looked at Joseph as if he were going to share something of importance. "A land for a people," he mused. "Just like the Germans and Italians. Only we – I will say we once, then you won't feel so alone – we have an extra problem compared to the rest. The Italians are already in Italy. And the Germans in Germany. We, on the other hand, are everywhere and nowhere. We will always have a better life here than withering in the Syrian desert."

"Reform Judaism has just erased everything about Jerusalem and Zion from their prayer books and they are winning."

"The Liberals. Here in Germany, yes. But do you know how many Jews there are in Russia? Millions! We are more divided than ever. None of us knows what we are. None of us knows where we are going. We have never been able to decide whether we are a people, a religion, or a race. I don't know either. I see the Jewish people more as a manifestation, a historical occurrence. And whether it has a future? Actually, the best question you can ask yourself is, what are we doing here? We are an anachronism. And the rest of the world treats us as leeches, outcasts at best. I think it would be best to stop, to close up shop. We've had our fun. It has only brought us misery. We will fade away and that will be that. The end of the Jewish problem."

Max's words made Joseph uncomfortable but he did not feel that this was the time to voice his disagreement.

Walking away from Max, Joseph felt his self-confidence increasing.

He wandered into another room, where his attention was drawn to a somewhat lost looking man, about fifty years old, who stood by himself looking at the paintings. Joseph walked over and introduced himself.

"Oppenheim, Moritz," replied the man. "I am a painter."

"I have heard of you. You are the court painter of the Rothschilds?"

Oppenheim affirmed it and pointed to a few paintings: "These are mine," he said with overt pride.

"Beautiful." Joseph meant what he said.

"And you? Also part of the Rothschild entourage?"

"No, I haven't made it that far yet. I am a writer." Joseph liked the man and did not feel like pretending to be better than he was. "Only beginning. I am from here, from the *Judengasse*, but I live in Cologne now."

"We all escape, don't we? Borne, Rothschild, you, me."

"My escape is not yet definitive, I think."

"I will tell you something. I think we will never get away from it entirely. And that's not so bad? It has brought us beautiful and good things."

"You know," said Joseph, "somehow it sticks to me. I thought I had renounced my Jewish roots, but they haunt me. I have to take more rigorous measures. Break away."

"I would be careful with breaking. Gluing is not easy."

Joseph felt relieved to be able to have a quiet conversation without any ulterior motives.

"This one is not yours, is it?" He pointed to a painting that hung prominently between two monumental columns. It was a portrait of a man with a flamboyant hat, half sitting on a bench in a pastoral landscape, thinking, looking serious and gazing beyond the viewer. He suspected who it was, but he did not want to commit a gaffe.

"No, that is the famous portrait by Tischbein. Our famous literary hero. A nice painting, I must say, although it is not my style. I did paint him once. It was interesting to meet him."

"You met Goethe?"

"Yes, not bad for a Jew from Hanau, right?" He laughed merrily, without resentment.

"How was it?"

"Hanau or Goethe?" he asked, still laughing. "He gave me the title of professor."

"Still, why do you stay here in Frankfurt? Shouldn't someone who creates such beautiful things be able to work for people of even higher rank? Italy, royalty."

"Given that we are talking about the Rothschilds, that higher level is relative. I do all sorts of things for them – buying art, painting, teaching. I'm one of the regulars. "The painter of the Rothschilds and the Rothschild of the painters," as someone quipped. This is my place. I have always remained pious. I want to build a bridge between the Germans and us, so that they will understand us better, so they will stop seeing us as a weird, dirty race. I intend to make some great works about the ghetto. Maybe idealized but that would be acceptable for this cause, I think."

"The ghetto was terrible."

"I have fond memories. There was so much love and respect for one another. When I recall my parents in that poor home, I see faith, love, hope, a longing for the good, and an awe for the higher." He looked at Joseph with melancholy eyes. "I sound like an old dreamer, don't I?" He smiled. "But what are we talking about now? Everyone is assimilating. The emergence from the ghetto is not an unmitigated success. We are on the verge of losing that Yiddish atmosphere forever."

"But as a painter couldn't you do what you wanted? Did you also have to break free?"

"I did. But I have never denied my origins. Not even in Rome, where I lived for years." He looked thoughtful. "Although, sometimes I had to compromise. In Rome I painted and copied numerous Christian scenes. Ah well..."

Oppenheim seemed to recall something. "When I was just getting started, we were assigned to draw a model for the first time. I was twenty, I think. Very pious and of course I had never seen a naked woman before in my life, not even my sister." Joseph nodded, encouraging him to continue. "I sat behind the easel in the studio and the most beautiful girl you can imagine, comes in. She just takes off her clothes, unabashed, and starts posing the way we had to draw her, a challenging pose to say the least. I can tell you, it took a while before I started drawing. I wanted to be professional, so I just did it. But all in all, of course, not very much in accordance with what the rabbis want. Nice story, right?"

By then they had come to another room where Joseph recognized a portrait of Heine.

"You know that I painted that?" asked Oppenheim.

"Yes. It's very good. I would dearly like to meet Heine."

"I have met them all. Zunz, the stubborn one. Börne, Heine, the troublemaker. But he is just a person like you and me. With his own pettiness. And an annoying whine every now and then. But of course, a genius of a writer."

Joseph couldn't care less what people would think of him in the future. Irritant, apostate, fake Jew, good-for-nothing, windbag. If he could achieve a status of genius like Heine, he didn't care.

The painter looked up when someone called him.

"Ah. It is time for the tableau vivant. I do the staging, one of my tasks. Don't you know the concept, depicting a painting in real life? A regular feature of the festivities here. It is highly amusing. I have spent the whole afternoon working on it. The setting is ready. I just have to put the characters in place."

Joseph had to admit that he did not know the phenomenon.

"Rest assured. We're not doing the *Death of Sardanapoulos*! In my modest wisdom, I have chosen a painting of my own. Just joking. Anselm Rothschild wanted this work in particular. I painted it twenty years ago and it now belongs to the Riesser family."

"I think it will be fun to witness."

"I painted the moment when a wounded young Jewish soldier comes home after his fight against Napoleon to defend Germany. On Shabbat, for heaven's sake! It is so cynical. Dozens of Jews fought against Napoleon for Germany, never realizing that they were contending against their own liberation."

Joseph nodded to indicate that he understood the irony.

"Gabriel Riesser wanted it as proof that we are real Germans. I also put in some other things. But everyone is entitled to his own interpretation of a work of art. It doesn't matter. Do you know Riesser? The nice thing is that he is here tonight. He is a great man, although I don't agree with him. He says that the Jewish people have ceased to exist and that it is only a religion. Just like the Catholics or the Protestants and that we can therefore be equal to the Germans. What do you think? Do we constitute a people or follow a religion? If we are a people, then you must agree with the opponents that we perhaps are not Germans."

"I think we are neither the one nor the other. It is more of a conviction. I just heard an interesting observation. We are a historical occurrence. With that we can be German and Jewish. Without a synagogue and without our own country."

"I must remember that. A historical occurrence. Nice. Very nice. That takes off the edge a bit and still gives us a special place."

The man who had called Oppenheim urgently wanted to say something: "Klaus can't participate," he says. "We must have a substitute."

"And is there?"

"Not really. I don't see how I can leave him out..." Oppenheim looked at Joseph, begging.

Joseph tried to look displeased, "What me? No, never."

"It's not that bad. Later, you can always say that you were part of a painting."

The idea was too frightful and too tempting at the same time. "All right, I'll do it. But only a role in the background, right?"

"Come, let's get to work. Don't be afraid!"

They went to a room at the rear end of the palace and Joseph couldn't help laughing when he looked at the scene. It seemed as if they had indeed stepped into a painting. A number of people, dressed in old and ostentatious garments, were nervously moving about in a secluded section of the room of about five by three meters. A curtain created a partition, as in a theater, and in front of it were rows of chairs. In the middle of the stage stood a table with an opened volume of the Talmud. There was a *kiddush* cup, salt, and two pieces of bread. A window had been painted on the right behind the table and on the walls hung all kinds of jewelry, a mirror, a portrait of the emperor. He even thought he could see Hebrew phrases.

"What do you want me to do?"

"Here you are near the bookcase. You are the little brother who turns away because the soldier has let him down." He took a red *yarmulke*.* "Put this on while I show you where to stand. Then we'll bring the rest of your clothes. I will show you what pose you should take. Don't forget, you'll have to hold it until I indicate that everything's over."

When Joseph asked how long that could take, Oppenheim laughed: "Not more than five minutes. In silence.

Joseph was not given time to reflect on this because Oppenheim immediately positioned him in the corner, in front of the bookcase. It was starting to get serious. Now someone brought over his costume.

"Five minutes left. All in place. Non-players, please remove yourselves, thank you."

Joseph put on a green gambeson and found himself balancing between a feeling of complete silliness and a discomforting recollection of his parents' home. He focused on the silliness.

"On your spot, now," he heard Oppenheim shout and at the same time the stage lights were put on from the sides. Two shielded gas lamps. The lights in the room itself were turned off, except for two candles at the entrance.

"Fine. Let the guests enter." Joseph heard some rumbling and sliding of chairs and then it got quieter. He heard Oppenheim make the announcement. The curtain opened and there was a loud applause, followed by a steady murmur. Joseph wanted to look at the viewers, but his gaze had to stay focused on the chair that he was touching with his right hand. The minutes slowly passed and while he crouched, frozen, he wondered whether any of this had a point. Other than entertainment, of course. But it did touch him. A soldier, a Jew who had fought for the

Prussians, who was wounded and now returned. A lost son who finally came home on Shabbat, lovingly received by his parents. Tenderness everywhere. Only the little boy who turned away. How had the painter made this up?

The curtain fell and Joseph could finally straighten his back. Oppenheim thanked them all and when the curtain opened again, the whole company bowed under loud applause.

"Thank you, *Herr* Socher, it has been a pleasure."

After this public stunt, Joseph did not feel like joining the party again. He said his goodbyes, went outside through the meter-high French windows, and came to the terrace at the back of the estate. The palace was built on a splendid location, at the top of a hill, with a view of the city on one side and the mountains in the distance on the other. A group of boys of about ten years old was playing around a fairylike gazebo. He recognized Edmond, the son of Jacob de Rothschild. The boy who had shook his hand at the *bima*. Joseph walked up to him. Edmond looked up.

"Please, don't tell us to go inside, sir," he said in French. Again Joseph mentioned that he preferred to speak German.

"I have the treasure map here," the boy said. "I had hoped that my brothers would help me find the treasure. But they're going to play in the park."

"May I see the map," Joseph asked.

"Careful, sir. It's the only one I've got."

Joseph looked at the paper on which were drawn a few vague lines and some words, but he couldn't make sense of it.

"Explain to me what it is all about, please," he asked in a conspiratorial tone.

The boy whispered in his ear, "Don't tell anyone. I dreamed it and I drew it myself as soon as I woke up. I just drafted the outlines, so that only someone who has knowledge of this matter will understand it."

"Of course, if it were completed, it would be too obvious for everyone," Joseph confirmed.

"You understand. You are smart."

"Those are your brothers?" Joseph asked while pointing at the other boys who were just visible in the park, among the immense trees.

"Yes. I'll have to do it on my own, I think. Nobody knows the place I am looking for. Would you come and help me find it?"

"Maybe it's not here in Frankfurt," Joseph suggested.

"You are right, I think. It has to be somewhere else. An unknown country. A magical place. Maybe it is near Paris?"

"Great idea. Paris it must be."

"Paris is far more beautiful than here. Will you come and see me to find it?"

"I will try. We have to make an appointment so that we can study the map and make a plan."

Apparently, he had completely won the boy's trust. "Here," little Edmond said, "please take the map, then it will be safe. I know it by heart, anyway. Nobody can take it from me. Later, we can have a good look at it."

Feeling honored, Joseph tucked the map into his pocket.

"Very good, sir. See you later. Alas, I really have to go inside now." The boy ran away, waving his hand.

Joseph felt for the boy as he walked back to the terrace. It reminded him of the time when, as a child, he had had a dream in which he had invented a fantastic game. The next day he had started the preparations, but by the time he finished, Rivka and Aron had decided that they had better things to do. They had left him with his dream for the rest of the afternoon. But the idea had been delightful and the hope itself had been worth the disillusionment.

Incarceration

After the daily interrogation they took him back to his cell. To his surprise he found a man lying on his bed.

"Shortage of space," the prison ward growled.

The man looked neglected, but more, there was something about him that caused Joseph to be wary. Maybe his clothes? Just too chic? Because he didn't want to converse, let alone argue, with an unknown criminal, he retreated to a corner and slept there, on the floor, that night.

Maybe his cellmate was a ploy by the guards? To pilfer information? Or perhaps the man was more innocent than Joseph. Did such a status exist? More innocent? Either you were guilty or you were innocent. More innocent was logically impossible. Besides, no one was innocent. From birth on, sins came. As a child, grabbing something that wasn't yours, an insignificant lie to your parents, innocuous offenses that carried the germ of greater guilt.

When he was returned after the next day's interrogation, his cellmate was gone. Joseph was relieved to have his cell to himself again. His cell? He was caught by this dubious thought – how awful to be happy with his own cell. Was this a sign that he had surrendered to the inevitable? To the absurdity? Was this a sign that he was regaining his dignity or was this the ultimate acceptance of prison life? He hoped they would leave him alone for the rest of the day.

He often tried to find a higher reason why he was here. He never succeeded but the attempts kept him busy for hours. Maybe this imprisonment would be beneficial for him in the end. Was it to test his strength? His stamina? Everyone was given the challenge he could handle, so he must be a great person. Who knows, perhaps he had to develop hatred so he could do something good with it? Maybe people would be nicer to him? Maybe he would write a book about it and that would provide him with a carefree life? Maybe it was all completely circumstantial, not related to his person at all. Anyway, if all of this had any meaning, it was beyond his comprehension. Maybe he would understand in the future. For now, once more, he gave up.

Perhaps he would never be among people again. Maybe he would just have to stare at the blocks here in his cell. Why wasn't one loose? He decided that if he ever built a prison he would put a loose block in it. That way a prisoner always had a possibility of escaping. It wouldn't be too obvious of course. The convict would have to work for it. But it would be inhumane to deny someone the hope of escape altogether.

(1856)

DUCK

One afternoon, after everyone else had left, Pennekamp asked Joseph to stay a minute. "We can celebrate your success with a glass of champagne. You've been here for a couple of years now and it has all turned out to be excellent. People take your writing seriously. Important people know the journalist Lichtman."

"Writer," corrected Joseph cautiously.

"Writer, then, if you are so committed to that."

Probably because of the success of his journalism, Pennekamp had published a short philosophical essay of Joseph's earlier that year. Despite its total lack of success – the only reaction had been a lukewarm positive review from an unknown professor in Heidelberg – Joseph clung to the title of writer.

They sat down between the printing presses and type cases. Pennekamp took a bottle out of the cupboard and proudly showed that it was a quality wine. Then he reconsidered. "Maybe the wrong kind for you. This champagne is certainly not kosher."

Joseph dismissed this with a shrug. "Who is still worried about that these days?"

"Jews perhaps," Pennekamp replied with a smile.

The bottle popped and the champagne sparkled in their glasses.

"Just asking, Lichtman. What are you actually going to do with your Jewish identity?"

"Nothing," he said, surprised by the question and the choice of topic. "Should I do something about it? I thought it didn't matter to you." He took a sip. The subject was awkward.

"Right. It doesn't matter to me at all. I just wanted to know, whether you are still religious or perhaps even following the laws. Really, pure interest. You don't have to change anything for me."

"Thank you. That's nice to hear. Most of all I am very grateful that I can work here. That you give me this freedom."

"That is not an answer. Maybe you should consider a career in diplomacy, my boy."

"With your permission, I hadn't finished yet." The champagne and

Pennekamp's reassuring words had their effect, but he wondered why his boss was so interested in his Jewish comings and goings. "I wanted to say that I feel completely at ease, although I sometimes have the impression that others are more concerned about my situation."

"There are some who do care about your being Jewish, I fear. That is why I am asking you about it. You can do whatever you want, but you will always be judged because of it. Believe me."

"Do you really think that it limits my opportunities?"

"Maybe, maybe not. Remember what Heine said about baptism. It is the entrance ticket to European culture. Abandon your naiveté." He held back for a moment. "Look, what we don't want is the old Jewish mentality; the bearded rabbis, to put it bluntly. But with eager, enlightened Jews, it's a different story. They have a lot of potential. You agree with that, don't you?"

"Certainly. I have also completely renounced the Talmudic culture of seclusion."

"Fine. Let's be honest. We have a liberal spirit. Assimilation and equal rights are the slogans. And medieval situations do not fit in anymore. If you insist on being different, you cannot demand equal treatment." He let go of the seriousness of his voice and said: "It is time that you really take some big steps. That is why I wanted to speak to you today. Joseph belongs at the Egyptian court."

"Johann."

"We both know who you are. It doesn't matter."

Joseph drank his glass and stared at it with an avid look hoping for a refill. Pennekamp topped off their glasses and said, "You have developed a taste for it, haven't you?"

Joseph shrugged his shoulders and returned to the subject, "I have noticed that you have a considerable knowledge of the Bible."

"I do, but I can just as easily refer to Greek mythology. Although everything in those stories ends badly. No redemption, no salvation. I will say that much for your people, their hopeful view is unique in the world."

Joseph did not know whether Pennekamp was being sarcastic or serious. Was there latent condescension in his irony? He considered his position safe enough to ask him an honest question. "Can't people live in multiple worlds?"

"Ah yes. That would be nice. On *Sankt-Nimmerleins*-Day. [9] Maybe that is too Christian for you," he said, smiling. "I mean that it is about as likely as the Messiah's showing up tomorrow. But to give you a real answer. I don't believe that anyone even wants that. People want to live in their own world. I don't mean the enlightened Jews, of course, but the rusty Orthodox ones. They will never cross to the other side. That would mean betrayal. And the gap is too wide. Building bridges, maybe for some, but closing the gap? Castles in the air. On the other hand, with all those innovative architects today, you never know."

It took a while for Joseph to grasp the jest, but then they both laughed.

"Listen. I have big plans for you. I would like you to write a regular page about art and culture every week. Page three of the Saturday edition. You can determine for yourself what subjects will be interesting, and review them. An exhibition, a new book or anything else that catches your attention. But keep away from firm statements about politics or religion. That only leads to cancellations. For starters, next year I want to send you to Paris as correspondent. That's where the action is."

"Paris! As a correspondent. Thank you so much. I won't let you down."

Pennekamp shone. "Do you know what? Come and dine with us next Sunday."

In Pennekamp's house there was the smell of clean. In the large high living room, the table was elegantly set. He was the only guest. To Joseph's relief, Horst and Hilde were not there and no one mentioned them.

The Pennekamps spoke French and it was all Joseph could do to follow the conversation. By now he had studied enough French and English that he could read proficiently and even write reasonably well. But a proper conversation was something different. Nevertheless, Joseph found himself enjoying the conversation. They ate an excellent soup and then the main course was now served. *Canard Lardé a la Moutarde Ancienne*, an old, regional dish from Metz where Odette was born; duck larded with mustard. Joseph saw the duck, layered on all sides with bacon.

Joseph let himself be served, not yet sure what to do. Pennekamp looked at him with encouragement. The last thing Joseph wanted was to offend his host and employer, so he took up his cutlery in the hope that he might be able to eat between the bacon strips without being noticed. The duck was not a problem and even the *treife* gravy was not insurmountable. But Pennekamp kept looking at him.

"*Bon appetit*," said Joseph.

"*Bon appetit*," replied Pennekamp. He suddenly seemed almost worried. "We assumed that you were no longer guided by archaic dietary regulations."

"No, of course not," Joseph slowly said. He took a piece of bacon on his fork and put it in his mouth. He swallowed it without really biting. He looked at Odette with his most cheerful face.

"*Delicieux.*"

"Enjoy," said Pennekamp and he stuck an immense piece of meat in his mouth.

"Take it easy," whispered Odette.

With full mouth, the publisher beamed: "Delicious." And as if a danger had been averted, he added in German: "To the rest of our lives and a fantastic collaboration." He washed the meat away with a big gulp of wine.

Joseph suspected that Pennekamp had intentionally tested him. Whether Johann Lichtman was only assimilated in word or in deed as well. He also raised his glass: "*prosit*," he said with his best smile.

The next morning, he woke with a troubled mind. He had a slight hangover, but that was not the problem. He often drank heavily. Bad dreams had plagued him. This had also been happening more often of late. Perhaps there was also an unconscious mechanism that made him feel guilty. His father had once said that he would do everything he could to save his skin and that of his family. Except eating pork.

Joseph tried to relax. In a few months he would be gone. To Paris.

One day, a few weeks later, when autumn was well on its way, there came a knock on the door. Joseph had spent the whole afternoon browsing reluctantly through a book that Pennekamp had asked him to look at. *Landscape Illustrations of the Bible. The Finden Collection.* "Perhaps it's something to publish in German," he had said. "You, with your Bible knowledge, might have an easier time assessing it. It definitely has some good prints."

To his surprise, it was Rivka. She was alone and looked neglected.

After they embraced each other, she said, "I wanted to see you again and to find out how the others are doing. Papa and Nathan. And Aron," she added.

"And that's all? For that you travel from Paris to Cologne?"

"Yes," she said. "I guess."

He assumed they would have more time together so he didn't ask any more questions. But he was convinced that there was something wrong. He told her that their father regularly wrote letters from Frankfurt. "The last one was about the construction of the synagogue. I don't keep up exactly, but papa mentioned the fight concerning the new building. I don't quite understand all the fuss – people who had given money, then new plans, then the construction that had been halted, and now there is another completely new synagogue, for the Orthodox, but who has to pay for it. Synagogue politics. I send back pretty bland responses. What else can I do? Offer a discourse on Spinoza?"

"How is Nathan doing?"

"Angry at me. And also at you. But he manages, says papa. Why don't you write them yourself?"

"I did, but I never get any answer. They really threw me out, unlike you."

"Probably they think that you have fallen even lower than I."

Rivka nodded. She had written to Joseph about her baptism and marriage to Rainer Wolfing, but not in detail.

"That baptism was not a big deal." She was clearly trying to trivialize it. "I had to read some things and then they sprinkled some water over me. I didn't even get immersed in a pleasant warm bath like the *mikve*."* She waited a while. "I think Rainer is cheating on me."

Joseph didn't know what to respond.

"I suspect he is unfaithful, but I don't want to confront him yet. What will I do if it is true? I don't know anyone else in Paris. I have nowhere to go." She stopped.

"What can I do for you?"

"I can't go back to Frankfurt. I can't admit I failed. You never would have if you had not been a success here in Cologne, would you?"

"You didn't fail."

She looked away and said nervously: "I just wanted to talk to someone." She now looked him straight in the eyes. "I might have made the wrong choice." She started to sob and Joseph hugged her. "Can you forgive me?" she asked.

"What should I forgive you for?"

He waited a while and then tried to take away some of the weight: "Maybe we can debaptize you."

She had to laugh through her tears. "More of your nonsense." Joseph gave her a handkerchief and she dried her tears. But she apparently felt better now that she had poured out her heart.

"If you allow me to stay here for a week to recover my strength, things will improve, I am sure. But not too many questions, agreed?"

She grabbed the book that was lying on his desk. "Are you doing *t'shuva** too?" she asked, laughing as she looked at the pictures of the Holy Land.

"How so?"

"A book about the Bible." She browsed through the pages. "Lovely there. With those palms and those hills. Exotic. I would like to visit those places someday."

"It is at the bottom of my list, to be honest. I think they have presented that wasteland a little rosier than it actually is. Heavily romanticized."

"Since when are you so cynical? Take another look."

Joseph looked over her shoulder. The prints had the same dreamy and mystical connotations as the prints of the Rhine Valley he had seen at Holstein. It was romantic and adventurous, but he felt no attraction to it. Maybe she was right and he had become a cynic.

"An Arab prince like that might be very interesting," said Rivka.

"You'd better be careful. From what I've read, you don't want to fall into their hands."

She gazed, captivated, at some other plates and then said seriously, putting the book aside: "Saturday is Yom Kippur."

Without any real interest, he replied: "Really?"

"Shall we go?"

Joseph looked as if he didn't understand."

"To *Shul*. To the service."

"Why? I don't belong there and you certainly don't."

"I want to taste the atmosphere again. Maybe it's nostalgia. It gives me a safe, protected feeling."

He thought for a moment. If he was strong enough to enter a church, a synagogue shouldn't disturb him at all. "If you want to go, I'll go with you. But only for the last part. To sit in shul all day seems somewhat overdoing it. I will look for my prayer shawl. I hope I can still find it," he lied. He knew exactly where his *tallit* was.

"All right, only *Ne'ila*.* Joseph, you are a good brother. Thank you."

"I have to go. I have an appointment with Pennekamp." He stood up, poured himself a glass of wine, and drank it in one gulp.

Rivka gave him a doubtful look.

"What?" he asked.

"Just. It is still early."

"Don't worry. I know exactly what I'm doing. A drink makes me stronger. More confident. Makes everything slightly easier." He grabbed his jacket and walked out with determination.

During the week Rivka got noticeably better and Joseph began to hope that it might have been just a temporary breakdown after all. As Yom Kippur approached, Joseph started to get nervous. Would they recognize him? Did he know people who went to shul, to the old shul? He knew that some went to the Liberal synagogue, but did anyone go to the Orthodox service? Probably not, but Yom Kippur was different. That day had a special status for many.

He felt somewhat hypocritical, not so much because he was no longer religious, but because of the simple fact that in the afternoon he had an extensive lunch, with wine and, as dessert, coffee with digestives, and as a result, he was rather tipsy when Rivka and he walked to the synagogue. Would people notice? The food probably not, but the drinks? It was his first time in the Orthodox synagogue in Cologne. It was so crowded there that no one noticed him at all. He pulled the *tallit* over his head.

Again, he was struck by the messiness of the service. But just as he expected to be annoyed by it, a feeling of solidarity overwhelmed him. Or rather, a feeling of regard, yes, even respect. These were no lazy followers, as with the Liberals and the Church, where everyone walked well within defined lines. Everyone here was involved with themselves, a little ahead of the prayer leader or a little behind, sometimes out loud, sometimes muttering, with a sound like a bluebottle fly or a loud howl of sorrow and despair. But at the same time, they needed each other. On their own they couldn't do it. People who chose to form a group, not just a group of people.

The call of the *shofar** filled the room, and while the lamentable tone lasted, a shiver went down his spine. Next, in contrast, a cheerful song started. *L'shana haba b'Yerushalaim.*

After the service Joseph wanted to go home immediately. He felt miserable. His throat was sour and dried out and his stomach seemed to be in knots. A cool beer would be the best medicine. He found Rivka and together they squeezed through the crowd that was standing outside to say the blessing for the New Moon. He felt how an arm was laid on his shoulder.

"Joseph? Johann?"

He turned around and thought he saw Max, but in religious camouflage. Then he recognized that it was Max's brother, Avraham. Next to him stood his wife and daughter. He remembered her, Miriam, from the café where they had met Schopenhauer. She had to be about sixteen years old now and for what he could see she had become a very pretty young lady. A little apart from the family stood another man, clearly recognizable as *Ostjude*, a Jew from Russia or Poland. He wore a long black coat, and on his head he had something of a bear's cap. His face was largely hidden behind a long black beard and ear locks that fell to his chest.

Avraham wished Joseph a good year and introduced his family. Joseph courteously replied that he had heard nothing but good about them and in turn he introduced his sister.

"This is Rav Yermiyahu Silberman," said Avraham. "He is from Lublin, Poland. He travels with a group that tries to convince us to go to Palestine." Avraham turned to the rabbi in Yiddish. "Correct me if I am wrong."

With a heavy, warm voice the man replied that he could not have put it better.

At first, the man dispelled every inclination Joseph might have had to identify with Judaism. Worse; he feared that others might see the *Ostjude* as the default Jew and then would regard Joseph in the same way. There was no point in fighting for equality for years when suddenly a number of fanatics from the East came forward and antagonized everyone.

"Next year in Jerusalem. You just heard it," said the Rav with a cheerful smile. "Do you want to do *Kiddush Levanah** now," he asked Joseph.

"No, I'd rather not," he replied. The last thing he felt like doing was praying to the moon.

"I did it last week, following the practice of the *Gaon of Vilna*."

"Smart. A wise man," was all Joseph said. He felt extremely uncomfortable and hoped that no acquaintances would pass by. He was ashamed and he felt even worse about being ashamed. The man did not deserve to be judged by his appearance. But when someone suggested that he and Rivka participate in the festive ending of the fast in the community room, he resolutely declined.

"We'd rather go home."

Avraham invited them instead to their home. Joseph saw Rivka looking at him, begging.

"All right. Thank you. Lead the way. Will Max be there too?"

"No, Max is skipping this year," Avraham said in a serious tone. He kept looking at Joseph and then a smile appeared on his face. "Max has skipped every year so far. But I am glad that his best friend is accompanying us."

"Best friend." Was it just a manner of speech or was Avraham relying on something Max had said? In any case, he felt deeply honored. He absolutely didn't know what to do with Rav Silberman. For now he just had to swallow his annoyance about the hat, the black coat and the *peyot*.

As they walked to Avraham's house, he decided to be straight with him.

"I have to admit that I was not there the entire service. And I did not fast either."

"I had a hunch," said Avraham. "It's fine. You came. That's what counts."

"Fasting on Yom Kippur is pointless," Joseph raised.

"Eating on Yom Kippur is equally pointless." Rav Yermiyahu joined the conversation. "A few hours later you're hungry again."

"But at least one feels good then. You don't. You are starving."

"I feel good precisely because I fast," said the man, giving the impression that he won the argument. They both laughed and let the matter rest.

The home of Avraham Ben Tov was a veritable mess. There were piles of clothing everywhere.

"I am a clothes merchant," Avraham declared, superfluously.

"I noticed. My father is the same. In Frankfurt."

"Max told me."

How much did this man know about him? He shouldn't say too much. They came to the back room and every step increased Joseph's sense that he was entering his parents' house in Frankfurt, which did not even exist anymore since his father had moved. The smell of second-hand clothes evoked images of his youth. He looked at Rivka and said, "You wanted nostalgia? Well, you can't get more than this."

The family sat down at the long table covered with a white cloth, and a variety of dishes were served. Without any semblance of order, people ate everything as one course. Soup and the traditional Jewish stew. The dessert, pastries, and dried fruit were on the table from the beginning. But the atmosphere was festive. The two pious men kept up a constant chatter in Yiddish. Joseph sat opposite them and was ashamed of his first thoughts about the *Ostjude*. However, he kept a low profile and just let everything happen. Miriam came by asking if he had eaten enough or if he wanted anything else. He felt a bit shy with her presence but was happy to tell her, with complete sincerity, that everything was excellent.

"Maybe a *schnapps*?" he asked her.

She nodded and came back a little later, smiling, with an almost full glass of cognac.

"One hundred percent kosher," she said softly.

Joseph thanked her, then turned his focus back to the conversation of the two men. He pulled out his tobacco and relaxed complacently while puffing his pipe.

"The unity of our people must come first," he heard Rav Silberman say.

"At this moment things are only getting worse. The groups are drifting further and further apart," answered Avraham.

The rabbi continued imperturbably, "Then comes the first phase. But it will happen slowly. First the phase of Joseph." Joseph looked up, disturbed, unsure whether they were discussing him.

Rav Yermiyahu noticed. "Relax. I am talking about the *Mashiach ben Yosef*.* The first phase of our salvation. The one we have to do ourselves. After that *Hashem* will help us and the *Mashiach ben David* will come. That will indeed be a miracle. We will hear the *shofar*! Now we have to convince our people that the time has come when we ourselves must act. It is up to us. We have to convince the great nations because we cannot do anything against their will. And we must be careful not to raise false expectations. One Shabtai Zvi is enough."

They laughed. "Beautiful thoughts, but too idealistic I fear," Joseph said.

The rabbi supported his vision with Talmudic texts that Joseph vaguely recognized, but which didn't mean much to him. The conversation continued for a while, and Joseph's attention began to drift.

The Rav turned to him. "Avraham tells me that you are a journalist. Maybe you would like to do something for us? Write an article to make our people in Prussia aware of *Eretz Israel*?"*

Writing a pamphlet for the ingathering of the exiles was about the last thing Joseph wanted to do. He demurred gently, saying, "Who knows? I would have to structure my ideas a bit more. But it could be done."

Fortunately, the rabbi let the subject rest. He now started a passionate discourse regarding the importance of setting aside a tenth of one's earnings for *tzedakah*,* which was a condition for the Jews to be allowed to return to the Land.

"Do you want some more coffee?" Again it was Miriam who asked the question.

"Yes, please. Thank you. But then we'll leave, won't we?" He looked at Rivka for an answer. She nodded. "We still have to build a *sukkah*," he joked. They all laughed.

When Joseph and Rivka said goodbye at the door, Yermiyahu gave him a firm handshake. "Maybe you are not ready for a return, but I imagine one day you will."

"I think it's extremely unlikely, but you are free to think that way."

As they walked back home, Rivka said, "Did you notice how that girl was taken with you?"

"Which girl? Miriam?"

"Don't pretend you didn't notice. Of course Miriam."

"I noticed her. Yes."

"She is good-looking and one day you will be looking for a wife."

"She is nice, indeed. She is going to be a beautiful young woman. But the thing is, she is more *frum* than my older brother. And that is not going to change."

Rivka smiled at him while she was teasing. "We will see."

A few days later, Rivka left for Paris, feeling much better. The farewell was short. Joseph assured her that she could always rely on him, but Rivka replied that she was strong and that things would turn out well.

"You have helped me. I'm going to make some important decisions when I'm back home."

Joseph looked curious but she felt no need to elaborate. "You'll hear from me in not too long. Thank you brother."

"I'll come and visit you as soon as possible."

"I have been thinking, Joseph." He noticed that Elsa used his Jewish name, something she had never done before. "I've had so many misfortunes in my life and I've always stood firm. I have adapted to the circumstances. Have identified with the culture. I myself was a figurehead for the enlightened spirits. Maybe I have been lying all the time, and in my heart I am still that girl from the ghetto of Frankfurt who can't live without her family. I have lost everyone. I am alone. You are here. But you will go your own way. I can't expect you to care about an old woman." Joseph wanted to object, but she didn't give him a chance. "It doesn't matter. It is important that you live your own life."

"And Max?"

"Max is not like me. He looks forward, ahead. He is an optimist. And he has no place for a woman in his life. Besides I am a lot older." She nodded gently. "But Max is a good man. And I will always be grateful for his friendship and the beautiful hours we had together."

"You sound as if you are saying goodbye. You're not ill, are you?"

"Not physically, no. But mentally I am worn out."

Joseph did not know what to say. The air in the room was heavy. Outside it had already become dark. Gusts of rain ravaged the windows.

"I have been thinking," she started again, as if her previous thought was not what she had wanted to say. "I've been brewing a plan. A wild plan." She waited for a moment. "I don't know. It feels as if by announcing this news, there won't be a way back." She took a deep breath. "I want to go to Jerusalem."

Joseph's mouth fell open with disbelief: "Jerusalem. Why on earth?"

"You know that I have recently been more involved with our religion. Synagogue visits and other things. But it's not comfortable, not right. People in the synagogue stare at me. They don't trust me. I don't feel at home. I am a stranger in a strange country."

"If you want something new or you want to leave Cologne, why not America? There are plenty of opportunities there."

"In America?" She laughed without joy. "America is for those who want to start a new life. I want to end my old life."

"But in Jerusalem they will be even more unfriendly than here in the synagogue. Only religious fanatics from Russia go there."

"You probably wonder where this reversal has come from. First the Christmas tree and then the *Kaddish*. You could write a book about that." She took a deep breath. "I've thought a lot and read a lot lately. I have looked into our sacred texts again. They were still in the attic. I have read the diary of an Italian woman who went to *Eretz Israel* and who felt completely free there, as a religious woman. I keep coming back to Rachel *Imenu*, our mother. And the misfortune that befell her. So long childless, then dying prematurely, not buried with her family. Strange as it may sound, I find it inspiring. Maybe I can do good works. In Jerusalem the conditions are quite bad, I hear. I have money. More money than I need. And who knows, one day you will come to visit me and write the last chapters of my memoirs. What do you think? Is it time to do *t'shuva*? Go to the land of our forefathers and die in Jerusalem?" She got up and started pacing back and forth. "You don't have to say anything. I've actually already made up my mind. I plan to go and visit Rachel's burial place. We will see what comes next. Either here in Germany or there. Maybe then, it won't matter that much anymore."

As she looked at Joseph, she smiled, "Don't feel badly. It has nothing to do with you. At least, you are not responsible for this." And in a more recognizable, authoritarian way she said: "Don't try to talk me out of it. You know how stubborn I am. Actually, I wanted to ask you to come along, but hearing your reaction I realize it's pointless. Still, you can think about it."

"I don't want to disappoint you, but *Herr* Pennekamp has just promised me a post in Paris." He looked guilty.

She comforted him by gently patting him on his arm. She got up. "I am tired. I'm going to rest now." Stately as always, she left the room, leaving Joseph in total dismay.

He sat for a moment and then left, feeling depressed. It felt as if he had read her obituary. If there had been anyone who had always been as steady as a rock, stronger than anyone else, it was Elsa. How could he not have seen this coming? He remembered the evening they first said *Kaddish* together. He had noticed how upset she was at the time, but had ascribed that to the memory of her deceased husband, not to a newly awakened religious consciousness. They had repeated the ritual more often. Joseph had always kept his mother in mind and assumed that for Elsa it was nothing more than a distraction. It could have been the Pater Noster for all he knew. What an enormous miscalculation. Should he tell Max about this? He had forgotten to ask if he should keep this a secret. Was it a confession only intended for his ears? Should he try to stop her?

Elsa Blumenreich left for Palestine the following February. Max and Joseph saw her off at the train station. The departure was less strenuous than either had expected. Elsa was in high spirits and looked strong, confident in her decision. She carried a small suitcase with only some bare necessities. She had already shipped her belongings to the "Promised Land", after giving away most of it to charity institutions. Once Max had reconciled himself to the idea of her going, he had made sure she would find a good home in Jerusalem when she arrived.

Max shouted, "Don't go out alone," as his last piece of advice as the train started moving. They ran alongside it, but as the wheels picked up the pace, they had to give up.

"Come and visit me," was the last thing she called, leaning out of an open window, her voice almost completely drowned out by a loud rush of steam and the rattling of the wheels.

Max and Joseph looked at each other, laughing nervously, and they decided to have a good schnapps to toast her well-being.

"Who would have thought? Who knows where we will wind up?"

"Take it easy, Max. First Paris."

"Strange, I really didn't see this coming."

"Did you try to persuade her to stay?"

"Briefly. But I saw there was no point. With all my rationality I still can't fight against higher authorities. I don't think I will ever see her again."

Incarceration

What if all that was left of his life was to kill time until time killed him. Or perhaps somehow, because of some misunderstanding, he had ended up trapped in a parallel universe. He would have to find the entrance again.

What genius move was God making by placing him in a cell? If there was a god He had to have a plan. At least, if it wasn't the god of Spinoza. Something like this could never have happened to his brother, Aron the Pious.

Why did his thoughts keep coming back to the year in Paris instead of the years before in Germany? Was it guilt? In Paris he had not really been a light to the nations.

"You petered out," he said out loud in the middle of the night.

"Shut up, I don't want to argue with myself," he shouted at the walls.

"You're just not yourself. You are a great derivative. The High Art of Self-Absorption. You did everything you could to fit into the cliché. You agreed with the right people, you dressed the way you thought they would accept; your bent your opinions and views to match those of the people you wanted to impress; you did everything to be salonfähig. Joseph, Joseph. Come back to yourself.

Think of your mother."

"Leave my mother out of this," he shouted. He stood up. This became too serious. He was having conversations with himself out loud. "I am myself. I am a writer," he continued with complete determination. "I am a writer whom people take seriously. People know me. They come to me for advice. I know all the great ones."

"Then write something decent, you writer! Write. Don't dump your failure on me."

Lying back on his cot, he calmed himself down a bit. He decided that he should tell his story. It would be difficult in his cell without pen and paper, but he could practice memorizing parts. He remembered Max who had said, when he was still living in his attic room, that a vagrant was not taken seriously. Maybe it was different for a prisoner? Freedom caused laziness. When he would be given a second chance, he would try to be better. He promised. But to whom? To himself. Did that make sense?

(1857)

HIGH ART OF SELF ABSORPTION

On the train to Paris he inadvertently thought back to his trip to Bonn years earlier. That short trip had been endless, full of promises and hope. Full of Maria. This time he was an established journalist riding the international train from Cologne to the capital of Europe. This trip was nothing more than inevitable. The iron colossus rushed across the German fields towards Belgium. There it shot through despondent forests of gloomy dark spruces that slowly turned into the lazy French flat land. When he got off the train in Paris, Joseph was so exhausted that he had hardly any energy left with which to admire the metropolis.

Paris turned out to be a large construction pit. Everywhere there were holes, ditches, and fenced off areas. It was much worse than anything he had seen in Frankfurt or Cologne. Max had told him about the great urbanization plans of Napoleon III and Baron Hausmann. Now it seemed as if the whole city was being overhauled. Via the dug-up Boulevard de Sebastopol, he walked towards Rue de Rivoli, stepping over the tramps and beggars. "Why don't they do something about this," he muttered to himself. He waved off a beggar and decided that he could do nothing better than to wash off the dust of the journey with a good glass of wine. Wasn't France the wine country *par excellence*? Joseph found a nice table on one of the many terraces; a perfect spot from which to take in the city. He was in no hurry. The only immediate plan was to visit Rivka as soon as possible. He enjoyed the radiant sun on his face and the glowing wine that heated his body.

As he let his eyes roam the busy street and the unrelenting stream of people, Paris presented itself grand and phenomenal. This city could give him everything. It was the center of the world. This was where everything happened. This was where everyone either came from or was going to. Germany had begun to get on his nerves. He was often bored and when he went for some alcohol for distraction, Max was always quick to rap his knuckles. Too fast and too often. His spiritual mentor had been interfering a little too much lately. It was nice to be away from Cologne. Nobody to interfere. A few hours later he got up, his head spinning and his legs a bit wobbly, but in good-humor as he walked to the hotel that Pennekamp had booked.

Because Rivka lived a considerable distance from the actual center of town, he left early the next day. He was looking forward to seeing her again. After searching for a while, he entered a narrow street with high houses on both sides. She had written him that they lived on the second floor. He rang and waited. A housekeeper opened the door and told him in the most unfriendly way that nobody was home. *Monsieur* Rainer Wolfing didn't live here anymore. When Joseph indicated that he had not come for him but for Rainer's wife, the woman laughed with contempt. "That one? She's gone into the monastery. Just ask the parish priest." With a grin she asked: "Do you want her? I think she was for sale. A truly sensual type. A real Jewess." And with those words she closed the door.

"Wait," Joseph yelled, stunned by her answer, but the woman did not come back. He tried to understand her words, but sense eluded him. A monastery! What was going on? Why had she not told anything about this in her letters? He remembered her agitation and the state in which she had come to Cologne last year. Thoughtfully, Joseph walked to the church down the street. He found the priest cleaning the candelabras. The man looked up as if surprised when he saw Joseph, but he tried to be helpful.

"You say you suspect that your sister has gone into a monastery," he repeated unnecessarily and with an unusual sense of drama.

"Yes, she lived here in this street; she was married, but I have no idea where she is now. Renata Wolfing is her name."

"I can ask around," the man solemnly said. "Come and see me again in a few days."

Unable to wait, Joseph went back to the church the next day. He was welcomed by the priest who was in the company of a nun.

"Have you found her?"

"Mother Superior Anna can tell you more."

"She is in our convent of the *Sisters of Zion*," the nun said.

"Is that far from here? Sion, isn't that Switzerland?"

"It is a monastery in the holy city where our Savior sacrificed Himself for our sins," she responded with conviction.

Joseph found the vague clues irritating. "What do you mean?"

"Jerusalem."

"What would she do in Jerusalem?" His thinking became increasingly confused. He began to sweat. "Wait. Really? She is in Palestine?"

"Our monastery in Jerusalem is primarily intended for Jewish converts who have found or want to find the way to true faith. We help them. The convent counts many nuns who have fled from France, as well as fallen women like Renata." The nun gazed at Joseph serenely for a long time. Then she continued. "As far as I know, she embarked for the Holy Land a few months ago. Sister Berthe, with whom I spoke, told me that she wanted to pay for the enormous sins she had committed after her divorce. Of course, out of mercy, sister Berthe did not tell us any details. Renata has repented and her sins have been forgiven. Who are we to rake them up?" The woman hesitated for a moment. "There was a scandal, I heard." Her voice dropped to a whisper. "She had to leave."

Joseph wanted to think calmly but his stomach was churning.

"That is all I can tell you." The woman turned around to leave. The priest shrugged his shoulders to show that he had nothing to add.

"Wait. What was the name of the monastery, again? *Sisters of Zion?*" The nun looked at him and nodded.

"I am indebted to you." Joseph took some money from his pocket. "Here, this is for you. Make sure it will go to a good cause." The nun thanked him and Joseph left, completely aghast.

So many questions. Jerusalem, of all places! The nun had called her a fallen woman. He had to inform Elsa. Maybe she could help. He remembered the afternoon in Cologne when they had looked at the sketches of the Holy Land. It had enchanted her. The land of milk and honey.

He decided that there was no point in trying to contact Rivka's husband, Rainer. From what he had learned, Joseph guessed that the man would probably not be very helpful. It might get nasty. It wasn't worth it.

•

Joseph had sent a couple of letters to the monastery but had not received a reply. He had also written to inform Elsa of the situation, but he had not heard from her either. Palestine seemed to be a dark hole into which both had disappeared, and very slowly it dawned on him that he had to accept to their disappearance from his life. First Elsa, now his sister.

He hated the world, he hated monasteries, he hated Paris, and above all, he hated himself. Whether it was because of his disappointment in Rivka, her alleged fall, her absence, or perhaps his powerlessness and frustration, he found himself more and more often in bars with a large glass of absinthe in front of him.

This afternoon he had chosen *Le Procope*, a small café on the left bank where the artists and the revolutionaries met. It was not far from the apartment he had found, on the corner of *Boulevard Saint Germain*. The hotel where he first had stayed was too far away from the place where it all happened. He wanted to be in the heart of the world. But so far it had given him little joy. His daily activities were not much more than a visit to the café where he had long futile discussions, some writing in the afternoon, supper in one of the many restaurants in the district, and then evening entertainment in the form of theater, opera, concert, or a more intimate evening in the private spheres of the cultural elite. The evening was invariably drunk away into the night with another visit to *Le Procope*. It was significant that the bartender called him a good friend.

The city offered the chance to submerge oneself in anonymity. Joseph was absorbed into the crowd and gradually became invisible. On the other hand, the metropolis provided the natural habitat for someone looking for an audience. The streets with the cafés and terraces and the omnipresent gas lamps in the evening were there for people who wanted to be seen. The theaters were full of people who came to be watched and adored. A performance of their own self. Mirrors were ubiquitous. Everywhere Joseph's own image confronted him. How he saw himself depended mainly on the time of day and the number of glasses of absinthe he had drunk. The later it got, the nicer the guests, he laughed. As continents were discovered and the world became smaller, it also became more narcissistic and he participated gladly. In this liberal artists' environment, Joseph felt free, completely in his element. He had no desire to return to Cologne. When he went out, he dressed according to the latest fashion, complete with top hat.

Pennekamp had given him carte blanche when it came to subjects for his articles.

•

Joseph passed many hours in *Le Procope*. Usually, he sat with men who enjoyed discussing theories and conspiracies throughout the afternoon, all with the goal of resisting the new capitalism and imperialism of Napoleon III. They barely dressed better than the clochards and their hair and beards had probably not been in contact with water for weeks. But their conversations were full of passion and courage, they all drank a lot, and Joseph gladly joined them in his lost hours.

The leader of the troupe, Jean de Nanterre, had long, spiky gray hair and sunken cheeks, and in his equally gray beard one could see the remains of yesterday's dinner. But the man was an extraordinary orator and certainly no fool. Joseph found it all a nice distraction and it was more fun than drinking alone in a café. Generally, he had the acute feeling that it was all about nothing. But the emptiness of the conversations gave him the opportunity to float along in the intellectual intoxication of Marxism, nationalism, and all the other isms. After all, they remained salon revolutionaries.

Either because he thought they were wrong, or because he wanted to fuel the discussion and be just contrary, he always liked to assert exactly what he knew would send the others off the deep end. "Devil's advocate" was too weak an expression. Joseph wanted to be the devil himself.

"Everyone," said De Nanterre, "is involved in nationalism. But I say, the time of nations will come to an end. Cosmopolitan, international, global thinking – that is the future."

"Then we will be a huge uninteresting one-size-fits-all," Joseph argued.

De Nanterre looked up, disturbed. He highly appreciated open discussions, but such a response to these clearly correct ideas? "No, not uniformity," he responded, irritated, "unity."

"Roots are important. To know where you came from. Otherwise, we are like grass on the roof without connection to the earth. We will wither."

"Every nation its own land with its own laws? Everyone only concerned with his own blood and soil? Is that what you advocate?"

"Perhaps. I would argue that it is in distinction that greatness and originality arise. It is conditional for art. Every great plan begins with differentiation. Universality and similarity only result in mediocrity." Joseph considered pointing out that in the first lines of Genesis, God created the world by separating things over and over again, but he suspected that this would make little impression in this atheist group and would rather constitute an argument against him.

De Nanterre spoke cordially. "Lichtman, you don't understand that here in France we are light-years ahead of the primitive ways of the Germans."

Joseph thought that highly amusing, but he did not want to spoil the atmosphere. He didn't really have to win. It was a game. So he kept it to himself that this man sought to win his argument by making a distinction between the French and the Germans. Joseph murmured something and then toasted on the future. The group agreed and moved on to the next drink and discussion.

•

One day he decided for a change not to go to *Le Procope* but to *Café Riche*. *Grand café Riche* was the place where the crème de la crème of the Parisian art world met. Writers, painters, philosophers, everyone who counted, went there. Joseph again took part in the discussions but also kept his distance. Better that they ask questions about him than that they know the answers.

He saw Flaubert talking at the bar and wanted to join him, but as the poet was just about to leave, Joseph merely greeted him and then looked around for other prey. The art collector De Bellio? No, although the man was very nice and Joseph had great appreciation for him, he didn't want a conversation about painting today. Further on, at a table in the corner, he saw the writer Jacques Poilvé, sitting with his friends Pierre Larrochelle and Erneste Lirac, two lesser-known painters. In their company he also recognized the actress, Isabelle Michel.

Joseph had joined them many times before and usually had a good time with them; especially when they aired their fanatical views. They tolerated him despite his German origin and despite the occasional objections he made to their convictions. The three were very determined in their contentions, especially when these concerned themselves. They were geniuses. In the café hung life-size portraits of the three of them, and Isabelle Michel did not object to seeing her portrait as a bathing nymph in full glory prominently above the bar. "That makes it easy. You can see me in the flesh," she mocked when asked about it. Joseph approached slowly, wanting first to hear what they were talking about.

"I read a beautiful premise yesterday," said Poilvé. "From a German philosopher, nota bene. Schlegel. He states that artists are to humanity what humanity is to the rest of creation. I definitely didn't want to deny you that one."

"Completely right," Larrochelle confirmed. "We are the chosen people. We are inspired. But we have to find our way in solitude."

He looked sadly at his glass of absinthe in front of him. "It is larger than us. We cannot resist our vocation."

Isabelle Michel only looked at him with great admiration.

"We are rebels," Poilvé continued. "But not like those social agitators like Jean de Nanterre. We are rebels for the good of humanity. It doesn't matter if someone thinks I am good or bad. I'm superior to that."

"Perhaps we should write a pamphlet," Larrochelle suggested.

"*Fabuleux*," said Lirac. "With all our principles."

Poilvé sniffed. "Lirac. Don't get carried away, man. We have no principles at all. But we could use a slogan. Something in the spirit of 'We romantics claim the right to go our own way. Not to be hindered by theoretical rules or social conventions.' What about that?"

"We have the right to express our individual sensitivities," Lirac stated. "The people are just vulgar."

Isabelle Michel tried to say something but couldn't manage it. During the conversations she had opened her mouth further and further in adoration for these artists, without any sound coming out whatsoever, beyond the occasional cackle. She was usually speechless when subjected to so much talent.

"Maybe we can call our group the anti-vulgarists," Larrochelle proposed. He looked at the others triumphantly. They stared back as if Larrochelle had committed a faux pas, then burst out laughing. Lirac patted Larrochelle on the shoulder. "Who knows, Larrochelle, if we ever start a group…But I think a group is a contradiction to our previous idea."

They toasted and left the idea of a pamphlet at that. One more item that would never see the light of day, Joseph thought. He laughed.

The others looked up. "Ha, Lichtman. We hadn't seen you. Come join us. You have that mysterious smile again. What do you think about all this?"

"The pamphlet sounds like a nice fit." Joseph considered his next remark. "But still, you want to be seen and read. And at the same time, being popular is a dirty word."

"An artist who is successful is not a genuine artist," Larrochelle said. "He closes the door on real artistry."

"Philistines, that's what they are," Lirac said, raising his voice. Joseph looked at him. In his mind, the word opened a door to old texts, even though he knew that artists used it to refer to the plebs.

Poilvé continued more calmly. "We are entitled to offend the people. We are independent. We don't follow the money. We are separate from the world. People don't understand us anyway."

"Only when we are dead, will we be understood. It is tragic but true," said Lirac. He said it cheerfully, as if death could not come fast enough. "Take my paintings for instance. The establishment scorns them. Too little form, no content, or whatever they say. My time has not come yet. They don't see what I see. And what I see is the divine light of art."

Joseph shrugged his shoulders. Poilvé remained absorbed in his thoughts for a while, but Lirac continued. "I will give you an example. You probably know the old dilemma in art between line and color. Ingres against Delacroix. Rafael against Titian. Everyone tries to put it all in boxes. I, on the other hand, call it light, or nothingness."

"Nothingness?" Joseph sincerely wondered where the man was heading. He looked at Poilvé, who apparently wasn't entirely convinced that Lirac was making sense.

As the painter continued, his argument became increasingly incoherent. "Nothingness. For lack of a better word. Neither blackness nor darkness; something like that. Light creates darkness. I mean nothingness. Romanticism has burdened us with a whole pile of terms, ideas, symbols, concepts, you name it. But everyone keeps coming back to style. I hate style. I hate color for the sake of color and line for the sake of line. What I want to see is what shines inside me. And why can I see this?" He paused dramatically. Joseph assumed the question was rhetorical, but the man remained silent. "Well?"

"Light! Lichtman." With a drunken smile he continued: "Of all people you should understand this with your name." He looked around to see if his quip was successful, but nobody reacted. Apparently, his companions had not yet seen the light. "Because I see. I see the painting because light falls on it. I am the god who gives meaning to form and color. I cause the light. Art is the new religion, but not because there are believers, but because we artists are divine. Light is everything. And we, the visionaries of light, the gods of the new religion, will bring the new light."

Joseph nodded as if he understood but kept silent.

"The part about religion, we could use that," said Poilvé. "Those new gods, you may have come up with something there. Beyond that, I can't really make much sense of it. But everyone is entitled to their own brilliant, misunderstood moments." After that, he dropped back in his thinking pose. Lirac looked disappointedly at his glass, as if his comrades had left him in the lurch. Larrochelle tried to restore the cheerful mood by asking the waiter to refill their glasses.

Joseph pondered Lirac's jumbled words. Hadn't he once thought of light as a divine phenomenon of his own as well?

Hours later he traced his weary way back to his apartment.

•

After an evening of heavy drinking Joseph decided that he too should be the star of a painting; to have himself portrayed. After all, everyone of significance let himself be painted. Immortalized, not a temporary pose like in a tableau vivant. An acquaintance recommended Charles Beau, a second-class but affordable painter. The man had learned the trade in the studio of Eugene Delacroix and now worked mainly as a portrait painter for the new bourgeoisie.

Beau's studio was on an upper floor near Rue de Rivoli. It was in one of the new buildings. Completely in classicist style with austere ornaments. The first six floors all had small balconies with wrought-iron fences. It was impressive. On top were two more floors with smaller windows in the blue-gray slate roof. The studio had to be there. Joseph entered through the large door and without hesitation, started up the large baroque marble staircase that led to the second floor. From there he continued via a smaller staircase to the sixth floor. In the corner he saw a door with on it *escalier*, written in large letters. He went inside and a poor wooden staircase went up steeply. He started climbing but was exhausted after the previous climb. On the seventh floor he stopped. Would the painter do this every day? He had heard of an American invention, an elevator, which hoisted people up in an instant. Joseph looked around. Next to him was a window that probably offered a view of the city. It would be worthwhile to have a look. But when he stepped toward the window, he slipped, and ended up a few steps lower. He ignored the sudden pain in his ankle. Getting higher comes with a price. Half limping, he climbed the last stairs and sat down at the top to catch his breath. Again, there was a window and against his better judgment, he tried to look out in the hope of a magnificent view. He saw a tangle of chimneys and roofs. Everything at various heights interrupted by planes of bare walls. It was a rainy day and the gray light could not brighten the image. Shouldn't he be able to see Notre-Dame or at least the bend of the Seine somewhere? Disappointed, he turned to the door on the other side where a decorative sign indicated that he had reached the studio of Charles Beau.

The painter welcomed him kindly and quickly came to the point. What pose did he want to take? Tormented or exalted, the imprisoned freedom fighter or the misunderstood genius who completely ignored the viewer by dramatically looking over him beyond the painting? Perhaps as an Olympic god, as Pan naked and playing the flute or as Phaeton steering the solar car? Joseph eventually opted for a simple pose with his head slightly tilted downwards, looking the observer straight in the eyes. Haughty and penetrating. His hair a bit tangled, his face half in a mysterious shadow. A cravat loose around the neck, an open shirt. Above all, nobody could think that he would conform to the clothing style of the bourgeoisie. He belonged to the avant-garde. Not to the old romantics. The fact that the whole concept of avant-garde was a romantic notion did not bother him. It was an uninteresting footnote.

"You would look better with a moustache," the painter said. "Would you perhaps like to see some portraits for inspiration?" The man pointed at a number of paintings that were stacked against the wall.

Joseph chose the moustache that he thought fitted him best. Not too heavy, running slightly down around the mouth, thereby enforcing distinction.

"Do I have to grow it like this?"

"Whatever you want. In any case, I will paint it that way. You have made a good choice."

After a few visits to the painter, Joseph decided that he didn't really like climbing all the way up, and told him to continue on intuition and memory. The little room under the roof and the whole hassle had started to annoy him.

•

There was plenty of amusement and entertainment in Paris but Joseph was not happy. His visits to *Le Procope* became longer, often he ate in the cafe in the afternoon and stayed there until evening. Almost every evening brought a cultural event or a visit to the theater. There were literary soirees and openings to which he was invited and where he usually drank away his boredom.

During one of the opera performances Joseph recognized Jacob de Rothschild in the lodge. Joseph nodded and Rothschild nodded back. He immediately looked around to see if anyone had seen it. After the performance he noticed that the gesture had been seen indeed. People spoke to him as if he were the best friend of the Rothschilds. As if he really belonged to the higher circles.

A woman asked him, "Aren't you Johann Lichtman?"

"Yes, I am Lichtman," he said.

"Do you know him personally? I mean the baron."

"The baron. Of course."

"Amazing, my niece is a painter and it's really fantastic what she creates. Maybe you find the opportunity to introduce her?"

He declined and turned to a stranger standing next to him. A little further down he saw Jacob de Rothschild.

He nodded friendly and with a lot of bravura he said to De Rothschild in German: "*Gutenabend, Geehrter Herr Baron.* It has been a while since we have spoken. Was it not in *Schloss Grüneburg*? How is little Edmond doing? Not so small anymore, I reckon?"

Rothschild looked a little confused. "At my brother's residence? Everything is fine with Edmond. *Herr....?*"

"Lichtman. We had such enjoyment with the *tableau vivant* by Moritz Oppenheim."

"Oh yes, of course. Indeed."

Rothschild had his son Edmond with him and Joseph was introduced to him again. The boy was elegantly dressed and his eyes were sharp and clear. He was about fifteen years old now. Joseph recalled the park in Frankfurt when Edmond had shown the treasure map.

"I do remember that. Do you still have the map?"

"Sure," said Joseph. It is safely locked away in my home."

"Keep it. Who knows who might need it?" The boy turned to his father: "Papa, can we invite Mr. Lichtman to our house?"

"Tomorrow some writers and painters will dine at our house. You should come too. You are a writer, aren't you?"

•

Joseph's arrival at the Rothschild residence in Bilange Billancourt reminded him of the one five years ago in Frankfurt. Only he himself had changed. At that time, he had the ambition to use the invitation to advance in society, now it no longer mattered. Then he had been searching, now he felt only indifference. The evening was pleasant, but after a while, the many familiar faces made him long for the simplicity of the bar in *Le Procope*. At least nobody there scrutinized his behavior. Here he had to be alert at every introduction and an alcoholic faux pas was out of the question. Among the guests he saw famous people he did not yet know, but he did not feel like seeking introductions. He thought he recognized Rossini speaking with a writer whose name did not immediately spring to his mind. He turned around and almost bumped into the host.

"Delightful evening," said Joseph.

"I'm glad you appreciate it. My son is very fond of you. He is very interested in painters, writers, and that sort of people." He realized that it was not quite an appropriate expression and corrected himself. "You are different from the rest here. And everyone says that I have a very sharp gift of observation."

Joseph had forgotten how it felt to blush. At that moment Edmond came running up. Rothschild said goodbye and Joseph turned to the boy. "And, have you already found the treasure?"

"I don't know. Not here in any case. I am looking for other treasures." The boy laughed.

Joseph wanted to reply that it was easy to say that you have other interests, if you have the richest father in France, but he kept the thought to himself. Instead, he laughed along.

"I mean," continued Edmond, "life should be more than banking. I hope I don't have to follow in my father's footsteps. I would rather collect art or make wine or something else really crazy."

"It's not that crazy."

"Or help people. I am always ashamed when we go to the synagogue and I see the poverty of our people."

"Who knows? Someone with a lot of means can do a lot of good."

"You are smart. What would you do if you had a lot of money?"

A question of conscience. Money had not been a problem for Joseph since he had entered Pennekamp's employment. He was certainly not poor. The luxury of infinite wealth had never fascinated him.

"Maybe we are the same. I would like to do something good as well."

They said goodbye and when Joseph went to bed a few hours later, he was pleased to notice that he was reasonably sober for the first time since weeks.

●

Every week Joseph made sure that he sent his regular page three article to Pennekamp. It was the only connection he had left with his old life in Cologne, but he was very careful to maintain it, not only because of the financial consequences if he didn't. Even in his most tattered moments he scraped himself together to deliver a good article. The previous week he had written a piece about Heinrich Heine and the significance of his poetry to the relationship between France and Germany. While he was writing it he remembered that he had planned to visit Heine's grave once he got to Paris. A few weeks before leaving Cologne, he had heard that the most talked-about poet had died, and although Joseph had never met him, the news came as a shock. It was as if one of his loved ones had died unexpectedly. The end of an era. Somewhere in the back of his mind Joseph had promised himself that he would say goodbye to him in Paris. Why? And why had he never tried to visit him when the poet was still alive? There had been plenty of opportunities. Was he afraid that the hero of his youth would be tarnished in the flesh? Or that his own pretensions would crumble? He could no more ask for the permission to finish *The Rabbi of Bacharach*. He realized that he didn't even want to any more. In the past few years he had come to understand why Heine had left the work unfinished.

At the cemetery, a helpful official pointed him toward Heine's grave. Joseph had imagined an intimate moment, but as he approached, he saw two men standing by it. Joseph greeted them briefly and tried to concentrate on the deceased; he tried to recall verses and aphorisms but was distracted by the conversation of the two men. They spoke French, but he heard a distinct German accent.

"For Meyerbeer there is hope again, now Heine can't grind him down anymore. The death of one Jew is the bread of another," he heard the taller man say.

Joseph looked at them and introduced himself in French.

"Hess, Moses Hess," said the smaller one. The other man's name was Daniel Bloch.

"Did you know him well?" Bloch asked, looking at the grave.

"Actually no," replied Joseph. "I have read him all my life, but never met him."

"He was a great writer. The greatest of our time."

Hess nodded. He turned to Joseph. "Lichtman, isn't it? Aren't you writing articles for *Die Rheinische Zeitung*? Controversial!"

Bloch indicated that he had an appointment and left. Joseph broke the somewhat uncomfortable silence: "I have heard about you, *Herr* Hess, but haven't read anything you have written so far. My apologies for that."

"Doesn't matter. My older work is not the best either. I am now exploring fresh ideas. I hope to publish a new book soon."

"You were in the circle around Marx, weren't you? In Bonn?"

"Yes, but to some extent I have turned away from him. Disengaged is perhaps a better word. I have found a new way. *Derech chadash*. You're Jewish, aren't you?"

Was there no escape? He saw no point in denying it. He asked in reply: "You are using Hebrew?"

"Sometimes. I am proud of my origins. You are not?"

Joseph took a deep breath. "It depends." He decided to wait and see. "You don't call yourself Moritz anymore, but Moses?"

"Right. I stopped assimilating. As I said: proud." He waited a moment and then went on about something else: "I think I have read some of your articles. You write well. Beautiful writing, I mean. Much better than me. I don't write very well, but I do have good ideas."

"And I write well but have inferior ideas."

Hess laughed. "No, that's not what I meant, of course. Come. Let me invite you for an aperitif in the café."

They found a quiet table in the corner of a slightly run down café. "Your writing could use more content. Wait, before you strangle me. I have too much content but I can't write. That's a much bigger problem."

Hess made himself comfortable. "Do you have time? I'd love to share some thoughts with you."

Joseph took a big sip and said he didn't have to go anywhere.

"I have great ideas," Hess began. "Really. Karl Marx too, don't misunderstand me, but I think he's on the wrong track. He bases everything on materialism, on possession and property. On the classes. I believe that he is wrong. There is more. He renounces everything and ultimately has nothing left. Beautiful analyses, stunning structures, but then you stand empty-handed and you have to preach revolutions. His dialectical materialism is inadequate. But I respect his thinking. Also Hegel and all those others. With all due respect, but we Jews can contribute something they have overlooked. We have a decisive role in the overall scenario for a better world. In fact, we have had that role through the centuries, only nobody wanted to listen to us. And I understand why not. We have always been too busy with religion and *halacha*." He paused for a moment as if he wanted to see the effect of his statements.

"And what do we have that others don't have," Joseph asked.

"Ethics."

Joseph nodded and Hess asked, "I suppose you have read Spinoza."

Joseph quickly tried to remember what he had read at the age of seventeen. Evading the question, he said, "Certainly. Not someone with whom to show up at the old school." He invited Hess to continue.

"Ethics is our strongest asset," said Hess. "We have given the world something that wasn't there before. Let's keep God out of it. Righteousness. The Torah is full of *tzedakah* and *mishpat*, righteousness and justice. We have to propagate that. But instead of listening, the people laugh at us. They spit at us. How Jews stand in the world now is a sign of weakness. We are the scum of the earth. What we need is respect so that they will listen to us. And a vagrant is not respected, however brilliant he may be. We need to be a king in a palace. Having a place will allow us to express our thoughts. We must become a people with a land. We must be respected. And the great powers must help us to do so. Did you follow the Crimean War? The balance of power is changing. The whole of Europe is reshuffling. The Ottomans are collapsing. The Russians are done. We must place our hopes in France and England, perhaps even Germany. Countries come into being. Romania, Belgium. Italy will become a country soon. And we must follow. After Rome comes Jerusalem. We will settle in our old homeland."

He stopped to drink something, but Joseph left the opportunity to react unused.

"By the way, that immediately solves another problem. Jewish integration in Europe is doomed to fail. You can see the signs everywhere. A dead-end street. They simply do not accept us as we are. First, we were the wrong people, then the wrong religion. And they will come up with something else to keep us apart, to taunt us and to condemn us. I don't want to be there when the Germans start to give in to their hatred. Nationalism also has very dirty and nasty sides."

It was invigorating to hear a real fiery speech instead of the platitudes of De Nanterre and his group. Max had once advised him to dive into the subject of Palestine. Elsa had already gone there. Should he start thinking about it too? Was it perhaps not completely insane for the Jews to return to the old land that had once been given to them? Joseph thought of Yermiyahu, the man from the *shtetl*. He also had made a fervent plea for the return to the land. Two totally different men. One a religious dreamer and one a communist. But Joseph found the enlightened philosopher more compelling than the rabbi whose fate depended on all kinds of *mashiachs*. Fanatics were dangerous. Hess was interpreting the times and got his truth from historical knowledge, from observation and thinking, not from the ancient books, however valuable in their own right.

"It's all very interesting," Joseph said. "I recently met some other people who came to the same view but from a slightly different angle." He took a big sip. "I wonder what Heine would have said about it."

"I can't imagine he would ever forsake his dear old Europe, however much he hated everything," Hess said.

Joseph got up and said farewell. "I'll definitely think about it. I hope we will meet again."

But at home, the standard thoughts and objections sneaked back in again. All the shabby artists and frustrated revolutionaries here were creating their own new world. And among all the utopists in Paris, Hess took perhaps an even more unrealistic standpoint than all the others.

•

He had already been told several times to deliver the portrait. He decided to take the short road. In the distance he saw the cathedral of Cologne. The portrait was heavy. The terrain became increasingly hilly and before he knew it, he had begun a steep climb. He lugged the painting behind him. Wooded hills, as far as he could see. A bleak wind blew and it started to rain. He thought he could see people standing along the side of the road. Wasn't that Maria over there? He trudged on. "Why do I always have to do everything alone," he murmured. "Because you don't ask for help," the answer came. He looked up. "Because you think you know better," he heard the heavy voice say. A figure in an antique tunic blocked the path. The man wore a strange head cover and a large eccentric breastplate.

"I am the *Kohen HaGadol*.* You cannot proceed. Who do you think you are? What are you carrying?"

Joseph showed the portrait, but the image had changed. It now depicted Joseph himself as the high priest. "I have to put it up in Valhalla."

"That is idolatry."

"But I am part of it. All the great artists and great thinkers have been immortalized there."

"This is Jerusalem. This is the temple."

Joseph looked around. Bare mountains. A scorching high wind made the sand blow up. It was quiet.

•

Soaked in sweat he woke up. The article he had been working on stuck to his forehead. He had been having nightmares and hallucinations more frequently of late. It had to be the absinthe. The stuff could not be trusted. Maybe he should stick to wine and beer and perhaps also reduce the intake a bit. Paris had started to bore him. He had seen it all by now. Or rather, the cultural elite was starting to annoy him. With no demands on his time, Joseph sometimes spent hours watching the construction works that were being carried out everywhere. Sometimes he installed himself on a wall with a good view of a demolition site. He made sure that he had something to drink and then he watched the destruction of the area, mesmerized. Whole blocks of houses were flattened, streets were broken up, until one large void remained. All alone, he toasted to the new age.

•

A man with the head of a pig knocked on the door. He questioned Joseph about Rivka. His sister emerged from the half-dark, crying. Joseph heard the man accuse her of being Jewish. The Jews and the vagrants were all sentenced to death and as an extra punishment they had to watch each other's execution. The verdict was carried out in an empty square. He saw Rivka go up the scaffold. It looked like the *bima* in the synagogue, as if she were getting an *aliyah*. Blindfolded. She asked the man to remove the blindfold. Joseph saw her lips moving as Rivka muttered the *Sh'ma*. Then she was bent forward, placing her head under the blade. Joseph stood as if nailed to the ground, and could not turn his gaze away, no matter how much he wanted to. His parents suddenly stood next to him. Joseph tried to distract his mother. He had to keep this from her. His mother looked at him, full of compassion. "This is not what we had imagined," he heard his father say. "It is all Joseph's fault. He drove Rivka towards the path of evil. Why did he always have to know better?"

•

With a shock he woke up, feeling an immense sense of guilt. He couldn't sleep anymore and decided to sit at his desk and write his magnum opus. Other than a few unreadable loose sentences on crumpled leaves that the cleaning lady invariably had thrown away, he hadn't written anything personal for a long time. Eventually he wrote another essay. When he had finished, he looked at his sheets with satisfaction; in elegant letters on the first page the title of the essay, he had written *The Last Seven Words*. He thought with a smile of a sentence he had composed a few years ago. He read the piece again and was extremely pleased with himself.

Later that day, he walked to the house of *madame* Gicault, to attend a recital by the pianist, Fernand Le Pret. Joseph knew him vaguely from another evening, a few weeks earlier.

The last piece Le Pret played was *The Tempest* sonata. Joseph remembered that this music had always captivated him, ever since that first time at Elsa Blumenreich's. But now he felt nothing. He recognized that the man played it very well, perhaps not quite fast enough, but that could not explain his lack of sensation. His emotions did not match the emotions in the music. This was not right at all. Was it his fault? Was he completely numb or did his sacred art have a limited life span?

•

The following evening, he drank in a desolate café with a sleazy, blond woman with a deep cleavage who convinced him to go upstairs with her. In the end it turned out to be extremely disappointing. He paid her extra to let him sleep it off on her couch and, disillusioned, left the house at daybreak and crashed into his bed at home. He slept terribly.

Did he dream or was he back in the upstairs room with the woman? There was a knock on the door. No visits please. He staggered out of bed and looked through the peephole. It was the door of his old house in Cologne. There she stood again. That enchanting beautiful woman who often troubled him in his dreams. But this time, she looked terrible. Her dark, wild hair fell in lank strands over her pale face. Her eyes were like black holes, her red lips cracked, her clothes torn. Barefoot. Why was she this tattered? He now remembered that he had let her in before, but every time she had disrupted his whole life. She begged him to open the door to her. Just one more time. One more time.

•

To his delight and disappointment he didn't see any acquaintances in *Café Riche*. He ordered tea although he despised the drink. Something for bourgeois ladies on an afternoon outdoors or when you were ill in bed. Tea was pusillanimous. But he had begun to wonder if he needed an opinion about tea. Why should he have to have an opinion about everything? Couldn't he just let things be what they were? Or accept that it was totally irrelevant whether he had an opinion about it.

Somewhere it started to dawn on him that he couldn't continue this way. Whether it was Paris or he himself he did not know, but something told him he had to leave. A wild idea originated: maybe he could go traveling through Europe and write stories about his journeys. A new kind of journalism, named after its founder – *Lichtman literature*. In any case, he knew that he needed a new goal.

Thoughtfully, he stirred the sugar in the cup. The nightmare with the woman had frightened him. He saw the deeper meaning, but did not yet want to grasp its consequence.

These last years he had conformed to life as it had unfolded. Shouldn't he try to counter it? Not with a playful, sarcastic remark or an insider's joke. That was too easy. Was he a drowning man who didn't see the land nearby where he could rest and recover his strength? What did he see? Emptiness everywhere. But had he caused the emptiness or was he being pulled into it? Could he not set himself a higher goal? To try to find Rivka, for example.

Erneste Lirac, the painter, came in. Joseph hadn't seen him for a while. He quickly got up, walked away from his table and greeted the man.

"Bordeaux and two glasses," Lirac called to the waiter. Joseph agreed and the two sat down.

After a few glasses Lirac asked, "Tonight is the soiree at the Ferrières. You're coming too, aren't you? I'm planning to fly off the handle." He took a crumpled piece of paper from his inside pocket. "Listen," he said. And with raised voice he continued: "We artists are the chosen people. We are the elite. We are the members of the republic of art and literature. You, you are not part of it. You are excluded. It is not a profession to be an artist. Either someone is an artist or one is not. It is talent and a vocation. You are slaves. Artists are not slaves. They have infinite freedom." He looked at Joseph defiantly. "It will be up there in their faces."

Joseph laughed. "I can make a contribution to this stuff." He also started proclaiming with a fake heavy voice: "This is the golden age of the recognition of the 'I'. The ego. This is the perfection and celebration of the self." He looked at Lirac, who gently applauded and laughed. "More, more!"

"All right. Here we go." And again he changed his voice and rose as if to make an important announcement: "We are the priests in the worship of the individual. Everyone is searching for salvation, but you are only looking for your own salvation. We artists, on the other hand, are looking for greater values." Forcing his voice caused the last words to be lost in coughs. He sat down and, when the coughing had stopped, continued with a normal voice: "I recently wrote a piece about art and art lovers, but I didn't want to publish it. Too arrogant I think. You should read it."

"Let me read it before we go tonight."

They toasted and laughed.

"I'll come by at eight. Agreed?"

An hour later Joseph left the café, two sheets to the wind, and crashed on his bed.

•

"You too will be attending your farewell dinner, yes?"

"My farewell dinner? What? When?"

"Monday morning at ten o'clock. Everyone is coming, but of course you have to be there yourself; it's your farewell, your funeral."

Images of his funeral followed this surreal conversation. Initially he was excited about the celebration and the idea of his own death didn't upset him. He imagined all the attention he would receive; the atmosphere would be excellent and he would be the center of everyone's focus. He would enjoy talking to the guests. "You realize that everything will be over this afternoon?" one of them asked him. Of course, he knew; it was the reason for the party. But about halfway through dinner, it started to gnaw at him. The bitter truth prevailed. Melancholy and an immense sadness attacked him. It could have been so beautiful. He could no longer imagine that he ever had liked the idea of this farewell dinner.

•

Madame Ferrière was one of the new artistic benefactors and her soiree promised to be interesting. Everyone of significance had promised to come, but the dream had put Joseph in a bad mood. Lirac arrived just after eight. He had to wait while Joseph was fixing his tie.

"Can I still see that article?" asked Lirac.

"It's somewhere there, on that pile. But as I said, it is not suitable for publication."

"Can I have a look anyway?"

"Suit yourself."

Lirac was still reading when Joseph told them they should leave.

Lirac put the sheets in his jacket. "May I?" Joseph looked disapproving.

"I won't use it," the man promised. "Just to have something to read at home."

•

With great to do, they were welcomed into the Ferrières immense salon. Lirac was a celebrity within the small circle of the cultural elite and most people knew Joseph as well.

"Ah, wine," said Lirac, as the butler passed with a tray. "Leave the tray here. Even better, get a second tray." It took a while before everyone arrived. By then, Joseph had drunk too much and wasn't very confident about mingling with the guests. He decided to sit quietly near the piano. If anyone wanted to talk to him, they could find him there.

He couldn't lose the ill-defined thought that this was a farewell. The evening started with a performance by a baritone who sang Schubert lieder, and grabbing another glass, Joseph decided that he would leave as soon as the baritone had finished. But after the performance, Lirac took the stage uninvited and unannounced. The hostess didn't interfere. Something compelled Joseph to stay.

"The art of self-absorption and the redemption of the self," Lirac declared. It was noisy but some people looked up.

"Please stop," Joseph said softly. "You are making a fool of yourself."

"The high art of self-absorption," Lirac almost shouted now. It was so compelling that the audience fell silent. "Thank you." Lirac turned around and laughed. "This is about all of us," he said, quietly. He continued more loudly. "Dear artists, art lovers, buyers, shoppers, spongers, scroungers and sycophants." A smile appeared on his face. "Ladies and gentlemen, for a while I was torn between the desire to identify myself with the new generation of artists on the one hand, and on the other, a genuine feeling of guilt that it is all about nothing. A bubble in a glass of water standing sheltered from the wind on a sturdy table. While around it, in real life, a battle is raging. Nations fight, people get killed, the poor are suffering, people are dying of the most miserable diseases. But artists also claim their engagement with these tribulations. Yet, I say, from their safe protection, they are the same sort of academics as those whom they despise."

Lirac took a break to sense the mood.

"Despite this hypocrisy, I still choose the artist."

The man kept going and Joseph heard the previous afternoon's arguments about artists as the chosen people. He was ashamed because in his drunken state, he had given the man ammunition for this tirade. He noticed whispers going around the room, so he hissed at Lirac again, "Stop now, please!"

Lirac coughed and inspected the audience. A long silence. "Is there a more selfish pursuit than the salvation of the personal self? Who are you? You attach yourself to the famous. You think that art itself makes you better people. Your salvation. But you are just opportunists blowing in the wind. You all live in your own narcissistic world. My ideal of salvation is for all mankind. And later, in a hundred years' time, professors will look at my work, trying to analyze it, and they will all have to say, "it is great but I don't understand it.""

Apparently, he didn't know how to proceed. To Joseph's dismay he saw Lirac taking the article out of his pocket. "A great German writer said the following in his famous essay *Die Sieben Letzte Worte*," and he raised his arms in a big gesture inviting Joseph to the stage. Joseph declined with a sheepish smile. He only wanted to hide. Why was the man dragging him into this? As in a nightmare, he heard Lirac speak his words with a thundering voice: "Art is the corridor for the soul to make the impossible possible, to overcome la condition humaine. Art touches the soul. A work of art opens the doors to a better world. So my conclusion is – if you have a soul for art and you are an artist, do something with it and create. If you have that soul and you are absolutely not an artist, enjoy it and keep your mouth shut. If you don't have the soul, just keep your mouth shut. Seven words: You can stop just talking about art. I have spoken." Lirac strode off the stage toward Joseph. Joseph started to get up, but Lirac pushed him back down. Misjudging his position, Joseph missed the seat and fell onto the floor. He stood up again, swaying, dusted his clothes as if they had gotten soiled, and sat down in the chair with as much dignity as he could muster. After a moment of doubt as to whether he should punch Lirac, he reconsidered, got up, and left the room. From a corner of his eye, he saw the lady who had organized the soiree looking at him with disdain.

•

This unsavory episode required washing away, so Joseph went straight to a small cafe nearby where he would certainly not meet anyone he knew. Where he could forget and be forgotten. A few hours later he wobbled back to his building but slipped on the pavement and fell again just before reaching the front door. He hit the stones with his chin and for a moment everything turned black. His face was in the mud. He wanted to get up and look around. He lifted his head. There was no one. He thought he saw his mother lying down, a little further on. He remembered how she had fallen, once. The last year he was in Frankfurt. They had gone shopping together. His father was on one of his business trips. "Business trip," a ridiculous expression, nothing but buying even more rags than he already had in his shop. His mother and he had walked for hours carrying their heavy bundles. Just before they had reached home it had become too much for her and she had come crashing down. For a while she had remained motionless, then she had gotten up and continued as if nothing were wrong.

With tears in his eyes Joseph stood up and dragged himself inside. His mother's fall was one of sacrifice, his was preposterous. One thing had become clear by this evening and Lirac's act: He had to turn away from all this as soon as possible. Without undressing himself, he plunged once again into an inextricable web of nightmares.

The next day, to his surprise, he saw Max sitting on the terrace opposite his apartment. His friend was writing leisurely, a cup of coffee on the table in front of him. Of course, how could he have forgotten? Max had written him that he had to be in Paris for an assignment. Joseph greeted him profusely, not yet completely sober. Max examined him and shook his head, "If I didn't know you better, I would say that you are a hopeless case. By the way, I heard about yesterday's spectacle."

Joseph preceded him to his apartment.

"It was Lirac, not me. I just fell awkwardly," he defended himself.

"Don't try to be someone other than who you are, Joseph. You have completely surrounded yourself with nonsense and hot air. And with the wrong people. You are a decent boy. Behave that way."

Joseph plunged into his chair and poured in a drink from the bottle that he had left open.

"I am not aware of any wrongdoing." He reached out for his glass and wanted to make a toast.

In one movement Max stood up and grabbed his wrist firmly. "It is because I know you, otherwise I would have walked out the door straight away. Stop that!"

Joseph startled. He had never heard Max talk like this. He remained silent for a while. Max was right. He had realized it yesterday lying on the stones, but admitting it was difficult. He laughed nervously. "I know you are right. I have to leave here."

"From now on you must put an end to this supercilious and decadent life. I have spoken to Pennekamp. He has an assignment for you in Italy. In Bologna to be precise."

"Who on earth wants to go to Bologna?"

"Don't you start again! Then go to Venice or Florence. But make sure you become a *mensch* again. And don't let Anton down."

"Venice is a step backwards compared to Paris."

"Do you really only think about climbing up? Venice has been what Paris is today for five hundred years. The center of power, capital, art, and entertainment. Everything was there. Don't scorn that. You pretend that you love art so much. Now, there you can really indulge yourself."

"All old junk. Christian stuff. Probably they haven't really seen the light in Venice yet."

Max gave him a long, penetrating look. "Do you hear yourself? Light and Venice. You will be surprised. You are such a romantic. Go to Venice. Jump into the Canal Grande and deliver us from your illusions and delusions. Whole pilgrimages of artificial *weltschmerz*-idiots like you have finished their lives there." He stood up to leave.

For a moment, Joseph wanted to feel offended, but shame won. And at the same time, he was relieved that Max had finally dismantled his facade. He himself had not been able to do so. He had tried, or wanted to, but every time, had fled back into the fake world for protection. Max had opened the wound that Joseph had kept covered by intoxication.

"Forgive me, Max," he said with a broken voice. "I have indeed been an idiot. It will change. From this point on." Softly he said: "Let Pennekamp send me a telegram with the assignment. I'll go to Venice."

Max looked up as if someone had asked him what time it was. "These days you can take the train to Venice. Jacob de Rothschild has just bought all the Austrian railways in Italy. You will be safe. I know someone there. A good man. Elia Banco. He lives in the ghetto. Contact him. Maybe I'll visit you later. And, if I can give you some very important advice..." Max looked at his friend very closely now. "Leave the bottle for good."

Joseph nodded and looked away. He saw in the corner his portrait still in the wrapping that it had come in two days earlier. Max followed his gaze and asked what it was.

"A portrait. Of me. Let's have a look."

Together they unwrapped it and stared silently at the painting for a moment. Then they both burst out with laughter.

"Rarely seen such a hideous thing," said Max between the sobs.

"Rarely seen something so outrageous," admitted Joseph.

"And it doesn't even resemble you."

"That mustache!"

Again they roared.

"What shall I do with it?"

"Put it above your writing table and from time to time look at it when haughtiness creeps up. Or else you can always sell the frame."

"Worth nothing. As fake as the painting. Maybe burn it in the winter when it gets cold."

Suddenly a childlike enthusiasm took possession of him. He couldn't wait to go.

"Thanks, Max. You are a real friend."

He decided that he would leave the next day, first thing in the morning. First the mail coach over the Alps and then the train from Milan to Venice.

$$\overline{9}$$

(1859)

THE MYTH OF THE BRIDGE

With powerful bursts of steam the locomotive roared over the bridge of the lagoon. A triumphant feeling took possession of Joseph. No more need for boats. Trains made a mockery of all natural limitations. Its straight rails delivered Joseph to the old city on the water. Paradoxically however, in the end the tiny back streets of the *Serenissima* brought the triumph of modernization to a halt; against the maze of dead-end streets, it could go no further. "Once again I land in a slum," he noted ruefully to himself. He smelled the stagnation of the water. Because it was still early and the sun was shining, he gave in to the temptation to stroll through the city to the better neighborhoods of *Rialto* or *San Marco*, where he wanted to take a hotel room. Only after he had left the bright light and entered a dark alley did he realize that he had reached the less pleasant intestines of the city. Venice turned out to be a maze. Every time he thought he had found a passageway, the alley ran dead on the water or opened onto a dismal little square with no passage on the other side. Happening upon a small canal, he was fortunate to find a gondolier, whom he asked to take him to a decent hotel. Above all, one that foreigners frequented.

"*Ca' Giustinian*?" asked the man and Joseph agreed. Clumsily he climbed into the gondola. It was his first time in a boat. Nevertheless, after a while he got used to the swaying movement and the sloshing water and began to feel more at ease. Passing through a number of small canals, the gondolier brought them to the *Canal Grande*. Joseph now began to enjoy his little excursion. He adjusted himself as much as possible in his uncomfortable chair and he feasted his eyes on the view. The *palazzi* on both sides of the bank were magnificent.

Ca' Giustinian was a renowned hotel and Joseph immediately felt at home. His room was on the third floor and his first move was to open the man-sized windows. He looked out over the lagoon. The stretch of water offered him an overwhelming sense of space and vastness. Although there were no clouds to be seen, the sky wasn't blue, but a sharp, penetrating gray and white. The light seemed extra bright because of its reflection on the water. The blurring of the contours between air and water deceived the eyes. The city looked motionless while simultaneously oscillating on the water, as if it bobbed at anchor.

While he gazed over the church of *San Giorgio* in the distance and at the *Salute* to the right, Joseph was overwhelmed by the sheer impossibility of this city. In a marshy area, refugees had hid. Eventually they had founded a city. How many human lives had paid the price to make the marshes habitable and to overcome malaria? As the city developed, the people started trading. Eventually, the city's existence was justified. In fact, it became itself a refuge for the persecuted. From survival to life. And from simple existence to higher aspirations. Bigger and more splendid buildings, more and more people, ever-greater plans. It had become the largest and strongest city in the world. And now Venice was showing itself off in the gleaming sunlight. A dream that had become reality because people had wanted it.

A small bar located on the *Canal Grande*, where the quay ended on the large arches of the *Rialto*, had been his base for the first nights. A few tables and chairs on the waterfront and soft lights on the wall tried to suggest liveliness and to lure people. He had not yet succeeded in shaking off the dark mood of Paris and had started drinking again. He had looked into the mirror and had been shocked by the beggarly image looking at him.

Nevertheless, after a few days he decided to turn his mind to his assignment, the controversial affair of Edgardo Mortara. Six months earlier, the Catholic Church in Bologna had abducted a Jewish boy of six, and had kept him hidden in a monastery in Rome, allegedly because a servant once had baptized him. Under the eyes of the parents, the collaborating Austrian police had dragged the child out of his home. Both the Church and Pope Pius IX in person had sanctioned it all. The whole world had spoken out against it, except for a number of Catholic newspapers.

It didn't interest Joseph so much, but he got up and decided to visit Max's contact, Elia Banco, who lived near the train station – the place that Joseph had immediately branded a slum. The logical location for the ghetto.

Outside, he beckoned a gondolier.

"*Il ghetto novo?*" The new ghetto? Joseph had not even known that there was an old and a new one. Hadn't Napoleon abolished the ghetto? Were the Jews locked up again?

"The names are misleading," the gondolier explained. "Actually, the new ghetto is older than the old one." He laughed and continued to exhibit his knowledge. "And then there is the latest ghetto, *il ghetto novissimo*."

Joseph shook his head. What they hadn't come up with to put away a few hundred Jews. "Just bring me there."

They soon left the better neighborhoods and came to the more dilapidated parts of the city. In ever-changing angles Venice presented itself here as a broken display of pale surfaces. On the walls that rose out of the water, a vague pattern of sagging bricks was often visible under the crimson, pink or green of the flaked plaster. Skewed blue and white mooring posts tried to improve the appearance of the buildings standing in the light green water. The result was a picture of decay, although in some places a few details suggested the old glory: a pediment, a row of trifoil arches, some beautifully designed capitals.

Joseph got off at the entrance to the ghetto. From the swaying boat he climbed onto the quay and descended the stone stairs to the old point where the iron hooks of the former gate were still visible. Stooping, he walked through the dark underpass. This was more oppressive than his birthplace in Frankfurt. Here and there wooden bridges over narrow canals interrupted alleyways with forward-leaning houses. Again and again, that all-too-familiar smell. In places, high roofs stretched between the houses on either side. The dwellings were in poor condition. With small windows and low floors, they looked like dollhouses. How many people could you cram into one space? Here, as in Frankfurt, the Jewish quarter used to be sealed and guarded at night. Not to prevent anyone from entering to wreak evil, but to prevent a Jew from accidentally wanting to go outside. The *chutspah* of all this was that the Jews themselves had to pay for their guards.

Elia was a sturdy thirty-something, with reddish hair and a rough beard. He reminded Joseph of the images of Vikings he had seen, certainly not the type to expect here. But his voice was soft and he chose his words carefully. At the door, Joseph explained the reason for his visit. He did not forget to mention Max. Elia looked at Joseph for a long time, as if deciding what to think of him. Apparently, he decided in his favor, and led Joseph up to a small but comfortable room on the third floor. A small window overlooked the courtyard. In a blink, Joseph saw more of the same houses and floors, all connected by a tangle of clotheslines.

Elia pushed a stack of books aside, but the pile was too high and the upper ones fell to the ground. Joseph picked them up. They were in Hebrew. As he placed the books on the table, he thought he saw the name of the *Rambam*. When they were seated, Elia began telling about the Mortara affair, at least what he knew about it. Elia reminded Joseph of Max; not in appearance – the two had nothing in common – but in the well-considered words, the gentle way in which he expressed his thoughts.

Joseph quickly lost track because of the many details and the seemingly infinite list of persons: Inquisitors, police officers, Jewish lawyers, Bolognese judges, Jesuits, with Italian names that all sounded the same to Joseph.

He gently interrupted and told Elia that he would come back to this later with writing materials. Elia studied him again.

"Why do you want to write about Mortara?"

"I received the assignment from my boss, Anton Pennekamp. To be honest, the whole affair interests me only moderately. I actually have better things to do." He felt that his stupid arrogance had resurfaced. Backtracking, he explained: "I don't mean better. I usually write about art and philosophy. Not about kidnappings."

"You could philosophize about that kidnapping. Transform it into art. What it means in the greater picture. About freedom, repression, about the power of the Church."

Joseph reluctantly admitted, "First I will delve into the subject matter." He wanted to rise, but Elia stopped him. "You write for a newspaper in Germany? Have you considered writing for an Italian chronicle?" Then he asked: "Where do you stand in all this?"

Although Joseph did not quite understand where Elia wanted to go, he tried not to appear too negative: "I am German. I don't know what's going on here."

"Indeed, I know you are not Italian, but I think you are Jewish."

Joseph blushed as if someone had caught him stealing sweets. "And why do you think so," he asked as calmly as he could.

"The way you put the books back on the table. A non-Jew would most likely have turned them upside down."

"So, I betrayed myself." Joseph laughed. "Right, I am Jewish. Or rather, I was Jewish. I haven't done anything about it for years." He saw Elia's affable smile, which made it easier for him to make his request: "I would appreciate it if you would keep it to yourself. I don't keep it secret, but I don't walk around brandishing it either," he said, not entirely in accordance with the truth.

Elia now told him that the Mortaras were distant relatives of his. He saw the matter primarily as a desperate attempt by the Catholic Church to display its power. "It would be laughable if it weren't so awful. Everyone is engaged, not only the Rothschilds and the Montefiores. Articles are appearing in the New York Times. The Church is on its last legs."

"A cornered cat becomes as fierce as a lion," replied Joseph.

"Exactly. The Austrians support the Pope, but what they don't know is that they are digging their own grave."

Joseph's interest was indeed aroused now. "Do you still occupy yourself a lot with these..." He pointed to the stack of books in front of him. "These sages." He laughed awkwardly.

"Certainly. I think it is perfectly compatible with the struggle for a just Italy. They don't bite each other." He got up. "I think it might be interesting for you to meet some people. Come to *Da Gino* tonight. There we can eat and talk."

Da Gino turned out to be a restaurant like dozens of others in Venice. Small, and every square meter used to put tables. Joseph was early and ordered a glass of wine.

"Not kosher, my friend," was the friendly greeting when Elia came in. Joseph shrugged and wanted to say something, but at that moment two of Elia's friends entered. Giuseppe, a man with a heavy beard, small in size. The other man, Tonio, was taller, more like Joseph imagined an Italian. Dark, sleek-haired, a large but well-groomed moustache, and a smooth tanned skin. As they sat down, Elia introduced Joseph.

"He is Jewish," said Elia without much emphasis. From a non-Jew this would have antagonized Joseph, but now it sounded as if Elia were presenting him as a member of the family.

After listening to the men speaking for a while, Joseph dared to ask a question. "Who are you for and who are you against, actually? I mean, I understand the theory, but where do you stand in practice?"

Giuseppe nodded slowly. "By all means, it's not easy. Sometimes one's friend suddenly becomes one's enemy and vice versa. Napoleon brought the glorious Venetian Republic to an end, but he also freed us in a certain way. We, Italians, are a people and we are entitled to our own country, where we ourselves will determine what happens, not men in palaces or churches far from here. You will see that Italy will become a state. But unfortunately we need the help of the great powers. One thing is clear at the moment: The Austrians are the occupiers and they are in cahoots with the Pope. Therefore, we must place our hope in the French. The new Emperor, Napoleon the Third must take our side. That is also in his own interest. But he is afraid of the papists. Now with that boy's case," and he nodded at Elia, "everything might be different. There is a breakthrough. We need someone to set a spark."

They agreed that Joseph would write an article. Every little bit could help. As a German and a relative outsider, he could make a more profound impression than if Giuseppe were to write his umpteenth charge. Elia would translate it.

Walking back to his hotel late that evening, Joseph felt important. Despite his inebriation, he had a clearer picture of the situation. In any case, these men had won his sympathy. This was more tangible than the alcohol-driven bravado conversations about art that had swirled around him in Paris. He did not want to cast his mind back to Paris. Especially because that would reawaken his worries about Rivka.

The next day Joseph wanted to visit Elia again, but there were warnings of high water, *Acqua Alta*, a regularly recurring phenomenon in the city in the lagoon. Almost the whole ghetto was flooded, but nobody really cared. The residents laid down boards and kept walking. He sat down on a bench in the large central square and looked at the rising water with fascination. Occasionally he heard gurgling and swaying sounds as the water found its way to a passage. After an hour he thought that it must have reached its apex. The planks were now almost all under water. He liked the idea of the old disappearing, becoming hidden. Could a place make a new beginning? First, it seemed, there had to be chaos. But this flooding was only temporary. Although he hoped that the quarter would be rinsed clean, more debris would remain once the flood was gone.

After an hour watching the water, he decided to go back home and start writing. He had the article about Mortara completely in mind. A clear analysis, objective, above the parties. And while he felt sympathy for the Jewish parents because of the barbaric behavior of the Church, he did not want to raise any suspicion that he himself was Jewish.

While dipping his pen in the ink for the last words, Joseph knew that he had written a crystal clear, but cowardly analysis with a total lack of emotion. He put his pen down and stared at the text for a few minutes. To allow his thoughts to rest, he poured a large glass of wine.

This was a moral test case. He realized that he could not be aloof. He had to choose between himself and the greater good. Who was he actually? A nice Jewish boy from the *Judengasse*? A success in the literary circles of Paris? He drank another glass and everything became clearer.

Did he not feel anything for that boy? And his Jewish descent? Even if he totally neglected it, there had to be some solidarity. Where was his sense of justice? He must let his Jewish heart speak. Or simply his heart. Against oppression, against injustice. Not from his comfortable position as a secular journalist. His position was not that comfortable, anyhow. He could perceive it in the ghetto. It was only fifty years ago that they had been locked up there at night. They? The Jews? Did he not belong to them? He had to rage against the rulers, the Austrians. Against the French who helped them in name but at the same time were too spineless to stand up against that clown in Rome. Yes. Especially against the Church. The Church oppressed everyone, more than any other regime. Obvious to everyone, but now he could drive the point home by means of a *cause célèbre*. He had to make the world better! *Tikkun Olam*, restore the world. But how on earth could he improve the world when he was a mess himself? Maybe by not making it worse? His thoughts strayed to his little brother, who already was traumatized because Joseph had left home. What if you were cut off from your whole family like Edgardo? He had to write a better piece, committed. He had to stay true to himself. In the end he was a good boy from the *Judengasse*.

He started again. In one burst he wrote a flamboyant speech, emotional and extremely militant. When he had finished it, he put it in an envelope and in his euphoric intoxication, decided to discuss it with Elia immediately.

As he walked through the dark alleys and he tried not to hear the hollow sound of his footsteps, the feeling of desolation crept back in again. Far off he heard the dreary dirge of a lamenting gondolier. The reverberation seemed to come straight out of the grave. After a while he lost his way and tried desperately to retrace his steps. An alley seemed to offer him a shortcut to his hotel and he quickly walked through it; now forlorn, he wanted to disappear, to hide in his bed. But the alley dead-ended at a canal. Before he realized this, Joseph found himself standing waist-deep in the water. Numb, he stood for a while, shivering, then he turned around. The cold water had sobered him. It would be better to take a critical look at the piece in the morning. Perhaps it would be wiser to rewrite the more combative and inflammatory sentences. With chattering teeth, he tried to make his way back to familiar ground. As he walked, he squeezed some of the water out of his clothes. He shivered continuously and finally, with more luck than real sense of direction, he reached his hotel.

The article, redacted but still sharp, had been published and Elia and Tonio had come to pick him up in his hotel with the announcement that they would meet at *Da Gino*.

"You are a hero," said Tonio. "Nobody has ever defended our case so well. The Austrians will not be happy. Should something happen, you will be a martyr for us."

Joseph looked at Elia. "What could happen? Have I put myself in danger?"

"No worry," said Elia taking him by the arm. "Come, let's cheer our success."

The atmosphere in *Da Gino* was more unsettled than usual. The patrons looked up at the slightest noise. There was a lot of drinking. And whenever the door opened, a couple of sturdy guys immediately jumped off their chairs.

A boy of barely twelve years old came in and walked excitedly to Elia: "They want to arrest Giuseppe and one Johann Lichtman, a journalist."

Elia took Joseph by the arm again. "Stay with me, whatever happens."

Meanwhile, the men in the cafe had armed themselves with sticks and bottles. "Let's go to Giuseppe's house. We will give them a good welcome. Let's see any Austrian try to get past us."

Everything went too fast. Joseph tried to make sure that he stayed next to Elia, but in the narrow alleys, the group was forced to spread out in a long line. The mood was rough. Joseph was very woozy or excited, or both. At the end of an alley stood a group of policemen. Questions and answers that ended in screaming and snarling. It turned into a riot and Elia got into a brawl with an Austrian policeman. The bridge. Suddenly he had a vivid view of the bridge. Beating sticks. Bayonets. Was there a shot? Had he seen someone fall?

Part 2

1

(1859)

...AND THERE WAS LIGHT

Joseph was awake. Faint light fell into the dungeon. Although there was no specific reason for it, he had hope. He tried hard to give this feeling a rationale, and eventually found it in the behavior of the principal guard. Yesterday his attitude had been different; less sure of himself, less inevitable.

Because he wanted to hold on to the feeling, Joseph decided to break with his regular routine. He did not save the daily bread for later, but ate it immediately. Then, instead of lying down, he decided to walk around his cell. Five steps to the door, two to the left, five back to the window, and again two to the left. Fourteen steps in total. How much would it add up to? Seventy centimeters per pass? Almost ten meters at a time. How far was Cologne, a thousand kilometers? One hundred thousand laps. Was this pacing up and down with these calculations a sign of an imminent nervous breakdown or the first symptoms of a renewed will to live? Or was he just walking in circles?

Until now, every day he had been taken out of his cell for interrogation. Today they had left him to his fate. Another question: Was this the beginning of total oblivion or a sign that change was at hand?

He thought he heard something. Was it a knock on the door? For a while it was quiet, but suddenly the locks rattled. His regular guard appeared in the doorway. "Jew, you are free. You can go." Then, contrary to what he had said, the man locked the door again.

Joseph could not believe it. Out loud, he said the appropriate blessing in Hebrew. Agitated, he walked back and forth in his cell. Was this real? It hadn't been a hallucination, he wasn't that far gone yet. He convinced himself that it was true and wanted to prepare his departure. Laughing aloud, he had to admit to himself that there was nothing to pack.

For half an hour nothing happened. Was it perhaps a trick to weaken him? After another half hour, as he contemplated the absurd thought that they had better get on with the release because otherwise he would miss out on his soup and bread, he again heard footsteps coming along the echoing corridor. The door was unlocked for a second time and the prison guard entered with a bundle of clothes, his own clothes. For weeks these had no longer existed for him. In his other hand the guard held Joseph's glasses and an official document with a pen.

"Sign this and you are free to go."

While he signed, he asked to what he was actually agreeing.

"We will release you and you will not take any further steps against us."

That was fine with Joseph. He dressed in the presence of the prison officer. While the latter urged him to hurry up, he looked around in his cell, but now with a completely different perspective. He felt as if he were seeing the decay and destitution of these implacable walls for the first time. Sixteen days he had counted. An eternity. He could no longer imagine how he had endured this. How could people survive this for years?

The guard preceded him through the corridors. Joseph did not see anyone else and after a few steps they came up to a large gate that opened onto a courtyard that he vaguely remembered from the night he had arrived. "Here, hand this to the guards at the outer gate." The man gave him the document and turned back to the prison. With complete serenity, Joseph slowly walked to the outside gate. Somehow, he knew that there would not be any more problems. He was free and confident. He straightened his back. They had not managed to break him. As he walked through the large gate, the connection with his life was restored. He remembered the evening of his arrest. How he had been shoved through this looming entrance. The images that had not come in the dungeon suddenly poured into his brain, in exquisite detail. The bridge, the blow on his head, Elia who had pulled him along, his arrest. How they had dragged him through the alleys. Blood on his clothes, pain in his whole body. But he had told the truth. He had not been to Zorzi's. He was innocent. With some pride he realized that he hadn't betrayed anyone during all the interrogations.

He decided to go to his hotel first. He was, above all, hungry and thirsty. The prison guards had taken everything that had any value, his watch, his money. Only his identity paper had remained in his trouser pocket. Clearly, he had some organizing to do.

As he pushed his way through the crowds in the narrow alleys, he started to get nervous. He began to walk faster, almost to run, and suddenly he noticed that he was laughing, softly at first but then it turned into an uncontrollable roar. He forced the sound to stop, afraid of himself. He was hysterical. He had to calm down.

In the hotel the clerk gave Joseph the key and walked with him to his room. Apparently, he had no interest whatever in Joseph's long absence. They stopped in front of the door. Joseph waited, subservient. The clerk looked at Joseph. When Joseph still did not take action, the man pointed to the key. Somewhat embarrassed, Joseph laughed nervously and opened the door. He wanted to give the clerk some change but realized that he had nothing. "*Domani*, tomorrow," Joseph promised. Entering the room, Joseph locked the door behind him. He put the key in sight on his bedside table and then fell on his bed, exhausted. The walk to the hotel and the meeting with the clerk had demanded a lot of his nerves. He wondered how long it would take before he would return to the old way of doing things. Or would this trauma remain with him for life? Would he keep waiting for someone to open and close doors for him from now on?

On the table were a few letters. All from Max, nothing from his family or from Pennekamp. Max's words showed a lot of empathy. He had learned only recently of his terrible misery. If he didn't hear from him within a few days, he would come to Venice himself. Joseph looked at the day stamp. Three days ago. Maybe Max was already here. He would ask the clerk. Did it mean anything that Pennekamp had not sent a telegram? His family probably did not even know. All the better. And what about Elia, Giuseppe and the others? Should he visit Elia? He decided to postpone the meeting. He needed to regain his strength first. It would be nice if Max were here. He had to think less chaotically. With that wish he fell into a dreamless sleep.

The next day Joseph sent a telegram to Max with the good news of his release. He had also asked him to help out with some money and other practical matters. He decided to go to the ghetto, but he made a detour along the northern part of the city, where he never had been before. The quay was deserted and the lagoon stretched out in front of him in the sharp light. The water had a calming effect. He was convinced of one thing – he had to leave Venice. In jail he had realized that something was wrong beyond the imprisonment. The closed cell was only a symptom.

Time and again, the same idea haunted his thoughts: How arbitrary everything was. One moment you were free and the next moment you were in a dungeon with no laws and no way out. And then, beyond any comprehension, they let you go. For all he knew, they might have held him for a week, a year, or the rest of his life. There was no logic. It was all capricious. And actually, he thought, his whole life was a terrifying whim in which he had nothing to say at all.

In prison he had retrieved part of his faith, he thought. But it had been nothing but pure fear. A cry for help. Locked up in his cell, with nothing to lose, he had been easy prey for the old practices. Now that he could think freely again, the critical and cynical considerations came back. Yet he did not want to ignore this development completely.

One time, he had left for Cologne with the deliberate intention of making a new start. Now he could not see a goal. Going back and staying here were equally horrible options. He had to break with his past.

The glittering reflection of the setting sun on the water offered a fascinating play of light. And as he watched it, he realized that the entire phenomenon had been orchestrated just for him. In a direct line from the sun towards him. On either side of it, the water in the lagoon was black and gray. Only his presence and observation made the brilliant light. The whole spectacle, the reflection of light, the brightness of the water, was there because he was there.

"I didn't have the courage to contact you. They could have traced me. The greater good surpassed your individual well-being."

Joseph grudgingly agreed. They were sitting at the small table in Elia's apartment, where they had spoken the first time. It seemed another era.

"How was prison?"

"I don't want to talk about it."

"How is freedom then?"

"I have started to think differently about freedom."

Elia poured a glass of wine. "Here. This helps to relax."

"No, thank you. I'm going to take things a bit slower." He remained silent for a moment. "I don't know how to proceed."

"Before we continue, I must tell you something terrible."

"Let's have it. I can take everything at the moment."

"Giuseppe is dead. Officially, he hanged himself." Elia waited for Joseph's reaction. "But you and I know that he would never have done that. He was eccentric, but never suicidal."

Joseph had overestimated himself. The news popped in his head. Elia told the details as far as he knew. In the first week after Joseph's arrest, the Austrians had searched the houses of all members of their group and reported that they had found Giuseppe dangling at the end of a rope. They had him buried immediately. "As I said, I don't believe the official report. They killed him and didn't allow anyone else to examine his remains. There was never a doctor. That says it all."

"I never mentioned anyone. They learned nothing from me," Joseph hastened to say.

Elia let it rest. Again, he looked at Joseph. "You said you don't know what to do. I know what I want to do. I am more determined than ever to fight for the good cause. In Giuseppe's name."

"I don't know. It's devastating, this news about Giuseppe."

"The Austrians have just suffered a shocking defeat in Solferino. The *Risorgimento* is almost complete. *Viva Italia*. The French are helping us. Tuscany and Romagna are already liberated. Venice will follow. Italy needs us, now more than ever."

"Were you not afraid to be arrested?"

"You might not know it, but I have connections. Bargaining chips, that I can use at any time."

Joseph let the words sink in: "I wasn't important enough?" It was more a confirmation than a question.

Elia flushed. "You said it, not me."

Joseph accepted. "Actually, I even understand." He thought for a moment and then changed the subject. "I don't want to suffer anymore," he said. "Do you know what I really want? I want revenge. On those Austrians. For me it's all personal. What they did to me in prison was for Catholicism and the Pope. So for me, it's all one and the same. Nothing but revenge."

"Perhaps you can channel those feelings into useful actions?"

Joseph presumed that Elia would do everything in his power to get him back in the game. But he did not give in. "I don't want to stay here. I don't want to go back to Germany either. I feel tainted." He paused. "Do you think it could work – just to bury your old garbage, put a stone on it, and then be rid of it forever?" Elia had nothing to reply.

"If you don't want to go back to Germany yet, I have an idea," said Elia, after some time. "I have friends."

"Don't rub it in."

"I know someone. I can introduce you to him. The man owes me. Salvatore Conte di Monselice. He has an estate just north of Rome. He is incredibly rich and I think you could find some rest there temporarily. To recover from all the misery."

Joseph was quiet for a while.

"Tell me more about your count."

Elia continued: "He has a kind of palazzo near the *Lago di Bracciano*, just north of Rome, really huge. I think it's three quarters empty. As far as I know he is a decent, honest man. I once took care of something for him. He will surely give you a place to stay for a while. I would introduce you under a different name. Better that your real name is no longer used here."

"Should I keep my Jewish background a secret too?"

"I don't know. It might work to your advantage to admit to it.

Presuming you have become a pious Christian, of course. Say that you were baptized as a child or something. When you were nine, just like the Mortara boy."

"Then I wouldn't have to be on guard all the time." Joseph mumbled to himself: "Leucht. Johann Leucht. Use that name when you introduce me.

"Maybe it's the right thing to do. Take some time off," Elia said.

"Yes. Peace of mind... to write." Where no one would be nagging him.

Elia patted Joseph kindly on the shoulder. "All right, I'll go find out."

With a heavy heart Joseph said goodbye to Elia. He walked back through the hollow-sounding alleys of this city of past glory. The world was disgusting. There was no good cause whatsoever. Giuseppe had died for nothing. He himself had been in prison for nothing. Nothing made sense.

To Joseph's relief, Elia came with him, to make the introduction himself. The trip in the carriage to Rome was long but very pleasant. They followed the route via Bologna through the Apennines, then to Florence, through Tuscany and Umbria. The undulating landscape was beautiful in the early spring sun. Joseph regretted that they had a destination. He would have preferred to get out of the carriage, to visit the cities and to enjoy the landscape.

"Do you know Rome well?"

Elia described it at length and Joseph eagerly absorbed the information.

"The Pope first seemed to be a true liberal who was concerned with the injustice in the world. Someone who supported change. He even abolished the ghetto of Rome. But when the French had defeated Garibaldi and had helped him back into the saddle, he became even worse than his predecessor. He immediately reinstated the ghetto."

"You don't say? Really? Do they still have a ghetto here? In this time?"

"As I said. Reinstated by this Pope after the failed struggle for freedom. A few years ago."

"But isn't it more the idea of the ghetto, like in Venice?"

"No, the Jews are not allowed to settle outside. And I have heard that they still lock the gates at night. The way they have for centuries."

Elia told him that the Jews were required to go to Mass every Sunday for reeducation and, more, for the entertainment of the Christians. Not so long ago, the rabbis were chased through the streets on carnival days, in clown costumes, while the bystanders threw trash at them.

"The Pope is a great coward," he continued. "Disguised as a priest, he fled with his tail between his legs when Garibaldi stood at the gates. Too bad it was only for a short time. As I said, the French helped the Church back to power. Of all people – the French. Talking about revolution. The only thing the Pope could think of in his omniscience was to excommunicate everyone. Gone was the forward thinking; his return put the Church back fifty years. But in the end, he will lose. The Church state as we know it, is finished. It can no longer put the liberal and enlightened genie back in the bottle."

Joseph did not know what to answer. The rolling hills with the pine trees and the Mediterranean buildings charmed him but at the same time the stories he had heard in his youth disturbed this peaceful image. The Talmud described Rome as the epitome of evil. It was the source of institutionalized hatred for the Jews. One Roman emperor, Titus, had taken the holy implements from the Temple. His triumphal arch, with the relief of the Menorah, still told the story. Another, Hadrian, had razed Jerusalem to the ground and had forbidden Jews ever to take another step in their city. Even the image of the *Judensau* in Cologne had its origin in Rome.

Joseph looked from the open window of his garden cottage over the slopes of the estate. The villa was surrounded by a garden in which it was delightful to loiter, especially at sunset; an Italian courtyard with all the characteristic shapes and colors. He had placed his writing desk in front of the windows. During the day, the shutters made sure to keep out the sun and the heat, but still allowed fresh air to enter. As soon as the sun disappeared behind the hills, he opened them wide. Joseph could smell the scent of pine trees, oleanders, and other Mediterranean plants he did not know. This small home was quickly becoming dear to him.

He had been at the estate for a month now and had begun to recover. The cell with its misery had become a distant horror. From afar he had followed the recent developments in Italy and was pleased about the news that had reached him. Italy was unified, only Venice and Rome had not yet joined. The Austrians had had their comeuppance. Most of this information came from Elia's letters.

He particularly pondered the thoughts he had in prison. Shouldn't those considerations and intentions be the determining factors in his life from now on? For the time being, Joseph decided not to make any choices except one: He never wanted to be part of anything again. Nobody here knew him and he felt safe.

He had written a letter to Anton Pennekamp in which he described the whole unfortunate story. He assumed Pennekamp would support him, but his answer was cool. He understood Joseph's distress, but lacked genuine empathy. Max wrote him long letters about the state of affairs in Cologne but Joseph didn't feel he was missing anything important.

Il conte di Monselice was a kindhearted man. A stout fifty-year-old with heavy gray sideburns. Distinguished but not aloof. Joseph did not see him often. In the beginning the Count had asked him a few obligatory questions, and that had sufficed. It was enough for him that Joseph was a friend of Elia's. In the evening, Joseph ate with the staff in one of the halls on the ground floor. He rarely visited the first floor, the *piano nobile* where the Count and Countess resided. Joseph had heard from Elia that the Count's wife was much younger, but he had not seen her yet.

"Finally, rest. Rest and time to write." Maybe now he could start his great novel.

There was a gentle knock on the cottage door. Joseph opened it to find a servant, who said that *il conte* would like to invite Joseph for dinner. When the bell sounded that evening, Joseph made his way to the main part of the house. The Count greeted him warmly and Joseph followed him into the beautiful dining room. Everything radiated elegance and by extending a chair, a servant invited Joseph to sit on the long side of a table. It was set for three.

"We will wait for the *contessa*."

It didn't take long before Isabella *contessa* di Monselice entered. Joseph had expected the female version of the Count: A small woman, a bit weighty perhaps, charming but not earth-shattering. What he saw was breathtaking. He felt as if she, with her fragile figure, was claiming the entire space. As if an opera by Verdi had entered the room. Her unpretentious dress elegantly complimented her body; she had arranged her dark hair in a way he had never seen before. Her face was delicate, with refined features. So much grace was hard for Joseph to grasp. Exalted beyond the need for approval and elusive to his desire. He wanted to stay near her forever just to admire her.

Dinner was a joy. The staff served them a five-course menu with the most exquisite refreshments and dishes. The wine was probably excellent, but Joseph decided to pass, again. They talked about almost everything, avoiding only political and personal subjects. During dessert, Monselice presented the real reason why he had invited Joseph to dinner.

"I've heard positive reports about you. From Elia. And I like you; you seem to be a clever man: you don't ask too many questions. It made me think that you might be the person to fit right in with the plan that some friends of mine in Rome have developed."

He took a bite from his dessert and continued with his mouth half-full. "They want to go on an expedition. To the Holy Land. They haven't worked out the details yet. But if you are interested, I will introduce you to the leader of the group. His name is Bruno Ferretti, a highly qualified employee in the Vatican, an archaeologist, I understand. They are looking for a chronicler. You speak several languages, you are a good writer, and perhaps most important, you know Hebrew and you know the Bible, at least the Old Testament."

"Quite an undertaking," Joseph stalled. He wanted to keep a low profile for the time being. He did not feel ready for adventures yet. On the other hand, he could hardly control his feelings. A chance to see Rivka! That alone would make the expedition worthwhile.

Until now the *contessa* had only occasionally participated in the conversation. Now, she said something, her soft voice barely a whisper. She spoke in a dialect that Joseph did not know. He had already asked several times during the meal if she could repeat herself. It seemed inappropriate to do so again.

"Of course," he assented enthusiastically.

"That's settled then," said Monselice. "I will arrange a meeting as soon as possible."

Apparently, Joseph had agreed, but he did not dare to take his words back. The *contessa* smiled at him. He melted. How could he refuse such charm?

It seemed prudent to consult with Elia beforehand. At Joseph's request his friend came to the cottage a few days later.

"There's no going back, really. I said yes to the *contessa* and I wouldn't know how to retract my words." He kept the most important reason, the possible reunion with Rivka, to himself. He did not feel like telling his family history now.

"You know what," said Elia. "Give it a chance. Act as if you agree. You can always change your mind later."

"If you say so…The group is made up of precisely the people we abhor, the Austrians and the Papists."

"Monselice is a real Italian."

"I don't know where his preferences lie."

"That's unkind. After the hospitality he has extended to you."

"You're right. I'm probably doing him an injustice. It's just that I don't have that much confidence in people anymore." He paused, and gave Elia a meaningful look. "I have a different plan. A bit childish perhaps, but one never knows. This infiltration could lead the way to the revenge I am looking for. Besides, I have nothing to lose. It is better to keep myself busy than go back to Cologne right now. And I assume it would be difficult to stay on the estate if I said no to the expedition."

Elia smiled. "Very well," he said. "It's always good to attack the enemy from the inside." He changed the subject: "Did you hear the news about the Mortara boy? It seems that he is quite pleased with his Catholic existence. He has become a pious Christian in a monastery."

"So what on earth were we worrying about?"

"Well, it is a pity for the parents but it was the push we needed. The case itself was useful. Because of it the Church – the Pope and all his power – is on its last legs."

A few days later, Joseph learned more about the expedition. The destination was the vanished city of Capernaum on Lake Galilee.

2

(1861)

AN ABANDONED LAND

For three days now, the ship had been bouncing wildly on the waves. Joseph had fallen terribly seasick at the beginning of the storm. He tried to concentrate on meaningful and joyful feelings, but the nausea made positive thoughts impossible. He lay in his cabin listening to the occasional murmurs of people above him, on the deck. Were they praying?

Shouldn't he do something himself? Almost hallucinating, it struck him that he might be the sole cause of this disaster. Perhaps he should throw himself overboard in order to spare the others. But he was not ready for such a great sacrifice. In addition, that pack above didn't deserve it. And he didn't feel like paying a visit to the intestines of a fish.

The wood of the boat was squeaking. It had to be around three o'clock at night. Joseph got up and painfully dragged himself to the upper deck. Except for a few sailors, it was completely deserted. The storm seemed to have subsided a little. He managed to sway to the rail without too much difficulty. Joseph found that he was sweating, though he knew it was cold. It was April, shouldn't the weather be much better here?

Below him the water swirled around the bow and along the side. Large foam heads broke into thousands of drops, glistening in the weak moonlight. Nothing to be seen but the wild sea. He imagined what it would be like to be swept overboard. The impact on the hard water. The ice-cold immersion and the currents that would grab him. Joseph shivered and felt a new respect for Jonah. But Jonah had fled from the Holy Land. It was good that the others knew nothing about him. If it was God's intention to teach him compassion, then better not with these ruffians.

"Tomorrow morning we will reach Haifa," said an unexpected voice behind him. It was Bruno Ferretti, the leader of the expedition.

"All the better," replied Joseph weakly. "I have had it. Two weeks at sea is more than I can bear."

Ferretti was a fleshy man with dark hair, a moustache like a broom, and the puffy face of someone who enjoyed the good life too much. He looked like the pretty boy who had not kept the promise of beauty. A long lock of black hair fell over his forehead, so that he had to tilt his head back and turn his dark eyes downwards when he wanted to speak to someone; it gave him a haughty appearance. Joseph remembered very clearly the first words Ferretti had spoken to him: "Actually, I am both the instigator of the idea and the leader of the team. At first, I was planning to do most of the tasks myself, but that would have been too much. Sometimes you have to give others a chance as well, although I know I would do it better myself."

To Joseph's annoyance, the man stayed next to him at the railing.

"Well, Leucht. What do you think? We'll show them, right?"

"Certainly," Joseph said with reluctance.

"You know. I am glad you're here. Kindred spirits always find each other. And I hardly speak German or English. It makes a better impression if an independent writer of your stature participates. As you know, I have decided to choose Capernaum as our goal. Do you know the place?"

"I've never been there before, but I know where it should be. At least, approximately."

"That's my man, now. We will become good friends, you and I. I promise you that."

Joseph was glad that the man did not give him a chance to respond.

"Anyhow, the Pope has given us carte blanche to come up with something spectacular, a find with an enormous grandeur. We are going to write history. The world will know who we are, just as the cardinal dreams. I can deliver to everyone, whatever he wants." He changed the subject. "The captain says that we might not be able to anchor in Haifa for a couple of days because of the storm. We might be forced to go to Yafo." Ferretti growled. "Then we will have an extra journey of three days extra over land."

"Is that a problem?"

"Do you have money to pay the caravan for an extra week?" Ferretti snarled. More quietly, he continued: "I'll find a solution. I'll butter up those natives."

Before Joseph could react, a new wave of nausea struck him. "I'm going to lie down a bit. I don't feel well."

"Just make sure you get better. We have not hired you for nothing."

Joseph was glad that his illness gave him an excuse to leave the man; there was some benefit after all.

Downstairs, the feverish hallucinations washed over him again. He saw himself standing on the deck with the world wide open before him. He could choose whatever he wanted, but suddenly realized that the boat was a cell. A prison at sea. He could not go anywhere. Some men told him not to be afraid. They carried him to the prison in Venice. He was safe. Solid ground under his feet. Food, drink. With a shock, Joseph realized that he was feeling nostalgic about the refuge of his cell. Did physical discomfort and illness turn the world upside down so fast?

Indeed, anchorage at Haifa turned out to be impossible. After a few hours bobbing off the coast, the captain decided to try his luck in Yafo. Although there was no real port there either, there was hope that the sea might be quieter. Joseph was hardly aware of anything. He remained below deck and although he had seen a glimpse of land, he was not well enough to get up. When he woke again, the sun had set and he felt a little better. He understood from the changed rhythms around him that they were at anchor.

Disembarking at Yafo was a nightmare. Indistinct shouting and complete chaos. But eventually, they all made it ashore in a number of sloops. Someone took Joseph to the primitive shelter where they would spend the night. He had a room to himself and he did his best to sleep. Several times he woke up from the buzzing of insects around his head and once he thought he saw a large black spider-like insect with wings crawling up the bare wall. The creature flew away as he rubbed his eyes to make sure that he was not hallucinating once again. Flying spiders. A promising land.

Joseph reflected on the events of the last few weeks. It all had gone fast. He had learned that one of the highest cardinals of the Vatican, Melchior van Schwarzenberg, had ordered the archaeologist Bruno Ferretti to find something special from the Holy Land. Ferretti had agreed to the challenge and had put together a team to embark on the search. His Holiness himself had approved the plan. It did not matter what or how he did it. Something tangible, something of value, a confirmation of the infallibility of the Holy Father, of Peter, the rock. A symbol of the Pope's everlasting regency. Joseph assumed that it all would become clear as soon as they reached the site of the archaeological excavation.

Eventually, Joseph saw the pale light of the day. Relieved, he edged himself off of the bed, wondering how to endure a week-long journey. Ferretti had boasted about the luxurious travel arrangements that he had made. Could Joseph have confidence in a swindler? He looked out of the window but couldn't see past the long wall of the opposite building.

Besides Joseph and Ferretti, the group consisted of a banker, Franco Padovani, and a priest, Enrico di Fonseca. Joseph called them the

Romans. There was also a Turkish dragoman, Mustafa, a nervous type with sparking eyes. He would leave when they had reached their destination. Five aides filled out the group – a cook, a translator, and three Arabs to help with all the routine chores including constructing and dismantling the encampments en route.

Padovani was quite young, somewhere in his thirties. He was a real bourgeois, well dressed and meticulously groomed, an Italian like the hundreds that Joseph had seen walking through the streets of Venice. He was the type who agreed with everyone when it was convenient. But Joseph took him to be a decent man, at least as long as nothing unpleasant happened. Di Fonseca reminded Joseph of a nibbling little mouse, who nevertheless might lash out fiercely. Joseph decided that he would not want to cross swords with him.

Finally, there was a British painter, Richard Walter Harrison, whom Ferretti had commissioned to make drawings and sketches of their discoveries. The painter had also studied the new technique of photography and Ferretti expected a lot from the potential. Harrison lived in Yafo, so he had come to greet the party; he would join them in Capernaum later. While the three Arabs were preparing everything for their departure, Joseph found some time to talk to him. "It is of no use for me to dig with you," the painter said, "you'll probably only find corpses, and I can't bring those back to life with my paintings. Better to come when there is actually something to draw or to photograph."

They were standing on the quay in Yafo. The storm had subsided somewhat and three ships were at anchor, all waiting to unload their cargo. Richard turned out to be a rough husk, but Joseph found it pleasant to talk to the painter. He had something of the rowdy, willing rascal who, after some rogue practices, had been given the choice to serve his sentence or to board the first ship that sailed. But Joseph was glad he was here. Somehow, he seemed to be a link with Europe, allowing Joseph not to say a complete farewell to civilization. It was a pity that he would not be joining the trip now.

The city showed its best side. In the sunlight, white houses shone on the hill, over which the old impressive fortress towered. Joseph vaguely thought he could see the cannons protruding. Colorfully dressed people from every region of the Mediterranean crowded the port.

"Splendid port, this," Richard said. To Joseph's ears, his voice sounded ironic. "I'll immortalize it. Imagine, Yafo, a beautiful harbor town, picturesque. In the middle, a steep rock. And then, above the rough waves, a naked girl chained to the rock, her face turned away, timid and anxious at the same time, at the mercy of the whims of the sea monsters." He paused, as if waiting for Joseph's reaction. "That

will make a sensation in the Paris and London salons, don't you think?"
He laughed. "Perhaps too wild for you? I didn't make it up myself. The
Greeks are the culprits. It is the ancient myth of Andromeda."

"I know. I would like to see it when it is finished," said Joseph
politely. "I mean, the painting. Not necessarily because of the naked
girl. I'm quite used to the salons in Paris."

"Don't worry. It is art. Everything is allowed in art. I wish you a
good trip. See you in Jesus' land." He nodded and tapped his straw
Panama hat as he strode away.

The first part of their trip was tedious. Ferretti rode with the Romans
in front on horseback; the others had donkeys. The Arabs walked next
to the additional donkeys, brought along to carry the tents, clothing,
provisions, books, and tools. They followed a path through the coastal
plain, parallel to the sea. On both sides were sand dunes, endless reed
beds, and marshes, as far as the eye could see. After a while Joseph gave
up trying to swat away the mosquitoes and other insects. Sometimes
they had to wade through swampy waters and it was here that the
Arabs first proved their added value. They knew every inch of land
and pointed out the dangerous areas precisely. Around eleven o'clock
they reached a low piece of land that was largely under water and
that, as far Joseph could tell, was covered with reeds. With a lot of
fuss, Ali, one of the Arabs, reported, "*Ghadir adim*, it's suicide to cross
this." The translator rendered it in modest language, but judging by the
ferocity of the pronunciation, the Arab had used stronger, saltier words.
Muhammad, another of the other Arabs, had already dismounted his
ass and approached Ferretti, looking ominous. Ferretti, however, did
not let this upset him.

"How much time would we waste on the detour?"

"Maybe an hour, maybe a day," was the phlegmatic answer from
Rachid, the third Arab.

Loudly and clearly, Ferretti stated that they could not afford to
lose more time. Muhammad raised his hands to heaven, screaming.
Superfluously, the translator noted that Muhammad thought that
attempting to cross was madness.

Ferretti ordered Ali to lead the way on his donkey. The man smiled,
"More money, *effendi*."

Ferretti just smiled, signaling that the negotiations were complete.
Ali started off, guiding his donkey at a sluggish pace. Slowly the
donkey's legs disappeared in the sludge. But a few meters further the
land rose again and they could see the rider continue steadily until
he vanished into the reeds. After about thirty anxious minutes he

reappeared smiling. "It is safe," he shouted. "I know this path. There are a few treacherous spots but it will be fine. Give me the money now, otherwise I won't take you through."

He proposed to start with the pack animals. Ferretti removed a large bundle from his saddlebag from which he took some banknotes.

"You get the rest when we are all safe across." He waved his hand in a hopeless attempt to keep the mosquitoes away. "Cursed land with its miserable bugs," he growled.

The pack animals followed Ali into the swamp. Joseph watched from a safe distance. He had little faith in the trail, but he didn't want to be a coward either. So, when most of the caravan had gone through, he forced his donkey onto the path, just behind the cook and some pack animals. Rachid calmly followed him, leaving Padovani to bring up the rear.

They moved slowly through reeds that now reached shoulder height. Occasionally Joseph saw a glimpse of one of the other pack animals, about ten meters in front of him. Joseph's donkey delicately picked its way along the trail of its predecessor, inching between the puddles and the swampy moss. A single misstep could be fatal, Joseph realized.

Suddenly he heard a shriek not far in front of him. Then the terrified brays of a donkey, as if the animal were in mortal agony. There was no point in speeding up to help. Quietly Joseph and the others in his group continued until they reached a clearing. It was covered with moss, but there was no way to miss the gurgling sounds emanating from under the ground at their feet. What or who had disappeared into it? Joseph shivered. With extreme caution they rode on, looking closely for any indications of instability in the ground. Not that it mattered, because the donkey had complete control over where they were going. The next half hour demanded the most of his nerves, but then the ground began to rise, and suddenly they emerged from the reeds. In front of him he saw the rest of the group. No one seemed to be missing.

"One of the donkeys slipped under its load and sank into the swamp," Ferretti said softly. "I think I should make the Arabs pay for it."

It turned out to be the donkey with all the kitchen utensils that had disappeared in the swamp. Joseph thought of the Torah text that speaks about raising an overburdened donkey, even it belongs to your enemy. He didn't want to get sentimental but his thoughts went to the poor animal, heavily laden, collapsing and perishing in the swamp.

Meanwhile a quarrel started between Ali and Ferretti when the Arabs learned that there would be no more money. According to Ferretti, they had not kept to the agreement. "When we're all safely across, I said." The pressure of the Turkish dragoman eventually forced the Arabs to acquiesce, but Joseph had the fearful suspicion that their loyalty had shrunk dramatically.

Joseph heard Padavoni murmuring behind him, "The Arabs told Bruno that the beasts were overloaded, but he said that he could not pay for another. An extra donkey would have cost ten francs. Now we have lost hundreds of francs in supplies." He nervously added, "And the donkey of course."

Apparently Ferretti was also tired of the situation, because he fired his rifle in the air. "We go on. I don't want to hear anything more about it." Joseph knew from now on that the gun by Ferretti's side would be loaded. Despite his aversion for the man, he had to admit that Ferretti showed perseverance and determination.

The sun was shining fiercely and by the end of the morning the heat became uncomfortable and unpleasant. Joseph had been riding next to Fonseca for a while, listening to the man's non-stop chatter. Joseph was uncomfortable with the priest but thought this could be a good opportunity to question him about his reasons for having joined the group.

Fonseca was only too happy to start. "The Church and the Pope are being threatened. The wicked want to force their ideas upon us. More than that, they want to make us disappear from the face of the earth. Their state, their schools, their universities, their newspapers, their judges, their freedom of religion – all these things they want to impose on us. Everything is liberal and godless. They infiltrate everything. That is why we must stand firm and not give way to the socialists, nationalists, and other modernists. They want a separation between Church and State, but that will never happen. They think they can win. But they have thought that before and every time we have come back stronger than ever. We have strengthened the Inquisition. We will not let our territory be lost. We will bring the apostates, the heretics, the Jews, and the other scum back to the right path. Whether they want it or not. We must defend ourselves and the best defense is an attack. Frontal."

Fonseca held back his horse. "Do you know that I spoke about this with the Pope personally? We are even going to publish a newspaper. That might be something for you too. You are a reporter, aren't you?" He had the exalted look of a man who was granting a favor. "You should look up Raimondo Zanchini when we are back in Italy. He has taken on the task of creating a daily publication in which we can express our political and moral views to the world. We are going to make solid, robust statements."

He paused briefly.

"To guide people in the right way, we need to highlight the success of the church," he resumed. "We need to look good. The form is as important as the content. The plaster might be even more important than the wall that it covers. People should see a radiant and cheerful Church, not a clique fighting in the mud. The rabble must regain confidence in us. Faith in the Faith. I cannot deny that the story of that Jewish boy, that Mortara, worked against us at first. But we were right. The boy himself proved us right by becoming a pious Roman pupil. But we need to do more." His volume now dropped to the level of a conspiracy. "We need a distraction from these things, and what could be better than something with a tangible religious impact? Something that we can build on. The memorial year for Saint Peter is nearing. Major festivities are in the offing. His Holiness thought it would be good to present something that shows that he has the right to be what we all know he is – the representative of Christ on earth, following in the footsteps of his great predecessor Petrus. A rock in these disconcerted times."

The priest made a cross to indicate that he thought his oration was completed. He clearly assumed that Joseph agreed with every word that he had said.

Joseph still felt a bit sick and was glad when the time came to dismount for lunch. The Arabs erected the meal tent with great efficiency and, as a crowning achievement, Fonseca proudly raised the papal flag at its top. Nobody could mistake the identity of this company. Joseph initially found it ridiculous that they had put in so much effort for a quick bite, but half an hour later, as he lay with a glass of lemonade in the tent's cool shade, he was grateful. These Arabs knew what they were doing and he decided not even to think of questioning them on practical matters. He realized that he needed to eat something and reluctantly swallowed a few boring, honey-sweet cookies.

The afternoon was a repetition of the morning, a monotonous bumping on winding paths between the marshes, but when the sun began to sink, they turned eastward, away from the wetlands. They passed a village of shabby mud huts and a mosque. Rachid, who rode next to Joseph, pointed. "Tulkarem," he said as if to impress. The name didn't mean anything to Joseph. He was glad when they just passed by because it did not look inviting. The road began to rise and slowly but surely the ground became harder. Soon they were on a path carved out of the hard limestone. Large boulders were everywhere, and it became harder to continue. Often, they all had to dismount to guide the donkeys around the obstacles. Only Ferretti and Padovani stayed on horseback and Ferretti noted with irritation that he was not amused by the delay. "Miserable land. Either you sink into the swamp or you break your leg on the rocks." In the east it became darker. Joseph thought he could see higher mountains in the haze of the dim distance.

Ferretti was discussing logistics with Mustafa and the Arabs. Eventually they reached a decision. "Here will be our first overnight stay," Ferretti announced. "We are above the unhealthy air of the marshes." They had reached a more or less flat stretch without much vegetation. Exhausted but relieved that this day was over and that he had persevered, Joseph collapsed on a strip of grass between the rough cacti along the path. He didn't have to help set up camp. He had asked Ferretti to leave him alone until he felt better.

Lying on the comfortable carpet, he watched the erection of the canvas structures. The Arabs' loud voices reverberated unceasingly, as if an entire army were preparing for battle. Guttural, arguing sounds, but nevertheless Joseph felt inexplicably safe. As if the tent shut out the undesirable immensity of the outside world.

The next day Joseph felt a little better and became more interested in his surroundings. Everywhere they went, he saw ruins that breathed desolation; the remains of ancient civilizations, as if the whole country had suddenly been abandoned and no one had ever looked back. Everything had remained as it was, fallen into decay.

"The land was never rebuilt," he heard Ferretti say. Joseph was now riding next to the leader, who told him all about what they were seeing. Again, Joseph was puzzled by the contrasts in the man. The knowledge he had versus the rudeness he displayed again and again. "To put it mildly, it is a mess, but a mess that is a paradise for archaeologists."

Not wanting to interrupt Ferretti's soliloquy Joseph replied briefly, "From the old prophets to the new."

"Incredible, what religion has done to this country. Here an archaeologist can find everything he wishes for. Biblical, Greek, Roman, Christian, Islamic. You name it and I will bring it to you," said Ferretti with a sly smile.

By the end of the afternoon Joseph's fever had gotten worse again. Overtired, he was shivering and sweating at the same time. The journey was beginning to take its toll.

In the east, threatening clouds piled up.

"Rain is coming. And it is another hour to Jenin," Ali said to Ferretti.

"Let's press on then."

"We won't make it before the rain starts. We have to make camp now."

"I'm still the leader and I decide that we'll continue to Jenin," Ferretti said curtly.

Padovani joined the conversation, "Shouldn't we listen to the Arabs this once? They know what they are talking about."

"In Italy, *Signor* Padovani, there may be reasons why I have to listen to you." He laughed. "There I have to comply. Here, I am the boss."

Padovani shrugged his shoulders to show that he would not argue. Joseph felt sorry for the man and wondered if Ferretti's words referred to more than just the hierarchical position.

To the west, the sun disappeared behind the clouds. Well before they had reached Jenin, the sky was completely black. Hell broke loose ruthlessly. Joseph could not remember ever having experienced such a thunderstorm. Ear-splitting eruptions came almost simultaneously with blinding flashes that cracked across the sky. In the broken air, the threatening rumble spread out over the landscape. An awe-inspiring game of giants. Visibility was virtually nil. In the chaos that ensued, Joseph sought the safety of Rachid's company, convinced that at least the Arab knew what he was doing. Soon, the Arabs dismounted and started to build the camp in the pouring rain. Ferretti stood by and watched.

"The last rains before the dry season begins," Rachid tried to add a cheerful note while putting large pegs into the ground. Words from the *Sh'ma* came to Joseph's mind for the first time in years. *V'natati matar ar'tz'chem b'ito yoreh umal'kosh* – "I shall give rain at the right moments, the early rain and the late rain." By the time the tents were complete, Joseph was soaked. He longed to feel the scorching sun of that afternoon again. Why did he have to get sick as a dog because of Ferretti's ambitions?

Later that night the thunderstorm stopped. Joseph woke up and after trying in vain to fall asleep again, he quietly crawled out of his bedroll and stepped outside. The sky was littered with stars. It seemed as if the thunderstorm had wiped the world clean. Everything breathed an ultimate serenity. With awe he gazed across the ancient landscape and stood there until the first glimmer of dawn.

Jenin reminded Joseph of the prints he had seen with Rivka. Which word had she used? Picturesque. Gray stone houses covered the slope, arranged around the white dome and the graceful minaret of the local mosque. A small river flowed through the village and a single palm tree enhanced the magical, oriental effect. After they had passed Jenin, the Jezreel valley opened up in front of them. On the west side, far off, the hills of the Carmel dominated the view. Directly in front of him, as they descended the slope, he saw Nazareth lying in the distance, its minarets sharply delineated against the northern horizon. Centuries ago, time had come to a standstill here.

Fragments of long-disregarded texts came to his mind. Jacob sending Joseph to S'chem. Dothan, where Joseph looked for his brothers. The well. Shaul fighting the Philistines. The vineyards of Naboth. Description of the Carmel Mountains. Apparently, he still remembered the texts well. But, as dry and boring they might have presented themselves once, now they seemed to spring to life. Joseph found himself overwhelmed with unfamiliar sensations. Maybe he had felt an opening to something like this in a concert hall or while reading a book, but this was different, it was the real thing. This was not an intellectual experience. It spoke right to the heart. It was like falling in love. Maybe all of the Jews from Frankfurt should come here on a compulsory trip to experience this and to give meaning to the texts.

Rachid saw him looking and pointed at the Carmel range. "*Ilia el Neby*," he said, nodding.

"*Eliahu HaNavi*," responded Joseph, smiling. It didn't matter much to Joseph that Ferretti might hear their conversation. The man knew his background. It might make him rise in esteem. "Almost the same."

"You call him *Eliahu HaNavi*? So, then you are *Yochanan*?" Rachid asked smiling, as he guessed at Joseph's Hebrew name.

Joseph didn't correct him and Rachid continued. "For us it is *Yuchanna*. We have the same ancestor. Ibrahim. Do you know what we call today's month? *Nissan*. Just like the *Yehudim*." Rachid was clearly proud that he could display his knowledge.

Standing side by side, they continued to discuss the similarities between Hebrew and Arabic. Strange, this man here with his donkey, sharing the same vocabulary as Joseph, born in Frankfurt. Everything was strange here. And even more so that Rivka lived behind those hills.

"After these rains, the Esdraelon plain is probably an almost inaccessible swamp," Ferretti said during their first stop of the morning. "We will head east from here to the valley of the Jordan River. Then we will go northwards, to the lake of Galilee." He pointed to the northeast. As if a child had drawn a mountain, a round hump protruded above the horizon. "That is Mount Tabor. There to our left," he pointed vaguely to the west, "there lies Armageddon. The location of the final battle."

Again images from the *Tanach** surfaced. But Joseph also remembered a conversation he had had not so long ago with Max in which they had discussed the political situation of the Levant. Max had spoken about the plain of Jezreel. This was the passageway from Egypt to Damascus and further, to Baghdad and even India. Napoleon had understood its importance. Hadn't the French fought the Turks here? Had the Brits helped the Turks or not? Hadn't Napoleon been stuck in the mud of the Kishon River in the same way as Deborah's opponents? How absurd was history. He needed to read the *Book of Judges* again.

The journey to the Kinneret took two days. They passed through the Jordan Valley with the mountains of Moab on their right and the rolling hills of the Galilee in the west. Tabor slowly disappeared behind them and the terrain became rougher again. From the top of a large hill toward the end of the second day, they finally saw their goal – the Lake of Galilee and, nearby, the alleged location of Capernaum. It was a sight from a fairytale. The town of Tiberias sprawled on the bank of the Kinneret's deep blue water. On the lake's far side, they could see the reflection of pink and lilac mountains dissolving with the darkening sky. A connection between heaven and earth. This is how it should be, Joseph said to himself, not knowing exactly what he meant. Their area of exploration was about ten kilometers north of the city. This time everyone agreed to push on, rather than spend the night in Tiberias. The stories about the city in ruins were not inviting; a hotbed of criminals and crooks, they had heard. It was dark by the time they finally reached their destination, but a surprise awaited them – three large tents flying the British flag. Ferretti was stamping his feet in anger. He insisted to Padovani that this definitely was the place that the authorities in Constantinople had assigned to him, fully in accordance with his request. But after Ferretti and Padovani went to meet the British, it became clear that they were already dug in and would not move. They had the permission, a *firman*, of the Turks.

Ferretti cursed. "I'll teach them a lesson, those damn English." But Padovani managed to calm him down. Joseph heard it all from the sidelines. He was grateful that they had reached their final goal and he did not feel like worrying about anything. The Arabs were setting up their own tent a little further off and Joseph was glad that he shared it with them. Exhausted he lay down on one of the mattresses.

A few hours later the voices of Ferretti and Padovani awakened him.

Ferretti had apparently come to his senses. He was convinced that further north there also would be enough to find. The source of this reliance was unclear, but nobody dared to question him. So a few hours later, in the middle of the night, the Arabs rebuilt the camp a few kilometers further north.

"Don't you think we're going to have problems with the Porte if we just start digging somewhere here. We don't have a *firman* for this area here," he heard Padovani say.

"Since when do you care about those Turkish buffoons? I think we can straighten that out with a bribe," replied Ferretti.

"And is there anything to dig up there?"

"We can't come back empty-handed," Ferretti reacted furiously. "If it were up to me, we would push those English into the lake."

"It's all fine with me, as long as we don't end up in a Turkish prison," sighed Padovani.

With a shake of his shoulders, Ferretti put the incident behind him. "Don't worry. The Church has a long and mighty arm. Tomorrow we'll do an inventory and get to work."

Ferretti was growing impatient. For two weeks now they had been searching and digging but the effort had not yet yielded anything. The days were hot but Joseph had made a comfortable spot for himself under a large fig tree. It was a good place to sit. The tree had a strong fragrance, and when Joseph closed his eyes and enjoyed the scent, Europe was far away. The landscape and the whole environment had an extremely calming effect on him, despite the immediacy of the expedition and Ferretti's fits of rage. Joseph diligently kept two diaries, one for himself and one for the expedition. He also made himself useful by studying old writers and texts, but the more he read, the more it became clear to him that they were in the wrong place. In the meantime, he wondered how on earth he could get in touch with Rivka from here, but he assumed that there would be an opportunity somewhere on the way back. Surely he could slip away when they no longer needed him.

"We need to go further north," he tried to convince Ferretti. "Where the Roman road ran into the lake." He took the book he was reading. "Josephus says...."

With a small gesture Ferretti exhorted him to silence.

"I know what I'm doing." Ferretti gazed at him for a long time. His look made Joseph nervous. Then Ferretti laughed scornfully, "Live up to your reputation as a writer." He turned on his heel and marched away, leaving Joseph feeling anxious.

Joseph considered mentioning his doubts to Padovani, but the latter was becoming more apathetic every day, overwhelmed with the fear that he would end up emaciated in a Turkish cell. Ferretti, on the other hand, grew more aggressive. Joseph really began to hate him. Soon the man's every mannerism came to bother him. Sometimes he watched him eat his soup, mesmerized. Carefully Ferretti took some liquid on his spoon, then he brought it to his mouth but pressed his moustache into it so that the hairs absorbed half of the liquid.

A bright change was the arrival of Richard Harrison, the painter and photographer. Joseph finally had someone with whom he felt comfortable voicing his thoughts. He told Richard about his doubts regarding the archaeological site.

"I know Ferretti. He will come up with something. You'll see what tricks he'll conjure before it's over. And what does it matter to you? Paid holiday." He smiled knowingly from under his eternal Panama.

At the end of another unproductive day Ferretti approached him. "I don't like to say it, but you were right. This is the wrong place. But we cannot give up. Going back to Rome empty-handed is not an option. There will certainly be no more money to fund a new expedition. And there's news from the cardinal. We have to come up with something quickly, otherwise he will cancel the whole mission, which means I can whistle for my money, and my reputation as an archeologist is down the drain."

Joseph nodded. He wondered why Ferretti came to share this with him.

Ferretti continued, murmuring more to himself than to Joseph: "There are no higher, noble purposes in archaeology. Archaeology is not a pure science as you might like to see it. Everything is politicized and everything is used to achieve political goals. Archaeology is a wonderful way to prove yourself right. Bring in your history. Produce facts." He looked haughty, as if he had prophetic gifts. "We are only at the beginning of this process. In a century nobody will know what was true and what was not. *We* can now determine the history of the future. And this what we are doing here is only small potatoes. You will see how the past will be abused in the future."

For a moment it seemed as if Ferretti wanted to continue, but he restrained himself. As he walked away, Joseph heard him muttering under his breath, "We will deliver to the Vatican. The higher goal. To the Pope himself."

The next day Joseph and Richard walked in the *shuk*, the market in Tiberias, something they often did to distract themselves from the boredom of the dig.

"Isn't that Ferretti, there? By that stall?" Richard suddenly exclaimed. Without waiting for a reply, Richard grabbed Joseph's arm and shoved him behind some carpets that were hanging for sale.

"Why are we hiding?" Joseph asked.

"I don't know. I want to see what he is doing here. It is not like Ferretti to leave the coolness of his tent to go shopping here in the Arab hustle and bustle. He is scheming something and it is always wise to be well informed."

Joseph saw Ferretti consulting with a merchant. A little later he left the shop with some jugs and rolls of papyrus, which he put in the sacks hanging from his horse's saddle before riding away.

Later that evening Ferretti visited Joseph again.

"You're the Bible expert. Can you show me some texts that the Christians use as a proclamation of the coming of our Savior?"

"Certainly. Why?"

"Not too many questions, Leucht. Do as I ask. You're being generously paid to be part of this." He thought for a moment, as if considering what to say and what not. "What did they speak in those days here? I mean when Jesus lived?"

"Aramaic."

"Right, also give me a few texts in Aramaic. You can bring them to my tent later tonight."

Joseph started to understand where Ferretti was heading. He decided to play along, but at the same time to make sure that the fraud could come to light with clarity, when appropriate. He wrote down some sentences from Isaiah about the coming of the Savior, which he knew Christians liked using. "For to us a child is born, to us a son is given, and the government will be on his shoulders. And he will be called Wonderful Counselor, Mighty God, Everlasting Father, Prince of Peace." He completed it with texts from the Talmud. That ought to do it. The Talmud would not be written for a few centuries, but it would make the fraud easier to prove.

After dinner, he brought Ferretti the rolls with the texts, then stayed in the shade of the tent to see what Ferretti would do with them. The light shone through the canvas of the tent and he could see the man's movements in silhouette. Ferretti was busy with the jugs and the rolls of papyrus. Suddenly he heard a few loud bangs and the sound of breaking pottery. Ferretti had apparently shattered the jugs. Eventually the expedition chief left the tent, carrying a big bundle and looked around to make sure that the area was clear. Joseph saw that Ferretti had taken his gun, and in case Ferretti discovered him, Joseph planned his retreat. But Ferretti quietly walked to the shore of the lake. Joseph followed him. In the dark, he could not make out the man's actions, but he assumed that Ferretti had submerged the whole package in the still water.

He rejoiced. Here was the subversive possibility to which Elia had alluded. The trip and the dig had distracted him from his reason for participating in the first place. Now, the situation was very clear to him again: revenge. On the Church and the Austrians and everything they had done to him. His sixteen days of imprisonment. Ferretti and this whole group of blowhards deserved to be punished.

For two days nothing happened and then Ferretti triumphantly summoned everyone together. With a flourish, he announced that he had decided that they needed to start searching in a cave further up the hill. He had a hunch that there might be something there. He stated all of this with such conviction that Joseph assumed that the others did not know about the fraud. Clearly Ferretti wanted to be more real than real.

"Do we participate in this?" Joseph asked Richard, as they saddled their donkeys.

"I draw a cave and a few crazy Europeans in Palestine. I know nothing. I am only recording this." He looked at Joseph with a grin. "It will all work out. The Turks are not interested in what is happening here. And the Europeans? I won't go there, so what could they possibly do to me?"

"I still have to go back."

"Do you? And have you done anything wrong? You gave him some texts. You didn't know what they were for. And anyway, why don't you just stay here? I think you would do fine, especially without that one there." The painter nodded vaguely in Ferretti's direction.

Ferretti interrupted their conversation: "Ready?"

"As good as."

A small party left the camp. Ferretti and Fonseca in front, then Richard and Joseph with the Arabs, and behind them Padovani. Slowly they climbed the hill. When it got steeper, they left the animals behind and made their way through the thorny bushes. Joseph heard Padovani grumble. "I hope this is worth it."

Ferretti heard it as well, but before he could respond they came to a large open site. On one side the mountain rose steeply; against it a landslide had left a pile of huge boulders.

"You two," Ferretti addressed the Arabs. "Remove that boulder." He pointed at an enormous round block of stone that looked like a cover. If anyone wondered why Ferretti had chosen that stone in particular, he did not speak up. The Arabs immediately set to work and with great difficulty they succeeded in rolling it aside. A gaping hole appeared behind it. Ferretti seemed to work himself into a frenzy. "I told you there was something here! I was sure of it," he screamed. "Harrison. Take pictures." Richard went to work with his equipment. Someone lit several torches.

"I will lead the way," said Ferretti and stooping down, he entered the cave with Richard close behind him. Joseph followed as third. Inside the cave, he had trouble discerning anything. The spooky light of the torches made grotesque shapes on the walls. As if blind, the group crawled deeper into the cave. The space grew narrower and narrower and the danger of the whole thing collapsing seemed very real to Joseph. He often slipped on the smooth, moist limestone. He expected to see cell doors along the walls at any moment. He wondered which was more frightening – the malice of the Austrians in Venice or the ruthlessness and indifference of nature here. Did Ferretti really know what he was doing? Or would there be a report in the newspaper in a few days' time about a group of missing archaeologists, most recently seen in a camp near the Kinneret? Was the man planning to bury himself in this underground dungeon in a great act of despair, at the same time taking the entire expedition with him into death so that it would be a glorious end and he would go down in history as a martyr among Catholics?

Joseph was relieved to discern a larger space ahead of them. There were boulders everywhere.

"Start digging. Just begin there," Ferretti ordered. Joseph assumed that the Arabs were digging for nothing. But Ferretti was a skillful director.

"All right. Next, the rocks there," Ferretti said when indeed nothing turned up.

Joseph was surprised at the effect that this entire orchestration had on him. Moritz Oppenheim would be proud if he could match this. When the Church staged something, it did it well. He did not know if he should burst out laughing. Mohammed was now moving the pile of heavy stones, one by one.

A scream. It was Fonseca. "There, there. There's something there," he shouted with excitement. Everyone cheered. Was this a performance? It seemed too real. Even Richard seemed caught up in the excitement.

"Careful," Ferretti cried. "Carry it outside, to the light."

After retracing their steps, the entire group stood in a circle, blinded by the bright light of day, and looking at a bunch of shards and pieces of parchment. Joseph had no doubt that these were the broken jars and the scrolls that Ferretti had bought at the market in Tiberias and submerged in the lake to age.

"Pictures! Harrison. Take pictures!"

Ferretti now took a piece of pottery in his hand. He held it out in front of him, in a pose most reminiscent of a fisherman who had just angled a three-pounder. Joseph wondered what Ferretti had written on it. As if Ferretti had read his thoughts, he said: "Leucht. You are going to decipher this. Tonight, I want to know exactly what these texts are about."

"At your service."

The whole group went back to the camp in a euphoric mood. Ferretti rode next to Joseph: "I want you to write a thorough scientific article about this discovery. Probably, with Harrison's sketches and photos, we'll have something to come home with." He spurred his horse to ride the front of the line.

Joseph wondered when he should make the scam public. It would be dangerous to do it now. Better for him to wait until they were back in Europe. At that point, he should not tarry; there should be no trace of suspicion that he had been complicit. But for now, it would be better to play along.

Later that evening, they were startled by an uproar. Agitated and bossy voices in Turkish. Joseph looked outside the tent and saw a few Turkish officers in an intense conversation with Ferretti. The latter turned away, seemingly defeated.

"This is horrible," he exclaimed. "They are confiscating everything. And I have to go with them to Jerusalem. It seems that we didn't have a *firman* to excavate here. All of that for nothing." Joseph saw him glancing at Padovani. What a performance this man put on.

Ferretti grabbed his head again. "All for nothing," he cried again, dramatically. Minutes later, the Turkish police took Ferretti away for interrogation. As Richard and Joseph watched them go, they recognized Ferretti's sardonic smile. He was sure he would laugh last. He saw himself already being hailed as the hero of the story.

"I would like to go to Jerusalem too. My sister lives there," said Joseph, after the group had disappeared into the dark.

"Your sister? Why didn't you say so before? We will leave tomorrow. I don't think we have a role here anymore. If someone interferes, you just tell them that you can do more for Ferretti in Jerusalem than you can here. We can meet up with the group again later in Yafo."

"Maybe we could ask one of the Arabs to come with us? For safety?"

"Excellent idea. Just arrange it."

"I'll ask Rachid."

That night Joseph slept better than he had since leaving Europe. He was relieved that the dig was more or less over and that he could quit the whole expedition. And now he was going to see Rivka.

$$
3
$$

AND A LOST CITY

The journey to Jerusalem led through a rough part of the land. The
desolate landscape presented little but barren rocks. Bushes with
prickly leaves and a single tree were the only vegetation in this dry and
infertile area. Yet the journey was pleasant. Richard and Rachid were
perfect travel companions and it soon seemed that they only needed no
more than half a word in order to come to a joint decision. Joseph had
already developed a soft spot for Rachid. The Arab was the paradigm of
modesty and simplicity, always calm and always ready with a solution.
Rachid told them that he lived with his family in Yafo. Four brothers and
three sisters. "At home I wear a turban," he said, "but I find this easier
for traveling," pointing to the light green cloth over his head, tied with a
simple cord. A long cloak hung loose around him. A double band with
a richly decorated belt around his waist held a sword and a pistol to his
body, ready for immediate use, if necessary. Rachid's face always bore
a faint smile. His skin had a mysterious complexion, between olive and
almond brown. His soft eyes twinkled or suddenly sank far and deep in
the unfathomable face. He was presumably a young man, contrary to
his appearance from a distance. All in all, Joseph found him a person
of an unprecedented grandeur, frightening for a stranger, reassuring for
a friend.

They reached Jerusalem two days after leaving the Kinneret. Rachid
explained that they would approach the city from the north.

"Look carefully," Richard ordered. "Only once in your life will you
see Jerusalem for the first time."

Joseph shrugged his shoulders. "I suppose that this first time will
also be the last."

"Perhaps." Richard sounded more serious than usual. "Jerusalem is
special. Whatever you think of it, the city is the center of the world."

"For the time being, let me grant that honor to Paris."

"Paris is a temporary phenomenon compared to Jerusalem."

After climbing a steep hill they reached the plateau with the first
views of the city. Joseph dismounted, determined to look without bias
or assumptions. He had to admit that it was magnificent. It resembled
nothing he had seen before. The first image was one of an inaccessible

fortress. All around it swirled the rampart of Suleiman, with the line of battlements that followed the hill, up and down, with the gates and the larger bastions as accents. The fortress reached its peak in the Tower of David rising from damaged walls. As soon as he trained his eyes beyond the fortress, the image grew inviting. An endless number of white roofs and domes spread out in waves, interspersed with minarets and towers. Everything gleamed and glittered in the sun. Through the heat and the clear air, even the smallest details stood out sharply. Past these lay deep valleys and dark, deserted gorges. They gave Joseph the impression that a circle of graves surrounded the city. A few paths weaved fruitlessly towards the gates of the seemingly impenetrable wall. The hills around the city had the same brightness, which the nearby gray-green olive trees enhanced. The sky was of the brightest blue he had ever seen. A refreshing wind brought just enough cool air. Joseph had never before breathed more benign air. So pure and fresh. It made him think of Rome, which he had visited once when he was staying at Count Monselice's. Perhaps it was the hills… But it was more hilly here, and the oriental buildings were completely different. Rome and Jerusalem. Funny that this was exactly what Moses Hess had talked about in Paris. Had he published his book already?

"I am supposed to tear my clothes. That's the Jewish tradition."

"What is keeping you?" Richard asked.

"A well-known scholar and poet of ours, Yehuda HaLevi, tore his clothes when he first saw the city. His response to reaching Jerusalem was to recite one of his own verses, but as he was doing so, he was trampled by an Arab's horse. At least that is how the story goes." He smiled. "So it's risky. Moreover, I have not brought much clothing with me. So… maybe next time." Joseph tried to keep his tone ironic and light, but he was touched by the sight and knew that had he been alone, he might in fact have ripped his cloak, if only slightly.

The group descended into the valley where there turned out to be no graves in the end and continued along the winding path, between the tents of the Bedouins with their merchandise and their sheep and donkeys, until they reached the blackened, worn Gate of Damascus.

The racket was phenomenal. When the Arabs of the archaeological excursion had erected the tents, heaven and earth had seemed to perish from the tumult, but it was nothing compared to the cacophony that overwhelmed Joseph here. Noise, voices, clatter. From all sides the clamor of screaming, singing, and arguing bombarded his ears. He found many of the sounds impossible to identify.

Passing through the gate didn't diminish the sensations. The houses stood high on both sides, adding to Joseph's feeling of claustrophobia.

Hanging above the passages and alleys, ripped tent cloths in all colors provided some shade. Joseph sensed action and excitement everywhere. Without Richard and particularly Rachid, Joseph would probably have felt very uncomfortable, but Rachid easily sent away the Arabs who swarmed around the group.

"Let's have coffee here," Richard suggested, pointing at a few low stones that stood like chairs in front of one of the buildings. "I'm knackered and I won't make it through this spectacle without stimulants."

"Let's go somewhere else. Here it stinks," said Joseph. "It's the smell of rotten meat and excrement."

"Get used to it. That is the smell of Jerusalem."

Despite the bombardment of his senses, Joseph wanted to be open to this new culture and he was curious. Sitting on the low stones, the three were almost in the middle of the street. They had to be careful that passers-by did not knock the hot coffee out of their hands. Joseph had the feeling that they blended in nicely with this environment. Rachid naturally, and he himself now rarely wore western clothes. With his Panama, cotton shirt, and three-quarter trousers Richard stood out in contrast.

"Boys," Richard started, "what do you think of a puff?" He clapped his hands and the manager appeared. "*Nargilah*," Richard ordered. Immediately a water pipe appeared, and they took turns smoking it.

While smoking and drinking, Rachid told stories that Joseph found even more surreal than the environment itself. At one point he took out a flute and accompanied his stories with the most sorrowful tones Joseph had ever heard. When he was done, they applauded him.

"Who would have thought that of our bold guide," joked Joseph.

"Appearances can be deceiving. Things are rarely what they seem," Rachid answered.

Somewhat later he dared to ask Rachid the question that was always on his mind.

"Rachid, do you know the Convent of the Congregation of Our Lady of Zion, here in Jerusalem?"

The man nodded. "It is near the Lions' Gate, sir. Not so far from here. Why? Do you want to go into a monastery?"

"I know someone who might be there. Is it safe to go check, do you think?"

"I will accompany you. You could get into trouble alone. Too much of a tourist." He laughed when he saw Joseph's indignation. "It takes more than some oriental clothes. You still think like a European. I do not blame you for that. It takes years to come to grips with the mentality of the Orient."

"I suggest we visit our hotel first," Richard said. "Time for some freshening-up and a cool drink at the bar."

Rachid agreed. Joseph looked at him, "And the monastery...?"

"Later. Tonight. Patience is particularly important. This is not Europe, time is of no consequence here."

Their hotel was close to the Yafo Gate. The city was a labyrinth, and close up Joseph thought it horrible. The streets were dirty and it stank like a sewer. Following his companions through the bowels of the city with his nose pressed shut, Jerusalem struck him as a large decaying cemetery. The last remains of decomposing life. Richard saw Joseph's face and laughed. "This is the Holy City whether you believe it or not. The center of spiritual life on earth, a dirty maze. They say that if you get lost here, there's no love lost between you and the city."

At the Yafo Gate the alleyway ended in a large square where Joseph found that he could breathe freely again. It was crowded and chaotic but in a cheerful way. The bright sunlight on the buildings and the sharp contrasts ensured that he got another, better image of the city. A Hungarian Jew, converted to Christianity, ran the hotel. The man provided everything they needed and when Joseph and Rachid later prepared to set out for the convent, they felt refreshed and rested. In his growing anticipation, Joseph was tense. This was the reason he had embarked on this whole enterprise in the first place.

"When we arrive there, will you keep waiting for me outside?"

"As you wish. Will it take long?"

Joseph hesitated for a moment but he was motivated by sympathy for the man and decided to confide in him. "My sister is in that convent. At least that's what I heard in Paris, a few years ago; I never received a response to my letters. I so hope that she is there."

"If Allah wills it."

"*B'ezrat Hashem*, as we say."

It had turned dark and because there were no street lamps, Rachid led the way, with a lantern in his hand. Soon Joseph had lost all sense of direction. Fortunately, they didn't have any canals here that he could unexpectedly walk into.

Down the hill, they reached a larger street. "*Tareeq al Alam,*" Rachid said quietly. "For the Christians, this is the Via Dolorosa. Here it is."

Joseph looked up and saw a large, quite new building. A sign said it was the Ecce-Homo church. Next to the big gate a small sign indicated that the monastery of the sisters of Zion was located here as well. He knocked on the door and after a little while a small hatch in the door opened. Two frightened eyes under a hood looked at Joseph.

"God be with you. Can I be of service to you," came a woman's voice, in French.

Joseph explained that his sister was in the monastery. Sister Renata. He had come all the way from Europe to speak to her.

"Sister Renata might already be asleep, but I will go and see." The hatch was closed.

After a few nervous minutes it opened again and Joseph saw two querying eyes in the half-dark. Were those his sister's eyes?

"Rivka?"

"Shhst. Joseph? Is that you? Don't call me that!"

"Please, open!"

He heard her say to the mother superior in French that it was all right. "He's my brother." Then the heavy door was unlocked. Joseph recognized Rivka, but at the same time there stood a stranger in front of him. She wore a light gray habit with a dark blue shoulder cloth over it. Her face was completely surrounded by a headscarf. He stepped forward to embrace her, but she put a finger on her mouth and whispered, "Not here. Come with me to my cell."

"Cell?"

"That's what we call it," she said. She laughed. "I'm not imprisoned if that's what you think. How did you get here?"

Joseph wanted to say so much, but first he turned back to Rachid and asked him to wait. Then he followed Rivka through the dim halls and corridors of the monastery. Rivka opened a door and they were in a small room, sparingly furnished with a bed, a table with some books, and a chair. There was no window. Rivka closed the door and Joseph embraced her.

"How is the family? Aron and Nathan? Is father still alive?"

"Papa is fine. Still in Frankfurt." Joseph briefly told what he knew, not hiding that he was not in close contact with them either. "I haven't seen them for more than two years."

"Don't tell him anything about the monastery. Tell him that I live happily in a village in the south of France or something like that. Maybe I can give you a letter and then you can mail it when you are in France."

Joseph nodded. For a long time it was quiet as they just looked at each other, happy and at peace.

After a while Rivka spoke: "So, this is where I am. How did you find me?"

"There is so much to tell. Where should I start? I am on an archaeological expedition as a chronicler. I'll explain it to you later."

It was clear to Joseph that neither of them really wanted to talk about the trials of the past years. Nonetheless he had to ask. "Tell me how you come to be here. It has been tormenting me for years. I do not see the connection between Paris and Jerusalem."

She looked away. Again Joseph looked at her for a long time.

"Here I have found peace."

"And now I come to disturb that peace," he tried in a cheerful tone.

"Don't judge too quickly." She observed him carefully. "Do you want to save me?"

"Yes."

She laughed. "Well then, my savior. Do you know what? If you tell me everything first, then I will tell my story afterwards. I promise. But it's late, the nuns are supposed to be sleeping. Come to the gate tomorrow at nine o'clock. We'll take a walk and then we can talk."

Joseph agreed. "It's so good to see you."

She embraced him again. Joseph felt her weight leaning heavily on him. As if she wanted to pass on the burden after all these years. Then she gave him a kiss on his forehead. "I love you, Joseph. See you tomorrow."

"I love you too, Rivka. I never want to lose touch with you again."

The next day they walked together through the Lions' Gate towards the Kidron Valley. A pleasant, refreshing wind was blowing. Joseph told his story, starting from the evening they had said goodbye in Cologne. Without hesitation, he told about how pretentious he had become in Paris and the subsequent disasters of Venice. He concluded with the expedition. "That's why I'm here. I'm not interested in that group. I only wanted to see you."

"So you too are employed by the papists," she said laughing.

"Now it's your turn."

Rivka stopped. She looked out to the east where the Mount of Olives stood out clearly against the clear blue sky. She took a deep breath and started: "Rainer was indeed unfaithful as I suspected when I saw you in Cologne. I threatened to leave him. His answer was: "Do as you please. You're not welcome anywhere. As soon as they hear that you are a Jewess and you have left your Christian husband, you will have nowhere to go. You will come crawling back." The next day I left. I couldn't find work anywhere, because I couldn't make up a conclusive story. I had no money. I begged. I had to. The best places for begging were in the center of the city. The rest I'd rather not tell. I focused only on the here and now. No thinking, no plans. Surviving."

Joseph burst out. "Why didn't you come to me?"

"When I closed the door at Rainer's, I burned all bridges behind me.

That must sound familiar to you. You also dragged stones in a church."
She waited a second. Joseph stroked her hand tenderly. "It's all in the past. For good," he said softly.

"In the end I wanted to leave. To go far away from Paris. I wanted to live, but not in sin and not determined by my past. Someone recommended these Sisters of Zion to me. They especially take care of Jewish women. They offered this way out. Jerusalem!" She looked at him with a sad smile. "I remembered that book of yours with the pictures that we looked at together. How beautiful Jerusalem was. How peaceful it looked."

She laughed. "If I had come here as a devout Jew perhaps. But in a monastery! But despite all the misery, the suggestion gave me a glimmer of hope. If only I had a past that did not cast its shadow forward."

"Let's never talk about it again," Joseph comforted her.

"Thanks. I never even want to think about it again."

"And you really want to stay in that monastery?"

"I've actually been quite happy since coming here. I didn't think until yesterday. Now I have to think again."

"Do you want to continue your self-punishment here? Why don't you come back with me?"

"I have an important role here."

"What, repentance?"

"No. Education," she said with strength. "Sometimes we convert people. But most of the time we work to improve the relationship between Jews and Christians. We believe in God's love for the Jewish people."

Joseph laughed. "Do you hear yourself? How did you get like this? A blow to your head?"

"I have had many blows," Rivka responded seriously.

"I find it hard to believe that you are seeking salvation from people who have done so much harm to us."

"I think everything has changed now. These are good people."

"But still... You exchanged a collapsing building for one on fire."

"I try not to look at the larger picture. Just, to keep my own world in order here. Helping people. I just want to be a good person. I think that's enough." She looked down and arranged her habit. "Again, these are good people here. Two Jews who converted to Christianity founded the monastery. Their motto is that God is faithful in His love for the Jewish people and will be faithful to His promises. But I am not engaged in the actual missionary work. I teach Jewish orphans in the girls' school. There are so many people dying here because of the miserable conditions. Poor hygiene, dirty water, malnutrition. There are those who claim that the Jews' miserable existence here is proof that they are no good. Are you still religious?"

Joseph ignored her question. "For me it is important that you are happy, Rivka."

"Are you happy?"

"In fits and starts," he replied.

"But you're going back soon. To Cologne?"

"I suppose so. I expect that we will go to Italy first. After that I will need to speak to my publisher."

They walked on but eventually came back into the city via the Zion Gate.

"This is where most of the Jews of Jerusalem live," said Rivka.

They walked down the alleys. There was garbage everywhere. There were places where the stench was almost unendurable.

"This is like...."

"Say it. It's worse than the ghetto where we used to play as children."

They walked on and Rivka pointed to a ruin. A once impressive building whose arches were still standing.

"That's the *Churva*, the ruin, the old synagogue of Rabbi Yehudah *ha-chasid*. They are rebuilding it. With money from rich European Jews."

"So something is happening? They do care about what happens here."

"I'm not saying they don't care. Shiploads of money come in. But too little is happening on the ground. Far too little. At least our monastery is genuinely doing something. If there is a mission connected with that, what does it matter? Nobody is coerced. We only give them the New Testament. Those people in France and Germany donate some money and leave it at that. Jacob de Rothschild has given funds for a hospital and a school here. I understand that a delegation from the Rothschilds came here about ten years ago."

"Who? I know the family."

"I know the Rothschilds," she mimicked, mocking him. "I believe it was the son of the baron."

"Edmond? No, he is too young. It must have been Gustave. Not that it matters. But at least they are doing something."

"The Rothschilds quarreled with Montefiore. About the honor of being the first to have a hospital. I don't know the ins and outs exactly. Everything was behind the scenes of course. Rothschild won. They started a school for twenty girls. But the Ashkenazim don't want to educate their daughters." She sighed. "So Montefiore started another project, a hospital outside the walls, but that didn't get far either. Of the original plan, they built just a few houses and a grain mill. And nobody wants to live there. It's far too dangerous at night. Even the Arabs are wary of leaving the city after dark."

"So now nobody is living there?"

"I think a few families. Montefiore pays them to. The mill no longer works. It was a well-meant project, but reality is different. People in Europe have no idea how it works here. This is the Middle East. You have to deal with everyone – the Ottomans, the Arabs, and the Jews themselves who do not want progress. It is a hopeless task. Everything has only gotten worse in the last few years. First there was a cholera epidemic, then the Crimean War, which left the Jewish community without money. It is misery everywhere. I don't think Jerusalem has a future. If God wants His holy city to become special, He is making it quite hard. Poverty and bloodshed, that's her history. No higher goals at all."

"And that girls' school of Rothschild. Maybe you can teach there? Better than the lofty educational cause you are now serving."

"I think the whole project is already dead. To be honest, I thought about asking whether I could start working there. But first I will wait and see. As I said, they hardly get any pupils because the Ashkenazim don't want schooling for their daughters at all and certainly not to learn the liberal novelties of the Europeans. All they want is more *halukkah*, the hand-outs that communities collect for them in Europe. That way they can quietly study Torah and die. As they see it, anyone who acts differently or wants something else is a threat."

They now went down a steep alley. Daylight hardly reached the ground because of the many arches and spans. The bumpy cobblestones, which probably had been there for centuries, were worn out and slippery. Rivka took her brother's arm.

"Where are we, now?" Joseph asked.

"Near the wall. If you listen carefully, you can already hear the lamenting. Maybe you want to go to the Western Wall?"

"I want to go to my hotel. Away from here." After a while, he asked, "Maybe I should do something about this situation with Rainer?"

"I am far away. I don't think it matters."

"But you wouldn't be able to marry again."

Rivka laughed. "One of the first rules of a monastery is that you cannot marry." More seriously, she added: "But I wouldn't even want to. I don't trust men anymore." She smiled. "Sorry Joseph, I don't mean that personally."

They returned to the monastery.

"Then this is farewell," Rivka said.

"Not forever. I will come back or maybe you will return. But I feel much better now that I know how you live here and that you are happy."

"Don't worry too much about me. I can cope, even with my feelings of guilt."

"Feeling sorry is pointless. I always hated *Selichot*.* And so did you."

They hugged each other and Joseph walked outside to Rachid who was waiting to guide him back to the hotel.

In the hotel he learned from Rachid that the authorities had released Ferretti on bail after the intervention of a representative of the Church and the Italian consul. The group planned to return to Italy in two days. They were also counting on Joseph for the return journey; Ferretti wanted to talk to him about the documentation of their archaeological find. Rachid invited Joseph to spend the last night in the country at his family's home in Yafo. Joseph gladly accepted.

"And what do you think of the Holy City?" Richard challenged him, as they sat quietly on the terrace of the hotel with a refreshing lemonade.

Joseph looked at the bare, dusty hills in the distance. "I have spoken with people in Europe who dream of the Jews' return to *Eretz Israel* as they call it. Not a settlement, not a poor existence in Jerusalem to die. No, a country with its own laws. A state for the people. One of them was a socialist and a nationalist, another was driven by religious motives. Each of them interpreted the spirit of the times in his own way – I have to say opposite ways – but they both think the time has come for us to come back." He laughed ashamed. "Strange. I don't know why I suddenly say *us*."

"Maybe this visit has awakened more than you want to admit."

"I don't know." Joseph tried to appear more rational than he actually felt. "I think the land, and particularly Jerusalem, is a mess. I have no illusions whatsoever that any of these ideas will be realized. No sensible person comes here of his own free will. Except perhaps a few fortune-hunters like you, Richard." He added: "Besides that, the Turks simply won't allow it."

"For me it is not a choice. I can't help but be here, in the Levant. Total love. I would die in Europe."

"Somehow I think it's time for me to go home."

"Then we will say goodbye, my friend."

"Goodbye. Although maybe it is farewell." He looked at Richard attentively. "There is someone else here whom I also wanted to visit. I asked about her, but they say she has moved away from Jerusalem. Somewhere near Bethlehem, perhaps. Her name is Elsa Blumenreich.

From Cologne. Of course, she could have changed her name. But I have to go back with the expedition now. I don't want to be stuck here."

"Maybe I can visit her and convey a message. Tell her you've been here." He laughed provocatively. "And that you hope to visit her next time."

"Next time?" He caught himself thinking that he somehow agreed to a next time. He had said it to Rivka as well. But how realistic was it to think that he would ever come back?

"Maybe you can bring her a letter?"

"I know what you're thinking. Let me tell you – someone who has been here will come back."

Both men stared into the distance unwilling to bring the conversation to a close.

"Do you already know what you're going to do?"

"I think I'm going back to Germany." Joseph thought for a moment. "I need a goal. I need to move forward. I need to get rid of the past."

Joseph found the journey back to Europe long and boring. He stood on the bow of the ship and peered ahead. His heart was heavy. Was it because he had left Palestine or because he was returning to Germany?

Thoughts of that last night, at Rachid's house, came to him. The visit had turned out to be one of the most enchanting evenings of Joseph's life. Rachid and his parents lived in a small building in one of the oldest parts of Yafo, on the hill. As Joseph had entered the front doorway, he felt that a new world had opened. Never before he had been received so cordially. He felt immensely honored. Rachid's father, Hassan, and one of his brothers, Jamal, were at home. Sounds of cooking came from the kitchen where the women were busy, but to Joseph's surprise he didn't see them all evening.

At first they had drunk tea with fresh mint leaves, sitting on a traditional rug in what could be called the living room. It was a colorful interior with carpets of all shapes and sizes against the low walls and on the ground. On them stood objects whose purpose Joseph could not even guess. Rachid's mother had prepared several dishes; specialties from the Levant, Joseph would have called them, but for Rachid's family it was their usual meal. *Baba ghanoush* and then lamb with *mezze*, a selection of side dishes. Rachid had told stories that would have been unbelievable or at least mysterious to the ears of Joseph the Westerner, but after the weeks he had spent here, he knew better. After dinner they had smoked a water pipe. Rachid had played the flute while his father sang, and Joseph had fallen asleep to the sound of the never-ending melancholy scales. But what had lingered the most – as he now smelled the penetrating, salty sea – were the sharp, oriental scents.

The whole expedition was very festively received in Trieste. Joseph was pleasantly surprised when he saw Elia standing among the crowd. Cardinal Von Schwarzenberg was present, as were also Count and Countess Monselice. Ferretti turned their arrival into a big show. Exercising his sense of drama, the expedition director told about the find and then gave the evidence to the cardinal. While he presented the accompanying documents, he called Joseph over. "Johann Leucht, our chronicler, helped with the scientific research." The cardinal took the time to thank Joseph personally and if Joseph had not known better he would have felt proud, especially with the Countess's gracious eyes on him. He was happy when the official ceremonies were over and he could leave with Elia. The Count and Countess had asked them to spend the week at their country house and the two men had gratefully accepted.

Over the next days Joseph wrote his article about the events as they had actually happened, about the fraud and the deception. He concluded with a diatribe against the hypocrisy of the Church and the intertwining of power and morality. Elia was satisfied, hoping that this might be a substantial blow to the Catholic Church, compelling the French to support Italy.

"I want to publish it tomorrow."

"Before you do, I need to explain to the Count and Countess what I did and why."

"I will accompany you."

"No. I will acquit you. Do you think they will betray me to the Austrians?"

"Frankly, I don't think so. But I have seen stranger things."

A servant let Joseph into the room where he had had dinner before his journey. After the obligatory acts of politeness, Joseph handed the article to the Count and asked him to read it. When his host was finished, his hand slowly went down and he looked at Joseph for a long time. He gave the paper to his wife who immediately started reading.

She had not finished when Monselice asked, "Why?"

"Because I think the Church and the Austrians deserve this, not to mention the way they personally treated me."

The Countess had also read the article now, and she looked Joseph straight in the eye: "Is this your gratitude?"

"I write nothing against you," Joseph defended himself. "That is why I am here. Distance yourself from that group. They are evil, not me."

"But you played along all the time just to take revenge. That makes you a bad person. We want you to leave now," said the Countess and she started to get up. But the Count interrupted her. "When will this be published?"

"It is planned for tomorrow. But I can probably hold back the publication for a few days, if you would like."

Monselice nodded, deep in thought. He called and a servant showed Joseph out.

Joseph immediately left with Elia and the day after he headed by coach for Germany, homeward. The problems of Italy were not his. He wanted to be far from Venice when the article came to light. He did not want to be stuck there again. They would certainly not have forgotten his previous stay. No, Italy was not safe until the Austrians and the whole Church was gone.

Back in Germany, he received a letter from Elia about the aftermath. The article had been published and it had caused a shock. Ferretti had been arrested and public opinion against the Church had increased. Monselice and the Countess had unconditionally chosen the side of the Risorgimento and were thankful for Joseph's warning. Joseph read about these events as if they were a story from another era. He had had his revenge but it had given him no satisfaction at all.

$$\overline{4}$$

(1862)

Back Again

The visit to his father in Frankfurt played out exactly as Joseph expected. He felt ashamed that it had been four years since he had seen him. The house still had the same furnishings and his father had hardly changed either. Joseph enjoyed entertaining him with the tales of his Palestine and Jerusalem adventures. Joseph could not tell the old man that Rivka was in a monastery. He had promised her and, more, he worried that perhaps his father would not survive the news. As agreed, Rivka had given him letters to post. She supposedly lived happily in France with her husband.

Aron was teaching at a *Yeshiva* in Frankfurt. He was married to Batia Kleinblatt and now had three children, all boys. They lived three houses further on. His father had recently celebrated his fifty-fifth birthday and although he was still healthy, Joseph was glad that someone who could look after him lived nearby. Joseph had to admit that Batia looked good despite her religious clothing. Of course he had not been to the *brit milah** of any of his nephews.

Aron was the only one of the Socher children who was still religious, because Nathan too had abandoned the faith. From one day to the next he had left the Jewish practice completely and now called himself John. He had taken over his father's business and had started a clothing store in London, *Sach Clothing*. While Joseph was riding through the plains in Palestine, Nathan had married a Christian girl, Penelope Pratley. His father had given up fighting it, but had refused to go to the wedding ceremony in a church in London. "So, he thinks it's better in distant London than in good old Germany. Let him go," his father said. Joseph could not completely disagree with his brother, but he said nothing. He realized that of the four children he was not even the one who had strayed the farthest.

The visit was not unpleasant but it didn't yield anything either. Their views remained unchanged and it turned out best not to really talk about anything, but just to stick to stories. Nevertheless, Joseph left Frankfurt with a sigh of relief, which slowly deepened into a darker mood during the train journey back to Cologne.

Joseph had now been back in Germany for two years, and time had passed like a sigh. He had taken up his life as if nothing had happened. He had even gone back to his old apartment. When he opened the door, he felt like he had been defeated. He was back in the house on which he had turned his back years before, with much fanfare, because something better happened for him. Paris – an opening to a new world. But it had turned out to be an illusion. Coming back, Joseph had had to walk through the door of the past again. He smelled the house of the past – the same stones, the same decor – but if there was a difference, it was for the worse; it no longer held the promise of those days.

Sometimes he browsed through the articles he had written in the past two years, seeking inspiration, just as he always thought he had written the perfect sentence and only had to look at his old notes in the cabinet to find it.

In the beginning he had been afraid that his abstinence from alcohol would also drain him of ideas, that his writing would prove to be a sober, boring affair lacking ingenious ideas and inspired thoughts. He was relieved to discover that the opposite was true. Now he could organize his sentences better. And looking at them again, Joseph had to admit that most of the things he had written under the influence did not deserve much more than the trashcan.

As he browsed from article to article, he noticed that, although the content varied – from the completion of the cathedral to Courbet's paintings, and from Italy's struggle for freedom to the demise of the mail coach with the arrival of the railways – his work had a specific undertone of alienation and soullessness. Of misanthropy and even cynicism. An objective reader would perhaps not even have noticed, but Joseph knew better. Now that he was trying to read the articles objectively, he could only conclude that the writer did not write with passion about his subjects. The text was to the point, and it had style, but there was no drive. Everything was detached, without involvement. Every opinion was autonomous. There was no greater meaning, no inspired strands that riveted the words to the world and to society. He was a chameleon who could take on all colors and he had just as easily written a militant plea in favor, as a tirade against the influence of the French on the Germans. Joseph felt that had he not penned these pieces, no one would have noticed or cared. *Beziehungslos*, without connection, orphaned. There was something missing but he had no idea where to look for it.

His ambitions had faded. When he had first arrived in Cologne more than ten years ago, he would have sold his soul for success and glory as a writer. But now he accepted that things were as they were. It was easier to be ambitious if the goal was far away. Then, the thought of failure had hardly any influence. The distance to the fictitious ideal was infinitely great. But as soon as the realization came closer, things changed. As the goal was no longer inaccessibly far away, the thought of failure became unbearable. Then it was better to stay put and do what you had to do. Ideals were for dreamers.

In Paris he had been full of himself. Much too full. But now he was empty, as he put it in one of his personal notes. Independent, strong, knowledgeable, successful, convincing, and above all, empty.

"Lichtman, we have to talk," said Pennekamp with his most reassuring voice, although it sounded a bit ominous to Joseph. They were in the publisher's office. Joseph had continued to work for the publisher after his return. "You are older and wiser, full of facts, accomplished and widely traveled. We will certainly benefit from that," Pennekamp said. Curiously, until now the man had not mentioned his imprisonment, but Joseph was more than happy about that. His journey to the Holy Land, on the other hand, had come under extensive discussion. Joseph had climbed up to the post of deputy editor-in-chief, which in practice meant that he was almost running the newspaper. Pennekamp was gradually withdrawing because of his age and ailing health.

"How are things? What about the family?"

Pennekamp had never asked about Joseph's family before and his doing so put Joseph on edge.

"Nothing special. The usual, sir."

"Good. Very good. And you, yourself? You're already around thirty, right? Do you have family plans?"

Joseph scrutinized Pennekamp. He shook his head. No, he had no plans.

Pennekamp offered him a cigar.

"Have you ever had wedding plans? Interest in the fairer sex?"

"Certainly, but the question of marriage has never arisen."

In fact, Joseph had decided that it was better to be alone. A woman would only demand attention, money, and time. He had managed well until now without one. In addition, he feared for his freedom. Under no circumstances was he prepared to sacrifice anything of himself. Once, for Maria, he had wanted to do so, but that had been a foolish infatuation. He knew better now. He needed only himself. He did not want anyone to impose on him a compelling rhythm like a metronome; his life had to be an infinite *rubato*.

"You know my daughter, don't you? Hilde," continued Pennekamp. Joseph nodded again.

"What do you think of my daughter?"

Joseph foresaw what was coming, although he could not believe it. This was unreal.

"I like her very much."

"Could she be a marriage candidate for you?"

He stuttered. "Why me?"

Anton confided in him. "It's not easy for her. You would be doing a good deed. The suitors are not exactly queuing in front of our door. We don't have any real capital so a candidate from the truly eminent families isn't realistic. You are precisely the right person. No financial problems. More, you are a decent boy, you work hard. As far as I know, you have always been very kind to my daughter. I think it would work." He waited as if to fathom Joseph's reaction. "But there is another reason as well. I don't have eternal life. To be honest, I feel weaker every day and I assume that the end isn't far. I want you to become family, so that you can succeed me in the business. As a son-in-law, there would be no question about your taking over. But that means a marriage to Hilde. Quid pro quo. I have always heard that Jews are good at doing business."

Joseph ignored the last remark. "Does she know about this? What does she think?"

"I mentioned it once and I don't think she has any problems with it."

No problems. As if that were sufficient for a marriage!

"I would like to live up to your trust in me. I am very honored by your offer," said Joseph to save some time.

"You are best qualified to lead the publishing house. I know that, you know that. But others? My son also has ambitions, and although I think he is a lesser candidate, I might eventually have to give him priority if you reject the proposal." Pennekamp was lost in thought. "That wouldn't be the best thing for the company." He laughed. "As you can hear, I'm not much of a businessman. I give up my conditions even before the negotiations have begun."

Joseph laughed as well. "Honesty is the best policy." Then, fearing that the statement might seem too light-hearted, he added, "I will seriously consider your proposal."

"I must tell you that there is something else. If you decide to marry Hilde, you will have to be baptized. But I don't think that's a problem?"

Joseph tried to hide his confusion. "I will think about it."

"Splendid. I have a nice idea. Why don't the two of you take a trip together. To see how you get along with each other, how things work out. I pictured a tour to Weimar. Afterwards, you decide."

High above him, the trees opened up in fans of branches on which the first new leaves announced themselves in a green haze. Underneath, between the rising trunks, it was empty and quiet. Sharp beams of light fell here and there on the ground covered with brown, rotten mulch. Joseph's feet sank into it. He remembered Elsa's *Waldeinsamkeit* and Friedrich's painting. This was indeed Germany. "*Warte nur, balde ruhest du auch.*" [10] He shivered. It was cold and he pulled his cloak closer around him. The wind was bleak, even for April. Spring had not yet begun here in Weimar.

He had decided to go for a walk on his own in the woods on the Ettersberg. The owner of the hotel where he and Hilde were staying, had explained exactly where Goethe had found inspiration. "In the beech forest under the large oak tree, where he met his Charlotte; *im Buchenwald,*" the man had told him.

Joseph did not care to bring Hilde, assuming that she would just blabber the whole time. In fact, he didn't care for Hilde at all.

He found the oak and sat against the trunk. Waiting. It was still early and there was no one else. After a while he decided that there was no inspiration. At least, no more than he found when sitting at his desk in Cologne, which wasn't replete with inspiration either. Neither Hilde nor the oak could be his muse.

Joseph and Hilde had been in Weimar now for a couple of days. They had taken the mail coach, because Hilde wanted to make a trip in the style of the famous. "This way we can be close to German art. Breathe the atmosphere of Goethe and Schiller, Bach and Friedrich." He had agreed. More significant disputes would surely be on the horizon. In any case, this time he did not have to sit on the box or get off before the end.

Since their arrival, they had already been to two musical soirees but they had not met any of the virtuosi who lived in the city. This evening they had been invited to the *Altenburg* and all of the important people would be there. The piano recital consisted of pieces by Schubert, Schumann, and Wagner. In the end the whole thing evoked a deep melancholy in Joseph. He felt as if hope had left this world.

At the reception after the performances, Joseph joined a few music connoisseurs who stood somewhat apart. He believed that he had seen one of them before, Schmidt was his name. The group was engaged in an animated conversation about the great romantic war that was raging in the music world, as if there weren't enough misery in the world already. Wagner on the one hand and Brahms on the other. All composers took Beethoven's music as their starting point, but each did something different with it. Joseph could not help but laugh. It sounded like the Liberal and Orthodox Jews with the Torah. Apparently, this was a universal phenomenon.

"There will be a big schism in German music," Schmidt predicted.

Another man turned to Joseph. "Pleased to meet you, my name is Klausen. Isn't it fantastic, Wagner's music?"

"Lichtman," Joseph replied. Quickly unearthing the old antagonism of his Paris years, he said, "That man is evil."

"I don't understand. What do you mean?"

"Haven't you seen his latest writings? His essay on Jews in music?"

"And what does Wagner write?" Schmidt asked now.

"Judaism in Music. How the influence of the Jews brings everything down."

"If Wagner says so, it must be true. He knows the music world like no one does," Klausen said.

"But apparently he didn't dare to write it in a personal capacity. He used a pen name," said Joseph, "not very sincere." He continued, "I have a completely different opinion. I believe that the Jews will add something fundamental to German art."

The men looked up taken aback. "Please explain yourself."

"Heine is of course the best example. More will follow. I think they have different ideas about art than the standard Romantics. Jews have other ways of representing things, symbols, abstractions. I think they will have a big influence."

"Yes, it will make them richer and us poorer," Klausen said, and both men roared. They indicated that they had seen someone else in the crowd and before he knew it, Joseph was on his own with Hilde. He looked at her and wondered again what had driven Hilde to agree with her father's plan.

"Don't do that when we are married," she said in an annoyed tone. He didn't know if he should laugh or get angry.

"We're not going to get married," he assured her. "And anyway, you don't want to marry a Jew."

"Don't you want to be baptized?" She seemed really surprised, as if she had offered him a huge bag of money and he refused it. The fact that Joseph did not want to marry her apparently left her untouched. "You are not really Jewish anymore. Moreover, everyone here sees us already as husband and wife."

He kept silent, but he knew that he would not convert. A marriage with Hilde was out of the question, and refusing baptism would give him a strong excuse without explicitly rejecting her. It was more than an excuse. Baptism was not an option. He did not want to be sprinkled by a priest. Judaism might be in decline, but he did not want to leave it. Christianity was not for him. If he believed in anything, it was in the God of Abraham. No other one. He did like that Abraham. Or was it perhaps love for his own people, for his family, for his upbringing, for the age-old tradition? Moritz Oppenheim's paintings of warmth and love in the old ghetto?

Joseph found Weimar very provincial and the trip a waste of time, and he was happy when they packed their suitcases the next day. As they neared Cologne, he noticed that the towers of the cathedral had grown higher and the middle section was now complete.

Joseph caught himself reminiscing more and more about the journey to Palestine. In his first year back, the memories had mainly remained subconscious. Sometimes one would surface at the smell of an herb, a sound reminiscent of the thud of walking on a dusty path, or the image of sharp sunlight on a late summer evening. When that happened, it sent him back, heart and soul, and melancholy took hold of him. He rationalized the reaction by reminding himself that life had been terrible there. Nostalgia was a bad counselor. But in truth, the gloomy light and the moist, wet smell in the streets of Cologne were not an appealing alternative.

Often when he was alone in the evening in his room, quietly puffing his pipe, Joseph imagined that he was smoking a water pipe with Rachid at the Damascus Gate. He could almost taste the strong, dark coffee. Cheerful oriental music swirled through his head; a few men got up and started dancing. Rachid looked at him and smiled. "This is life," he said, moving his head rhythmically to the music. Joseph would hold the vision for as long as he could. The memories were dear to him and the hopeless misery he had seen there, proved no antidote to his melancholy. The feeling sometimes stayed with him for days and despite everything, it made him feel better.

Sometimes he sought refuge in musical evenings. They were also heartwarming and inspiring, but in the music itself he often found an undertone of melancholy as well. Beethoven's piano sonatas or Chopin's nocturnes made him even more gloomy. Somehow, a light in him had gone out and, although he was aware of it, he had no idea how to rekindle it.

He wondered whether change would come by itself. Should he wait for it? Or should he take action? And what should he do then? Visiting people was often an obligation and it didn't really make him happy.

Usually Joseph declined invitations. The Pennekamps and the Löwes had their own lives and he didn't want to become part of them. Max was the exception to the rule.

One day he was sitting in his usual spot in the local cafe waiting for Max. Could it be? Could that woman who – with a flamboyant presence – had just entered, be Maria Löwe? He quickly moved out of her line of sight, and positioned himself so that he could keep staring, mesmerized. The confirmation came from the person who followed her. Werner, but in a modified version. He had become bulky and puffy. Signs of a life that was too good and too lazy. Joseph had heard that Werner had been assigned a diplomatic post in Vienna and had not been home for years. He was married. They had written a few times but for Joseph, the memory of his sister had always been in the way. Gradually the old friend had disappeared from Joseph's life. Maria had hardly changed. There was no nod to age, only to fashion. Her hair was arranged in the latest style and a distinctive necklace and wide bracelets decorated her white skin. A long violet silk garment with fringes to the ground and a soft pink cardigan that half covered her upper body gave her a posh appearance. Observing her attentively, he wondered what he had seen in her. But the compulsion, the lust to have her burst from deep within him, as if he had stored it like a dried flower between the pages of a book and now the page had fallen open.

Did he want to see her, to accept her unintended challenge? Could he bear the humiliation of her potential rejection? Joseph decided that he had nothing to lose. His social position was strong, he was a man of the world. And despite the many years, despite the distance, all the sensations of his crush, his obsession, returned against his will. Perhaps he was not master of his own will at all and Schopenhauer was more right than he cared to admit. He was not at all free in what he wanted.

Nevertheless, Joseph pulled his coat far over his shoulders and deeply covered his head with his beret when he tried to leave the establishment. He could visit Max at home.

"Johann? Johann? Is that you?"

No way back. Smiling in welcome, he said, "Look here. The Löwe family. What a pleasant surprise."

Werner was jovial as always. In the end, their conversation was confined to nothing more than recalling memories. After half an hour Werner said he had to attend to some business and left. Joseph was also planning to leave but Maria stopped him.

"Don't go yet. Will you order me something to drink?"

"Of course."

Nervously, he walked to the bar. He decided to have a glass of wine, just this once, to take away the edge of the encounter. But to his surprise, being alone with Maria wasn't awkward at all. She looked at him. Was it different than it used to be? Was she acknowledging his new, higher status?

"I hear you are doing well." Her voice was full of respect.

Did he have a choice whether to fall in love again? He had expected that he would be completely overwhelmed, should they ever meet, which is why he had not wanted to see her again in the first place. It was why he had kept Werner at a distance. Still, hadn't he been longing for this for years? Didn't she symbolize what a full life could offer? Weimar might have convinced him that he did not want to marry Hilde, but it had helped him begin to recognize the benefits of a companion. Someone who would be attentive to his accounts and experiences. At the Löwes he had to keep up appearances. During the expedition he had to remain inaccessible. With his brother Aron he had to be the intellectual, with Werner the cheerful boy. Even with Max, he was alert, aware of himself. There was always a pose. But with Maria, he now felt at ease. She listened to his stories raptly and satisfied his curiosity about what had happened to her in the intervening years. Maria had lived in Berlin all this time but her husband had died a few years ago from tuberculosis. Joseph spoke a hundred words about his adventures abroad and Maria was all ears. He kept silent about his prison story. With great pride and only slight exaggeration, he reported that Pennekamp had asked him to take over the publishing company and that his future was secure. When they said goodbye, his glass of wine stood untouched on the table.

He couldn't get Maria out of his head, so a week later he made the reluctant decision to visit the Löwes. Like his daughter, Maria's father had not changed a bit. However, they had taken a cat as pet, according to the latest trend. While Löwe was talking, the animal jumped onto his lap.

"We liberals are people of the world," he said with a lot of fuss, stroking the purring animal. "We are enlightened. We don't think in boxes. We have to educate the dumb masses that don't know it yet. But in the end, it will also become clear to them. Everyone will choose our way. No more dull bourgeoisie. Isn't that right, *Mitzi*?"

The cat turned her head to the man as if she agreed. Joseph smiled. To him, *Mitzi* represented the ultimate symbol of bourgeoisie.

In the following weeks, Joseph and Maria saw each other more often and Maria was always very attentive to him. Was she warmer to him than to others? Secretly, Joseph began to believe that there was a possibility. For Hilde he would not be baptized, for sure, but for Maria? Then he remembered Ferretti, Padovani, and all those other hypocrites of the Catholic Church. It would be difficult. He tried not to dwell on this theoretical game, but still the thoughts kept feeding his imagination.

"*Mitzi* died a couple of days ago," said Werner when Joseph next visited the Löwes. "Father is inconsolable. Maybe it would be better to come another time."

"For better or for worse," Joseph said, but when he saw Werner's look he understood that this was no laughing matter. "Can I help with something?"

"We're going to bury him. In the garden."

"Is Maria here?"

Werner looked at him disapprovingly: "No. I don't know where she is."

Joseph walked with Werner to the back door and in the small garden he saw Mr. Löwe standing with a shovel in his hands. He had a large hood over his head against the drizzly rain.

"Shall I do the digging?" offered Joseph

"No, this is something I have to do myself."

Joseph saw that the man pulled a few heavy tiles away from the edge of the patio and started digging. Next to him sat a bundle of cloth containing the dead animal, Joseph assumed. It started to rain harder. When Mr. Löwe had dug a large hole, he picked up the bundle and carefully lowered it into the dirt. He turned around, apparently overwhelmed by emotion. Werner put his arm around his father's shoulders. Joseph grabbed the shovel and looked at Werner askance. He nodded and father and son went inside. It was pouring now and Joseph wanted to finish the job quickly. In the pit lay the dead evidence of a modern, clean, well-organized household. He filled the hole and then dragged one of the tiles over it. He had had enough of this melodrama. He was prepared to go straight home, but from the doorway, *Herr* Löwe beckoned him.

"Thank you, my boy, for helping us in this difficult hour."

"It was no trouble," he replied. He told Werner he had an appointment. As he left the saddened family, Joseph wondered what was going on with the world.

"We have planned a trip with some friends this weekend," Werner told him. "Hiking in nature, a bit of hunting. If you want, I will also ask Maria. We will spend the night in a lodge of one of my friends. You want to join us?"

The plan was to take a long walk on Saturday in the fields south of Cologne. They would have a picnic en route and stay the night in the small hunting lodge. The weather was forecast to get better after days of rain. Spring was again long in coming.

Indeed, on Saturday the sun came out and it promised to be a beautiful day. Joseph was in high spirits. Besides from being together with Maria, it somehow seemed right for him to shift his thoughts with an outdoor activity. In addition to Werner and Maria, there were two couples Joseph didn't know and there was Brecht. A robust, tough soldier, his parents were the owners of the lodge.

During the walk Joseph tried to keep up with Maria as much as possible, without being too obvious. When she walked with the others, in front of him, he kept a close eye on her. In his jealousy, her every smile and compliment seemed a challenging flirtation. Sadly he noticed that he had not made much progress with her since his visit to the cathedral.

They had walked for a few hours when Joseph suddenly recognized where he was. The crossroads where he had gotten out of the carriage, long ago. The cross was still there. He remembered the dry winter air.

"Let's have our picnic here," suggested Brecht. The group spread out two large blankets and laid out the food. Joseph did not end up on the same blanket as Maria. When the meal was finished, he was the first to propose moving on.

A stretch of the path was flooded from the rain and Joseph wanted to give Maria a hand, but Brecht beat him to it. As Maria grinned, Brecht lifted her up and carried her across. While Joseph stood watching at the side of the path, he suddenly felt himself slipping. Unable to stop it, he sank into the mud up to his knees. None other than Brecht reached over to help him to get out. Everyone was laughing; Maria roared. Under normal circumstances, Joseph would have seen the fun of all this, but now it felt like the company was mocking him. And he also felt – on many levels – ridiculous. Nonetheless, he put on a brave face and laughed along.

"I hate swamps," he tried to say casually, while wiping off the worst of the dirt. A brown plant fiber stuck stubbornly to his shoe. With nostalgia he thought of Rachid. His trusted guide would not be a luxury now. With the memory, the window on that other world opened again. Werner patted Joseph kindly on his back. "Come on. We're almost at the hunting lodge. You can clean up there."

Soon enough, the group reached the lodge. Joseph washed himself as best as he could. He had brought no spare clothes and his trousers were too dirty to wear. He rinsed these into a bucket of water and wrapped himself in a large blanket, hoping that they would dry quickly. By the time he joined the others, they had already put the food on the table.

The whole evening his frustration only grew. Maria flirted with everyone. She was nice to him but he had to admit that there was no special spark. He was exhausted but did not want to go to sleep before anyone else so that he could keep an eye on her. Even if he didn't have a chance, it would be good to know that the others didn't either. Late in the evening Maria indicated she was going to bed and a little later he saw Brecht going upstairs also. Joseph did not want to know the sequel. He said goodnight to Werner and went to bed.

Half an hour later he woke up. For a moment he thought he heard a soft giggle. A thought that he absolutely did not want to pursue, poked at his consciousness again and again. They wouldn't? He dismissed the idea, then sat up straight, his ears straining. Nothing to be heard. He just had to go back to sleep. It was preferable not to know, so in his ignorance he could still think that Maria would not do something like that. It was better to live in a dream than to have full knowledge.

Joseph resigned himself to the fact that he would always remain a loser in the eyes of women; that had become very clear today. Or maybe he would always just be a loser. Here he was. An adult man who had experienced a lot; who had been invited by important people, traveled. And he felt like a fourteen-year-old boy who had given the wrong answer in the classroom. Where was his former boldness, his self-assurance? He just wanted to crawl away into a corner.

Back in Cologne a few days later, unable to shake the torment of the outing, Joseph decided to try his luck once and for all. He would never forgive himself if he didn't. This story had to be finished. The trip to Weimar had made clear that Hilde was not an option. But he didn't know how much pressure Anton would put on him. If he already had a fiancée, it would solve at least that problem. That evening he went to the Löwes to put out a feeler with Maria's father about a possible marriage.

For half a minute the man looked at him dead serious and then he burst out laughing.

"What, you? Marrying my daughter? *Herr* Lichtman, you must be drunk."

Joseph did not know what to say.

"Why?" he asked faintly.

"Because I don't want you in the family."

"Do you disapprove of me personally, then?"

"No. Because you are Jewish. I say it honestly." The man looked triumphant. "You see, your people are no good. You are not the chosen people at all. You supposedly represent God but see what you look like. Paupers and vagrants. That God of yours is doing bad business."

Joseph did not know how to react. It did not even occur to him to announce that he could convert. He was stupefied. He had gone through all the reasons for a rejection beforehand, but this was too absurd. "I thought you supported me, but you're cut from the same cloth as any narrow-minded bourgeois. Jews fine, but not too close. Not too high up, and certainly not in the family."

"Who do you think you are? Be gone. Burn in hell, that you will."

For a moment Joseph wanted to reply that there was no hell in his faith, but he kept quiet. This was not a competition to see who was the wittiest. This was not about winning or losing. This was just the end. He got up and took his hat. How could this man be the same as the man who had invited Joseph to drink with him, who had always received him so kindly? Could anyone change this much, or had it always been there under the surface? Did Löwe believe that no education, training, or experience could erase the brand? He could wash and scrub himself, but not even baptism would remove the mark.

In his anger, he decided to deal with everything at once. If he couldn't have Maria, then he didn't need anyone, particularly not Hilde. He felt obligated to report to Pennekamp that it had not worked out, although Hilde would have told him that already. When Joseph came to the house he saw that the curtains were closed. He knocked and Horst opened the door.

"Ah, Lichtman, quiet please, our father is not well. Maybe it's better not to visit him." That was fine with Joseph. He did not fancy a fight with Horst today.

The next day Joseph received a note from the Pennekamp family that explicitly asked him not to visit Anton because of the publisher's severe condition. But, after a few days, Joseph couldn't bear it anymore. He told Max and together they went to Pennekamp. Hilde opened the door, looking anxious. "He is dying. You can visit him for a moment, but keep it short." Her words were addressed to Max, as if Joseph were not there.

A bed stood in a corner of the drawing room and in it, Joseph saw the emaciated face of his publisher. The last thing he should tell this man was that he would not marry his daughter. At the bedside sat his wife Odette, who briefly nodded when they entered, but then fell back to herself, her eyes cast down.

With a weak voice Pennekamp said: "Max, Johann. Come closer. Why haven't you come before? But then again, perfect timing. The light is going out. I can feel it."

They sat down next to the bed. Hilde took a seat at the end. Again she expressed her concern that this visit was actually too exhausting for her father.

"Johann. I want you to run the publishing house. You are witnesses." He looked at Odette and then at Hilde. "Help him, right?"

"Of course, Vati." Max tried to tell a story from the past, as if the memory of good life could keep death at bay, but Horst's entrance interrupted him. He threw his jacket aside and whispered to Hilde with restrained anger, "I told you not to let Lichtman in. He only brings misery." Apparently it didn't matter to him that Joseph could hear every word.

"We will go," said Joseph. He took Pennekamp's hand and kissed it. "Farewell, my friend, and thank you for all you have done for me."

They left the house together, in silence. After a while Max softly said: "It looks like Horst is not very fond of us, nor is he charmed by the idea that you are going to lead the publishing house."

"But Mr. Pennekamp said it himself and there are witnesses."

"I only warn you. Just gird yourself."

The next day Max came to tell him that Antonius Maria Pennekamp had passed away at the age of sixty-three. The funeral was on Saturday morning in the church near Pennekamp's home, in the *Sankt Maria im Kapitol*. Joseph had passed it often and thought it a rather nice building. From its sides extended a few cheerful, round chapels and the stone itself had a warm color. But now it was different. Now he had to enter.

The interior was a relief compared to the cathedral. There was no attempt here to destroy the human dimension and to belittle the visitor with mystical megalomania. If the all-pervading smell of incense had not been present, Joseph could have imagined that this was a synagogue, but the choir, which started singing high above him as a sign that mass had begun, brought him back to reality. The church attendants came in and walked down the aisle to the coffin that had been placed in the middle of the church. The smell of the incense was overwhelming. Joseph slipped quietly out of the building. To his delight he saw Max standing, outside.

"Even too much for me," Max said with a sad smile.

"The building is nice."

"Anton certainly would have liked it."

They were still sharing memories of Pennekamp when the procession left the church for the cemetery. The priest walked in front, holding a cross high in hands. Next came the boys with the incense. Then, the coffin, carried by six men. Joseph recognized Horst. His face was expressionless. Behind it came Odette and Hilde. It was far too cold for a day in May. Joseph joined the line.

Max, standing next to him at the open grave, nodded at the coffin that slowly disappeared into the ground. "Funerals are okay, but I hate the burial. Too much personal mortality."

When it was all over, Horst Pennekamp came over to them. Turning to Joseph, he asked, "Can you come to the office tomorrow? We need to discuss a number of issues now that father has gone." The tone was businesslike, but Joseph heard hostility in it.

With a fearful premonition he went to the publisher's office. Horst let him in, but did not offer him a chair.

"I have had my lawyers prepare the paperwork for the continuation of the publishing company. You had better not have any false illusions."

Joseph quickly browsed through the papers but couldn't make any sense out of the legal language.

"What does this mean?"

"This means that I am the one hundred percent owner of the publishing house and that I and I alone, as director, am continuing the business."

"I have witnesses that your father saw me as his successor."

"My father was on his deathbed. He was no longer fit or qualified to make any serious decisions. Every judge will agree with me. Listen. I might allow you to write something for us occasionally, but I will never hand over our family property to a Jew. Over my dead body. You people must know your place."

Joseph stared around as if he was looking for inspiration in the shelves full of books that Anton Pennekamp had collected. How could that man have such a son?

"I have rights. I also helped him grow this company."

"We won't let you go empty-handed. My lawyers said that you could not challenge a dismissal, but that you had grounds to claim a financial compensation. I am reasonable."

"So?"

Horst handed him a piece of paper. "This is our offer. Take it. There will be no other."

Joseph looked at the paper and saw the amount. Redemption money. Should he not just walk out the door and spit on everything that happened here? On the other hand, living a good life was a worthy revenge. The amount was considerable; enough to ensure a carefree life for a number of years. He signed.

Max agreed that there was little to be done about it.

"Some people just don't like us no matter how hard we try. Just accept it."

"But I can't accept this."

"As a matter of fact you already have. But you will have plenty of opportunities to write and I will introduce you to other people. You don't have to worry."

Joseph did not share Max's optimism. "I've been thinking about it all. Assimilation doesn't help. You see the signs of hatred everywhere, against the assimilated and even against the baptized."

Max looked at him with compassion. "I don't know what would be a good choice right now."

Joseph shrugged his shoulders.

Almost as if speaking for himself, Max continued in a soft, sad tone. "Maybe we should just admit that Heine was mistaken about his baptism. For a long time I thought that rationality would win here in Germany. That it was just about social classes and standing and it would dissolve with socialism and enlightenment. But it has started to dawn on me that what we face is of a different order. It is a form of hatred beyond all forms. And if so, where does it come from?"

"The greatest champion of socialism is a hater of Jews. The greatest composer is a hater of Jews, you name them. When I read the great philosophers, I am impressed and then suddenly, completely unexpectedly, you come across their hatred of Jews. Voltaire, Kant, Fichte. Why do they resent us? What have we done wrong? Are we vermin? It's deeper than anything else. I am beginning to fear that Hess was right."

Max nodded gloomily. "I miss Elsa. It's strange that you didn't see her in Palestine."

Again, Joseph remembered the fragrances from the expedition, the images of dry plains, the reminiscences of distant views in unknown places.

That summer, Joseph went to Munich, alone. He had been invited to the premiere of *Tristan und Isolde*, Wagner's new opera. Mingling with the leading figures in politics and the important industrialists before the performance, he felt lost. The horn solo at the beginning of the third act, not only triggered the melancholy of Venice, but caused his whole being to sink into a gloomy abyss that took him days to climb out of. The opera was brilliant. The music overwhelming and superb. The infinite melody continued in his head for hours, despite its final resolution into a redeeming chord, in death. Was there no salvation but this? Was there no redeeming chord in life? If a few years earlier in Frankfurt, during *Lohengrin*, Joseph could have opposed the composer's self-centered philosophy of salvation, now this melancholy feeling perfectly matched his own situation. Like the lost lovers, he went into hiding in the night. In everything he did, he tasted the philosophy of that disgraceful man, Schopenhauer. He pictured him again with his dog in the café in Frankfurt, on that memorable day when everything had seemed possible. The opera visit with the *beau monde*, the evening of festivities at the grandiose court of the Rothschilds, the tableau of Moritz Oppenheim. Joseph had experienced it all, but nothing offered him a glimpse of dawn, not even the thought of Max with his cheerful wittiness.

In Paris, he could at least have blamed external factors, especially alcohol, for his desolate emptiness. Now, more sober than ever, Joseph saw shallowness everywhere. Here he was. He spoke several languages. His study and knowledge had brought him forward in the world. As the sorcerer's apprentice he had corrected his mentor, Max, more than once. Max had only encouraged it and was proud of him. Joseph had defied the "storm of adaptation," as Max called it, and had survived it with verve. He had not drowned in the higher circles. Even his imprisonment had eventually had a cleansing effect, a kind of catharsis. Not that he would not get angry again if he thought about it, but he had let it rest and understood it as a necessary evil that had made him aware of what freedom meant.

Yes, his experiences had made him rich in thought. They had sharpened his brain. Then, why this emptiness, this ungrateful feeling that it had all been for nothing? Was it because of these two unexpected and dramatic refusals, regarding marriage and work? Joseph had thought that his imprisonment was the absolute rock bottom, but it was not. Then he wanted to be released; he had plans, he had hope, albeit hope for revenge. But the revenge of the good life had not come. He only saw an abyss in emptiness.

5

(1865)

SHABBAT

"I'll be fifty-five next week and my family wants to do something special," said Max.

They were drinking coffee in their regular café one late afternoon in September. "As you know, my brother Avraham is very religious. So, he has offered to host a Shabbat dinner. In my immense wisdom, I have agreed to let them incorporate the festivities into the Shabbat meal. They will do it at my house to make me more comfortable." He winked. "But I want to invite you as well."

Joseph took this in slowly.

"I am inviting you for a Friday night dinner," Max explained.

"I am honored. But how are you going to manage that? I mean with *kashrut* and all," he asked.

"The Ben Tovs will bring everything. They will take care of it all."

"Splendid," said Joseph. "Again. A great honor."

A young lady opened the door. Joseph thought she looked vaguely familiar. Was this Max's niece? The modest girl in the café in Frankfurt, the day he had met Schopenhauer. And then there had been that remarkable evening after Yom Kippur when she had looked at him with admiration. Pleased with himself, he realized that he remembered her name: Miriam. Joseph took in the fine features of her face, and especially noted her soft, blue eyes.

She led him through the living room into the library. He saw Miriam's mother, Golde, busy with the preparations. The cutlery and piles of china were on the table and he spied Max, completely lost, following her with a tablecloth. He wondered whether it was the birthday that was causing all the excitement or whether this was the family's normal preparation for Shabbat. In the library, Avraham was studying. He looked up with a welcoming smile.

"I'll leave you here. We'll be busy for a while," said Miriam.

Joseph thanked her and sat down timidly. It felt like a mandatory audience, one he neither wanted nor was interested in; in the wrong place with the wrong person. Suddenly Max's library seemed strange to him. It had been a while since Joseph had been here and the smell of the books had grown even more intense. Soon Max came in with Avraham's sons, Gideon and Nathaniel. "They sent me away. I am completely useless." He laughed and sank down in a chair. "Such commotion."

"Let it go, Max," said Avraham. "More important, I am studying the passage again about the day God was defeated by the rabbis and smiled. A few things are still not clear to me. Maybe you can help. I need a voice from heaven, I think."

Max and Joseph moved closer and soon they all were engaged in an intense conversation about Rabbi Eliezer ben Hyrcanus and his bending walls, and the river that flowed upstream to prove his theory.

An hour later, Golde came to fetch them. The festively set table stood in the middle of the living room and Joseph recognized the accessories for Shabbat – the candlesticks, the wine cup, the salt, and the covering for the loaves. He wondered whether Max had borrowed everything from his brother or whether he had taken it somewhere from his attic. He could not remember having seen any of it before. He thought of his family who were sitting at a similar table some hundred kilometers from here, also ready for *kiddush*. Or rather, what was left of his family. Was his father alone? That image was too sad. No. Aron had probably invited him to his home. Batia Kleinblatt would light the candles with a little one on her arm.

"Here." Avraham placed a skullcap on Joseph's head. A big round one that covered all his hair. Max also wore one and Joseph noticed how much Max looked like his brother. Outside it was not yet dark, but it was certainly not light. One of those days where the light has no power and the day is a long twilight. Dusk was an orphan.

The women lit the candles and everyone wished each other a *"git Shabbos."* It was easy to fit in again. Avraham said he was going to *shul* with his sons. Max shook his head. For a moment Joseph was tempted. The whole atmosphere was inviting, but going to synagogue was one step too far.

During the *gefilte fish* – a dish that made Joseph smile, the taste of the ghetto – Avraham spoke about Rav Yermiyahu and his project for *Eretz Israel*. He turned to Joseph. "I understand from Max that you have been there. Tell us about the new light over Zion."

Joseph smiled. "A new light. Indeed, the light is not from this world. It is truly another world." He hesitated for a moment.

Everyone looked at him expectantly. "I will tell you what it is like there, a description that you cannot find in the travel guides." He tried to put a light tone in his words. "The Turks are incompetent, cocky, lazy scammers, the Arabs bloodthirsty violent robbers, the Jews are egoistic fools who are foreign to the world. The handful of Westerners either stand by in amazement or simply survive. Literally." He stopped to see whether his sarcasm came across or if he had to slow down. He decided to go on for a while. "All right. So much about the people. Then there is the place itself. It smells, it's dirty. There is disease and poverty. Everywhere, the houses are in ruins, no one repairs anything. Nobody works. Outside the cities, your life is not safe. From April to October the sun burns on your head with merciless force, the fields are brown, the trees are withered, and in some places the air is so moist that you can hardly breathe. In the winter, the rain turns the soil in a dirty reddish sludge and the land into a swamp, which in turn causes diseases and epidemics. In short, a disaster."

Cheerfully, he looked around. Did he see disapproval? Had he overdone it? "I am exaggerating, of course," he said. "As a writer you have to try to captivate your audience." The time had come to get more serious. "But for those who are receptive, it has many positive aspects. The landscape is stunning. The cities are like a fairy tale. Ali Baba and the forty thieves. It is exotic, you really can't compare it to the world we know. You can pick the oranges from the trees. The scents will stay with you for the rest of your life. The people are helpful and patient. You can spend hours dreaming without anyone disturbing you. It has a rich history that you taste in everything. If I didn't know better, I would say that I remember my stay there with nostalgia." He considered whether he should tell the deepest of his thoughts. "I can't let it go. Like homesickness, that longing. Going back there. Although it runs counter to all logic, I can no longer put the land out of my mind."

"It sounds like there is a lot to do," Max quipped. "Really something for a committed person like you."

Joseph laughed. "Maybe both representations were a bit exaggerated. But I assure you. It's hard there; not suitable for the weak."

"Are you going to tell us that there are giants," Avraham asked cheerfully. "Otherwise, it's better to send some more spies. Oh no, you might end up wandering in the desert for forty years as punishment!"

They all laughed. "No, worse. Turks," Joseph replied, "they are definitely worse."

"And what about the Jews?" Max asked.

Joseph continued, still more seriously. "There are many kinds of Jews who make the trip to Palestine. There are some who go there to die or only to be buried. Those I call the ghosts. Then you have those who sit there and study, and do no work; those I call the otherworldly.

Then there are a few who want to live there; the idealists. And to top it all off, there's a group of people who think they're just about to start an independent state. And that's a delusion."

Avraham looked at him critically. "And to which group would you belong," he asked.

"None of them. I don't belong to anything. I probably won't go back anyway."

"You certainly have to come by one day when I invite Rav Yermiyahu, so he will have this firsthand account. He will love it."

Joseph agreed to visit them next week.

"You live in the city center at the shop, right?"

"No, we moved. We now live in a new house just outside the walls. We use the old building only for the clothing business. You see, we are not against progress per se."

Miriam, who until now hardly had said anything, asked: "Uncle Max, talking about progress. Weren't you in Berlin at some meeting about that?"

Max looked joyful. "Yes, indeed. About industrialization and its impact on society, actually. I am writing an article about it. It was quite boring." He laughed. "Not much progress in the meeting itself." He sat up to get his audience's attention. "But Berlin is still fascinating. Even more so nowadays. I went to see a new museum. It's called the New Museum, very to the point. Immensely rewarding. Full of the latest finds of Egyptian artifacts. You would find it interesting, Miriam."

"Absolutely," Miriam said full of enthusiasm. "I read whatever I can find about the ancient civilizations." She looked as if she were about to say something of which her parents would disapprove.

"Don't waste your time on these things," her mother said. "Better study your *Tsenerene*." The name brought memories of home back to Joseph. He remembered how Rivka had to read this Yiddish study book for women. He heard Miriam agree to her mother's wish but her expression didn't match her words.

The conversation fell silent until Max raised a new topic about the Jewish community in Cologne.

The next week Joseph kept his promise. After a sturdy walk, he came to the street in the new neighborhood. Modern houses, built in the latest style. At least they had straight angles. A narrow path led to the Ben Tovs' front door and a small court lay in front with some shrubs around the edge. Peeking through the branches of the hedge, he saw the shape of a woman hanging up the laundry. He supposed this was Miriam. She wore a short-sleeved, white dress, with a small-waisted full skirt that reached just below her knees. It was Miriam, indeed. Even as he watched, she walked away, taking the empty laundry basket into the house. She soon came back with a new pile. Joseph smelled the freshly washed linen. Each time she had to stand on her toes to reach the clothesline, she extended her arms heavenward; then she gently reached down and smoothly grasped the next item. In Joseph's imagination, her moves formed a graceful ballet. It reminded him of a passage from the Talmud. *Tu b'Av*, the day of immense joy, in the middle of summer, when the unmarried girls from Jerusalem dance in the vineyards and the watching boys make their choice.

As he walked the path to the front door, he looked again. Now she was sitting on the grass next to the laundry basket, her legs folded underneath her. He had seen this scene before. On a print in the bookstore of Holstein.

"Joseph, come in," Avraham said as he led Joseph to his study. Joseph heard the outside door open and close again. Avraham stood up and called out in Yiddish into the hallway, "Miriam, would you bring us some coffee?"

"Right away, papa."

"We'll speak German," he said to Joseph. "That's easier, I think."

"Fine, my Yiddish is a little rusty."

"I have to apologize. Rav Yermiyahu won't be able to make it today, but let's talk anyway."

As they sat quietly in the comfortable armchairs, Miriam came in with coffee. She put away the tray and took a chair. She looked hopeful at her father, who nodded in a friendly way.

"If Joseph doesn't mind."

"No, on the contrary. The more the merrier, as the proverb goes."

After some small talk, Avraham came to the purpose of Joseph's visit.

"You've been to Jerusalem yourself?" he asked.

Joseph nodded as he carefully tried to drink his hot coffee.

"And to the *Kotel*, the wall?"

"There as well." Joseph put his coffee on the table and gave a detailed account of his voyage with the emphasis on Jerusalem, though much rosier than he had experienced it. "Of course, there are problems, especially practical ones," he added.

"You called the people who wanted to establish a Jewish state in the land, deluded, if I remember correctly."

"You recall rightly. It was said, however, in the heat of the conversation. I exaggerated. But in spite of that, I don't see it happening.

Everything points in the direction of trouble. The idea is certainly worth entertaining, but to put it into practice? I'm not going to become an advocate."

"Rav Yermiyahu and quite a few of his supporters would disagree."

"I know. I'll tell you what. He's even getting some unexpected support, Moses Hess, an old Marxist, has also come to the conclusion that a country for the Jewish people would be the best thing for the world. Mind you, *for the world*. Not just for us. Of course, all this from a socialist perspective. A light to the nations. The prophecy coming true... But I don't have to tell you anything about prophets, I suppose."

Avraham smiled. "I've heard of Hess. Never read him. Maybe I should."

"Frankly, his last book, *Rom und Jerusalem*, in which he discusses all this, is not very well written. In fact, he once asked me to help him make his writings a little more accessible." His gaze went involuntarily to Miriam and he realized that he had made this addition mainly to impress her. "Nothing came of it. I went to Italy and our paths diverged. I don't know what he's doing right now. I don't believe he has many followers. But I genuinely respect him." He took a sip. "By the way, it might interest you to see how the nationalist movement is manifesting itself in Italy.

Avraham nodded for a long time as if he were lost in thought.

"Tell me more about Jerusalem. After all, that is the holy city," he began again.

"What I haven't told you yet is that my sister lives there."

Miriam spoke for the first time now. Her eyes were shining. "Really? How amazing. Listen papa, his sister lives in Jerusalem. What is she doing there?"

Joseph was just considering what he should and shouldn't tell, when Golde came in.

"Miriam, weren't you supposed to hang the laundry?" she asked in Yiddish.

"I did, mama."

Golde looked for a moment outmaneuvered. "I'm sure there's still the dishes you need to do."

"I'll do the dishes later. I think it's so interesting. It's about Jerusalem. You know, Joseph's sister lives there."

"And she will still live there tomorrow. I think the dishes are more urgent than Jerusalem," Golde now said firmly.

"Go, help your mother, my love," Avraham said to Miriam in a sympathetic tone.

As they left the room, Golde said, "No good will come from girls getting involved in men's affairs,"

"Sometimes it's very hard to introduce new ideas," Avraham said when Golde and Miriam had left. "My wife isn't into modernisms."

They continued to talk about the situation in Jerusalem until Joseph indicated that he had to leave. But he would like to come back again.

From then on, he visited the Ben Tovs regularly. Joseph was grateful for the engaging distraction after his failure with the Pennekamps and the Löwes. The last thing he felt like doing was plunging into the social and cultural life of Cologne. The Ben Tovs offered a pleasant way to spend his time while giving him the opportunity to reminisce about Palestine. He liked Avraham. In a different way than he liked Max, but there was some resemblance in both their ability to put all the heavy stuff, all the fervent opinions, into perspective. Max had complained frivolously that Joseph had exchanged a Bentoff for a Ben Tov.

Somehow, he also liked it when Miriam – despite her mother's opposition – sat down with them. When she dared to say something, her observations were clever, and she had a broader range of knowledge than Joseph had expected. He thought that she combined some of Max's practical wisdom with a graceful softness.

One time, as he entered the Ben Tovs' house, he heard piano playing. He guessed it was Miriam. A Haydn sonata, he thought.

Golde greeted him. "*Herr* Socher, my husband is in the library. Would you like to follow me?"

After some time, Miriam came in and asked if she could join them.

"Was that you playing?" Joseph asked. "It was beautiful."

"Yes. Thank you."

In the unfolding conversation, Avraham touched on a sensitive subject, asking what Joseph thought about religious life. "In general," Avraham added, but Joseph could not deny that the peculiar smile indicated that the question was more personal than he had first realized. Normally Joseph would have been uncomfortable with the subject, but Avraham made him feel at ease. Even Miriam's bright, sharp look didn't upset him.

Joseph started with some vague remarks, but then decided to speak frankly: "For me it is mainly the ethical and philosophical side of Judaism that is attractive. Less the religious practice. Or maybe the spiritual, but not the theological." How far would he go? "To be honest it's hard for me to fit into a straightjacket. Not being able to move anymore. I need to explore. Like enjoying paintings, for instance."

"But art is something Christians do," Miriam said. "We don't." She blushed, as if she had overstepped her boundaries.

"But we *do*," Joseph replied, "at least we have done. Synagogues used to be elaborately painted. Depictions of people, Moses, Aron. I admit, sculptures, that's something else. But nowadays, everything is forbidden."

"Not everything is about beauty," Avraham said.

Miriam sang softly, hardly audible, "*Sheker ha chen, hevel ha jofi.*"

"Miriam," Avraham interrupted. "Don't sing please."

Miriam looked a bit guilty but Joseph also saw a little teasing. He knew the line. From the song, *Eshet Chayil*, chanted at the beginning of Shabbat. "Charm is deceptive, beauty vain." Yet he didn't want to give in so easily. He had dedicated most of his life to art and beauty.

"What's beautiful is beautiful," he said in a stubborn tone, not very original.

"True," said Avraham. "But not necessarily the most important thing."

Joseph didn't want to drive his point home so he changed tack and said, "But there's nothing wrong with reading books. With literature. That's for sure."

"I like reading," Miriam said. "After all, we are the people of the book."

"Yes, my love. But then again there are books and there are books."

He turned to Joseph. "Probably you have read a lot, all these years as a journalist."

"I have, indeed. And reading is the best there is." He smiled toward Miriam.

"You like music?" Joseph dared to ask.

"Certainly. As you heard, I play the piano. Max gave us the instrument." She looked with half an eye at her father. "At first, my parents weren't so excited about it. They thought it was something for the *goyim*, but now they even like it."

"We could go to a concert one of these days. There's plenty of them. We could go with Max," he hastened to add. Miriam couldn't hide her enthusiasm.

Joseph noticed Avraham eyeing him seriously.

"Maybe, you would join me in *shul* one day," Avraham asked.

"Certainly. I would be honored."

The next time he visited, it was Miriam who opened the door. She was busy tying up her loose hair. She led him in the back room.

"Papa will be home in an hour, I think."

"Shall I come back another time?"

"If you want, you can stay," she said. "I was just going to make tea.

Would you like some?"

"Yes please. A cup of tea sounds just right." He sat down on the comfortable couch in the corner. He sank into the unexpectedly deep cushions.

She laughed. "No one ever sits there."

He clumsily knocked over the cushions in an attempt to get up.

"I can keep you company if you want," she said.

"Of course. Please." He blushed. "I mean. If you don't mind."

"No, not at all. I was reading in here." As proof, she held up the book that lay on the table. Joseph read the title and recognized it. *Jenny* by Fanny Lewald. The book he had once accidentally taken from Holstein's bookstore and given Rivka to read.

"Great book," he said, trying to sound serious. "I am surprised you are reading it."

"How so? Have you read it?" she asked.

"Certainly," he said, "but I thought it's more a book fit for women."

"It's about independence. Women no longer need to be the desperate ivy trying to cling to the strong male oak."

"I don't see women as dependent plants," he defended himself. "I have a modern outlook."

She looked at him boldly. "But you think the book is not right for me?"

"No, No. Very suitable." He blushed again. "Not that I think you are a revolutionary or anything." It was becoming increasingly hopeless.

She challenged him. "And what *do* you think?"

She sat down next to him. Joseph moved further into the corner.

He answered nervously. "She is quite a free-spirited woman. Jenny, I mean. She rejects marriage all together. I wasn't connecting her with you, but rather with the Jewish environment and your family."

"Now you are making me very curious. You think it's impossible for a well-behaved Jewish girl to have an independent mind?" If he had not known better, he would have thought she was teasing him.

"I..." He stammered something inaudible.

But Miriam made another point. "If you were reading *The Three Musketeers*, I wouldn't classify you as a swordsman."

Joseph knew that there was nothing else to do but to admit frankly that from the beginning he had taken a stupid position. He took a deep breath and laughed. "You are too smart for me." He waited a moment. "Maybe we can start over?" He tried to show his most disarming smile. "You remind me of my sister, Rivka. She is a strong and independent woman. Maybe you'll meet her one day."

"Who knows." She got up again now. "But I didn't mean to embarrass you. My apologies."

"Are you leaving," he asked alarmed.

"I'm going to get the tea. You wanted tea, didn't you?"

"Ah yes. Lovely."

A little later she came back with the teapot and two cups.

"Shall we address each other more informal from now on?"

"Yes, please." She looked at him. "How would you like to be called? Joseph or Johann? We call you Joseph, because that's how Uncle Max introduced you. Most people call you Johann, don't they?"

"Don't care about most people. Joseph is perfect."

"I am glad," she responded. "I like Joseph better than Johann. Joseph was a really righteous man. I love his stories. All those dreams, and then in Egypt and with his brothers. Johann would be…" she thought for a moment. "Actually, I don't know of any nice Johanns."

"What about Johann Wolfgang von Goethe?" Joseph asked.

Did he want some sort of vindication for his lost discussion about *Jenny*?

Miriam smiled, putting down the tray. "Yes, but I don't like him."

"You don't like Goethe?"

"I read his book *Werther*. It's so extreme."

"*Sturm und Drang* they call it."

"If it leads to suicide, I would rather channel that *Sturm und Drang* into calm waters, don't you think?"

Joseph thought for a moment. "Perhaps you have a point."

As she sat down, she changed the subject. "I find it fascinating that you have been in *Eretz Israel*."

"Thank you, but I wasn't so positive about it."

"I would like to go there. My father too. To live there, even to resettle the land."

"With all due respect, Miriam," Joseph's self-confidence increased again, "it is one thing to make the journey there. To settle there is something completely different. Unimaginable actually."

"My mother is against it. She says the time is not ripe. The nations will prevent us from doing so. In the Talmud it says that three oaths must be fulfilled first – that we must not obtain it by force, that we must not go against the nations, and something about that we must not be too oppressed, I believe. My father says it could be a reason for divorce, but he loves her too much."

"You know what?" Joseph said. "I'm going to bring you some books with descriptions and pictures so you can get an idea of what it looks like."

Avraham had asked Joseph to join him for the morning service, so one Tuesday morning they went together to the new *shul* in the *Glockenstrasse*. It was the synagogue where Joseph had stood long ago on a Saturday morning – or should he say Shabbat again? Where he had decided that there was no way back. That the boat had sailed. Was he unexpectedly returning to the same harbor? Had he made an unnecessary detour or had that been the beginning of the search for this moment? Or did it not matter at all? When leaving home, he did not have to look for his *tefillin*. He knew exactly where he had put them, but the bag was dusty.

As he climbed the stairs, Joseph looked around. The onion-shaped minarets on the exterior evoked a vaguely oriental atmosphere and overall, it had too much of a Venetian church about it. Not a bad imitation of real Byzantine architecture in the middle of Cologne, he thought. In the past he could not have stopped himself from mentioning this, but now he kept the thought to himself. He decided that his conceitedness would probably never leave him entirely, but perhaps he was improving. At least he recognized it.

Avraham had his fixed spot in the front and Joseph took the seat next to him. He would have preferred to sit somewhere quietly alone, further toward the back of the room. Just as he was about to start the regular rituals, a man sat down on his other side. He had a reddish burly face. His eyes continuously panned from right to left above a pair of round glasses. He nodded kindly. Avraham had already completely immersed himself in the prayers, with his *tallit* pulled over his head.

Joseph started to put on his *tefillin* and for a moment he looked for the words that accompany it. While he was clumsily wrapping the straps over his arm while at the same time browsing through the prayer book to find the right page, he saw his neighbor moving to help. Joseph shook no. The man then turned his attention back to his own prayer book.

The service started and Joseph's old routine quickly resurfaced, but after a while he lost his place. Perhaps they had different customs here than in Frankfurt. He leafed backwards and forwards through the *sidur*. Again, the man next to him offered to help. This time Joseph accepted and soon picked up the service again.

When it ended, Joseph felt pleasantly satisfied. It was nice to hear the prayers again and to be part of a *minyan*. The man next to him stretched out his hand, "Shmuel Finkelstein. I don't know you. Are you from Cologne?"

"Originally from Frankfurt." This, he hoped, explained why the service had been unfamiliar. "Joseph." He didn't feel like saying Lichtman, but Socher really was from a different era. Instead, he said,

"I'm a family friend of the Ben Tovs," pointing to Avraham who hadn't finished yet.

"Welcome. Isn't there a new rabbi in Frankfurt, Rabbi Hirsch? A bit of a new wind, I have heard. Somewhat radical?"

"It's not so bad. He is of the opinion that Torah goes very well with worldly society. Normal *and* Jewish!" He hoped the man could follow his humor. Finkelstein smiled, as if he had, then headed off.

Meanwhile Avraham had also finished and he patted Joseph on the shoulder in encouragement.

"Well done," he said. "It wasn't that awkward, I hope?"

"No, no. Not at all. I liked it, actually."

"Beautiful." Avraham seemed to be considering something. "Would you like to spend the next Shabbat with us? Ever since the boys left the house, it's only been the three of us. We could set up the guest room so you don't have to walk home and you can stay with us all day."

Joseph accepted the offer.

"Which *parasha* is it this week?" he asked.

"*Lech Lecha.*"

"Ah yes, of course, it's my birthday next week."

A little overconfident, he asked whether he could read from the Torah. "I think I remember the portion well enough."

"If you want, sure. But, I have to ask, what's your motive? A good show or a deep conviction that it's good to read Torah."

Joseph hesitated for a moment. "If I'm honest, a little bit of both."

"Do it when it's only for the appropriate reason. "One who makes unworthy use of the crown, shall pass away," it says. And we wouldn't want that, wouldn't we?" he said with a smile.

Joseph smiled. "You're right. You are a wise man."

Friday afternoon, he packed his stuff for the Shabbat visit at the Ben Tovs. He had talked about it with Max who was delighted to hear of his planned stay there.

"You will go to synagogue as well?"

"Of course. The whole family goes."

"Are my cousins there?"

"No, only Miriam, I guess."

"Very good," Max said with a smile. "Should we look in the Talmud for reasons to go?"

"I don't understand."

"The time you went to church, you remember. You had to find some excuse."

Joseph laughed. "No, I don't need the Talmud now. I hope I can manage the *sidur*."

Miriam stood just behind her mother at a table with the candles. She wore a long white dress with a purple waistband. The sleeves were like veils, transparent, with delicate pearls. She had elegantly put her auburn hair up with a small bow. No further adornments. Her straight posture was graceful and at the same time as proud as a classic statue. She tilted her head modestly downwards and covered her eyes with her hands after she had lit the candles. Gently the women murmured the blessings. Joseph watched motionless and silent. He had been in this scene before.

When they came back from *shul*, Avraham asked Joseph if he would like to make *kiddush*. Joseph hesitated. He had not drunk wine since Venice. Would he drink it now? Avraham looked at him warmly, "You haven't forgotten the words, haven't you? You can read them?"

Joseph decided to accept the honor. The request moved him and he was sure that this was the right thing to do. He lifted the cup. The words had power beyond their meaning. With increasing assurance, he recited them and when he drank a sip of the cup, he saw over the edge how radiantly Miriam was looking at him.

The conversation during the meal was lively. At one point, Joseph asked Miriam what she was doing. Did she study or work?

"I am very busy with some charity projects," she replied.

"What kind of work?"

"Raising funds. Doing chores for old people. Different things."

"But what I mean is, is there something you really want to do for yourself?"

"This is for myself. It's such rewarding work."

"I thought it was more like something you'd do on the side."

"Perhaps. But for me it's enough."

"You know, I once delivered the magazine of the community. When I was about eighteen. With my little brother. But to be honest, I got paid for it."

"You have to tell me everything about your family."

"Then we'll need a week, I'm afraid," he said cheerfully. "I've already told you that my sister lives in Jerusalem. She works in a school there." He talked at length about his parents. As he mentioned his mother's untimely death, he felt the sadness coming over him. He found consolation in Miriam's eyes. He continued about his two brothers, emphasizing Aron's piety and Nathan's success in London.

"We are a bit scattered right now," he said. "To get the family together you have to search all four corners of the earth," he added for a laugh.

"A real diaspora," said Avraham who just had finished a discussion with his wife and now turned to Joseph and Miriam.

"Yes, it would be nice if we were all together again. But who knows?"

"That opportunity will surely come," Miriam said.

Later that evening in bed, he reviewed the dinner in his mind. His memory mostly dwelled on Miriam's lovely face and her courteous and charming manner. Her delightful image remained with him, bright and clear. It generated a yearning, quite different from the desire he had felt for Maria. Miriam's simplicity and intrinsic beauty evoked feelings of tenderness. He felt only the desire to be with her. He remembered the sudden feeling of emptiness when she had left the table during dinner. It dawned on him that he wanted to share his life, to share himself, with her.

Why hadn't that occurred to him before? He tried to analyze the matter rationally and came to the conclusion that she was far too religious for him. And he would never want her to break away. But together with Miriam, something new could emerge. His existential loneliness could be lifted. He could become a better man.

She was so beautiful. Why had the scales only fallen from his eyes now? Was it because he was still recovering from Maria's glare? And a strange romantic notion that true love could not be reached in this imperfect sublunary world? Had he been so prejudiced that he couldn't think of an Orthodox girl as a candidate for marriage? Or was it a symptom of his old arrogance? That a woman could never be a comrade in life. Only just an extension of himself? He had wanted to be with Maria, but that had mainly been physical attraction. Even if they had married, Maria would only have been an extra. Convenient and pleasant. But in the end Maria would have had to adapt to *him*. And of course, in his fantasy, she would have. She'd have to fit into his life. Joseph hadn't actually ever thought it through that far. In contrast, Miriam could be an antagonist, a respected partner, who would bring out the best in him.

Whatever be the case, he'd fallen in love with Miriam. He tried to get his thoughts in order. It all came so fast. Nevertheless, he had the paradoxical feeling that he had calmed down while being swept away by the current.

The family went to shul on Shabbat morning. Joseph sat next to Avraham. The Torah scroll was taken out and Joseph received the honor of the seventh *aliyah*. It had been thirteen years ago. He went up the *bima* under the immense cupola and he felt pride. Avraham was already up there because he had received the previous *aliyah*. As they stood there, they smiled at each other. Without really looking up, Joseph saw in the corner of his eye that Miriam was watching. Had he gone back to being the good boy from the *Judengasse*? When the service was over, the men joined the women and Joseph welcomed the company of Miriam's soft, blue eyes again.

After lunch, Avraham and Golde retreated for an afternoon nap. Joseph went to his small guest room, but he could not sleep. Dressing again, he went downstairs and saw Miriam reading in the living room. It was half dark, but not gloomy. The peace of a Shabbat afternoon. He thought that if they opened only one curtain, the light would flood in. As it was, some bright beams found their way to the carpet.

"You know what?" Miriam suggested. "We could go for a stroll in the park."

They went to the new city park nearby. It was beautifully designed. The city had done its best to recreate nature. Joseph and Miriam walked side by side. She made him forget himself. There were young couples all over the park. Would an outsider see him and Miriam as a couple? He had never dreamed of himself walking next to a girl in a park. Strange in itself, because it was probably an image that all these boys and girls had cherished from childhood. Had he been so self-involved that he had never even contemplated it?

Was he supposed to hold her hand? Instead, he asked, "Can I offer you my arm?"

"Later," she said. Her eyes smiled at him.

After they had passed a fountain, they saw a small zoo. Miriam was excited. "Come, Joseph. Let's go." She took his hand and almost hauled him to the low fence of the zoo. Some ponies were there and a little boy was trying to feed one of them. He couldn't reach the animal's muzzle. His mother was carrying a baby in her arms so Miriam asked whether she could help. She lifted the boy and the pony ate the sugar cube from his hand.

The mother thanked her and they walked on. It was quiet for a while, but it wasn't an awkward silence. Joseph enjoyed every second; just being with her was enough.

They reached a small pavilion. It was a bit elevated from the rest of the park. Narrow steps led up to a quaint coffee and teahouse. The sky was already dimming and all around the pavilion lanterns had been lit. People were drinking and chatting at nicely arranged tables. It all looked very festive.

"Maybe we could drink tea there? It looks very pretty," Joseph said.

"It's Shabbat and on top of that I am quite sure that it is not kosher."

"Yes, of course."

Twilight was now setting in.

"We should go home for the end of Shabbat. You already missed *Mincha*," Miriam teased.

"Now I feel really guilty," he answered with a laugh. He promised he would improve his life. As they turned away, he saw a gleam of light through the silhouette of the trees in the distance.

"Isn't that the full moon rising?" he asked.

"Tuesday is *Rosh Chodesh*. New moon. Or do you think nature has adapted to our situation?"

"No. I suppose it hasn't. But it would have been nice, wouldn't it?"

He was happy, even to be trumped by her. It did not matter to him that he had made himself slightly ridiculous. She had not rejected him. On the contrary. This had to go on forever. It would heal all his scars. From now on, evening would never again be melancholic but would always hold the promise of a new day.

The next morning, he poured out his feelings to Max. Max listened, amused, and when Joseph had finished, he said, "And what do you want?" Teasingly, he offered, "Should I come and support you when you ask her hand?"

"You think that I should ask her to marry me?"

"I think you should marry her!" He laughed heartily. "In the end, that's what you want. All you want is to be with her."

"But her family is so religious and I still don't know her that well."

"Add some water to the wine. Metaphor of the wrong religion, but anyway. You be a little more religious, she a little less. And then you can get to know each other. I think it would be fantastic if you married her."

"Really? You do?"

"I have known Miriam all her life. She is a special girl. A will of her own, mind you! No wonder she has refused all of the marriage proposals so far." His eyes sparkled. "We would be family, Joseph. After all these years." He patted Joseph on the shoulder. "But that should not be a reason to marry her, of course." He got serious again. "I think it would be very good and beneficial for you."

"So you think I should ask her? How should I tackle this?"

"I must honestly say that I don't have much experience in that area. You know what? Just tell her the truth."

"The truth! Have you gone completely *meshugge*? Never."

"I mean it. Women are usually charmed by that."

Joseph considered the idea. Telling the truth. About Paris? About his drinking? There was so much he rather not even think about, let alone tell Miriam. To distract himself from these thoughts, he said. "May I ask you something. You and Elsa formed a beautiful couple. Why weren't you together?"

"Age, my boy. For you, everyone is probably an old sock, but Elsa is almost fifteen years older than I am."

"I always wanted you to be my father."

Max shook his head. "You shouldn't say that. You have a father. You can't forsake him."

Joseph sighed and nodded.

"I think you are each other's salvation," Max continued.

Joseph gave him a questioning look.

"Don't get me wrong. You will make sure that she doesn't fade away in Cologne. She has a mind too independent to let perish here in an arranged marriage. I think my brother agrees, only he is entangled in tradition, the pressure to do things as expected. His two sons are learning at the *Yeshiva* and are probably going to be more Catholic than the Pope, so to speak. I suppose her mother will be the biggest problem. She doesn't like the idea of her daughter being snatched by some wild man."

"I see what you mean. But I won't snatch her. She is completely free," riposted Joseph. "And I'm not a wild man."

"In her mother's eyes you are worse than Genghis Khan. And that is also what Miriam finds fascinating."

"Do they know about my prison story?"

"I haven't told anyone."

"I would appreciate it if you would keep it to yourself. I will tell it in good time, but it's not something I'm proud of. I know what it was. You know what it was. But I actually have a hard time disclosing that I was in prison. It's a dirty stain that I prefer to cover."

Max promised not to mention it ever.

"She is too beautiful for me," he confessed.

Max hesitated, so Joseph knew he was right. "Maybe you deserve her anyway. And beauty? Heavily overrated."

"Shall I keep all the *mitzvot*?"

Max shrugged his shoulders. "I can't help you with that. What should I say? Do this, do that, don't do that. What would Miriam say if I would advise you, for example, to leave your *tefillin* in the cabinet? Just discuss it with her."

"I don't want to burden her with my problems. I want everything to be good. I want to make her happy."

Max sighed. "Joseph, grow up."

"I think I will do as much as is desirable and feasible," Joseph said, intentionally vague. "I will certainly keep the Sabbath. Shabbat is a blessing. No work, no news, nothing to worry about, only rest."

"*Kashrut?*"

"Miriam would take care of the food."

"Three times a day prayers?"

"As I said, desirable and feasible."

"I won't ask any further," said Max with a grin.

"You haven't said why it will be beneficial for me as well?" asked Joseph.

"Get off your high horse and fill in the blanks yourself, my friend."

That same evening Joseph returned to the Ben Tovs. Avraham told him that Miriam had gone out with her mother, some charity project. They would not be back until after ten. "I want to have a serious talk with you," he said.

Joseph followed Miriam's father into his study. It took Avraham a while to start but when he did, he came to the point immediately. "I would be very sorry to see Miriam marry a non-religious man."

Joseph wanted to react but Avraham gave him no opportunity.

"That's why I asked you to come to the synagogue. I have noticed how the two of you get along. It's good, but she is inexperienced. You are desirable in her eyes, I think." He smiled. "Sometimes things develop very quickly. We want to rush to do a *mitzvah* but we should take the time to do it right." He waited a moment. "I would, of course, let her choose freely. I respect Max too. But think carefully, before you start anything."

"If you know why I am here and you haven't shown me the door, does that mean you would give us your blessing?"

Slowly Avraham started laughing, "Yes, I will give you my blessing, and I'm going to see to it that my wife does the same. Not an easy task, mind you." He looked at Joseph intently, gazing straight into his eyes. After a few seconds, Joseph looked away. He didn't feel guilty but it was as if in a flash all his thoughts had been revealed to Avraham.

"Don't be afraid," he said. "When I saw you the very first time, that Yom Kippur evening, I paid attention. I know that deep down you are quite a good boy."

"Quite," Joseph dared to ask. "Not just good?"

They both laughed. "Max has been telling me things. No details. Let's leave it at that."

Joseph was worried but the joy of Avraham's approval overcame any concern. He nodded in agreement, still smiling.

"More important," continued Avraham, "I trust my daughter's

judgment." In a cheerful gesture, he raised his eyebrows. "Not so bad, don't you think, for an *Altglaubige*. Relying on the judgment of a girl, just in her twenties."

"In a word, progressive."

"Max and I of course have different opinions sometimes, but you have been his best friend for years and that says a lot. And the last weeks have confirmed my opinion."

"Thank you."

Joseph couldn't sleep that night. He had come up with several detailed scenarios how to approach her. Now he tossed in his bed, the thought of asking to marry her terrifying him. He was sure he wanted her, but couldn't let go of the idea that she wouldn't want him. What if she rejected him? He would be devastated. And that chance was not unreasonable. What had Max said? She had refused many good marriage proposals. A mind of her own. He had seen it and it was one of the most fascinating aspects of her. But maybe she didn't want to be married at all. It wouldn't even be about him. After a few hours he was so exhausted that he nodded off, convinced she would reject him.

The next morning he went back to the Ben Tovs. Still not sure how to approach her, Joseph had brought a new book with pictures of the Holy Land. It would be a good start to talk about *Eretz Israel* and then see what would happen.

"It would be nice if we could walk there together, don't you think?" She pointed to a plate of the Dead Sea. "It's beautiful."

"Would you really like to be with me? There, I mean?" He grabbed her hand. Impulse or not, it seemed the right thing to do.

"I would like to be with you. Not only there," she replied.

Joseph reached for her other hand, then firmly held her hands in his. "Are you sure? I haven't been able to think of anything else."

"I am hopelessly in love with you," she said. "That's my answer."

Her face was radiant. They kissed each other.

When he walked back home in jubilation, it seemed as if his life had not existed until now.

"Who would have thought it could be so easy!" he said to himself.

During their engagement, Joseph visited her every day. When he woke in the morning the day brought that feeling of expectancy and possibilities. He was always a bit nervous when he went to her house, but when they were together he was completely at ease. It didn't matter what they were doing, laundry, or reading, or just drinking coffee. It was all good. Very good.

To show that he was returning to the faith, Joseph went back to wearing a head covering and let his beard grow. Not the rough bristles of the Orthodox, but a civilized, neatly trimmed beard such as the artists had in Paris. He also tried to go to the synagogue every day. Miriam drew his attention to the fact that he shouldn't smoke on Shabbat. He complied.

Everything now was focused on the wedding. Of course, it would be an Orthodox wedding canopy with all the trimmings, in the synagogue. Joseph had briefly advocated another location, somewhere outside the city. Maybe in the beautiful valley where the carriage had dropped him off. An inn had opened there. But in the end, he understood the impossibility of this idea, and the compelling logistical and religious reasons had made him agree to the synagogue on the *Glockenstrasse*.

One evening, when going through the guest list with Miriam, Joseph let slip that he was not sure whether his brothers would come.

"But surely you're going to invite them, aren't you?"

"Of course," he said. "But Nathan might not come over from London. I didn't go to his wedding. And as a matter of fact, I didn't go to Aron's either. Of course I'll invite my family. It's such a pity you never knew my mother. I think you would have liked each other."

He doubted whether he should invite the Löwes. Father Löwe was out of the question, but Werner and Maria? Would he want to see Maria at the moment of his greatest happiness? The girl he had adored in a church? Too many painful memories. He decided to write them a letter to report the planned marriage. They would probably not even answer but he would have done his duty.

On the day of the wedding, his father, Max, and Aron with his family accompanied Joseph to the *shul*. The sarcastic thought about the architecture – was it only a few weeks ago? – came to his mind. He smiled.

"What is so funny," his father asked.

"Nothing. A stray thought. It doesn't matter."

His father gave him a penetrating look. "Yossi, you always will be an odd boy, but I have the feeling that you will land on your feet."

He was about to respond, but Max punched his side and he swallowed the comment. Meekly he said to his father, "Yes *Tate*, I think everything will be fine."

"Wait. Don't move. I want to bless you."

He felt his father's hands on his head and heard him say the words in Hebrew: "May the Lord bless you and protect you; may the Lord make His face shine on you and be gracious to you; may the Lord turn His face toward you, and grant you peace." Humble and grateful, Joseph accepted.

He was standing under the *chupa*, the wedding canopy. Max and his father were next to him. Miriam appeared at the end of the aisle with her family. Veiled. A haze of light and happiness. Holding her parents' hands, she moved closer. Behind her came her two brothers. She stood next to him under the canopy and through the veil Joseph saw that she was smiling. The rabbi gave him a ring, which Joseph slid onto Miriam's finger. Under the *tallit* that the rabbi draped over them, they disappeared briefly into their own little world. Blessings were spoken. Max did his best in Hebrew. Everyone sang and at the right moment, Joseph crushed the glass with his foot. "*If I forget thee Jerusalem, let my right hand forget its skill.*" After the ceremony, they joined in the singing and dancing. They saw happy faces, they heard warm wishes, shook hands, and accepted "*mazal tovs*" from all sides. Through it all, they were the center of infinite bliss.

Later, Joseph found that he did not remember the rest of the evening well. It was like a dream, a hallucination, but unlike the images he had seen in his deliriums in Paris in which everything had ended badly or was encased in cynical black. Now everything was pure, blessed and, above all, real.

The weeks after the wedding were even more like a fairytale. Miriam moved into his rooms. Joseph alone no longer existed. There was shared love and attention, tenderness and excitement. Seeing her in the pale moonlight after another passionate night made him fall in love with her all over again. They would be one forever.

6

(1866)

SO THE SUN STOOD STILL

Still no land in sight. Joseph stood on the bow of the Greek steamer and peered over the black water. He drummed his fingers on the railing and every now and again looked behind him. Even in this dark hour before sunrise it was warm. He was grateful for the strong breeze that kept him awake. The journey had been a joy. Although it was unbearable to stay in the direct sun for more than a minute, they had been able to spend most of the time on the deck, where the crew had hung screens and sails against the sun.

Avraham and Max had decided to honor Miriam's longstanding wish and to offer the newly married couple a trip to the Holy Land. Joseph wondered whether Avraham might have a hidden agenda – if Miriam found the land to be interesting and worthwhile, it would help the cause of Rav Yermiyahu. The thought did not bother him.

Of all cities, they had embarked in Venice. But the city was now part of the free and independent kingdom of Italy. There were no Austrians to be seen and Joseph finally felt confident enough to disclose his Venetian tale to Miriam. They were sitting on a bench on the *Riva degli Schiavoni*, diagonally opposite hotel *Danieli*, where they had spent the night. *Danieli* was one of the most luxurious hotels in Venice, and Joseph, despite objections from Miriam, had insisted that they would stay there. But now neither Miriam nor Joseph looked at the hotel. Their gaze was on the monumental building next to it, the *Palazzo delle Prigioni*.

"All's well, that ends well," Miriam said.

"Unbelievable that I was imprisoned there for two weeks. Sixteen days. *Palazzo* they call it. *Carceri*, that's what they are. Dungeons. Underground. Although, more under water. The stench. Terrible. I could never have imagined that I would sit here with you one day." There was a strong breeze blowing and he planted his hat more firmly on his head. "When I was locked up there, I did not think I could ever be happy again. And just as I experienced the misery then, now I am relishing the happiness. Letting it dominate me completely." He looked at her. "It's important to recognize happiness when we have it.

You never know what can happen. Your life can be destroyed in one moment. Maybe that was the lesson I had to learn here. To recognize happiness. To see what is good."

"You know, there's more to you than meets the eye. At first I was afraid to dig, but I'm glad you told me this story."

"There is nothing left to find. From my foolish drunken adventures in Paris to my imprisonment here and from my church visit in Cologne to the bizarre expedition in Palestine – you know everything now."

"Quite a husband I have!"

He made a face. Her compliments usually thrilled him, but sometimes he wondered why she admired him so deeply. Was it his wild lifestyle, so different from anything that she had experienced? But he didn't want that kind of life any more. He just wanted to calm down after all the turbulence of the past.

"I see life as a patchwork. All the pieces merge seamlessly and with some good will, you think you see the whole quilt. But I know better: They are all separate pieces. Cutouts that a child has stuck together." He looked at Miriam and wondered if he would bore her with these kinds of musings.

"But do you think that is bad?"

"Bad? I don't know." He smiled and embraced her. "Come, let's be happy."

Miriam was still asleep. She wanted to rest on the last day before their arrival. Joseph had not been able even to doze, so had been standing since midnight at the front of the bow in eager anticipation of the first sign of land. The sea breeze blew toward him and aroused a self-assured excitement in him. He was without fear. He had already been here. Surely he would become her support and safety in that strange land.

This visit would be different. Five years ago he had been ill and had hardly been aware of his arrival, and they had almost carried him to the hotel. Now the country was full of promise, waiting for both of them. He had decided not to visit the places of the fiasco at Capernaum. They would set their base in Jerusalem and make trips from there. Their time was limited anyway. They had three weeks. One thing was certain: Above all, he wanted to see Rivka again. Would she have left the monastery? Would she like Miriam? At sea, full of enthusiasm, he had told Miriam his plans and described the places they would visit. He had also mentioned that he wanted to write a travel report on the Land of Israel right away and perhaps publish it.

In the first light of dawn he saw a vague outline in the distance. The Greek sailors burst into action. It rapidly became lighter; this was not the slow dawn of Europe. Soon he could see the gray-blue contours of the land and, slowly but surely, more details of a city became visible. He rushed down to call Miriam, but ran into her already climbing up to the deck. Together they looked towards the city that now emerged clearly. In the bright light, straight walls rose from the water like a fortress and above these, white houses piled up on the shining hill. In the northern area he thought he recognized the hotel where he had stayed last time.

"Magnificent! So exotic!" he heard Miriam say.

He bit his tongue against the cynical, "Just wait until you smell the streets there," saying only, "Yafo, it's a beautiful sight."

He knew that the city looked far better than it really was, but it was not difficult for him to pretend that he was seeing it for the first time. Maybe it had been hazy then. In any case, the country presented itself differently this time, and much better.

The steamer slowed down as they drew near the coast with its perilous rocks. The anchor was dropped. On the quay, people were preparing for their arrival. A long rowed boat approached them, with a few men in colorful wide trousers who made noise for ten when the boat came alongside the steamer. The memory of Venice came back for a moment. The smell of the water, but now with an oriental fragrance.

More sloops drew up and a couple of Arabs climbed aboard the steamer. In the consternation, Joseph almost lost sight of Miriam. A sturdy Arab wanted to pick her up and put her in a sloop, but Joseph intervened. Someone from the hotel was supposed to bring them ashore. In the corner of his eye he saw that their suitcases had already been put aboard another boat. Joseph tried to clarify things when he was tapped on his shoulder.

"Mister Socher? My name is Mustafa. I am the servant of the Hotel Jerusalem. Come with me, please." Joseph saw a small man with an elegant Turkish mustache, dressed in a long, discolored robe with big puffed sleeves. He was wearing a fez and Joseph hoped that he would be reliable. "I'll make sure the suitcases will be delivered to the hotel," he said in fluent English, although with a Levantine accent. "We have a separate boat for the hotel guests." The man snapped his fingers and immediately three others came to help them to disembark. Before Joseph could object, one of them skillfully picked Miriam up. Miriam smiled and gestured at him to be quiet. "I am not that delicate," she shouted, dangling in the arms of the large man. Joseph ruefully accepted the fact that his plan to keep Miriam away from the rough population as much as possible had failed immediately. Soon it was Joseph's turn and eventually everyone was aboard the sloop.

The boat navigated through the rocky surf to the quay where they could disembark by themselves. They watched as the porters piled all the suitcases together in a large stack. Now from all sides, more porters, seamen, and travel agents appeared, each apparently trying to out-yell the next. Some of them seemed to decide that the suitcases were public goods because they started to look for useful things among them. Mustafa intervened and posted a few men as guards.

"We have to arrange the customs facilities first. Do you have some extra money? Francs please." He winked. "*Baksheesh.*"

"Yes, I remember," mumbled Joseph, handing him some. Mustafa quickly walked toward a small building not far away.

He looked at Miriam who returned his gaze cheerfully. He was glad that she seemed to enjoy this turmoil and cacophony.

A few minutes later Mustafa returned with a Turkish official. The man whistled and two other men in uniform immediately loaded the suitcases onto a mule. Two horses were brought for Joseph and Miriam.

"We will see the city later today," Joseph promised. Their journey took them northeast, over the sun-drenched road through friendly orchards and inviting plantations outside the Yafo wall. The sharp shadows made it difficult for their eyes to get used to the light. When the land sloped slightly, the alluring ridge of Judea appeared on their right in the hazy distance. Miriam pressed her hat further over her eyes.

"We should build our house here," she exclaimed in delight.

In the distance the German-American colony appeared. The Hotel Jerusalem, their destination, stood out from the other buildings. Its stately three stories were embellished with an awkward mix of French, Italian and Oriental styles, but in this setting it had the appearance of a palace. Inside, the staff received them graciously. The owner offered them a cool drink, which they were happy to accept. When they finally entered their room, they embraced and fell exhausted on their bed. Miriam started to laugh, "this is exactly as I envisioned it."

He kissed her. Within a minute they were both sound asleep.

Joseph woke to a strange sound that nevertheless was vaguely familiar. He felt completely disoriented. The sound came again. It was the *muezzin*. He opened his eyes and saw the last light of day coming through the high windows. As he saw Miriam lying next to him, he realized where he was. Softly, he woke her.

"Come, we have to meet someone. At least I hope so."

Miriam asked him where they were going but Joseph only winked and said: "Just wait and see."

They left the hotel and headed back on horseback to the gate of Yafo, relieved to find the horses so docile. From the gate they followed the path to the highest part of the city. Joseph prayed that the man he wanted to visit would be home. Before their departure he had sent a letter, but there had been no answer, which he hoped was just due to the unreliable postal services.

It had to be one of the streets here. Joseph had assumed that he would recognize it immediately, but he was taken aback. Either his memory had betrayed him or a lot had changed since his last visit. And all houses looked similar. But suddenly he recognized a door. He pushed aside the curtain covering to the entrance of a house. Behind it stood a dim room.

"Is anyone here?" He knocked on an overhead beam.

"One moment," sounded a voice from out back. Joseph recognized the timbre and soon Rachid's energetic shape appeared.

"Rachid, thank God that we see each other again." They embraced each other. "Please let me introduce you to my wife, Miriam."

"Joseph has told me so much about you," Miriam said.

Rachid thanked her with a modest nod and a smile.

"I did not receive your letter until this week, Sir Johann. But, of course, I will accompany you."

"Wonderful! By the way, is Mr. Harrison around?"

"No, he went on an expedition in the Sinai. He is not expected to be back for a few months."

"It's a pity." Joseph shrugged his shoulders. "Then we will do without him. Six o'clock at our hotel tomorrow morning? Oh and, from now on, please refer to me as Joseph." In response to Rachid's quizzical look, he commented enigmatically, "that was then, and this is now."

The next day Rachid was there with two fine horses. In addition, he had arranged for a few extra mules to carry their suitcases and other belongings.

"The journey will take about fourteen hours," he said to Joseph.

Miriam had undergone a metamorphosis. She looked like an oriental princess. Wild and exotic, with wide green flowing trousers, a beautiful loose white blouse and a purple scarf tied around her neck and shoulders. A single dark strand of hair fell loosely from under the large straw hat that partially covered her face. In nothing did she remind Joseph of the girl who he had seen mumbling her silent prayers, dressed in her black religious dress in the synagogue of Cologne.

"I love you, my Sheherazade." Of course, he then had to explain who Sheherazade was, but he enjoyed these moments.

"How do you know all these things?" she asked.

"I sweated my guts out all the years that I worked for Pennekamp in Cologne. He thought I was a clever boy but with a lack of general knowledge. I wanted to be as well read as the others. I plowed through the books at night so that no one could catch me as illiterate. Most of all, I learned from Max."

"With Uncle Max? How funny." She stopped for a moment. "He really sees you as his best friend."

"Max is the best that ever happened to me in my life. Except you of course," he rushed to say. "But I also got to know you via Max, so." He thought for a moment. "That knowledge. I like to show it off but frankly knowledge is greatly overestimated. You, Miriam, you have an abundance of insight and understanding, which is much more important."

After riding for half an hour they saw the minarets of Ramle in the distance, fiercely contrasting against the hazy blue sky that vibrated in the heat. A group of pine trees and a single palm tree gave exactly the right contours to the landscape.

"Richard could really make something of this," said Joseph as they approached the city. Time and again he took out his map to see where they were. With childlike pleasure he enjoyed the adventure the map promised.

"Just look at the real world instead of spending all your time on that map. Are you afraid we'll get lost? Rachid really knows what he's doing." Rachid confirmed that they were in safe hands.

Joseph remembered little Edmond Rothschild with his treasure map in a park in Frankfurt. Had he ever found his prize? By now he would be a man in his early twenties. He would probably have discovered the treasure in the vault of his bank. Joseph put the map away again and looked at the distant hills beyond Ramle. But a little later he proudly pulled it out again, as they came to a junction. Rachid confidently chose the right hand path.

"Are we not going through Ramle?" Miriam asked.

"If you want. It's the other path. But there is not much to see. More of the same, more Yafo."

"Then let's continue," Joseph decided. "The holy city calls us!"

"Don't mock it," Miriam said. "Or you will end up badly."

"Then I will take you down with me in my wickedness." He blew her a kiss and urged his horse to take the lead. "Come on. We still have a long way to go."

Beyond Ramle they climbed gradually to higher ground and went into the hills. The path meandered between the chalk cliffs. The horses seemed sure of their steps. The air became purer and clearer. The humidity disappeared and breathing became a pleasure instead of an effort. The colors were a beautiful mosaic of light blue, green and white. Here and there were villages to be seen, as if a child had been playing with small white cubes and stacked them randomly against the hills.

Suddenly the horses and donkeys stood stock-still. A dull rumble sounded from under the ground, as if a monster were trying to break through the earth's crust. Then the animals started to tremble.

Rachid was the first to take action. "Earthquake," he shouted hoarsely. "Try to get on a flat piece of ground. Not under the trees!" His actions matched his words and just as Joseph and Miriam tried to do the same, the earth moved. Miriam screamed. A strip of dirt sank half a meter and then shot up again. Trees creaked around them. A few fell, their roots pointing skyward. Miriam shouted again as her horse ran off in full gallop. She hung on desperately. Without hesitation Joseph urged his horse after hers. He jumped over low bushes in a steep descent; in front of him he saw Miriam, who was somehow still on her horse. They soared over stones, rocks, and low vegetation, and missed a solitary tree by a hair. Soon the ground was firm again, but the horses ran on. They had now reached a *wadi* and Miriam's horse apparently decided to follow the riverbed. Joseph began to lag behind, probably because he was still trying to control his horse. Suddenly he heard a shriek in front of him. He hurried on and saw Miriam lying on the ground in a heap. Her horse, still shaking, stood next to her.

"Oh, my God, Miriam!"

She looked up painfully, with tears in her eyes. Joseph jumped off his horse and tried to take her in his arms. "Don't. It hurts. Everything hurts." She laughed through her tears while she rubbed her lower leg. "I think it's not too bad." She sighed. "I was terrified."

"Me too." He looked at her leg, but couldn't see anything else except some grazes. "Can you move your leg?"

"I think so, but it hurts." With a twisted face she stretched her leg. "It's getting better already."

"We have to take care of you." Miriam's clothes were torn in several places and she had scratches on her arms and legs. She tied the fabric together with a few knots.

Now that Joseph had recovered from the first shock, he inspected the surroundings. They were in a sheltered valley with steep limestone walls on both sides. In front and behind them the prickly but lush vegetation of mulberry and cactus figs blocked the view. Here and there trees unfamiliar to Joseph had tried to find a foothold in the dry riverbed. It made a peaceful impression, especially after the wild pursuit. In the quiet, they could occasionally hear a cricket or a bird. A weak wind carried sharp, unknown, but pleasant smells. "It's beautiful here." He sat down and looked at Miriam. "What do you think we should do? Go back, wait for Rachid, or try to continue? Are you fit to ride?"

"Don't worry about that. What do you think Rachid will do? Try to find us?"

"Yes, I think so. But it might take a while. You could walk for days here without seeing anyone."

"Please, let's wait for him."

"Then we had better go up that hill. It has a wider view."

In the distance they heard sheep bells and a barking dog. After that it was quiet again.

They led the horses out of the *wadi* and climbed up the steep slope, while holding carefully onto the thorny bushes. Miriam was still limping a bit. Their feet sought hold on the rough uneven limestone. Exhausted, they ended up under a broad tree from which they had a panoramic view. Still raw with emotion and also struck by the breathtaking beauty of what they saw, they sat for a while without saying anything.

"Strange," Joseph said. "This country has two opposing aspects. You can see hostile deterrence and grim desolation, but with the right attitude the landscape becomes peaceful and friendly, even idyllic."

"It is so beautiful here," Miriam said.

Joseph agreed. "I never saw a place like this. So harmonious. I feel whole. At one with the world, at one with you." After some time, he continued. "This is a crossroads. Not a loose point in time. Not even a continuous line. All is open. I am not afraid of anything. Wherever we go it's good. It doesn't matter."

"You could say it is a miracle that the horses have taken us here." Miriam said. "Otherwise we would never have discovered this place."

Joseph looked at his vest watch but discovered that it no longer worked.

"Look," Miriam said with a smile and she pointed, "The sun also stands still."

"If we want to arrive in Jerusalem before dark, it may have to stand still a little longer," said Joseph smiling. He felt that being here with her would be the ultimate ideal for the rest of his life.

After some time they heard a familiar voice calling in the distance.

"Rachid, we are here!" Joseph shouted. Finally, they saw him, leading his horse and the mules on the reins, searching his way in the dry bed.

"God is blessed," Rachid cried. "You are both unharmed."

Joseph and Rachid embraced each other.

"We must leave immediately if we want to reach Jerusalem before dark," Rachid said.

It turned out that the sun had just continued its course. They descended again to the bed.

"We will follow the *wadi*," said Rachid, "its path heads exactly the right way. It can't be more than an hour."

"Let's hope we don't get assailed."

"I don't think anyone lives here. It might become a bit more dangerous as we draw closer to Jerusalem. I'm more worried about our water supply."

Despite the irregular terrain they made good progress. The wadi eventually turned into some kind of path. As it started to get dark, Rachid said they were nearing the city.

"Do you see that building over there, Rachid?" asked Joseph. "With that cross on top?"

"I've never seen it before," Rachid replied.

Miriam came up next to them and wiped the sweat off her face. If she had looked like an Oriental princess that morning, now, with the scarf tied around her forehead and the torn clothes, she looked more like a member of an Assyrian gang of robbers. Dark smears of sand ran across her face.

"Generally, the Christians here can be trusted," said Rachid.

"Maybe we can spend the night there," Joseph suggested.

As they approached, they began to see more details of the building. Joseph could not resist showing his knowledge of architectural styles. "Those volutes on the façade show that it must have been built after 1500. It cannot have been from the time of the Crusaders."

Miriam looked at him, mockingly. "Do you really think that this knowledge is going to help us somehow?" Joseph stuttered a bit and Miriam continued: "Maybe it was taken over by a gang of Bedouin bandits."

But the monastery was completely deserted and the empty spaces made a ghostly impression. Joseph thought of the cathedral of Cologne. But this was scarier because somehow it was alien to their wondrous experiences of the day.

"Maybe we can see more from the bell tower," Miriam said. The depressing atmosphere of the building had not taken hold of her.

On top they saw, to their relief, the lights of a city in the distance. It could only be Jerusalem.

"Come, let's go. Maybe the gates of the city are still open."

But it took another hour before they had found the right way and when they finally approached the city in the plain before the Yafo Gate, they knew that they were too late and that the city was closed.

"Nothing is going to change that," said Rachid calmly. "It is the will of God."

Joseph looked at Miriam: "I have experienced this before. In Cologne. I spent the night outside the walls. It was the night they robbed me of everything. The drawing of my parents. I told you about that, didn't I?" Now he felt the same kind of tension and excitement as then. An open future.

"Yes," Miriam said. "I thought it was a beautiful story. You told it rather well. You, losing your past."

"I don't want to lose anything now," he said. He let his gaze wander over the walls once more. "What do you think, Rachid? Shall we wait here for the morning?"

In response, their loyal guide started to unpack all the baggage and began to make a provisional bed in the shelter of a gnarled olive tree.

"It's better to stay here," he said.

Against his better judgment Joseph pushed forward. "Let's just knock on the door and tell our story. Maybe the gatekeeper will take pity on a woman? I don't feel safe outside."

7

A DESERT VISION

The Turkish gatekeeper was adamant; no one entered the city after the gates had closed. But when he saw that Joseph and Miriam were refusing to leave he eventually provided an alternative, suggesting that they try the new buildings, outside the walls, near the mill. *Mishkenot Sha'ananim*. The man pointed vaguely to the southwest, where Joseph saw the silhouette of a mill stand out against the evening sky. He remembered it from his first visit. "There," the gatekeeper said, "among your fellow believers, you might be more successful." The way he said it made clear that he thought very little of any of them.

Rachid did not feel comfortable with the idea, but he reluctantly agreed to come along. The three of them dragged back down the hill to the valley, to start the steep climb to the small community.

"I assume no one will be eager to let us in."

Joseph remembered what Rivka had said. These houses were built by Montefiore, but they were difficult to rent out. Nobody wanted to live outside the walls. Far too dangerous. He looked at Rachid, who evidently knew the question that would come.

"I'll wait here. Just try. I guess it would be the same the other way around."

They knocked at the first door. No reaction, although Joseph thought he saw a movement behind one of the windows. "Let's forget it," Joseph said. "No one is going to answer. And I can't blame them. I wouldn't open the door for some strangers either."

"But hospitality is one of our most important virtues," Miriam replied. "Have you forgotten what Avraham did when he saw the three strangers coming?"

Their third attempt was more successful. Someone opened the door just a crack. Joseph saw a stout man with a long white beard. He was wearing his tzitzit over his large belly. After Joseph had explained who they were and what had happened, the man introduced himself as Yankele Goldstein and called his wife, Rochele. She was dressed in the tradition of the small Jewish towns in Eastern Europe.

"Newlyweds. *Mazal tov!*" she exclaimed. "And then on a honeymoon to Jerusalem. Come in."

"We've already eaten," said Yankele, "but we probably have some cake left from Shabbat." He turned to his wife. "And maybe some wine too." Extra candles were lit and Rochele brought food and drinks.

When they had begun to feel comfortable, Miriam ventured, "our guide… He is still outside. May he join us?" Miriam asked.

"Of course," said Yankele hospitably. "If you trust him, we trust him."

Rachid entered reluctantly, with an awkward smile on his face. He exhausted himself in gratitude. Soon they were enjoying what was nothing less than a little feast. Joseph did not know what to say, as undoubtedly, the family was not rich. Miriam, however, seemed to feel at home immediately and asked a lot of questions. The Goldsteins had left Vilnius some ten years earlier. Their eldest son had been killed in the Crimean War, fighting for the Russians. At all costs they wanted to prevent their other sons from being dragooned as well, as they would probably have faced a similar fate. They had heeded the recommendation of the head of the *Yeshiva* and left for Palestine. They left precipitously and had arrived in Jerusalem without any possessions. At first they had lived from the contributions, the *halukkah*, but Montefiore had opened Yankele's eyes.

"By putting these buildings here, the man has changed history. There is no way back. I don't know if I agree with all of it, but I started to think. And then I started working. I am an assistant in a small printing shop in the city."

"Is it hard to survive here?"

"I'll tell you a secret. We even get money to live here. If you have the time one of these days, I will be happy to give you a personal tour. Then you can see what we have accomplished and what the future might bring. Unfortunately, not everyone is convinced of this."

"We'd love to come back again," Miriam replied. She looked at Joseph. "Right?"

"Certainly. Certainly. I find it all very interesting."

"The day after tomorrow is *Tisha b'Av*. Maybe the day after?"

"Indeed, better not on a day of mourning."

He offered them the master bedroom, but Joseph would not have it. "We'll sleep here, on some cushions." Miriam thanked them again for their hospitality.

"You have a nice family and a nice house," Joseph said. "May it be blessed for as long as you live."

Rachid thanked them as well and made himself comfortable on some cushions in a corner.

Later, when they were alone, Joseph said: "So, happiness is possible here." The unconditional warmth and affection reminded him of the Yom Kippur evening at the Ben Tovs. He smiled thankfully at Miriam who took his hand and said, as if she could read his thoughts: "It reminds me so much of home."

"Maybe we are indeed one big family?"

In the early morning, they said goodbye and went back to the gate that was open now. When they finally arrived in their hotel room, Rachid took his leave as they were safe within the walls.

"Now our holiday can really begin. Well, except for the fast tomorrow," Joseph said.

He opened the windows and sniffed the air, full of scents that brought to mind his first visit to the city in the same hotel.

"I would like to visit Rivka," he said.

"Certainly and afterwards we could walk to the Western Wall," Miriam replied.

Half an hour later they arrived at the gate of the monastery in the *Via Dolorosa* where Joseph had found his sister five years ago.

"Renata is no longer in our monastery," said the nun who opened it.

Joseph looked surprised. "Good news or bad news?"

The nun seemed offended and said sullenly, "I will bring you to her." She did not say another word, but marched off down the street. Miriam and Joseph followed her silently. Not far from the monastery, the nun knocked at the door of an old building.

"She lives here, on the second floor," she said.

The door opened and an old Arab looked at them for a long time. The nun spoke with him in Arabic. Before they had a chance to thank her, she turned around and was gone. The man growled something and then led them up the stairs. On top of the portal he knocked on a door. They heard stumbling and someone asked a question, also in Arabic. Joseph thought he recognized his sister's voice but he was not sure at all. The door opened slowly and cautiously a head appeared.

"Rivka!"

"Joseph! Is that really you! What a surprise." Rivka opened the door and Joseph saw that she was no longer wearing her nun's habit, but a strange colorful mix of western and oriental clothes. It looked good on her. Her dark hair was not covered. She looked at Miriam.

"This is Miriam, my wife."

"Well, well, brother."

Rivka embraced her. Miriam blushed.

"But please enter. Let me make you some coffee."

The room was small but pleasantly furnished.

"Nice! One wouldn't expect such a nice place, so high up," Joseph said.

"The higher you go up in a building, the better they get. More air, more light. More privacy. Different than in modern Europe. But everything here is different from Europe," Rivka said, then adding, "and more expensive. So, as you can see, I am doing well. But most people here don't want to be on their own. Most things, people do communally, Jews as well as the Arabs."

"Like in the good old *Judengasse*," Joseph said cheerfully.

Rivka proposed that she would first tell her account: "My story is simple. After that you can tell yours." She sat back: "I took your advice to heart. I left the convent. The other sisters respected that."

"And now?"

"For the time being I am teaching French at a Christian girls' school."

"I'm glad to hear that," Joseph said. "If I may ask, why did you leave the monastery?"

"You may ask and I will tell you one day." Rivka smiled. "Not now. I'll tell you something else. Some time ago I met someone at school who knows you, a lady from Cologne. Esther Perachim."

"Elsa," Joseph exclaimed. "*Perachim*. Flowers. Blumenreich. It makes sense. What a coincidence."

"It's not that coincidental. Jerusalem is quite small and if there's another German walking around who's also been baptized, there's a good chance you'll run into her. By the way, she did not want to be reminded of that. She stopped working for the school. She has moved to Bethlehem."

Joseph looked at her in amazement.

"Esther, or Elsa as you call her," continued Rivka, "has spoken to me at length about you. It was so much fun hearing stories about you, here, so far away from Germany."

Joseph looked slightly alarmed: "What kind of stories?"

"All kind of things. About your friend Max, about our family." She laughed and looked playful. "Yes, she repeated to me everything you told her. No harm," she hurried to say. "All good things. No evil speech. And she said you had a weak spot for me."

"Miriam is Max's niece."

"How nice!" She looked at Miriam. "I think my brother should be the happiest man in the world."

Again Miriam blushed.

Rivka laughed. "It is so nice to see you both." She poured more coffee and made herself comfortable in her chair. "Tell me everything."

For quite some time, they sat and talked.

"We will spend more time together?" asked Rivka.

"For sure. We are going to visit the *Kotel* now," Miriam said. "Would you like to join us?"

In the sharp light of the afternoon, they descended through the alleys to the ancient western wall, but Jerusalem still did not give Joseph a special feeling. Little had changed since last time. Everywhere people were trying to sell something – rosaries, pearl shells, stones of the Dead Sea; everything was displayed on the street in a chaotic mess. When they came to the Jewish quarter, boys stopped them on every corner, hands outstretched for coins. Perhaps there were more shops than last time, stone cutters, wine sellers, horse renters. But there was nothing that kindled his enthusiasm, not even the *Kotel*. They passed the *Churva* synagogue. Rivka pointed out that it was only two years ago that the synagogue finally had been consecrated. "I think it is the highest building in Jerusalem."

When they arrived at the wall, they saw dozens of men and women in the narrow space in front of it, facing the wall, praying with fervent movements.

"I do not believe in holy places," Joseph said. "I do believe in the power of experiences in specific places. Like the hill by the *wadi* where we sat. That moment was divine. I find it hard to feel or find any holiness in a wall. Do you mind?"

Miriam only said: "Everyone is entitled to his own opinion."

Thinking of that afternoon, Joseph asked Rivka about the building they had seen when they got lost.

"An abandoned monastery. About an hour's walk to the west."

Rivka shook her head.

"It was really a ghost building," Miriam said with a smile.

"One day we will go back together to see whether it was real," Joseph promised.

"The day the sun stopped," Miriam continued. "We will never forget it."

After they promised to spend more time with her soon, they took their leave from Rivka and got back to the hotel.

"I really like your sister. I think we will become very good friends."

Joseph nodded as he looked at her, feeling that he was indeed the happiest man on earth.

The sun shone mercilessly on the fast day of *Tisha b'Av*. Joseph stayed in the hotel and tried to sleep as much as possible. He wasn't insensitive to the remembrance of the destruction of the Temple, but did he have to suffer because of it in 1866? To keep alive the memory of a distant past that had come to an end rather dubiously? Nevertheless, he fasted together with Miriam, who could apparently endure anything without difficulty.

The day of mourning was different from what it had been in Germany. There you could identify with the exile and the misfortune and there the lamentations of Yermiyahu made an impression. Now they were in Jerusalem. Didn't it make more sense to build a future than look at past destruction? And hadn't the Jews deserved having the Temples destroyed, he asked Miriam. Both the first and the second one.

"Aren't you being a bit harsh?" she replied.

"*Sinat chinam*, baseless hatred, and a society that was corrupt, masquerading all its faults by playing nice in the Temple. That was why the end came. It's all in the Scriptures."

"Yes, I know, but do you really have a heart of stone?"

"I am sorry. I am just thirsty. Let's go to *Mishkenot Sha'ananim* now," Joseph proposed, to give the conversation a more positive direction. "The nice people we met there are both in the past and the present. They grieve, but in the end, they are not fatalists."

"I don't know whether they will welcome us today. But let's try. I do think it's a wonderful idea."

Without rushing, they made the walk to the buildings outside the walls. The sun was burning and it was hard not to think of water.

The Goldsteins received them, but because of the fast day the atmosphere was solemn. Joseph heard weeping in the back room. He looked at Yankele with a questioning face.

"We are very personally affected by the destruction of the Temple. It is the saddest day of the year."

"I know. I know," admitted Joseph.

Miriam said she would stay with Rochele. Yankele went ahead and led Joseph to the other room. A group of men were sitting on the floor. One of them read lamentations and *kinot*, sad poems. Most of them swayed back and forth in rhythm. Occasionally a person wailed with sorrow and grief. Most of them had tears in their eyes. Joseph felt uncomfortable. "Maybe it's better to leave? Come back later?"

"No, we will sit in the kitchen. Would you like to study with me? Read *Eicha* again?"

Joseph nodded. He did not see Miriam anywhere, but someone told him that she had gone to the neighbors with Rochele and her daughters. Joseph sat with Yankele for the rest of the afternoon, leaning over the book, reading and discussing the heartbreaking lamentations of Yermiyahu about the lost greatness of Jerusalem, the bereaved city that had become a widow. No comfort there.

At first he resisted the texts and the whole idea of reading them here and now. If only they had visited Rivka instead; she was probably drinking some refreshing lemonade right now. But gradually his resistance faded. It had been a long time since he had really read these texts and doing so in this context made an impression, especially while accompanied by the moans and cries that occasionally came out of the back room. Joseph realized that he could never mock this. These people experienced the destruction as if it were happening today. Slowly but surely the sonorous tones of the lyrics engulfed him and the time flew by. It was late in the afternoon when the women came back. Miriam smiled at him. "We're going to clean up a bit."

Around eight o'clock the fast ended, and Miriam and Joseph joined the Goldsteins for a light meal. The food and drinks tasted better than ever. They felt like survivors. Yankele turned very talkative. "For most people it is even sadder than for us."

Joseph asked what he meant.

"Everyone believes in the coming of the *Mashiach*. Only, most of them are convinced that we cannot influence it. They are waiting for a miracle. And then all will be well. I think, on the other hand, that we can speed up the coming by rebuilding Jerusalem."

Joseph remembered the words of Rav Yermiyahu after the Yom Kippur service in Cologne. Here were apparently more representatives of this ideology. Joseph wanted to say that he was not so concerned about the coming of the Messiah, but understood that voicing the thought in this company would not be appropriate. "Rabbi Akiva said that one of the two seats in heaven is for King David. Mankind is sitting next to God in ruling the world. But on the other hand, Rabbi Akiva backed the wrong horse when he supported the uprising against the Romans."

"Very good. You have learned well," Yankele praised. "But a lot is happening. Europe is finally interfering. In France, the *Alliance* is busy. They are collecting money in the United States."

Joseph remarked that it was all too small in scale and not supported by a real vision. "With all due respect, building a few houses here will not change the situation."

"You are right," Yankele admitted. "Money alone is not enough. And even if everyone did their utmost, we would still need a miracle to make the vision a reality. But people can do a lot. We have to take those first shaky steps."

"As long as the great nations don't support it, you won't achieve anything."

"Great nations are relative," argued Yankele. "The great empires of the past no longer exist, yet we do. Since the Damascus story, something has changed. And since the baptism of that Italian boy."

Joseph smiled at the thought of Edgardo Mortara, remembering his tiny role in the story. He also knew the other story, that of Damascus. In 1840 a number of Jews were wrongly accused of the ritual murder of a priest. They were tortured for days and two of them did not survive. It had become a scandal in both England and France. Even Montefiore had tried to interfere. The accusation was that they had used the priest's blood to make *matza* dough. Joseph shook his head sadly. That ancient disgusting lie had also been the source of Heine's tale of the *Rabbi of Bacherach*. He remembered his arrogant thought of finishing the novella. His childish desire to see the place at the Rhine. Strange that here in the hills of Jerusalem he was thinking back to that misty journey, and to Heine and his story. Then, it all had been a game, but here the pieces fell into place. The people mourning the destruction of the Temple, the patron Montefiore who had built the house where he, Joseph, was now. The Goldsteins who had fled from evil and at the same time sought redemption. These people were real. This was not an exercise in piety or involvement. Joseph was grateful that he had seen a glimpse of the grief and a spark of the future of these people.

They picked up Rivka before leaving for Bethlehem to visit Elsa. Rivka had gathered some information and the German consul had provided a precise route description. To his relief Joseph found out that Rachid was still in the city. The reliable guide offered to accompany them. The road was dangerous and a man and two women would be easy prey for robbers.

Just outside the town, Rachid drew their attention to a building at the side of the road, a small dome on a square base. Rachel's grave. Some people, mostly women, were deeply immersed in prayer and meditation. Joseph had difficulty imagining Elsa among them.

"Let's have a look," Miriam suggested.

"Do you believe Rachel is buried here?" Joseph asked Rachid.

"We call her *Rachil*," Rachid replied. "Yes. I believe so."

Joseph walked to the building. Rachid believed in it, so why would he try to dispute it?

"Should I believe it?" he asked when they were walking around the building.

"That's up to you. You are free," Rachid said. "Tradition is important and according to tradition this is the grave of *Rachil*. It is what it is," he added.

"Why are so many women here," Miriam asked.

"She is their source of inspiration," replied Rivka, "The tears of Rachel are a connecting element. The mother who will bring her children home. Many women make the trip to this tomb every new month."

A moaning woman approached them and asked if they wanted to buy a few red strands. Rivka took out some money and gave it to her.

"I still don't get these red strings on the wrist. It reminds me of some kind of rosary. Why do believers always want to hold something?"

Not long after leaving the tomb, they reached a small white house standing apart from the others in the valley. It could hardly contain more than two rooms. So this was where his old benefactress from Cologne lived. They saw a woman outside, chasing the chickens into the run. Could it be?

"*Frau* Elsa. *Frau* Blumenreich," Joseph called.

The woman looked up. Joseph was sure she was not Elsa. It couldn't be. A tanned face wrapped in a frayed cloth. A long, rather shapeless, brown robe to the ground. Sandals at her feet.

"The Holy One be blessed. Is this really you, Joseph?" Her voice faltered.

"It's me." Joseph descended his horse and embraced her. "This is my wife Miriam." Miriam curtsied and gave her a hand. "Rivka, my sister, you have already met, I heard?"

"Indeed, indeed." She took off her headscarf and tried to arrange her hair a little. "Please, go inside and Saïda will make tea. In the meantime, I'll clean myself up a little." A young girl appeared. Elsa said something in Arabic and the girl laughed.

"*Sie, Willkommen*," said Saïda in broken German. "Please tea?"

The interior was one big oriental feast of exuberant shapes and colors. In the middle was a low table with a water pipe. Pillows lay on the carpets. Apparently, the only thing Elsa had not been able to part with was her portrait, which hung pontifically on the main wall of the house.

Elsa came in. She was now dressed in more European style, with a skirt and a simple sweater. Joseph noticed that she had put on a little make-up. Elsa smiled, obviously pleased to have them there. "You never expected to see me in a place like this, did you? On that day you came to visit me at the *Heumarkt*."

"I certainly did not expect this. But it all looks really cozy and inviting." Joseph then pointed to the water pipe. "Do you use it?"

"But certainly." She called her helper again. "Saïda is my support and helper in domestic affairs. She lives in the small village nearby and her parents and I have become good friends. Her father is more or less the police chief there. He always complains about the Turks. But then again, everybody always complains about the Turks, so what else is new. Her mother does the laundry for me and some extra things."

Miriam asked: "Do you feel safe? All alone and so far away from everything?"

"Safer than I could ever have been in Cologne. Everyone knows me and they constantly keep an eye on me."

"How are we going to make this credible in your memoirs?"

"That's your job. I don't know how it all will turn out. But I trust you will make the end as sparkling as the beginning."

Joseph nodded. A feeling of sadness washed over him; this was the last place he wanted to think about her end. He looked out of the window over the hills of Judea. In the distance the sharp light fell on a few houses between some rough low vegetation and the rocky slopes. As the prayer put it, a good, desirable, and spacious country.

When Saïda had poured the tea a little later, Joseph said: "Isn't she a bit young to be working for you?"

"She is lucky to be with me. In Jerusalem, as a twelve-year-old, she probably would already have been married. The age at which these children are getting married is outrageous, not only the Jews but also the Arabs here."

Elsa took a sip of tea in her own distinguished manner, with her little finger up, and started her story. "I don't remember what I've already told you in the letters, but I'll tell it briefly for the others." She still loved to create order, even when it was not necessary. Her order. "As you know, I wanted to go all the way back to our faith. I expected Jerusalem to be the best place for that. I found a nice home in a small house in a Muslim neighborhood. But it was expensive, overcrowded and it smelled very bad. I occasionally would go to the Wall but I soon ceased doing that. They always throw garbage at you there."

She looked at Rivka. "I wanted to help set up a Jewish school. But then the Orthodox rabbis began to distrust me. I was Christian, I lived among the Muslims and I behaved like a Jew. They were suspicious of a German witch who had converted to Christianity and was now doing *t'shuva* in the Holy Land. They don't take women seriously anyway and the regulations they imposed on us only got stricter and stricter. If I had stayed, I would have had to accept that, since for the Jews the Orthodox community determines what happens in Jerusalem. So I left."

She looked at Joseph, as if reading his thoughts. "I hear you thinking, why didn't she come back to Germany?" Elsa shook her head. "This land has become too dear to me. And to deny it to myself because of those people was not something I could live with."

She still radiated such authority that no one dared to interrupt her. "As long as the ultra-Orthodox are in charge there, I will remain at a distance. I am practical. I can't get them out of Jerusalem and for sure I can't change them, so I decided to move. Look at this beautiful place. I feel at home here. I have help from the locals." She laughed. "I became an Ottoman citizen. You hadn't imagined that, I guess?"

Rivka looked worried. Joseph noticed and asked what was wrong.

"It doesn't have to mean anything," answered Rivka. She turned to Elsa: "Then you no longer have the right of protection. You are a toy for the Turkish authorities."

"But then at least I could live where I wanted to. And I wanted to live here, near my Rachel."

She relaxed. "Enough about me. Tell me about you and your lovely wife." She looked a bit impish, "and tell me especially about what that crazy Max is doing."

They talked until dusk. Rivka said it was safer to get back to Jerusalem before dark and Rachid agreed with her. The farewell made Joseph melancholic. It felt sadder than the farewell at the station long ago in Cologne, possibly because they had not seen each other for so long.

"You're going to come back," Elsa predicted. "You're made exactly from the stuff that can't resist this." Both Miriam and Joseph laughed. Rivka looked cheerfully. "That is exactly what I tell him all the time."

They mounted their horses and Joseph gave a sign to Rachid to lead the way. Before a sharp turn in the path blocked his view, he looked back again and saw Elsa standing in front of her house like a phantom from the past.

The last day of their honeymoon they had reserved for a trip to the Dead Sea and a visit to the spring of Ein Gedi. Joseph was struck again by a feeling of nostalgia; his awareness that the journey was almost over stabbed him like a physical pain.

They left before the sun was up because it would be a long ride through the desert. For the first time they went eastward from Jerusalem and as they descended, the land became rougher and more desolate. There was hardly any vegetation left. The parasols were no superfluous luxury. Ibrahim, a local guide who knew the area through and through, led them. Rivka had decided not to go along. She had been there once and had got a minor sunstroke.

Deeper and deeper they descended. Joseph knew that their target was three hundred meters below sea level and when he reported this to Miriam, she said she could feel it. "As if we are descending into a salt mine. But it is exciting."

Not much later, they saw the sea below them. The contrast in colors was overwhelming. Deeper blue Joseph had never seen. In the water, the pinkish mountains on the other side were reflected. The sky was transparent, as if the heavens had opened. No painting could match this beauty. Miriam held her breath.

"This is the most beautiful thing I have ever seen," she said.

The world seemed to be reduced to its elements – air, water, earth. "Indeed, it's almost too much," he said. This view went beyond any definition of aesthetic delight. Every now and then they stopped to admire the impressive landscape.

When they reached the water, they continued, parallel to the shore. Between the white rocks and holes a primitive track led them southward. On their right, grim ocher-brown mountains stood as guards. It reminded Joseph strongly of pictures he had seen of the Valley of the Kings in Egypt, where one astonishing discovery after another had come to light. Joseph suspected that in the caverns he saw here, a lot could be found as well. Better to keep Ferretti far away, he thought with a smile.

Suddenly the guide pointed up to the right side, to the mountains.

"Ein Gedi," he said simply.

Joseph tried to see an opening somewhere in the ridge, a gorge, valley or passage, but the mountains seemed impenetrable.

"We leave things behind here. We put up tent when we get back," said Ibrahim. "Now still beautiful light. We go up."

Joseph nodded. They took the essentials with them, some food and especially the water bottles. The heat was overwhelming. The guide urged his mule and they went up a winding path. After a while they had to leave their riding animals behind. It was too steep and too narrow.

"Above water, springs of *Dawuud*, your King David," the guide solemnly said. "But difficult, especially for ladies."

Miriam looked offended, but said nothing. They followed a dry bed and made their way over the rocks. There was more vegetation now, which indeed indicated the presence of a spring, and as they climbed between the large boulders, the soil became damp. They had to be careful not to slip, but a little later the *wadi* opened. In the sharp light they saw a pool of clear water, fed by a small waterfall on the other side and shaded by steep golden brown rocks and plants hanging over the water.

Miriam shone: "This is a scene from paradise."

Joseph nodded. "David was not so crazy after all. I would also like to sit here and write."

"He was on the run. Hiding. It wasn't all fun," Miriam said.

They looked up because of a sound followed by the clashing of stones.

"Goats, kids," the guide said. "We disturb drink."

"They will have to wait," Miriam said. "I'm going to refresh my sore feet first."

"And drink. I could swallow this entire pool of water."

They made themselves comfortable on the waterside and brought out their food. Miriam took off her boots and waded through the water. In the middle of the pool she stood, the water up to her knees: "Come, this is delicious." Joseph followed her. The cold water around his feet refreshed him. In the middle of the pool they embraced.

"If we ever get sad or downcast back home, we should remember this," she said.

After eating a little and drinking of the clear water, they refilled their bottles and continued. The climb now became even steeper, but as they looked back they realized that it would be worth it. Sometimes they caught a glimpse of the motionless Dead Sea, which deepened in color with every step they took. The unrelenting mountains on the other side of the sea seemed to be getting higher and higher and now that the sun was in the west, they were becoming increasingly more pink and radiant.

When they finally arrived at the springs, they were at least a few hundred meters above the plain of the sea. A large waterfall crashed down and the air was saturated with moisture. They stood on a kind of barren platform above the spring and had a clear view to all sides. All around them the desert stretched out. Motionless and eternal. Desert was different from anything Joseph had ever experienced. There was no transience here, as there was in a November evening in Germany. There the movement of things was frozen, fixed, thereby paradoxically strengthening its volatility. Here in the desert was the link between all times, an overarching time. Desert was everlasting and age-old. This was, this had been, and this would be.

Joseph pointed to the east: "What a view. This is visionary. The mountains of Moab." Then he turned his gaze to the south. "And there are the mountains of Edom. You can't get any more biblical than this."

After an hour the guide told them they had to return. It was important to descend in daylight.

While they reluctantly started down, Joseph said: "I was thinking up there. Do you remember what Rivka said about Rachel's tomb? As a symbol?"

Miriam nodded.

"All those Jews who want to return to the land and are trying to inspire others. They need something of this stature. What I mean is that they have to come up with something good. Not only with statements about how bad it is in Europe, but how great it is here. Ferretti's party were crooks, but in some respect he was right. He saw things very sharply. Like the meaning of historic symbols, the enormous value that comes from them. Think of those women at Rachel's grave. Ferretti wanted something to get the Church back on its feet. He did not succeed, but the idea was good. This could be a symbol for the Jews."

"What do you think of the Temple in Jerusalem? Isn't that a symbol?"

"For many too religious. And apart from that, the Temple isn't there anymore." Joseph continued, now speaking more to himself. "Funny. Max is turning out to have been right after all. I have to occupy myself with real Jewish history. I am going to write a novel about this place. Finally I have found my subject."

Sitting in the small encampment that evening, Miriam fell into a more melancholy mood. "We have to return to Germany the day after tomorrow. Let's agree here and now that the darkness of Europe will never get to us again, even when it surrounds us anew."

Joseph reached out and held her tightly. He knew all too well what Miriam meant. He saw the danger of blending in again. At first he would resist, to some extent; he would still know that Cologne was not his place. After that he would give himself over to it and conform to it until he didn't know any better, pulled down, in the black hole, adding his own weight to the load. Was it strange for them to think about these things right now? Or did light and beauty make everything more poignant. From here he could hardly understand the heaviness of Europe. But he understood why freedom after captivity had been so disappointing. It had been a freedom that didn't lead to anything. During the expedition with Ferretti he had sometimes had a vague feeling that he belonged here. Now he knew. This was the watershed.

"I don't think we can go back. I have to be here. We have to be here," he solemnly said. "Not the way your father wants it, not the way Moshe Hess wants it, nor as the Gaon of Vilna pictures it. Not as an unwelcome refugee nor as a religious idealist dreaming of building something. Just as it is. I have to be here. I feel it. Here I feel alive." He looked around. "Something has changed. We will come back here. We can go back to Germany, but we will always be here in our hearts and minds."

The steamship that would take them back to Europe lay anchored in Yafo. On the quay they said goodbye to Rachid and Rivka. The buzz was overwhelming. Another ship had just arrived with an evangelical group from America.

Joseph asked someone in the crowd with an impressive uniform what was going on. He turned out to be the British consul. "Americans," the consul said. "The Christian Lovers of Zion of a certain George Adams. They have come to the Promised Land to seek their salvation."

The whole bank was full of wooden beams and planks, slats and plates. Joseph laughed. "Those Americans do it the high way. Not a suitcase with a few clothes. They just take their houses with them."

Miriam winked. "Maybe an idea for when we come back?"

8

THE LAST TIME

They bought a floor in a stately building on the *Holzmarkt*, by the
river. The location seemed perfect – on the edge of the city but at the
same time right in the center, which ended on the river. The economic
boom had reached Cologne and the city council had decided to build
the new harbor right there, so there was construction everywhere.
Despite this, Joseph and Miriam found the place extremely suitable.
They had a spacious room with large windows overlooking the Rhine,
and a small bedroom at the back. The room came fully furnished with
antiques from the Empire period. Paneling of ocher wood running the
entire length of the walls tried to make it all a bit lighter. Heavy carpets
covered the wooden floor. There was an option to buy the upper floor
as well; an opportunity for enlargement, Miriam jested.

Joseph found it difficult to resume his daily life after Palestine.
Nonetheless, he started writing again, about all sorts of subjects.
Pennekamp's newspaper was of course, out of the question, but Max
had introduced him to other newspapers and periodicals, both in
Germany and in the Netherlands, so Joseph had no problem getting his
work published. There was also some translation work and the monthly
stipend he still received from Elsa, along with Horst Pennekamp's dirty
money, to make sure that no financial cloud fell over them. It was the
real clouds, the heavy autumn clouds hanging low in the sky day after
day, that bothered him. Although it might not rain for days, everything
was always moist. As if the ground breathed mist. As if the cold was in
the matter itself.

In November there came a fancy invitation. Joseph recognized his
father's handwriting; it hadn't changed in twenty years. And if that were
not enough to let him recognize the sender, the opening words were
in Yiddish. How many people did he know who still used that? His
father was to be sixty in a month and the whole family was invited to
celebrate a festive gathering in Frankfurt. In a separate note, Aron told
him that even Nathan was planning to come from London with his wife
Penelope. He had not managed to reach Rivka. Reading this, Joseph
felt a sting. He still kept her stay in Jerusalem a secret from his family.
Maybe now it was time to inform them.

More news came two weeks later. One afternoon Miriam came

walking into the room and demanded his full attention. As Joseph put his pen down and watched her attentively, he suddenly guessed what was coming.

"I am pregnant."

He got up and hugged her for a long time. "This is so beautiful. Since when do you know and when does the little one come?"

"The doctor says that our little one will come in May. If God wants it."

"I think he wants it. I hope so."

Again he took her in his arms. "You make me so happy. Do your parents already know?"

"No, not yet. What do you think? Shall we visit them tonight and tell them?"

"Splendid. And surely we'll get a genuine traditional meal," he joked.

The existence of this new human being made Joseph more at ease with the idea of a family reunion. This was news. The momentousness put all stupid questions aside and he could not wait to see the amazement on his older brother's face. Aron would never have expected that the rogue Joseph would become a decent family man after all.

The reunion was held in the house in *Ostend*. When Joseph entered, he knew immediately that he was at home. His mother had hardly lived here and yet, even after all these years, her scent was present. He had little time for nostalgia because he was instantly welcomed by his little brother, who now definitely deserved another predicate. Nathan was an adult man who towered above him. He had short hair and a well-groomed beard. He had all the attributes of a handsome young man who could drive the girls crazy. The features of little Nathan, however, were still present. Joseph greeted him warmly. Nathan quickly introduced him to Penelope, his wife. For a moment Joseph thought he could discern Maria in the blond locks and in the facial traits, but Penelope was sturdier. It was mainly the broad gestures, the exuberant clothing, and the appearance of nonchalant worldliness that reminded him of her. For a moment he was thrown back into old thoughts. What if old Löwe had not been a miserable man and Joseph had married Maria? No Miriam, no visit to Palestine, no baby coming, but a worldly existence separate from Judaism, as part of the bourgeoisie of Cologne. He saw the parallel paths that had presented itself to him. Infinite happiness took possession of him. Thank God, Miriam had come into his life.

"So, you must be Penelope," he said in his best English. She laughed and answered that she had heard a lot about John's older brother. "I was dying to meet you," she added. "You are the traveler, I understand, the brave reporter."

"I don't know if I'm so brave."

He turned to Aron who was hovering in the background with Batia and their four children. Any grudge he might have held against him immediately disappeared. The resentment he had felt earlier in his life melted away when he looked his brother straight in the eye. These were good people.

"Our globetrotter," Aron said cheerfully. "Tell me, what does the east wind bring us?"

"Mainly dust and sand." He hugged him. "We can talk about it later in detail." He looked around to look at Miriam, but to his delight, he saw her crouching down to play with the children.

"Where is Papa?"

"Where do you think he is? He's stuck to his chair. I even wonder if he will get up when *Mashiach* comes," Aron said.

They went to the living room where father Socher sat with his eyes closed, gently nodding, in his old tattered chair. The same chair in which Joseph had huddled in as a child. It had probably not been shifted by as much as an inch since the move from the *Gasse*.

"Yossi," his father said softly when he had opened his eyes. "I hear that you often visit our land. I am so thrilled." His eyes glowed even more when he saw Nathan. "What a day. All the children come to visit me. *Baruch Hashem.*"

"How are you Papa?"

"I am fine, my boy. A little forgetful and I don't hear so well anymore, but I don't complain. They take good care of me. Aron comes by every day and the *kehilla* also does a lot. I only have to be five minutes late for morning prayers and they're already banging at the door." He laughed laboriously. "Unfortunately, I can't do anything without their knowledge." Joseph took his hand and kissed it. "Nice, papa. I think of you every day in my prayers." His father nodded as a sign that everything was good.

A little later they were all sitting in the living room. Aron had opened the curtains completely and a weak sun tried her best to make the scene even more cheerful. Joseph saved his news until they all had calmed down a bit.

"Miriam is pregnant. In May we are expecting a little one, God willing."

"*Mazal tov,*" came from all sides. Miriam glowed.

"It is a pity that Rivka is not here," Nathan said. "Has anyone heard of her lately?"

"I had no address," Aron said, "or else I would have sent her an invitation."

This was the moment. Joseph could no longer remain silent.

"I know where Rivka is," he said quietly.

The others looked up.

"I have spoken with her. In Jerusalem."

"Jerusalem? How did you know? Why didn't you say anything," Aron asked.

"It was when we were on our honeymoon. I wanted to wait for a good opportunity to tell you."

Aron stared in disbelief. "What is she doing there? Is she still with that man, that Rainer?"

"No. That was over before she went there. She is very religious and found Jerusalem the best place to do justice to her faith. She works as a teacher at a girls' school."

Their father had also heard: "Our Rivka in *Eretz Yisroel*. In the holy city. *Baruch Hashem*. I always knew that she was a woman of valor." He dozed off for a while and then opened his eyes again. "We will include her in our prayers." Joseph did not know whether his father remembered that Rivka had been baptized, but he decided not to point it out.

His father continued: "*Eretz Yisroel*. That would be something, wouldn't it, Yossi? A place to stay forever. A place to rest forever."

Did he mean to be buried there or to spend the rest of his days there? Joseph nodded.

The women began to occupy themselves with dinner and the brothers stayed in the living room. It became quieter now and the conversation was about major events and changes in the world: the American Civil War, the Suez Canal.

"You know that we have trains under the ground in London," Nathan said. "To go from one part of the city to another. The Underground. Fast and efficient. The future is going to bring a lot. We are planning to start a department store in New York. There is the future. We already have a floor in a new building in mind. An eight-floor building. Can you imagine? And then you go from one floor to another with an elevator." Nathan turned to Joseph. "You should see New York and write about it."

"I've heard stories about it. Also of the civil war there of course. It must have been bad. The world is changing. One can hardly follow what is happening in Europe. Countries are bursting out of the ground like mushrooms. Italy, Belgium."

"And Palestine?" Nathan asked. "I have heard that there are Jews who want to start a state in Palestine. You have been there. What do you think?"

Joseph scratched his head. "I don't know. The problem is that those who want, cannot, and those who can, do not want. I think it's far from becoming reality."

"But there is a lot of buzz about the roots of a people," Nathan said. "To belong somewhere. Nationality, identity is important."

Joseph looked closely at Nathan: "Are you still interested in the tribe?"

Nathan looked a bit embarrassed. "I am not very much into it. Nobody bothers me about it. For me it is something from the past. Like you think back at child's games. That was fun then. But be honest. I'm not going to play in the street with a hoop any more either. But somehow it is a part of one's identity."

Joseph nodded. "Nationalism is certainly a driving force. But for us? Without the secular world and their idea of nationalism, the notion of going back to the land of our forefathers might not even have arisen at all. But at the same time, nationalism creates the greatest anti-Jewish sentiment."

Aron now also joined the discussion: "It's better to wait until the time is ripe."

"You mean, wait for Divine interference?" asked Nathan.

"Then we can wait a long time," Joseph said. "Don't you know that joke about the *Mashiach*?"

Aron seemed a bit irritated. "Which one?"

"In this *shtetl* a man who has just lost his job, comes to the rabbi for work. Of course, says the rabbi. We need someone to greet *Mashiach* when he comes. It is badly paid, but on the other side, don't be disappointed, it is a job for the rest of your life."

Nathan roared out. Aron smiled hesitantly.

"Ah, come on, Aron," Nathan said. "That was a fun one."

"I really think it is wrong to interfere with the Divine plan," Aron responded.

"But what is the Divine plan?"

Joseph added, "What if there are signs now that you haven't noticed? Divine signs?"

"As there are?" Aron asked.

"Perhaps God sent this contemporary nationalism to show us the way. After all, He remains hidden but He must find a way to rebuild that Temple of His."

Nathan laughed again. Joseph looked at his older brother and felt a bit sorry. He merrily patted him on the shoulder. "Sorry, Aron. I mean well and I know you mean well too."

Aron laughed and the tension was gone. At that moment Batia and Miriam cheerfully came in to report that dinner was ready. It seemed that the women had become best friends in the shortest time. During the meal, the atmosphere became more and more relaxed. It was like old times.

Their father was sitting quietly. He seemed to be happy. He relished that his three sons were involved in conversations about Jewish affairs. But he didn't realize how different his sons had become. Happiness was a great good. Knowledge might cause unhappiness. He didn't need to know. When the brothers mentioned certain things and names, their father nodded with conviction and muttered approvingly.

At the farewell the next day Joseph invited everyone to the *brit milah* of their son.

Miriam disapproved. "You see, you prefer a boy!"

Joseph took a deep breath, "I mean, of course, if there is a *brit milah*, then you are all invited."

It was a boy. Joseph and Miriam's son was born on the fifth of *Iyar** of the Hebrew year 5628, the year 1868. Labor started in the morning and Joseph paced the room for hours waiting for good news. In the late afternoon the midwife asked him to call a doctor.

"Nothing serious," she said. "More a precaution."

Finally, late in the evening, came the liberating sound of a crying baby. A little later the doctor appeared and nodded reassuringly. "It's a boy. Mother and child are doing well."

Joseph pronounced the blessing and rushed into the bedroom. Miriam lay in bed, still perspiring, holding a small bundle of blankets in her arms. She smiled weakly. Joseph kissed her and looked at the little one. It was incredible. So small. It was alive. It was his son.

"Do you want to hold him," she asked.

Joseph knelt down and took the baby in his arms. He brought his nose to the baby's face and sniffed. Through his tears he saw eyes looking curiously at him.

The midwife came in. She smiled as she made the bed.

"This is incredible," was all Joseph said. He repeated it at least another thirty times that evening until Miriam asked him if he had anything else to say. Joseph shook his head and said, looking at the little one, "This is a miracle. It is incredible. Thank God."

"Miracle or not," said the midwife. "We all need sleep. So if you want to excuse us."

"Of course, of course," Joseph rushed to say. He caressed Miriam once more and said, "You are incredible too."

The next day, after a night during which Joseph had barely closed an eye, the doctor came by.

"We have to talk for a moment," he said seriously. "It came close, but in the end everything went well. Especially because of the latest developments in science. That's the good news." He took a break. "But, I am afraid that your wife will not have any more children. There was a complication. But you have a healthy son."

Joseph sighed. At that moment, he was not interested in the future; he was completely happy with the existing situation, but he did not want to appear insensitive. "Have you already told her?"

"Indeed. She took it wonderfully well. She is happy that this boy was born healthy and she thanks God for this miracle."

"That makes two of us."

Miriam had to stay in bed for a couple of days because of the loss of blood, and Joseph was there day and night to be of service to her. The little one was lying in a small crib next to the bed and Joseph stood up every few minutes to have a look.

"We still haven't chosen a name," he said.

"I was thinking of Moshe. The way he is lying there in his small basket. What do you think?"

"Perfect. You are exactly right, Miriam. Moshe it shall be." He got up again and looked at the baby in the cradle. "Moshe." He waved. "Hi Moshe." After a while he said: "We have to take care of the *brit milah*. Do you think we should invite the whole family?"

"Invite them and we will see who comes."

The *brit* was performed on the eighth day in the synagogue after the morning service. Nathan had congratulated them in a telegram but apologized that he really couldn't leave his business unattended. Aron was on a study trip with his *Yeshiva* in Lithuania and Joseph's father was too fragile to travel.

"So much for my family," Joseph said. But Miriam's family was there and Max also came. He had asked Max to be the *sandek*, the man holding the baby. The whole procedure took less than ten minutes and then there was a small meal. Miriam was exhausted by then and they were glad when they could finally leave.

"It will take some time for me to get back in shape," she said feebly when she sank into the chair at home. Joseph put the baby in her arms and she gently hummed the little one to sleep. Joseph smoked his pipe and sat opposite them, happier than ever. An awareness of his own relativity and the mystery of life came over him.

A few months later Joseph was surprised to find an invitation in the mail asking him to an appointment with Horst Pennekamp. It had been a long time since he had thought about the family and the publishing house. Certainly he had not written a word for the newspaper since Anton's funeral and fortunately he had not run into Horst or Hilde over the years. He had seen them a few times at the opera or other musical evenings, but he had carefully avoided them, the same way as he had avoided the Löwes. He had heard that the siblings Pennekamp had remained unmarried and still lived together in Anton Pennekamp's old house. Pennekamp's wife, Odette, had returned to France. Of course he didn't feel like going at all, but his curiosity won out.

Horst Pennekamp sat at the desk in the office where Joseph had often spent time with Anton and where once he had even pictured himself sitting. The contempt was apparent on Horst Pennekamp's face – here was the one whom his father had chosen over his own son to run the company. Worse, this man had rejected his sister. Horst did not stand up, nor did he ask Joseph to sit down.

Without any further ceremony he started. "My father was apparently not the only one whom you deluded. Do you know anything about a dead supervisor in the cathedral? Long ago, around 1852. Around the time you squirmed yourself into our lives. Are the bells, the alarm bells, ringing?"

This was about the last topic Joseph had expected. Had that disgraceful Braunberger betrayed him in the end? But then Braunberger would have incriminated himself as well, so that was not likely. Joseph decided to pretend that he knew nothing and certainly not to show his aversion or fear. "What on earth are you talking about?"

"I have a good friend in a high position at the police and guess what? He knows something about you. From those days. Here in Cologne." He scoffed. "I thought, let's ask the perpetrator himself. And give him the chance to find a safe haven. Benevolent, isn't it?"

Joseph suspected that Horst had heard something but still did not know exactly how matters stood. If Braunberger had betrayed Joseph, Horst would have been more certain.

"Wasn't that case closed years ago?"

Horst was apparently enjoying this cat and mouse game and continued, "I think some vivid testimony about your character by a respectable man like me, would make the police connect the dots. So far I haven't done it. It's up to you whether I do."

Joseph stared at the greasy wallpaper with its monotonous motif of yellowish leaves. The room felt as if no fresh air had entered it for years. "I have nothing to do with all this. What do you want?" he asked.

"That you leave. That I never see you again. That my sister never has to encounter your smug face again in the audience at the opera. Not in Cologne, not anywhere in Germany."

"You must hate me very much. Revenge is a bad teacher."

"I don't just hate you. I hate all of you." Horst Pennekamp had now given up all restraint. "A new wind is blowing. We Germans don't want you people anymore."

"Thanks," said Joseph. "Thank you for your clarity. Until today I had some doubts, but now I know for sure."

Without saying another word, he left the office. The question of whether Braunberger had betrayed him was not his main concern. There was a nastier aftertaste. A new wind was blowing indeed. A very unpleasant wind. It was no longer personal prejudice. It had become a larger political thought. Institutionalized hatred of which the Judensau and Luther's writings were only a prelude.

But in the end, one thought took possession of him. As Joseph walked home, he carefully prepared his words.

Joseph was most solemn when he entered the apartment. He saw Miriam sitting in front of the window with little Moshe on her lap, looking outside, as if they were both carefully studying the steadily falling rain and considering what to do about it.

"It is time to find a safe haven for the phantom people. We are going to set a good example. We're going to stop wandering. Think of the words of Yechezkiel. Even if we don't deserve it, God must and will take us back. It will be blessed. What do you think?"

"What are you saying?"

"Your father will weep with joy and your mother with sadness."

She jumped up with the little one in her arms, ran toward him, and gave him a kiss. "Yes! With all my heart."

"Of course there are a lot of things to be arranged." He laughed. "It won't be easy."

"I can't wait."

"Where would you like to live?"

"Perhaps Jerusalem," Miriam said.

"I don't know. Or Yafo. Would you like that? I think it's a good place to start. I always have imagined us living in a small house near Yafo, in the middle of the orchards, where in the evening, while puffing my pipe on the terrace in bliss and writing a brilliant observation, you rock the baby to sleep."

Joseph shared the decision with Max who immediately came up with a thousand counterarguments.

"You are looking for misery again. After fifty years, we have finally made a start with civilization. In Germany we have just escaped all diseases, poverty, crop failures, famine. We have taken a step towards modern life. And what do you do? Going to a backward country with only the prospect of misery."

"It's better to be poor there than unhappy in Cologne."

"How are you going to support yourself?"

"I assume I can write. There are a few Hebrew magazines and newspapers there and I could learn the language and write articles; your proposal from long ago to write in Hebrew is finally taking shape."

"You know," Max tried, "there is a new magazine in Vienna. Maybe it's something for you. It's called *HaShachar*, all in Hebrew. Published by a guy called Peretz Smolenskin. I don't think it can hurt to talk to him. Smolenskin's slogan is that the Jews as a nation are entitled to national independence."

"Yes, he might love the idea of a correspondent in Palestine."

"A man on the spot would be a plus, indeed." He made a face. "Oh dear, I just gave you another means of supporting yourself there."

Joseph looked closely at his friend and mentor: "You have to understand, Max. I don't just want to leave here, I really want to go there. And so does Miriam. That despicable son of Pennekamp was just a messenger."

"I understand." Max arranged some papers that were in front of him.

"Why don't you come too?" Joseph asked.

"No. I have absolutely no added value there. And I will tell you something: I can't suffer. Hunger, poverty. I can't even see it. Makes me depressed."

Joseph let it rest. "There is an Englishman, Charles Warren, who is digging in Jerusalem. Serious excavations. Maybe I can work for him. I have experience in archaeological excursions."

"Isn't your experience a bit tainted?"

"Anyway. I think there is work in abundance."

"Roll up your sleeves then."

"No, there must also be people who instigate, describe, whatever."

Joseph thought for a moment. "Perhaps I am beginning to believe in nationalism. For us. Moses Hess is right. People used to hate us because of religion, now because of our nose. It has become a racial issue. Now that we are assimilated, they argue that we are undermining the Germanic spirit and nation from within, simply by acquiring civil rights. Ergo, assimilation does not help."

Max responded philosophically, "God has grossly overestimated Himself. He started something that got terribly out of hand. First the creation, then that people. Now He is a step behind and He is trying to extinguish fires everywhere. I feel sorry for Him."

Everything was arranged and the day of departure arrived, the 26th of April. Max accompanied them to the train station. Miriam and Moshe boarded first and Joseph knew that he could not tarry. It was hard for him, this farewell. And possibly it was even harder for Max.

"Do something sensible there," said Max light-heartedly.

"I'll try," said Joseph, suppressing his emotion. He grabbed something out of his pocket and gave it to Max.

"I wrote a farewell poem."

"To me? We weren't that intimate, were we?" said Max laughing.

"No, to Germany. I want to call it *Shir HaGermania*."

"Oh boy. Who knows in which of the holy writings it will be included?"

They hugged once more and Joseph climbed the stairs.

"Come and visit," Joseph shouted.

With a dull thrust of steam, the train started to move.

They sat down heavily on a wooden bench. After the exhausting train journey, they were once again in the waiting room of the shipping company in the port of Venice. Joseph would have preferred not to visit that city again, but Elia had promised to meet them to say goodbye. It would be a very welcome distraction during their eight-hour waiting time.

The reunion was cordial. Joseph introduced Miriam and little Moshe.

"I see that you have become an adult man. In more than one sense," Elia whispered to Joseph. "Smarter than me, in any case." Joseph laughed sheepishly. They sat down at the table of a small sidewalk café in the port and enjoyed the cool morning air.

"Venice is beautiful this time of year."

"I don't know whether Venice can ever captivate me again," replied Joseph.

"Well said. Very nice pun." He nodded at Miriam with a question on his lips.

"It's all right," said Joseph, "we have no secrets."

"I understand. But everything has changed now. Italy is independent!

Italy is one and Venice is part of it. We have a king. Can you believe it? And you contributed to that as well."

"Mostly in a passive way, by being locked up."

"Martyrs are important," said Elia merrily. "And your expedition probably helped as well. Honor to whom honor is due." He waited a moment. "And now you are going to Palestine just as I thought you had become a wise man."

"Yes, we are," Joseph replied proudly.

Elia held back for a moment. "I can't follow you, neither literally nor figuratively. What on earth are you going to do there?"

"I don't know, frankly. Living with my family. Writing."

"Believe me, Joseph. That fight is not worth fighting. A rearguard battle. This year, here in Italy, we finally got civil rights. Late, but perhaps not too late. At least we have them. Disraeli, a Jew, is Prime Minister in England, Cremieux is at the top in France. The Rothschilds are the richest people in Europe. Jews can study at any university, they have reached the highest levels of society. Even in your beloved Germany it looks as if the Jews are obtaining equal rights."

"The love between me and Germany has somewhat cooled down, I can tell you."

"You know, I like the idea. A homeland for the Jews. I fought for a similar cause. A homeland is important, but I am an Italian. Not a Turk, or Arab, or whoever lives there," he said. "There is nothing there. It makes no sense. No country, no people, nothing to fight for. And I don't want to be remembered later as some silly *Don* Elia di Banco, the general who was attacking windmills."

They talked on for a while but eventually the time came to part. Another goodbye. New life came with a price.

More and more people registered to board the ship. Joseph tried to ascertain where they came from. He heard Yiddish, Ladino, Hebrew. But also French, Italian, English, and German. It seemed to him that from all corners of the earth these people were gathered here to start the journey to the Holy Land.

Their luggage was minimal, just a few pieces. The choice of what to take had kept him busy for a long time. An existential decision. Physical matters were a derivative of the mental state. It would be more than simply missing a music score, a photo, a book. What could you take with you to a new life? Didn't Rashi say that Avram, with his *Lech Lecha*, gave up all his possessions? He wanted a past that did not cast any shadow forward when he moved. Crossing over to the other side.

In the end there were two large suitcases with their clothes and

Joseph's old trunk, which, while still in Cologne, he had stuffed with relevant things, as he put it to Miriam. He just had to take some Western culture with him. Hardly any clothes; after all, once there, he planned to dress according to the oriental norm.

Miriam sat next to him with little Moshe laying in her arm.

"So this is it," she said solemnly.

Joseph had intended to make the most of this final moment. To get through it very consciously, but he kept getting distracted. He tried to concentrate on the immense step they were taking, but then someone would ask him what time it was or the purser would summon him to confirm for the umpteenth time that they were also passengers. Practical reality overtook the dream. But was that bad? Miriam looked dreamily in front of her. She seemed not to worry about anything. Following her example, Joseph set himself the new goal of not getting annoyed anymore. He started playing a little with Moshe and tried to make the baby laugh.

Eventually their names were called and they boarded. Their cabin was on the lowest deck. A small primitive cabin, not at all what they had booked. Again Joseph forced himself not to take umbrage. Miriam lay down on the bed with Moshe and Joseph sank into the only seat.

"Relax Joseph," Miriam said. "We are finally going to leave."

From above came the sound of the horn.

"You're right. This is it. We are leaving."

Part 3

$$\frac{1}{\;}$$

(1871)

A Rock with a View

Rivka Socher was sitting on a large lime boulder just outside
the Jerusalem wall. In front of her lay the valley, while to her
left, on the side of the hill, she saw the new buildings of *Mishkenot*
and the windmill. They still had not succeeded in getting it to work.
Looking to her right, she saw families walking through the Yafo Gate
with loaded donkeys. Passing the silhouettes of the buildings in the
Russian Orthodox quarter, they were heading to a newly developed
neighborhood. *Nachalat Shiv'a*, the Inheritance of the Seven, was a
recent attempt by a group of Jewish adventurers to create a dignified
existence outside the walls of Jerusalem. She could not blame them;
others – mainly non-Jews – had done it before. Living conditions in the
city were degrading and the rents were high. Maybe she should think
about moving herself.

She often came here when she wanted to reflect. Next week Joseph
and his family would come. For good. When she had received the
letter with his decision a month ago, Rivka had felt both stunned
and overjoyed. But the letter had evoked thoughts about matters long
forgotten. The change would undo the break with her past; her brother's
arrival would re-connect her to her old life. What had he said? "Won't
you just do *teshuva* and just become part of us again?"

She was content now. The land had been good to her. She was a
teacher at a Christian school and had come to know a lot of people.
Being familiar with the ins and outs of life in the old city, she was
independent but, at the same time, she was part of everything. Most
of the people she dealt with respected her, especially the Christian
teachers and authorities. She had learned to speak Arabic fluently. The
Sephardic Jews were friendly. They dressed like the Arabs and were
very down to earth. Actually, they *were* locals. The Orthodox Jews from
Eastern Europe clearly were not. They were different and sometimes
annoying, but in the end that did not bother her too much. She had very
few dealings with them, since they lived in isolation from the rest of the
city. Nor did the Turks bother her, that bunch of useless supervisors.
Placate and appease them and they would not interfere. The Arabs were

generally benevolent. After the difficult start, she had found her place as Rivka or Renata, depending on the conversation partner. With the arrival of her brother, she might have to re-think this. After all, Joseph was quite a busybody, she thought with a smile. She kicked at a loose stone and listened as it rattled into the valley.

It grew darker. She got up and left her thoughts for what they were. The most important thing now was to welcome her brother, Joseph.

2

A PLEASING COUNTRY

"We have to make their arrival as festive as possible," said Rivka to Rachid when she visited him in Yafo. She had already started some preparations on her own, but of course she had contacted Rachid. Rachid was now married to his childhood love but still lived in the same house in Yafo. They had already found a nice home for the new immigrants. An upper floor on the hill in the oldest part of the city.

"Maybe I should stay here for a while," said Rivka a few days later, when they were waiting for the ship on the quay. "To help them adjust."

Rachid had arranged a sloop to take them off the boat personally. They had filled the cupboards in the new house with provisions for at least a week.

"Joseph! So this time it is for good," said Rivka as she embraced him. Then she greeted Miriam. The latter handed Moshe to her and Rivka immediately fell in love with the little one.

"How old is he now?" she asked.

"He will be three this year."

"He is so cute. He looks like you, Miriam."

"Don't tell Joseph," said Miriam laughing.

Rachid greeted Joseph. "You have become wise, my friend. Good to let us know long beforehand that you were coming," he said. "We have arranged a home for you. Later you can decide whether you want to stay there or move on."

"My, Rachid, you are marvelous," said Joseph. "Everything is going to be fine."

They carried their suitcases through the narrow streets to their house on top of the hill. Everyone was in the best of moods; even the mess in the alleys couldn't spoil it.

"This is *Gan Eden*," Miriam said in disbelief, when they were sitting on their rooftop terrace a little later, sipping a cup of tea with mint. "We are so blessed. Look, Joseph. What a view."

With a broad smile Joseph said: "This is not just good. This is very good. I intend to say the full grace after meals and bless the country from now on. It would be ridiculous not to say thanks here.

"I assumed you were already doing that."

Rachid's first recommendation was that they involve Chaim Amzalek in all their affairs. Amzalek was a Sephardic merchant who over the years, had gained the trust of both the Arab and Western inhabitants. He knew everyone and everyone knew him. In addition, Amzalek could count Moses Montefiore among his friends. His roots were English and the family had originally come from Tunis. His father had run a small trading house from Jerusalem. Chaim himself had moved to Yafo after his father's death.

His house was just outside the old walls. Miriam enjoyed the walk down the streets as they went to visit him. She saw the dirt and noticed occasionally a gust of pungent odors, but these did not bother her. This was not a neat neighborhood in Cologne. This was the Levant.

"With whom do I have the honor?" Amzalek asked. He was a small, amiable man, completely dressed in the oriental style. His English was impeccable.

"Most people know me as Johann Lichtman, but it's actually Yossi Socher. Joseph. This is my wife, Miriam."

He bowed courteously and said, "Welcome. You are an asset to the land."

The conversation was animated and in a short time they got a lot of advice.

"We really want to fit in," Joseph said. "Absorb life here."

"Then maybe you can change your name to something less Ashkenaz. More Hebrew. Like Shachar. Shachar means dawn."

Joseph let the name echo in his head. And to Miriam he said, "What do you think? Miriam Shachar?" Miriam nodded, smiling. "Thank you. It will be Shachar." He repeated softly. "Joseph Shachar."

When they walked back to their roof house, Joseph found himself in an odd mood. Yafo, could it ever feel like home? He remembered Max's words. Going to a backward country with only the prospect of misery.

"You heard what he said. Sieve water before using it," he reminded Miriam, smiling. "There is a lot to get used to. And much to learn."

Miriam pointed to the hills in the distance: "Do you know that our ancestors walked there? Our *Avot*?"

They spent hours on the roof terrace. Because their house was on the hill they had a panoramic view of the landscape; in the west, the sea and in the east, the hills of Ephraim. When it was really clear, the mountains in the distance showed all their details – a small village, a green plain, a minaret, chalk plains. On hazy days the mountains were only vague silhouettes against the sky, suggesting an undiscovered landscape behind them.

"I've been thinking for a while about that building on that hill," Joseph said to Miriam one late afternoon, when they were drinking their tea. Moshe sat playing in the corner of the terrace, as content as any toddler could be. Joseph pointed to a distant hill, where a bright spot of light suggested the reflection of the last rays of the sun on a wall. It seemed as if a big bonfire had been lit. "You can only see it when it reflects the sun, exactly from where we are. During the day it is one with the mountain," he pondered without looking at Miriam. After a while he said, "We'll probably never know what it is."

"You should ask Amzalek. He will know for sure."

"But then the pleasure will be gone. Now it can still be anything. A sanctuary, an old fortress, a monastery, perhaps an ammunition depot, who knows? With imagination I can do anything. Knowledge always falls short."

Their first summer went by and, after *Sukkot*,* the sticky heat ended and the evenings became chillier. It was dark by six o'clock. Rivka had long since returned to Jerusalem. Above the hills in the distance Joseph saw constellations he thought were familiar. The constellation Orion had always been standing recognizably straight above the horizon in Germany, but here in October the hunter lay on his side and it took a while before Joseph realized he was looking at the familiar stars. Everything was the same but different.

One morning, it was barely light, Miriam woke up with a shock. What was that noise? A torrential shower like nothing she had ever experienced before. She quickly dressed to go outside and experience the phenomenon. In the doorway she almost bumped into Rachid.

"Come," he said. "I have to show you something. Your husband and son also have to come. Hurry."

Joseph dressed slowly. He didn't feel like getting up at all with this weather. When he looked out of the window, it seemed as if he was in Germany.

"Where are we going?"

"*Wadi Misrara.*"

Joseph shook his head.

"Come on," Rachid insisted. "It doesn't usually last long."

Via Nablus Road they rode out of town in the pouring rain. As they reached the top of a light hill, they suddenly saw a wide river in front of them, almost thirty meters wide. This was where the *wadi* had been. Miriam remembered how it had looked in the summer. Bone-dry. Cracked earth between hundreds of stones and boulders. Here and there, some thorny, withered bushes and some tough pale grass. Now there was this wild stream of brown water.

"Look Moshe. It looks almost like the Rhine," Joseph said.

Miriam gave him a sarcastic look. "Seriously? The Rhine?"

Joseph laughed. "Okay. Slightly smaller. The Main."

Miriam turned to Rachid. "Thank you, Rachid, for showing this to us."

It kept raining all day and Joseph and Miriam were afraid that it would last for weeks as in the old country. Rachid had told them that winter did not count for much – a few days of rain, usually lovely sunny days in between, but they had experienced too much autumn in cold Europe not to look back with nostalgia on the carefree warmth of the recent months.

In the evening he lit the firepot in the room and they warmed themselves.

"I'll put Moshe to sleep," Miriam said. She picked up the little one and took him to the bedroom. A little later Joseph heard her humming. Was that Mozart? Joseph was touched. It had been a long time since he had heard music. Real music, not the extravagant tone scales of the Arabs in the coffee houses or the unknown Sephardic chants of the synagogue. He missed Chopin, Liszt, and especially Beethoven. To hear Miriam singing Mozart was tantalizing. In response, Joseph himself gently began to hum Beethoven's seventh symphony, thinking that to hear it again, he would probably have to travel three thousand kilometers. And he hadn't seen a decent painting for centuries. When Miriam came back into the room a little later, he tried to find support for an idea that was beginning to take shape.

"I do miss European culture a bit, like a good concert. Somehow, I feel cut off," he said.

"It's hard to whip up a symphony orchestra."

"We could organize a recital, a piano recital, Mozart, Beethoven, Liszt."

"For some reason I assume those things don't work here."

Joseph looked crestfallen. "I suppose so."

"But I'll help you with everything, of course," Miriam quickly said. She didn't want to disappoint him. "How do we get a piano?"

"I'll ask around. Maybe those German settlers in Sarona. What do they call themselves? *Templers*? In any case, Chaim said that it might be interesting for us to get to know them." Joseph referred to Amzalek, who had become a good friend.

"What do you actually know about those people?"

"Not so much. They are German Christians. They have come here to experience the end of time. The coming of the Messiah or whatever."

"Don't mock it. Bear in mind, your own sister also converted."

"Don't remind me. But I don't think these *Templers* are missionaries. They prefer to stay among themselves. I heard they were kicked out of the main church. But they believe that the time of the Savior is approaching and that the Jews, with their return to Palestine, are the first indication of redemption."

"Well, be that as it may, they do a fine job by arranging everything the Turks are too lazy to do. The carriage service they maintain between here and Jerusalem is fantastic."

"I will visit them. Maybe they can rent us a piano." Joseph thought for a moment. "If I can arrange a piano, would you like to play? Maybe you could expand your old repertoire a little. Chopin and Liszt?"

"I can try, but I think it's too difficult for me. First you find the piano, and then I'll do my best."

The next day, the storm was over. The clean, washed air was brighter and more blue than ever, and everything felt refreshed. The sun shone in November with a force they had never experienced in Germany. They decided to do nothing else for the whole day, and enjoy the sun on the terrace. Joseph had just submitted some articles, so could take the time. At the far end of the terrace, Moshe was busy investigating a line of ants marching over the wooden fence. In the sharp light Joseph could look further into the distance over the hills than ever.

Miriam brought coffee and as she sat down and stretched her legs, she said, "Marvelous. What a blessing this sun is." She pointed at the trees in front of their terrace. "With all that green you would think that spring had begun."

"Indeed. That idea of necessary decay every year might be an interesting philosophical concept, but it's not my cup of tea." He looked lovingly at Miriam. "I am still amazed that we are here. Just see us sitting here. I still can't fully grasp it."

She pulled him close. "Not everything is within our grasp."

"Do you know what I sometimes find hard to believe," he asked. "That I am *me*. Being here."

"Now you really are talking in riddles."

"What I mean is, when I think of myself, I see that young boy in Cologne in his little room, who wanted to conquer the world. And now I am sitting here, almost forty. I have a wife, a child, a house. I have emigrated to another country, to this place. I know this is me, but it's hard to imagine that it's all real." He picked up little Moshe and put him on his lap. "If someone had told me back then that all this would happen, I would have told him he was completely insane. I wouldn't have believed it. I know everything happened, but still, I don't believe it."

"You are strange," she grinned. "Moshe, don't listen to that man!"

Rachid accompanied Joseph to the German colony of Sarona. "Germans need pianos to survive," Joseph said cryptically to Rachid who nodded, although he didn't really seem to understand what Joseph was talking about. "In the mean time we can see how they are doing," he continued.

They rode through the neatly maintained streets of the new settlement.

"This is how Germans manage this. *Gründlichkeit*, thoroughness."

But despite his ridicule, Joseph had to admit that the *Tempelgesellschaft* had done a fantastic job. There was a clean main street with spacious stone houses on both sides, two stories high. The most striking thing was that they were standing straight, European-style, with sloping roofs, large, neatly washed windows, and even windowsills. The colony had only started a year earlier but the work had borne fruit. The *Templers* had planted trees everywhere. If the sun had not warmed them so pleasantly on this November day, he would have thought that he was somewhere in a city in the Rhine plain.

"Smart," said Rachid, pointing at some of the newly planted trees. "Eucalyptus. Against swamps. Against disease."

"Good to remember." Joseph nodded appreciatively.

They easily found the leader of the *Templer* community, *Herr* Hoffmann, who was very courteous. To his surprise, Joseph actually enjoyed speaking German again with a stranger.

"We were able to realize our ideal here," Hoffmann said. "Our dream was to go to the Holy Land and help prepare for the ultimate salvation."

"That sounds beautiful." Joseph smiled.

"We are building a new Christian world in this place. The beginning of the end time, when everything will be perfect. The last judgment is near."

"Sarona is a jewel," Joseph evaded.

"With blood, sweat, and tears," Hoffmann continued. "Too many people have died building the community."

Hoffmann said he was too busy now, but he would be happy to give them a tour if they would come again. The piano was no problem at all and he also knew a good pianist in Jerusalem who would surely like to play for a small fee. He would put them in touch with each other.

They said goodbye. From the corner of his eye, Joseph saw someone crossing the street and with a shock he thought he recognized him. Was that Christian Braunberger, his colleague stone-*shlepper* from the cathedral of Cologne, the man with whom he shared the secret of the supervisor's death?

Rivka visited a week later. She was not doing much at the moment, and it seemed more pleasant to spend the winter in Yafo than in cold Jerusalem. Joseph and Miriam had a spare room in which they had invited her to stay for as long as she wanted.

"As a matter of fact, I am considering settling in Yafo. Amzalek asked me to work in his business as assistant," she told Miriam. The two of them had gone for a stroll and were now standing at the port, overlooking the sea. "I can help you with the house. And with little Moshe."

"I would love to have you close," Miriam replied. "It's good to have some female company."

"A bit bored with my brother?" Rivka asked, laughing.

"No, no, not at all. But he is often occupied with other things."

"He helps you, doesn't he? If not, I'll have a word with him."

"No, he's really exemplary," Miriam replied, "but he's getting restless. He's looking for a new challenge. The first fascination of living here is fading away. The naive feeling that everything we did was blessed, as in childhood."

"That sounds as if reality has sunk in. Only then do you really begin to adapt to the country."

"Quite right," Miriam said. "I think it is different for me than for Joseph." She stopped for a moment. "The thought of a greater spiritual task, if there ever was one, has faded. I just want to build a home. No mission, just to live here." Miriam was vainly batting at the insects that swarmed around her. "The world is bigger than we are, I know. But for the moment I would like to keep it very modest and small: Joseph, Moshe, you. That's it."

"I also survived here by shutting myself off in the beginning," said Rivka. "Coerced to some degree, but still."

Miriam looked at her compassionately. "It must have been hard."

Rivka's gaze went over the Mediterranean Sea. Further, towards the hazy western horizon. To the Land of Evening. Memories surfaced. Fourteen years ago she had left. She seldom wanted to think about it. Europe stood for so much, but for her most of it was dark. Baptism, betrayed love. Few peaks and too many deep depressions. How she had slipped away anonymously from that drizzly harbor in France, wrapped in a brown cloak. She had hardly spoken to her peers, a group of nuns from Lyon. How she had landed in Yafo one chilly morning. They had spent the night in the chapel of a church and the next day had made the journey to Jerusalem, on donkeys. Late in the evening they had arrived at the monastery in the *Via Dolorosa* and she was given a private cell. Exhausted, she had fallen asleep on her bed until the bells had awakened her the next day. The first months she had hardly eaten or spoken, but eventually she recovered, thanks to the kindness and empathy of the sisters, most of whom had gone through similar ordeals.

"It was hard," she said. "When you said goodbye, after your honeymoon, I was sad. But I knew you would come back."

Miriam asked the question that had intrigued her for a long time. It seemed like the right moment. "Why did you leave the convent?"

Rivka thought for a moment. "Joseph's visit, I think, was decisive. Living with the nuns, my roots no longer existed, but when he suddenly stood there in front of me, I knew I couldn't deny them. Joseph has always been a catalyst for me. He opened my eyes the first time in Frankfurt so long ago." She told of her visit to Cologne when she had proudly informed him that she would be changing her name to Renata.

"I've hated that name for so long now. The nuns helped me reconcile with it." She remembered the way they had pronounced it softly and subtly. "But with Joseph's arrival a change came. I remember what he said in the convent at our farewell. "Guilt is useless." But I knew that I was responsible for my choices. I started to think again about my parents, my brothers. For a long time I had tucked them away. You have to understand that I looked up to my two older brothers. But Aron had become more and more boring. Joseph was the creative eccentric. And he gave me direction by choosing the unusual path."

"But there was more. Not everything is Joseph's fault," she said laughing. "I was willing to engage myself with the humanitarian causes of the order, but I could not identify with Christian theology. I even started to resent the liturgy. 'This is the body of Christ' and things like that. You know what I mean."

"Honestly, I don't know at all," Miriam said. "But I can imagine."

"No of course you don't know. In the end, I am too worldly for a convent. It was a necessary period because it let me regain strength. But I want to live a full life. Christianity and the monastic life were alien to my inner self."

After a brief moment of silence, Rivka continued. "There were also a few specific events that pushed me away. But I don't know if I should share them."

"Your thoughts are safe with me."

"I know. Of course. You should know, I'm still grateful to the nuns. And they're doing a fine job. They have a role, a good role. To put them in a bad light now would be unkind or even ungrateful."

"You may be right," Miriam said. "No *lashon hara*."

"Let's leave it at that," Rivka said.

But Rivka's memories took her back to Sister Emmanuela, a fanatical nun who claimed she had seen the Virgin Mary. She had set herself the crucial task of taking care of a Jewish orphan girl. In spite of her misery, a happy child. The girl had an open mind and was perceptive. Her name was Rachel, and Rivka liked to spend time with her. Sister Emmanuela had been extreme in her callous attempts to convert the child. In the end she had succeeded, but a few days later the girl had run away. Eventually she had been found dead outside the walls of the city.

"I found the courage to leave the monastery. And now this country, yesteryear's place of escape, has become my safe home. Even more so now we are together here."

Miriam smiled. "That goes for me as well. I feel safe with you."

"Thank you. I look up to you. So calm. So spiritual, yet with both feet on the ground."

"I'm not so sure about all that. It hasn't been easy."

Rivka looked at Miriam. "I ended up on my feet. You will too."

"We have already learned to live with some of the less pleasant aspects. The heat and the humidity of the long summer and the insects. They are a real plague."

"As far as that's concerned, it would be better to live in Jerusalem."

"I don't think Joseph is up for that yet."

"I don't think he will ever be ready for it," Rivka said. "Even I am coming back to the plain."

"Do you know what surprises me? That nobody cares about all these rows and skirmishes you hear about. They are really commonplace."

"I know. As you said, at times it is best to close your eyes to the shortcomings in a childlike way. Blind faith."

Their house became an open door for the few Europeans who lived in Yafo and in this way they got to know more and more people. Richard Harrison had come back again. The painter was often traveling, but sometimes he hung around in the city for weeks, ostensibly doing nothing at all. He had no accommodation, so he asked if he could temporarily move in with Joseph and Miriam. He slept on the terrace in the hammock he had brought along. For Richard this behavior was routine, for Miriam it was less regular, but for the time being she didn't want to let it bother her. Joseph tried to reassure her.

"Richard is impulsive, for sure. But he would not hurt a fly."

"He is too much of a slacker. And he drinks too much. I don't know if I can trust him."

"He sometimes reminds me of Max."

"Uncle Max! How can you say that?"

"The same kind of relativism, maybe?" Joseph looked at her in the hope that she would agree. He did not feel like having this conversation.

"Uncle Max takes his distance to get a better perspective. Richard just detaches himself from everything."

"I think it's not that bad."

He wanted to see Richard as Max's successor, but maybe that was wishful thinking and Miriam was just plain right.

Joseph, Richard and Rachid were drinking coffee in their regular cafe. The café-owner brought them a new hookah.

"Life is good. I know, it's a cliché but still," Joseph said.

"Indeed, although there is always something to be desired, of course," replied Richard. "Like more cash, for instance." He grinned. "How do you manage, if I may ask?"

"You may. I write regularly for some of the German newspapers. They pay well for so-called realistic stories from the Levant. With an oriental touch, exactly as they like it. I don't fabricate anything but to say that I am exactly telling the truth?" He laughed. "But, thank God, we don't need to rely on that right now. We still have some reserves."

In the distance someone started to play a lamenting clarinet and someone else joined in with wild drumming.

"Impossible to hear anything decent here," Richard complained. "Something other than those shouting Arabs who in the end turn out only to be ordering coffee." He drank a sip and then apologetically said to Rachid: "No offense."

Rachid laughed a bit uncomfortably.

"Richard is just talking rubbish, Rachid," Joseph quickly said. "You know how he is. Impulsive. Doesn't think so much."

Rachid turned to Joseph. "Perhaps you should come with me and get to know the local culture better," he suggested.

"Yes, thank you, Rachid. I would like that. Maybe we could visit a mosque. I'm in favor of the new immigrants getting along well with the Arabs. I even think we should learn Arabic. You can't settle somewhere and then not be able to communicate with the local population at all."

"I think you are right."

"But on the other hand we shouldn't adapt too much, lest we start shouting at each other when we want some sugar in our coffee!" Rachid laughed as well.

"Tell me, Rachid. You must have thoughts about what this stream of strangers means to you, to your country, and to the people."

Rachid shrugged his shoulders. "There is enough space for everyone. For Christians, for us, for you. And overall, living together works out well. Even in Jerusalem." He thought for a moment as if considering whether to continue. "I just don't think the Ottomans are the right people to govern this country. They are brothers in faith, but they are not interested in the land. They only see it as a moneymaker. And they are corrupt to the bone. In their time here, the Turks have ruined the whole land. No replanting, no renovation. They even impose a tax if you plant a tree. Everything is neglected. If another people were in charge here, this whole region could be blooming. He sadly added: "But the Arabs are too docile. They show too little initiative."

"But what about those sheikhs with their gangs of robbers? They are not docile at all."

"Those are bad, yes. They should be brought to justice. But in Europe there are bandits and robbers, murderers, and rapists too. That doesn't make the Europeans bad. But there is change. It has become safer." Rachid stood up, while explaining like a schoolmaster how improvement had started with Ali Pasha in the forties. And then, it had taken a long time before directives from Constantinople reached Jerusalem, not to mention the wild areas in the south and east. There the local sheikhs were still in charge. Rachid's solution was simple. "More of these bandits should be beheaded. At the gates in Yafo and Jerusalem you sometimes see their heads hanging."

Joseph applauded. He was impressed with Rachid's knowledge.

The recital would take place at Chaim Amzalek's house. About thirty chairs were put on the veranda. They had first wanted to have it on their home roof terrace, but it would have been too difficult to get the piano up there. Miriam and Rivka had provided some festive lighting and decorations: a number of colored lanterns in the overhanging branches and some large torches stood around the terrace. Richard had taken care of the drinks. In addition to wine, he had managed to get his hands on a few bottles of good whisky. Miriam saw that one bottle was already half empty. Richard fancied a drink too often.

The greatest delight of the day was Elsa's arrival, care of the carriage line from Jerusalem. She was in her seventies and she had difficulty walking. Her face had sunk a bit more since the last time they had seen her. But she was as enthusiastic and determined as ever. She had turned down the request to play a piece, but when she saw the piano, she sat down on the stool and looked at the keys long and carefully. She looked up and smiled. "It's been a long time." She leafed briefly through the scores that lay on top of the piano and took a few sheets. "Let's try one more time." The melancholic sounds of Beethoven's *Sturmsonate* filled the space. Her fingers knew exactly what to do, but the age weighed in. After a few bars she stopped.

"That's no longer for me," she said cheerfully. "And how did it sound?"

"It was as if I was back at the *Heumart*, so beautiful," said Joseph.

"Good. Very good. But you are here. Don't forget that."

Indeed, it seemed as if Joseph had been back in Cologne for a moment. He saw the hills in the distance but in his mind, he was in Elsa's living room in Germany on a Christmas evening.

The company sat down in the garden where they enjoyed the last rays of the sun.

"You are following the same process I did, I understand," said Elsa, teasing Rivka. "First part of the tribe, then out, and now slowly slipping back in again."

Rivka laughed. "I don't know if it all happened so consciously and to be honest, I don't have a clue in which state I am right now. We will see."

"Fine. Then give me a *schnapps*," Elsa said.

Richard filled the glasses and put the bottle next to him.

"*L'chaim*, friends."

"*L'chaim*, Elsa."

She made herself comfortable in her chair.

"Are you completely all right there, in Bethlehem?" Joseph asked. "You are not getting any younger."

"I can take perfect care of myself, thank you. I feel very young."

Joseph laughed. "Don't forget I write your memoirs. I know your age."

"Shht, you watch out," she warned. "It's all right. My Saïda takes good care of me. Traveling and things like this are getting a bit difficult, but I didn't want to deny myself the pleasure." She looked with resignation for a moment. "But I do miss Max," she admitted. "His cheerful company."

Richard had an idea. "What if I come by now and again and make a virtue of necessity by immortalizing you in a beautiful portrait?"

"That has been done before."

"My art makes everything else pale," Richard said, too loudly.

Rivka proposed a different idea. "Wouldn't it be better if you moved to the center of Bethlehem?"

"I don't want to hear about it. Soon you'll put me in some home for the elderly."

At that moment Amzalek joined them. He looked serious. "I

heard what you said. Recently there have been more reports from Bedouin gangs traveling around the hills around Jerusalem. Robbery and manslaughter, as if nothing has changed in twenty years. Maybe Rivka's idea is not so unreasonable."

But Elsa did not want to hear about it.

Gerhard Sotter, the German pianist, arrived with his wife and the evening began. Suddenly a huge bang sounded. Miriam jumped up and looked at Amzalek in panic. The latter laughed. Rachid was also laughing and Miriam understood that, whatever it was, they were not worried. "The end of *Ramadan*. That is indicated by the shooting of the cannon at the harbor."

"So many countries, so many customs," Miriam joked, but the worry had been real for a second.

"Well," Joseph said, "we'll take that as a sign that we can start."

Only a few locals had come. There was Rachid with three of his companions, a couple of men Joseph knew from the coffee house, and a few tourists on their way to Jerusalem.

He asked Amzalek, "Are we expecting anyone else?"

"I'm afraid there won't be many more. The Arabs are not interested and I have heard that the synagogue warned its congregants not to attend. Before you know it, women might start singing and dancing!"

"Well. We can't be worried about that right now. Let's start," said Joseph. He positioned himself on the edge of the terrace, prepared to give a formal welcome. He had to wait a moment because a few people arrived at the last minute; *Herr* Hoffmann and a few families from Sarona. He appreciated that they had come. He could not see their faces clearly in the half darkness, but he also thought he had seen the man who looked like Braunberger.

"Dear people." He coughed. He hadn't done this for a long time. "Ladies and gentlemen, we are delighted that you all have come for this special evening." After uttering some more generalities, he said: "Please welcome with a heartfelt applause our first pianist, Mrs. Miriam Shachar, who will perform a Mozart sonata."

He sat down in the audience next to Moshe who said: "Papa, you are really good at this."

"Thank you, my son. It was not such a big deal."

Miriam sat down behind the piano and started playing. She had chosen a simple sonata by Mozart and Joseph enjoyed her beautiful playing. After the applause, she indicated that Gerhard Sotter would take over. The pianist from Jerusalem played pieces by Beethoven and Liszt until the intermission. Joseph turned around and saw in the doorway of the terrace the silhouette of the man who resembled

Braunberger, the phantom from Cologne. He took a closer look and concluded with relief that it was someone else.

After the break the repertoire was lighter. The pianist played some Schumann and Chopin waltzes and Richard asked Miriam to dance. It was the last thing Miriam felt like doing. Despite her opposition, Richard grabbed her and started to waltz. With a forced smile Miriam looked around for help. Joseph was about to step up when Richard swung her around a few times in his awkward drunkenness. He slipped and could just hold his ground by grabbing Miriam in his fall; he pressed his hands directly on her breasts. Miriam found him repellent. She suspected the incident had been no coincidence. They took their places again, straightened their clothes as if nothing had happened. To Miriam's relief she saw that Moshe had not seen anything of the incident. He was completely absorbed in some wooden sticks in the garden. Joseph sat down next to her, but Miriam was looking straight ahead. "That is why women are not allowed to dance with strange men. The rabbis were not so backward after all."

Miriam decided that she didn't want to have anything to do with that man ever again.

One morning Miriam came into the kitchen and saw Moshe sitting at the door. The boy was staring intently at something on the ground and as Miriam approached, she saw that the object of Moshe's interest was a cockroach. The animal lay floundering with its legs up, spinning slowly as it tried to turn over and put itself back on its feet. Moshe did nothing. Very occasionally he raised his hand as if he was shaking it.

"Look, mama, he's waving at me."

Miriam squatted next to him and looked at the cockroach. Then she stood up, opened the door and kicked the little creature out.

"Mama! What have you done?"

"It's a cockroach, Moshe. We don't want them in the house."

"But he was my friend. Didn't you see him waving at me?"

Miriam realized that she might not have acted in the subtlest way. A little more empathy for her son would have been appropriate. She opened the door, with a vague plan to pick up the cockroach and put it back by the door for a while. But the bug was nowhere to be seen. Probably the kick had been hard enough to send it down the stairs.

"I'm so sorry, Moshe," she said with remorse. "I will make up for it. Really."

"Then maybe we can have a dog?"

Miriam laughed at her son's clever negotiating tactics.

"Certainly." She sighed. "We will look for a dog."

Despite Joseph's opposition, they acquired a dog. A small dachshund. Moshe decided that the animal was called Benny. When there was no one around, Joseph sometimes caught himself talking to the animal. He looked at the dog lying at his feet.

"So, what should we start writing about? Not expecting an answer from you," he said softly to the sleeping animal. "About the dog's life you have? Or that we all have?"

He wondered about the animal. A miracle how the animal looked and behaved, but at the same time the dog didn't understand anything about it. How it went aimlessly from one side of the room to the other. There was absolutely no logic in what it did. What was its drive? Joseph wondered whether a more highly developed being would say the same about him.

Joseph wrote a lot; every week he sent several articles to Max, which he usually read in print a few weeks later, when he picked up the parcel with the newspapers from Germany and Europe at the Turkish post office at the harbor. But that was not what he wanted. It partly covered their expenses, but there was nothing in it that he thought had real value. Or was even worth preserving and reading again after years. No, he wanted something grand – the old dream of finally writing his book.

3

(1873)

DEATH AND DESTRUCTION

The following year, Chaim Amzalek was appointed British vice-consul and he invited Joseph, Miriam and Rivka to the grand reception in the official residence. Rivka immediately merged with the crowd and was soon engaged in a conversation with some people whom Miriam and Joseph didn't know. They themselves stood a bit apart, watching the attire of the guests and the splendor of their clothes with amazement. From all parts of the country, people had come to celebrate the joyful occasion. Arab sheikhs, a single Turkish captain with his personal guard, Bedouin chieftains, British officers, representatives of all the major European countries, religious leaders of numerous faiths and partitions. It was a spectacle to remember. Amzalek himself, although small in size, looked impressive in his British uniform.

"What a land in which you can assemble a crowd like this," exclaimed Miriam. "I've never seen so many different kinds of people gathered before."

"Well. I'm glad I don't bear the responsibility for them," answered Joseph.

Drinks in hand, they approached Amzalek.

"Congratulations again on your appointment," said Joseph. "You have invited all sorts and conditions of people."

"I didn't invite them all, not by a long shot. Here in Palestine, everyone just shows up if they think it will benefit their cause."

Joseph nodded at a man who was standing alone. He was dressed in European style, distinguished and – although it was barely possible – he looked like the odd man out. "Who is he, if I may ask?"

"Ah. That's *Monsieur* Netter. Charles Netter. From France. One of the men of the *Alliance Française*. Haven't you heard, they actually started their school, just south of Yafo on the road to Ramle. An agricultural school for Jewish boys. It is heavily financed by Edmond de Rothschild, I understand. Charles is really an excellent man. I will introduce you."

Amzalek promptly did so. After he walked away, Joseph asked Netter in French whether the lessons had started, saying that he would like to come by to watch the proceedings.

"Ah. There you have my weak spot, right away. We did a fantastic job of arranging everything, just, no lessons. A problem, one could say."

"And why?"

"There are no students," Netter responded with a forced smile.

Joseph raised his eyebrows.

"They are not allowed to attend by their parents, who think this kind of teaching is pointless. Working the land to support yourself is a grotesque concept according to certain Torah scholars in Jerusalem. Besides they think that I am a *maskil*. An enlightened modernist. The most severe condemnation you can get from the Jerusalem circles."

Joseph saw the anger in his eyes.

"But you certainly have to come," Netter continued. "We have called the school *Mikve Israel*. After Jeremiah. By the way, your French is excellent."

"I lived in Paris for a while. I was on good terms with Jacob de Rothschild, the father of your patron. What I understood by the way, if I might be candid, is that neither he nor his son were initially very charmed by all these plans."

"But that is changing."

"All the better!" Joseph wanted to encourage the man. "I think the school is an excellent initiative. I'd love to visit it."

They said goodbye. Joseph couldn't help but think Mr. Netter looked miserable. As if the climate here didn't agree with him.

"I hope he succeeds," Miriam said, when the two of them were standing quietly in a corner. "And if I may, I would like to visit the school too. We can take Moshe, make an outing of it."

"Yes, of course, I hadn't thought of that."

One day, as they were walking through the plantations north of Yafo, just outside the walls, Miriam pointed to a little house that could just be seen between the orange trees. "How lovely!"

"It's a ruin," said Joseph, dismissing the idea.

"Then we will renovate it." Miriam looked at him. "We've always wanted a house near the orange groves."

"All right. We can ask if it is for sale. For my wife and my child, I will make a sacrifice and drag stones again," he said with a smile.

Joseph talked about it with Rachid, who said it would take a lot of hard work to make the place habitable. Rachid advised him to check it out properly. Water was vital. "Tell the owner that you are interested, but first you want to see whether the well can be cleaned from the rubbish and stones."

The owner, a merchant from Yafo, agreed to this deal. Soon, Rachid had arranged for some Arab workers, and under his supervision the work progressed smoothly.

"I am going to have a look how they proceed with the well," Joseph said to Miriam. "Maybe I can help."

"Be careful, you are not exactly a renowned handyman," she said laughing.

Accompanied by Moshe, Joseph came by frequently to see how things progressed. His son was almost four years old and had an immense interest in everything his father did. The Arabs sweated while hauling the big rocks away. Despite Miriam's admonition Joseph suddenly wanted to be part of the action as well.

"Watch me," he said confidently to his son and stepped onto the bricked edge of the well to help with the work.

"Beware, *effendi*," shouted one of the Arabs. "Not good. Do not stand on it."

But it was too late. Joseph felt the wall buckling beneath him. He toppled and desperately tried to grab the edge. One by one the blocks of stone rolled into the well. With a crash, the last one broke off, and screaming, Joseph fell with the stones into the dark hole. He heard Moshe yelling. His own shriek bounced off the walls around him. It was not very deep; about four meters and blockages and protrusions in the well broke the severity of his fall, although they caused a lot of scratches and some more serious cuts. He landed quite softly on a damp bed of grit and plant debris, almost a mattress. It was dark but looking up, Joseph could see the light that marked the well's mouth. He began to notice a stabbing pain in his left wrist.

"Moshe. Help. Get Rachid." He heard his own voice echoing.

"Master. I am coming down," Rachid shouted.

"No, stay there, Rachid. I'm fine. Throw a rope. Then I can climb up."

Almost immediately, he saw the dangling rope. He grabbed it, but he could not use his left hand and with his right hand he had too little strength.

"You will have to pull me out," he shouted.

"Tie the rope around your waist."

He wound the rope a few times around his waist and under his shoulders.

"Pull!" He felt the rope tighten and slowly he went up. He tried to help by walking along the side of the well. Five minutes later, he reached the opening and four pairs of hands grabbed him. Soon he was lying exhausted on the ground. "I hate enclosed spaces."

"You were lucky," said Rachid.

"I fear I have broken my wrist," he reported, clutching his arm. "I should have listened to my wife. Why do I always fall, Rachid?" he asked, dismayed.

"He who climbs will fall," responded Rachid laconically.

Joseph wondered if this was an Arabic proverb or Rachid's evaluation of Joseph's life.

Still Joseph couldn't sit by and in the following days he turned his thoughts to the house's backyard. He imagined putting the finishing touches to the fence of what would become their private garden. He hoped to train vines to grow on it and to plant a large fig tree in the middle. Rachid now thought that the well would give water. When it did, they would proceed with the purchase of the house. Joseph's thoughts went to Elsa, remembering how she had succeeded in turning her house into a pleasant home.

That afternoon, Joseph said to Miriam, "I want to visit Elsa again. I have almost finished her memoirs and I want to discuss things with her. I haven't seen her since the recital. I'm also curious to see if those robber gangs have been caught yet. You know that Amzalek sent someone as an extra guard to keep an eye on her."

Miriam said that she preferred to stay with Moshe.

"I'll ask Rivka if she feels like going," said Joseph.

When they arrived at Elsa's house, Joseph and Rivka sensed that something was wrong. Elsa loved everything clean and tidy, but it seemed as if a hurricane had raged through the house. The doors were open. The tent cloths, hanging out against the sun, were torn and all kind of bits and pieces were scattered around. In a frenzy, they stormed into the house, but froze at the sight that met their eyes. In the middle of the small living room were two bodies. Elsa and Saïda, barely recognizable in all the blood. Their clothes were mostly torn off. In the corner lay the mutilated body of a man. Joseph thought he recognized Khader, the man Amzalek had sent. He shivered, and despite all his instincts that told him to look away, he came closer. Elsa's face was upward, her eyes wide open. He took her head in his hands. Slowly he closed her eyes. As if from afar, he heard Rivka shouting, "Joseph, Saïda is still alive. Quickly. We have to get help."

Suddenly he came back to his senses. "I'm going to the *kfar* nearby. Will you stay here? Lock yourself in this room. Don't touch anything. Don't make a sound. I will come back as soon as possible."

Rivka said nothing. She grabbed a few sheets and covered the bodies. Like a madman, Joseph ran down the hill through the stinging and pungent plants. He did not notice. Tears flowed down his cheeks. "No time now. Not yet. Concentrate on Saïda." He saw a group of Arabs at the first house. Could he trust them?

"Come, come, great disaster."

Apparently his command was so convincing that three men immediately grabbed their donkeys and followed him. The way back seemed to take longer, far too long for Joseph. What if the assailants were still around? Rivka! Again and again, he urged his companions to be quick. He shuddered when he entered the house.

"Rivka!"

"I'm here with Saïda. She has regained consciousness. She should be taken to the hospital immediately."

The men were efficient. Somehow, they hung a few slats between two donkeys and on top of it they attached a mattress. Very carefully, they carried Saïda outside. It was the first time Joseph saw what had been done to her. Her clothes had been torn and her arms were covered with blood. Joseph saw that the lower part of her leg was dangling loosely from her body. He arranged the blanket better.

"Hurry," he called out to the men, "two of you bring her to Jerusalem. The other should go to the village and get more help."

He gently took Saïda's hand. "Hang in there. You'll be all right."

Despite the pain, she managed to show she understood. Joseph knew nothing better to say than, "We will come to Jerusalem as soon as possible."

The men lifted the maidservant on the improvised stretcher and left immediately. It would probably take more than two hours, but Joseph hoped they would arrive in Jerusalem before dark.

Now that Saïda had been taken care of, he returned to the living room where Rivka was trying to wipe the blood from Elsa's face with a damp cloth. Tears now flowed over his face without reserve.

"Elsa. Of all the people in the world, this had to happen to her."

He looked around and saw the painting of the young Elsa Blumenreich lying on the ground, slashed. All the cupboards were open. Plundered.

"Why did these bastards have to do this to her? And to Saïda? Couldn't they just take Elsa's stuff and leave? Why this barbarity?"

He looked at the covered body of the Arab boy. Rivka stood up and hugged Joseph.

From the village, a group of people came to help. They all expressed their abhorrence and the women immediately started to wash the bodies. The men started to shut up the windows and doors with large wooden panels. Joseph sat down on a chair, no longer able to think or act. Half an hour later, the German consul arrived with a Turkish policeman. The consul turned to Rivka, whom he knew from her work at the school. "We will find them and we will make them pay, but I know that will not bring Mrs. Blumenreich and Khader back. It is better for you to go now."

After some time, Joseph stood up as if under a spell. He looked around for Rivka. Apparently, she was busy outside. She was made of tougher material than he. He looked out over the landscape. The serenity he saw there was a stark contrast to the images in the house. How was this possible? He was witness to a massacre. Murder, rape.

"Come," the consul said to him. "Ride with us to Jerusalem. These people can be trusted here."

Saïda's father had arrived and the consul turned to him as well. "Please, sir, come with us."

Joseph stared again at the house of Elsa's dreams, near her beloved Rachel. With Rivka's support, he turned away sadly, and they took the path to Jerusalem.

Saïda's recovery was progressing well, but they wouldn't know for months whether she would be able to walk again. Khader was buried the next day according to Muslim customs. Joseph and Rivka were present and Rachid came as well. The following day, Elsa was buried in the Jewish cemetery, despite the protests of a number of Orthodox rabbis who thought there was no place for a Christian there. Joseph would not concede and pleaded with all his Talmudic knowledge. Miriam also came, without Moshe. There were also a few people from Jerusalem, including the British and German consuls. Joseph said *Kaddish*. After the burial, he saw Richard Harrison standing in the background.

"I had to come. I have visited Esther quite often, lately," the painter said. "We got along very well."

"This is the worst hour of my life," said Joseph.

"I know. It is terrible." Richard swallowed with difficulty. "I am going to honor her with a magnificent painting. The best I have ever made." Weakly, he waved his hand and left.

Joseph decided to keep saying *Kaddish* for Elsa. In addition, he continued working on her memoirs. One evening, some weeks later, he was startled by a knock on the door. It was Richard with a huge pack under his arm. He looked pitiable.

"Come in," invited Joseph.

"No, thank you. This is for Esther, Elsa. Together with your memoirs this will keep her memory alive."

He turned around and disappeared before Joseph could say anything. He stared after him into the darkness, then closed the door.

Miriam called from the kitchen, "Who was that?"

"Richard Harrison."

For a moment it was quiet. "What did he want?"

"He brought something." Miriam entered the room while Joseph unwrapped the painting. He leaned it on a cabinet and the two of them stood for a while looking in silence.

"It's beautiful," whispered Miriam.

"Indeed," Joseph said with a sob in his voice.

In the idealized, rolling landscape of Bethlehem, Elsa stood in front of Rachel's grave. Soft golden yellow light fell over the scene. Harrison had captured Elsa with her elegant posture. Her face was radiant. The powerful features were those of the wrecked portrait of her youth. The cathedral of Cologne shimmered vaguely in the dissolving mountains in the background.

A few days later Joseph received a letter from Max. The news of Elsa had obviously not reached him yet, which made reading his words even more distressing. Max wanted to come soon; he was eager to see his old friends again. Especially Elsa.

Max wrote about the state of affairs in Europe. The war with the French was over and Jews now really had equal rights in Germany. Cheerfully he wrote, "And guess what? Germany has won the war. Bismarck is our genius. *Treaty of Frankfurt* of all places. Abraham Geiger is founding a Jewish school in Berlin and has explicitly asked about you as a possible teacher. A royal position with ditto salary. I just mention it, although I don't expect that you will consider it seriously."

Something fundamental had changed. The fairy tale was over. The radiance had disappeared from life. The same morbid thoughts of that gray day, when he had returned from Munich after the premiere of *Tristan und Isolde*, got hold of him. But then, everything was centered on himself, now it was universal. Life could never be the same again after the massacre in Bethlehem. Joseph had expected difficult times, but more in a cultural and social sense, like being visited by nostalgia. But this? This was utterly senseless. Everything felt futile.

He forced himself to remember the thoughts of Ein Gedi, the watershed moment. But that feeling, which had stayed with him for so long, now faded in the face of reality. In the first years after their immigration, reality had not touched him. Sometimes he had even consciously looked away from it. Now it assaulted him harder than ever. Was everything just built on quicksand, on a few loose pillars that could so easily be overthrown?

In the evenings, when Moshe was in bed, Joseph continued to edit the memoirs. When they were done, he contacted Max about publishing them. Max wrote that he was devastated about Elsa's death but nonetheless he added in a cynical tone that no one in Germany cared to read old, outdated memoirs. Everything was focused on the future. The past of a Jewish woman, anchored in Napoleonic times, converted to Christianity, but eventually returned to that archaic religion, even renouncing Germany? No, in such a story no one had any interest.

Miriam and Joseph were downcast for weeks. The weather had no consideration for their depressed mood. Each day was brighter than the last. But the sunshine lacked the power to pull them out of their lethargy. It was hard to think about anything else. In an attempt to cheer Miriam up, Joseph said: "Think of Moshe."

"Yes. And how he will probably come to grief."

"Better times are coming. I am certain."

"I am still in shock," Miriam said. "Sometimes I am simply terrified."

"Perhaps we have to provide meaning. Make sure her memory inspires people to do good."

Miriam pointed to the piano. "I don't even feel like playing any more. It reminds me too much of her."

She sighed and looked at Moshe. "Come here, little one, come on mama's lap."

"Shall we take a look at our new house?"

"That's what I wanted to talk to you about." She waited for a second. "I am not sure that I want to live there anymore. It frightens me that anyone can just walk in there."

"We've invested a lot." He looked at her and saw the fear in her eyes. "I suppose we can get out of it. I'll talk to Rachid about it. He always has a solution for everything. We haven't signed anything yet. As an explanation, I can say that the well is not yet giving water."

Some days later, Miriam came to see Joseph in his study. "I have received a letter from my parents. They beseech me to visit them again. There is a good reason now. My cousin Moti is getting married and the whole family will be there. Also Uncle Max."

It was quiet for a while.

"I do understand if you don't want to go," she added.

"Honestly, I have to admit that it doesn't appeal to me. Although, seeing Max would be nice." And he hastened to say, "but if you think it's important, we will go of course."

"It might be better that you stay here with Moshe."

Joseph wanted to interrupt her, but she gave him no chance. "I've already thought it through. I would only be away for a month. Two weeks in total for traveling and a stay of two weeks. I really want to see my parents again."

"Of course." He got up and walked to the fence of the terrace and looked out over the plain. "But you, alone on a big boat and then in Europe? Do you think that's a good idea?" He looked at her for a long time: "You've already thought all this through, haven't you? Hmmm."

"Rivka will look after you. Really, I don't mind if you stay here."

"I wasn't really concerned about myself but more about you."

"I've told you before: I'm not that delicate."

Two weeks later Miriam left on the steamboat to Thessaloniki, from which she would take another boat to Marseille. The last part would be by train. She had arranged everything with Thomas Cook, a trustworthy agency. Joseph and Moshe waved goodbye from the quay. Rivka was in Jerusalem on an errand for Amzalek.

"So, young man. That leaves the two of us," said Joseph, when the ship disappeared in the distance.

"Now we are going to do fun stuff," the boy said.

"Yes, like cleaning, going to bed on time. Those kind of things."

Moshe looked miserable. "You are even stricter than mama."

The first Shabbat, the two of them had lunch on the terrace.

"Can I go play with my friends?" Moshe asked after they had finished eating and had cleaned up.

"Sure. Have fun." He called after him, "Be home on time. Before the end of Shabbat!"

"All right," the boy responded from afar.

It was quiet. Joseph sat down comfortably. He looked around. The feeling that he was really alone suddenly struck him. From a mild sense of concern, this turned into an unassailable melancholy. He had never experienced this before here. Loneliness. Would he allow the feeling to continue? Could he even stop it? Was it interesting to feel this way?

"So this is it," he said, barely aware that he was speaking to himself. "Here I am, alone, and it will always be like this." He imagined that no one would ever come back. Miriam would stay with her parents in Europe. Rivka would go back to the monastery. Elsa gone forever. Moshe? He would continue playing with his friends forever. Joseph petted the dog, which had curled up next to him.

"This is how it always will be," he said to the animal, doing nothing to counteract the melancholy. In an almost unnatural way, he wanted to experience the terrifying and thoroughly depressing feeling completely.

After a while, however, he decided that he had had enough. He had become too sad. Joseph wanted to get his writing materials but realized it was Shabbat. He grabbed a book instead, and half an hour later he was sleeping peacefully, with the book on his chest and Benny snoring next to him.

$$\frac{4}{}$$

(1874)

To Jerusalem

Miriam returned a few weeks later. Seeing each other again was wonderful. The Shachar family was reunited. But Joseph soon noticed that Miriam was very quiet and at the same time, rather nervous.

"Not much has happened here, to be honest," Joseph said. They sat on their bed.

"Did Moshe behave?" she asked.

"Exemplary. He helped with everything."

She smiled. "He's a good boy."

Joseph waited for her to continue, but she kept silently staring at the window.

"How are your parents?" he asked. "Tell me about Germany."

"Not now."

"Have you spoken to Max?"

"Yes." She paused for a moment. "I'll tell you all about it later."

A couple of days passed and Miriam remained very reticent. Often her thoughts seemed to take her far away. Joseph could startle her just by entering the room. He talked about it to Rivka.

"Maybe she should have something to keep her busy," Rivka said. "A job?"

"She's already got her hands full with Moshe and the household. Maybe she should do less. Have some rest."

"Women sometimes want to do more than just the housework."

"I know. I didn't mean it like that. I'm just worried. But I could ask around."

In the following weeks Miriam seemed to cheer up, but sometimes she still was moody without any particular reason. She spent most of her time with Rivka. In the evenings she sometimes played the piano but only when no one was in the room. Towards Moshe, however, she was as caring as always. Joseph asked her now and then if there was something wrong. Whether something had happened back in Germany, but Miriam denied categorically.

"What should have happened? Everything's fine," she answered bluntly.

"Let's go for a walk," he tried, one evening. He was glad she agreed. They passed the market where the merchants were dismantling the last stalls, stacking wooden crates on the pavement. With each sudden loud bang Miriam jumped. She looked really frightened. Joseph let it be, afraid it would upset her more, and only said, "Let's get away from this noise."

When they were back home, Joseph withdrew into the study and a little later he heard her playing the piano. The Haydn sonata he had heard her play the first time at the Ben Tovs' home in Frankfurt. It seemed centuries ago. He went into the living room and Miriam stopped immediately.

"Please continue. It's beautiful. It's nice that you're back at it again, although I thought you didn't like this piece anymore. Too much Germany."

"I can do whatever I want, can't I?" she said. "I'm not asking you what you're doing all day."

"Sorry, I didn't want to upset you."

"I'm not angry. I need more practice. It's too late to play anyway."

"Did you play at your parents?"

"No."

Joseph waited and then tried: "What was it like living there again for a while? You haven't told me much about it yet."

"Not very nice. Papa was away a lot." She closed the lid of the piano. "Anyway, I'm glad I'm back home."

"That's good to hear. I worried now and then. Maybe you miss your parents a little?"

"No, certainly not," she replied.

Joseph let it rest. Things would improve in time. At least she was glad she was here. That was important.

Joseph heard from Rachid that Richard Harrison was back in Yafo, and the next day they met for coffee.

"I have missed you," Joseph said. "I miss a comrade to discuss things. Miriam is mainly busy with Moshe and the little things."

"You shouldn't meet me, without your wife knowing, I mean," Richard replied.

"She would have objected immediately. If I bring it up delicately, afterwards, I might contain the damage."

"Your choice."

"I know. My choices are generally not that strong. But I have missed our conversations. And you were here from the beginning. For me, you are part of the country, like Rachid. Without you I probably would not even be here."

Richard laughed. "Don't get worked up. I just don't want to be involved in your marital quarrel afterwards."

Joseph changed the subject. "Do you remember that we spoke about making a trip through the country? Turning those experiences into a book? A travel description with sketches. You as the painter and I as the storyteller. I would like to proceed with that. I need a challenge."

"And how are you going to sell that at home? That you need to go away every now and again on a business trip for a few weeks?"

"No, I would be honest about it. But before I raise it with Miriam, I want to know if you're still interested."

"Certainly. It still sounds like a splendid idea."

At home that evening, Joseph decided not to beat about the bush. "I met with Richard Harrison today. I would like to do a project with him."

Carefully he explained their plan, but Miriam wasn't really interested and said that he could pursue it. But there was no question of leaving for a longer period. She suggested a compromise. Joseph could cooperate with Richard, but not go on a long journey. His place was with the family.

"All right." He was glad and relieved that she was in a good mood and had accepted the idea so easily.

"There is something really important, we have to talk about," Miriam went on. "School. Moshe is almost five years old, so it would be good if we started thinking about his education."

Miriam took her time. "I have talked about it with your sister and she would love to help. We want to start a school. We already made plans. It would be good for the whole community if there would be a decent school here."

Joseph looked bewildered, not so much because of the thought but because of the diligence.

"Magnificent. I think it's a great idea for you to work together. I am just amazed at the speed with which everything is happening."

"Don't you worry about that. We thought about naming the school after Elsa. *The Elsa Blumenreich School*. A school for boys to begin with. Later we could start thinking about a girls' school. One step at a time."

"It's a splendid idea. Elsa would have been so touched. She loved *Bildung*!"

It was a word that Joseph had so far only reserved for himself and that he had not thought about for years. *Bildung*. What would they teach

Moshe? English, German, Arabic, French? Yiddish? Mathematics, Talmud? Would it make sense to let him play the piano or to teach him about paintings in this country? Or was it better to train him in a simple profession to secure his future? One thing was out of the question. No continuation of the *shmatte* trade here in Yafo.

"It's good that you're excited as well." She became serious again. "There is a lot to do. We have to make a lot of decisions. Which subjects? Who is going to do what? Where? Money of course. We need books."

Joseph agreed. He hadn't seen Miriam so passionate for a long time. Perhaps this was just what she needed.

"Rivka might be able to borrow books from the settlers in Sarona," Miriam said. "She has already been in touch with them about it."

They found an empty office in the harbor that they could use as a classroom for the short term. They put the name of the school in capital letters above the entrance. In a kind of founding ceremony, they hung Richard's painting on the wall. A meeting followed in which they discussed the curriculum. Rivka had succeeded in borrowing a number of books from the *Templers*, but Miriam found that they had to reject most of them because they were too Christian.

"Are we going to teach in Hebrew? Or in Arabic," Rivka asked, "Or maybe better, French?"

"Hebrew is fine, as far as I am concerned," Miriam said. "Then everyone will at least understand each other on a basic level. I am hoping that the Ashkenazi children will come as well."

"And there will be a lot of general education," said Rivka.

"Indeed," Joseph confirmed. "When you try to understand how a steam engine works, religion shouldn't play a role."

"Or should it? Isn't everything supposed to be permeated with the divine?" Miriam asked.

Rivka considered the point for a moment. "Maybe so. But they get separate Torah lessons." She continued, "I could go to Jerusalem to see if I can get cooperation from my old school there?"

"From your monastery?" Joseph asked.

"Yes, they had good teaching material. Better than what we have here. Now that I think of it, do you know a man from Sarona, called Schönfeld?" Rivka asked.

"No sorry, I only know their leader, that Hoffmann guy. Why?"

"I have the feeling that Schönfeld is trying to help me a little too emphatically, if you understand what I mean."

"Do you want me to talk to him?"

"No, I can handle it myself. Just wanted to tell you. I'm not looking for a German admirer who is waiting for the Savior." She laughed. "I've suffered enough from both, admirers and saviors."

"Shall I come with you to Jerusalem?" Miriam asked, picking up the subject again.

Joseph looked concerned.

"Don't you worry," Miriam said defiantly. "Maybe it would be good for Rivka not to go to the monastery alone." She looked at Rivka for affirmation and Rivka nodded with a smile.

When Miriam saw the battlements of the walls of Jerusalem, she tried to pull herself together. She felt scared. She could no longer go on this way. Since Elsa's death, irrational fears had surfaced at the strangest moments. A fear that death was all around. And her stay in Germany had put everything on edge. She planned to confide in Rivka today.

They arrived at the monastery on the *Via Dolorosa*. Wedged between the intrusive buildings, Miriam noticed the arch spanning the street.

"Still from the Romans, from emperor Hadrian," Rivka said pointing to it.

"He wasn't good for us. Wasn't he the one who plowed the whole city over?"

"As far as I know, yes. Anyway, that devastation was a long time ago."

"Some misery will never disappear."

"Wait here," Rivka said, changing the subject. "I'm going in to ask whether we're welcome. Whether the abbot or anyone else can see us."

Miriam stayed behind in the street. Suddenly she saw a hooded figure in an open window in the arch. The man was completely dressed in black. He stared right at her. She shuddered. The sudden appearance frightened her. The man looked a bit like Joseph. Her gaze went to the door in the hope that Rivka would come back. When she looked up again the figure had vanished. Had she been hallucinating? At that moment Rivka appeared.

"The abbot can see us in half an hour," she said. She observed Miriam closely. "What is wrong? It looks like you've seen a ghost."

"Nothing. Not really anything at all," Miriam replied. Tears sprang to her eyes. Rivka saw them.

"I'll tell you in a minute," Miriam said. "When we're inside. I'd like to see where you lived all those years."

"Five years to be precise."

"Unbelievable. Come, lead on," Miriam said.

They walked through the narrow, low corridors. They smelled stale, a combination of damp stone and incense. The walls were built of heavy dark brown blocks. There was hardly any light. On the right,

Miriam saw a large room at the end of a similar corridor.

"The refectory, the dining room," Rivka explained. "The food was actually quite good. I suppose a lot better than what most people in Jerusalem have for supper. Not kosher, I daresay, but you can't have everything." She laughed then saw Miriam's troubled face. "I'm sorry, it's not the time for quips."

"No, never mind," Miriam said. She looked around. "Is there somewhere we can sit quietly?"

"We can see if my old room's still available." She walked on and turned into another, even lower corridor. "Let's see, it's around here somewhere. It all looks so much alike."

They came into a hallway with open doors on both sides.

"I don't think there are many nuns left," said Rivka, "they have a new building. In Ein Kerem, outside Jerusalem. I think most of them have moved there."

She went into a room on the right. "This one's empty," she said. "It wasn't mine, but that doesn't matter. They're all about the same."

They entered a room no more than two by three meters. There was no window and the only light came in through the doorway. "Leave the door open," said Rivka. She lit a candle. The interior was even more spare than Miriam had expected, a bed, a table and a chair. A large cross hung on the wall. There was a kind of lectern with a mat in front of it.

"For prayer," Rivka said superfluously. "I was never very precise in it, I must say. The liturgy of Christianity never spoke to me."

"How were you able to survive here," Miriam said in disbelief.

"You can get used to anything." She pulled up the chair for Miriam and sat herself down on the bed. "And now you're going to tell me everything."

"I don't know where to start," Miriam said.

"What has changed?"

"Actually, nothing's changed. I have changed."

"Start with what just happened out on the street. Then maybe the rest will come naturally. It looked like you had seen the devil himself, that's how pale you were."

She told about the frightening apparition. Then, taking a deep breath, she went on. "I'm so scared." Again, tears came into her eyes, but now she didn't try to hold them back. Rivka hugged her tightly. With shaking voice, Miriam continued. "I can't be strong anymore. Too much has happened. It all started with the murder of Elsa and the rape of Saida. I'm so scared," she repeated. "Stupid things that I would have dismissed in the past are suddenly important now, threatening. In my dreams they come back like birds of prey that surround me and bend over to peck at me. Signs of doom. I keep looking over my shoulder and don't trust anyone anymore. And I keep having these moments of pure panic."

Rivka tried to dry her tears. She waited for Miriam to compose herself.

After a while Miriam continued. "It is awful. I get so tense that I can hardly breathe. I had expected that with organizing the school and the daily work, everything would go back to normal, but these attacks are still coming back. It has to do with everything that has happened here and especially what happened in Germany."

"In Germany?"

"Yes. When I was visiting for my nephew's wedding."

She sat straight. "I'll tell you everything, but please don't say anything to Joseph. I don't want him to know. Not yet." She swallowed and swept her sleeve over her eyes. "Of course, my parents welcomed me warmly. They pampered me. Wanted me to feel at home. They had already heard about Elsa's murder. Through Max. Papa left the second day. He was busy winning souls for his project: convincing people to go to *Eretz Israel*. I was at home with my mother most of the time and she started talking. The first day she was sympathetic about what happened in Bethlehem, but soon she started to point out that probably it was the way of the land. The barbarity, the lack of civilization. She understood why we wanted to be there, but there was someone else involved we should think of. One who couldn't speak up for himself. Of course, she was talking about Moshe. In the end it came down to her belief that it would be completely irresponsible to leave the child in a country with such thugs. I would come to regret it very deeply, if we stayed there. She didn't have any specifics but she made it clear that things would end badly, especially for Moshe. She forgave me for not being able to read the signs, even though they were clearly on the wall. Someone was needed to bring me out of my fantasy, and regrettably, as she said, it had to be her. She even brought in all kinds of theological reflections. Trying to hasten messianic times was a doomed mission, she said. And her little grandson would pay the price. I don't think she herself understood anything she was saying."

"But your mother thought it was a good thing that you came here, didn't she?"

"My father did, but my mother always had her reservations. But she submitted to my father's will."

"Please, go on."

"I started to feel worried at first and then guilt crept in. Guilt of leaving Moshe in such a barbarous country. In the beginning I was able to counter her attacks, but I got weaker. After a few days I had no strength left to oppose her. I just sat there and listened. Mum and terrified.

And then she started to give me alternatives. I should stay in Germany. She would arrange for everything. It wouldn't be a defeat. Just the wise thing to do. Better to stop halfway than to persevere in an error. The time wasn't ripe. Perhaps we could try it again later, when Moshe was older. Maybe the situation in Palestine would be better then." Miriam stopped to take a deep breath. "Europe was the secure haven. It was so much safer there. In Cologne, there was progress and civilization."

"But what about Joseph and Moshe?"

"She had it all planned out. First I would extend my stay in Cologne. Then extend it another time, and then we would send someone to fetch Moshe. And Joseph. She clearly thought of Max. He would be able to convince Joseph."

"Terrible!"

"I went to talk to Max. Especially to ask him not to go. To get Joseph, I mean."

"And what did he say?"

"Do you know Max?"

"No, not really, just Joseph's stories."

"Max is my uncle and he has become sort of Joseph's second father. He is his anchor and always has the right answer. But also for me, Uncle Max is important. He is always cheerful and so smart. But when I asked him now what to do, he had no answer. That said it all. I think he was still very distressed about Elsa."

Again she started crying. Rivka sat next to her on the bed and gave Miriam her shoulder.

"How did it end? You came back. That's clear."

"My nephew's wedding was a day before I was supposed to leave. My father came back for Shabbat. I didn't have the energy to talk to him about it. Or, more accurately, I felt ashamed about the whole situation. A voice in my head said that maybe my mother was right. I had really started to think that I was an awful mother to leave Moshe in such a place. And that I was responsible for the horrific ending that inevitably would come."

"And?"

"My mother was as peaceful as a lamb during the last day. But the damage was done." She held back for a while. "You know. I am not a dreamer. I see the misery and the bad things here too. It's not that I close my eyes and don't see the reality. My mother managed to catch me at the right moment in the right place. Eventually, I took the train and the boat. I kept telling myself, "You have to go back to fetch them. Think of Moshe."

"Back here, I abandoned the whole absurd idea of going back," she continued, "but then came the phantoms. The murder of Elsa still haunts me every day. Sometimes I only see doom and gloom. I'm scared all the time. I try to be as normal as possible with Moshe, but I am excluding Joseph completely. I'm afraid I haven't been very nice to him lately."

"Then talk to him about it."

"I don't know. I'm afraid that he would immediately get on a boat to Germany and make a stink there." She laughed through her tears.

The arrival of a nun interrupted their conversation. "This is a private room, mind you." And then suddenly her face lit up. "Sister Renata. How nice. It's so good to see you!"

Rivka greeted her warmly and introduced her to Miriam, "This is Sister Clara. One of my friends here. She has helped me very much. Especially in difficult times, she was my support."

Addressing Sister Clara she said. "I wanted to give my sister-in-law a glimpse into the lives of the sisters here."

"What are you doing these days," Sister Clara asked.

"I live in Yafo. We want to start a school there. That's why we are here. To ask the abbot whether we can borrow books. I think it's about time for our appointment."

"I'll take you to him."

The conversation with the abbot was fruitful and when Miriam and Rivka said goodbye, they were loaded with books. On their way back to Yafo, Miriam said, "I am happy that I told you. You are stronger than I am. You can think out of despair, I can only think out of hope. From despair, I only see more despair. You can make it anywhere. Evidently, as it turns out, I can't."

Rivka shook her head.

"No really," Miriam continued, "I am adventurous, for sure, but there are limits. When I used to lie in bed as a child, I'd always see forms haunting my room. I drove them away by crawling under the sheets or sometimes by building a story around them and giving them a friendly meaning. I thought I had conquered that fear. Maybe I overestimated myself. When disaster really strikes, there's no place to hide. Let's face it, the fear of being killed here or worse is very real."

"I agree that the danger is real, but maybe the fear can be contained. First of all you don't live in the wilderness, but in Yafo. And you were weak and alone in Germany. The most important thing now is to talk to Joseph. He will understand, I am sure of it. He has gone through some things himself."

Miriam hesitated. "I think he needs someone strong at his side."

"You won't be strong unless you tell him. Believe me."

Miriam promised she would talk to Joseph. "He sees me as his rock, you know. I am sure that he can manage on his own, but he doesn't see it that way. Of course he's got the wrong end of the stick." She laughed.

"I assure you. You'll be stronger than ever."

"I feel very relieved. Really, so much better. Anyway, I am not thinking of leaving here, no way. Here's home. With Joseph and Moshe. And with you."

That week, after the morning service, Rav Yehuda, one of the rabbis of Yafo, asked Joseph to stay. Joseph was curious to learn what he had to say, because although he knew the man well enough and thought him sympathetic, he had had few dealings with him. The small group of Ashkenazim in Yafo seemed exotic to Joseph. In Frankfurt, the Sephardic Jews had been the aliens. Some Sephardic merchants once had visited his father and they had seemed stranger to Joseph than the Christians around the corner. In Yafo, however, the Sephardim were at home. Joseph prayed in the Sephardic synagogue, but – as always – he did not really want to belong to any group.

Rav Yehuda quickly got to the point. "A messenger from the *Beth Din* of Jerusalem has just arrived and he has bad news, at least for you."

The rabbi chose his words carefully. "There is a problem with the school. Specifically with who will teach there."

"They don't know anything about me."

"It's not about you. It's about your sister. Isn't it true that she converted to Christianity?"

Joseph waved his arm. "A youthful sin. In order to get married. She left that all behind her a long time ago."

"But she was in the convent of the *Sisters of Zion*. That's right, isn't it?"

"Bygones."

"Not for the rabbis. They will not allow her to teach at a school where Jewish children attend. They plan to proclaim a *cherem*, on you and the school if you proceed."

"My family is being thrown out of the Jewish community?" Joseph asked, trying not to give in to his anger. "Let's try to stay reasonable. After all, you are not responsible. Which *Beth Din* are we talking about? There are so many."

"One of the strictest. Headed by a rabbi named Benyomin Jacobson."

Joseph nodded long and slowly. "Doesn't matter. All this has no effect on us, on what we do. They can proclaim *cherems* as much as they want. As far as I am concerned, they can prophesize that the world will perish." He thanked the rabbi and immediately went back home. Rivka was with Miriam on the terrace wrapping books.

"The fanatics in Jerusalem are going to pronounce a ban on the school." He told them what he just had heard. When he had finished, everyone let the words sink in.

"Maybe I should withdraw," Rivka said slowly.

"Never ever," replied Joseph. "We will not grant them this victory."

"We or you?" Miriam asked. "Maybe it's not about defeat and victory. Not everything is about you." She got up and said, "I am going to see where Moshe is."

Joseph fell silent. Miriam was right, but she had answered so fiercely. He tried to focus on the subject. Indeed, it was not about him. But asking Rivka to step back? Sacrificing his sister to appease the fanatics? He shook his head with frustration.

Later, Joseph started writing a libel article about Rabbi Jacobson and his followers, and soon found himself expanding to write about all ultra-religious Jews as a group. He was fierce and indiscriminate. Probably some frustration about the estrangement between Miriam and him seeped in as well. As he was not planning to publish it, he did not hold anything back. He found it a gratifying way to channel his anger, but as he wrote he found himself becoming angrier and angrier. He used everything he had at his disposal. He remembered a story Rivka had told about a *Yeshiva* teacher who had laid his hands on a girl. Another story about prostitution in strict Orthodox families to earn some extra money. He called the piece "The Hypocrisy of the Zealots". Everything had to be covered up all the time, he wrote, because the shock of this kind of report in the newspapers would be devastating to the image of Jerusalem's holiness. And the Orthodox Jews were receiving support from the Ottomans, an unexpected source. Two groups of hypocrites who had found each other. Joseph concluded with the statement that, together with those Jewish extremists, the inadequate Turks should also be taken down.

He read the piece when he had finished it. Instead of picking up the pen to edit it, he sat down and just enjoyed reading it. He laughed. It was too harsh. He was trying to decide whether to throw it away immediately or whether he wanted to rewrite it later, when Rachid entered and announced that someone had arrived from Sarona. Joseph left the article on his desk and went to the door.

To his surprise, it was the man who resembled Braunberger. Would this keep haunting him for the rest of his life? "Gerhard Schönfeld is my name," the man introduced himself politely and removed his hat. "I heard that Renata Socher would be here?"

Joseph didn't know what to do. He was in a bad mood. So this was the man who was pursuing Rivka. Should he treat the man in an unfriendly manner so that he would stay away forever or was it better to let his sister handle this matter? He led the man into his study.

"Would you at least call her Rivka, please? I will get her."

Rivka was in her room at the back of the house and immediately said that she would rather not meet the man.

"Should I kindly send him away or in such a way that he doesn't come back?"

"You are my big brother. My decisions in this area have been disastrous so far, so please do what you think is best."

Joseph returned to his study with peace of mind.

"My apologies, but I think Rivka doesn't see any possibility of receiving you at the moment. And as far as I know, this also applies to the future."

The man immediately understood that he had been rejected and seemed not to handle it well.

With restrained anger he said, "I wanted to help. You don't see it for yourself. You must be helped."

"We are not really waiting for this kind of condescending help," Joseph replied, getting up and opening the door.

Schönfeld paused a moment, then continued angrily. "You think you are so exalted. See what has become of you. Wanderers, the lowest class of society. One can smell where the Jews live." Joseph shrugged his shoulders not understanding where this hatred suddenly came from.

"Would you please leave," he just said in a low voice.

Schönfeld took his hat and walked to the door where he turned around. At that moment he saw Rivka in the hallway. This seemed to help Schönfeld get a grip on himself. He looked at Rivka and stammered, "I really only wanted to help. You must be helped, you see. I thought you had the same ideas as I do. If I had known that I would upset you, I would never have come. I hope you will forgive me. I was blinded."

Joseph looked down. What a spectacle the man was making of himself.

"Perhaps it's indeed better that you not visit us anymore," said Rivka. "Do you understand?" She looked at him with piercing eyes and Joseph himself was almost afraid of her. He had never seen his sister like this before.

Schönfeld nodded. Her gaze softened. Joseph shook his head. He knew Rivka. She had already forgiven him.

Schönfeld left the house.

Rivka heard Schönfeld's words echoing. "You must be helped. The situation of the Jewish people is temporary. They, you, will be absorbed."

"You must know," she said to Joseph when they were alone, "so often, after leaving the monastery, I have felt tested or even attacked from all sides, quizzed about my baptism, about my origins, about my life before Jerusalem."

"I can imagine."

"That statement he just made, 'you must be helped.' I think I have heard it dozens of times, in one way or another. And I always told them that I already had been absorbed, and had left it at that. I decided not to worry about where I belonged anymore. And it worked."

"Have you entirely abandoned the idea of love and marriage?" he asked.

"I had to take a vow of chastity when I entered the monastery." She laughed. "Actually, I didn't know what I was thinking then." Then she continued, serious again. "In a way I stick to that idea. But now it's my own choice. The disappointment of the past has been too devastating to admit any new upheaval." As she continued, she spoke softly. "To use an understatement, I never spoke a lot about what happened in France. It was terrible and, mind you, I am speaking about the time before I left Rainer. Almost every day I paced our apartment waiting for him to come home and imagining him with someone else. I think that was the worst part. The consuming jealousy. No freedom left. Caged. He liked it that way. To have his wife enslaved at home to control. To get rid of my anger and bitterness, I wanted to sink my teeth into the carpet and bite off a square. After I left him, my situation was pretty desperate but at least I was free from the hatred, and could make my own choices."

Joseph nodded in sympathy, as she continued in a resolute tone, "That's why I think I will never surrender again to a new alleged love."

"And children?" Joseph tried. "You love children."

"Moshe is probably the closest I will get to having my own child. I love that boy so much. And I know that I want to be a good aunt to him. You can call me an old spinster, but I see myself more as an independent woman. Perhaps a role model for the girls here who are far too submissive. I spoke to Elsa about this a few times. She was made of the same metal." She smiled. "I can always go back to the convent if I feel lonely."

"You'd never!"

Later that evening Joseph looked for his diatribe against Benyomin Jacobson and his group of fanatics, but he couldn't find it anywhere. Had he thrown it away? The wastepaper basket was empty. Didn't Miriam empty it every night? He shrugged his shoulders. No loss. It was far too wild to even start editing. It would be better to sit down and quietly write a decent piece.

The threat of the *cherem* kept haunting him. Excluding Rivka? There should be another way. Perhaps they could go to Jerusalem and defend their case. Maybe the judges of the *Beth Din* would be more reasonable than he expected.

Miriam failed to see the need. "Don't you think it will blow over if we keep Rivka out of it for now? Maybe it would be for the greater good? She has already volunteered to drop out of the school, at least for a while. I don't want all this conflict."

"It's a matter of principle."

She got angry. "Why are you so hopelessly stubborn? I just can't believe that you don't understand."

Joseph sighed deeply. "Perhaps you're right. But I think that first we should try to have a serious chat with those people in Jerusalem. It probably won't make a difference, but I think we owe it to Rivka to protest."

"If you want."

A little later, after Miriam had tucked Moshe in, she said: "I apologize for my angry words just now."

She waited a second.

Then she asked. "Can we talk?"

5

Jerusalem Revisited

A week later Joseph and Miriam were striding through Jerusalem, huddled closely together because of the cold. It was a rainy December evening. The wind cut through their clothes. There was mud on the streets and despite the cold, the air stank. Rivka had stayed with Moshe. It had seemed better not to involve her in this visit and besides Joseph had thought that after Miriam's opening up, it would be good for the two of them to take a trip together. But the weather seemed an unexpected spoiler.

"If only we were back in Yafo," Joseph thought out loud. There the mornings already held the promise of spring. Here it was still the heart of winter. He shivered.

Until now he had kept himself far from the extreme Orthodox Jews in Jerusalem, but even from a distance he had gotten to know the relationships between the communities there. The views of the *Chassidim*, of their opposers the *Mitnagdim*, and of course, of the original Jewish population, mainly Sephardic Jews. The non-conformist views, the poverty, the division of the money. The intransigence. But he had never really had to deal with it.

"Do you remember that *Tisha b'Av* afternoon?" he asked Miriam. "I sympathized with the Goldsteins, their community. I loved it, sincerely. I may not agree with everything they say, but it made an impression. They stole my heart then. And now they are trampling on it."

"Those are not the same people, Joseph," Miriam said. They walked on, heavily bent forward against the wind. "Could we visit the Goldsteins again?"

"Better not now," he replied. "We should not let our judgment be clouded by our well-meant intentions. My heart must become hard. Just like Pharaoh's."

He laughed but Miriam shook her head. "Please behave when we are there."

"Don't worry. But, be honest, that was a funny remark."

Miriam gave him a scathing look. "I'm afraid you're going to make a scene because you just happen to like doing that."

"Of course I won't. Listen. I see it this way: we are currently engaged in a fight with an institution. Not with people. And I need to keep those separate. I want to confront this man, this Jacobson, with what he is doing. And that has nothing to do with the Goldstein family in *Mishkenot*. You also want the school to open and Rivka to teach there. This is the last chance to get these people on our side, or at least not opposing us. Otherwise we'll just do it without their approval. This is a trip to Canossa, you could say. We mean well but it's not that simple. Everyone here is arguing with everyone, and will until the end of time. And in the end, the hostility will remain and it will lead to nothing."

Miriam nodded and her expression softened. "Well put, Mr. Teacher. But first tell me where Canossa is."

He smiled. Long ago, before Joseph had returned to his parents' home for the first time, he had heard Max use the term and now, after all these years, he enjoyed being able to explain it to his wife. He told her about the German Emperor's journey to the Pope who made him wait in the snow for days. Joseph added, "I just hope we won't have to sit at the gate for three days in this grueling weather."

"Do you remember when we couldn't enter the city?" Miriam was daydreaming. "It was so beautiful then."

"It's still beautiful, isn't it? A lot of misery has happened, but we are still good."

They walked on.

"Maybe we should get back to that place where the sun stood still," Miriam suggested. "When everything was blessed."

"I think everything is still blessed. But sure, we will. Perhaps after our conversation with the rabbi. It probably won't yield anything, so we'll need something pleasant afterward."

"You're already assuming that it will amount to nothing. Give them a chance," Miriam said.

"Maybe. But I won't let myself be lectured at. Do you know what? If the conversation gets out of hand, you can end it by sitting down next to the rabbi. For sure he'll go running out of the room."

Joseph pointed in the distance. "Look, there is our hotel."

Rav Benyomin Jacobson, *dayan* of one of the religious courts of Jerusalem, lived in a small house near the Western Wall. He opened the door himself and led them into a spartanly furnished room. This could be by choice but more likely it reflected poverty. Joseph started in Hebrew, assuming that German or French would be too worldly. But the rabbi interrupted him almost immediately.

"Where were you born?" Jacobson asked in Yiddish.

"Frankfurt."

"Then there is no reason not to have this conversation in Yiddish."

Joseph took a deep breath.

He explained the situation. Miriam and Rivka, pious people, Jewish, wanted to start a school for the small group of Jewish children who could hardly get any education in Yafo. As he spoke, he became increasingly convinced of the fairness of the plans, and he could not see why Jacobson should not acknowledge this as well. When he had finished, he looked at the rabbi expectantly. Jacobson stroked his beard for a long time.

Slowly he began to talk, "I understand that this lady is not Jewish." He paused for a moment and just as Joseph wanted to object, he continued: "In fact, she has worked in a monastery to win converts for the Christian faith." His voice gained strength. "Under no circumstances can we allow her to teach at such a school."

"She is my sister. She is as Jewish as I am," said Joseph.

"With the clothes you are wearing? To me, you look very much like a *goy* who has no business here at all."

Miriam spoke before Joseph could explode. "If his sister would step back, there wouldn't be a problem?"

"I would have to check what lessons would be given. What are your plans?"

"We want to offer a broad education. Torah and Talmud, but also Languages and Mathematics. Maybe Arabic. General education."

"Science pollutes the Torah. They cannot be together."

Joseph had listened with gritted teeth. "To invent an engine, you first need to know the basic principles of physics."

"If you say so."

"And what about *Torah im Derech Eretz*; the *Mishna* in *Avot*. Torah with the modern world together. The much-praised Rabbi of Frankfurt, Rabbi Hirsch, has even made this the paradigm for his congregation."

"We don't live in Frankfurt, we are here in Jerusalem. Here, studying Torah and Talmud is the only proper way to acquire knowledge. I have no dealings with this rabbi in Frankfurt." He began to get up as a sign that the conversation was over. Joseph saw that it would be useless, but still he wanted to make his point. "When you think as a relic from ancient times, you have no future. In the end you will lose."

The man smiled, condescending. "Without these ancient relics, as you call them, our people would have long since ceased to exist. And you would never have been born in the ghetto of Frankfurt."

"Fair enough. You don't respect Rabbi Hirsch. But what about Shimon bar Yochai? What God says when he despises the world. "Have you come out of your cave to destroy my world? Go back to your cave!"

The rabbi gave him a contemptuous look: "Don't talk about things you have no knowledge of."

"You are a *Tzaddik im Pelz*. [11] You are a hermit. You think only about yourself. Just like Noach. You put on a thick coat to keep yourself warm. Instead of lighting a fire to warm others."

"How dare you abuse our own stories for your heretical ideas? Please leave now."

As Joseph walked out with Miriam, he raged, "These people are backward. I did not travel thousands of miles to come to a copy of the *Judengasse*. Or worse."

Miriam tried to curb his anger. "Let it go, Joseph. There is no point in getting worked up about this, when you were expecting it to begin with. Leave it alone."

"All they do is beg. And in that way, everyone here is a pauper. They do absolutely nothing for themselves." He gave a laugh. "To learn Torah. I am so fed up with it. Do you think the whole community here is nothing but sages?" He stopped and took a deep breath. "They want to transform this whole land into one big ghetto. And they will impose a ban on anyone who wants something else. One cannot do anything or they interfere."

Bitterly disappointed and frustrated, they walked silently back to their hotel.

"I have made up my mind," Joseph finally said. "I hope you'll agree. We have to step back from the whole mess here. We'll deal only with ourselves. In Yafo. Far from all the religious violence, literally and figuratively. And if there will be fractures, so be it."

"I've been saying that all the time."

"We start the school and let the *cherem* come. That way Rivka doesn't have to quit." He continued after a short pause. "They are trying to make us feel guilty. And I don't want to feel guilty. We support our community, in order for our children to have a school. We even came to this forsaken country. I shouldn't say that, but sometimes it feels like that. We're obstructed at every turn. And Elsa was murdered… Maybe your mother was right. Maybe the time is not ripe for us to live here."

"Please, leave my mother out of it," Miriam said angrily.

"She barely agreed to let you marry me. A Jew who strayed from the right path. The last thing she expected of me, or of us, was that we would put your father's ideas into practice."

"Don't talk that way about my mother." Miriam continued. "We have just put that whole story behind us. We are both in a pesky, cynical mood."

"I just wanted…" He paused. "Let it go. I'm whining. I'm angry and I just wanted to lash out. I apologize. I shouldn't have said all this.

It's those fanatics who drive me mad. We just have to stay away from Jerusalem."

"This visit was doomed from the beginning. You knew the outcome. You did it only for your...," she paused, looking for the right word.

"Just say it," Joseph insisted. "I deserve it."

"For your ego. To have your judgment confirmed. To justify your anger."

They were startled by the shouts of a man who hurried toward them. "Are you a doctor?" the man asked in Yiddish. Joseph presumed that the man would have accosted anyone who was not wearing a black coat.

"No, but what is the problem?"

"I think my wife is dying. She is pregnant. You must help."

Joseph looked at Miriam and she nodded.

"Lead the way. We will see what we can do." And whispering to Miriam: "Wouldn't it be better to get a doctor right away?"

"Let's see what's going on first."

"Thank you. My name is Dovid. Dovid Gans."

After a rapid walk alongside a dark wall with hardly any windows, they saw an underpass opening onto a courtyard. They entered one of the doors. The room was even more poverty-stricken than Rabbi Jacobson's home. On the floor and against the wall were worn bedspreads; on an old mattress a woman was lying, rather a girl. She looked pale as death and her face was sweaty. Next to her, on the ground, sat a man and a woman. In a corner were two more men. "Her parents," whispered Dovid. "And that is Shmuel. He usually knows what to do when someone is ill. But now? I'm afraid my Malke will die."

Miriam knelt beside her. She felt her pulse. "Joseph, get a doctor immediately. Maybe ask the consul. He lives nearby."

Joseph rushed to the consul's house. His pounding heart reminded him of the minutes of despair at Elsa's house.

Moments later, he returned with a doctor, whom the consul had called up in a hurry. Dovid was walking back and forth nervously with tears in his eyes. "I think it's too late. Malke. Malke."

The doctor knelt beside her and a little later, he closed her eyes.

"I can't do anything anymore," he said softly.

Joseph and Miriam accompanied him to the courtyard.

"She should have been treated in the hospital," the doctor said. "Here, in these unhygienic conditions, no one can recover from dysentery."

"Why wasn't she taken there," Miriam asked. "There are decent hospitals here, aren't there?"

"Only one small Jewish one but it doesn't function very well. There are Christian ones, but the Orthodox are afraid that the patients will convert."

"But if the choice is life or death," Joseph exclaimed.

The doctor sadly shook his head and left.

Joseph and Miriam didn't know what to do now. Should they stay and comfort the family? They went back inside. Dovid was sitting in a corner, together with the others. He was saying prayers and seemed barely aware of what was happening. The man who had initially been present as some kind of doctor, now stood up. "We have to do something about the unborn child," he remarked, unruffled. "Could you perhaps take Dovid and the others outside?"

Joseph looked at Miriam. "Go, I'll be there in a minute." He stayed as the others left. Now, Shmuel walked out, and returned a little later in the company of an older woman carrying a broom. All of a sudden, Joseph understood what was going to happen. He did not want to see it. The child would be beaten to death in the belly. As he slipped out, he heard the dull blow of the broom on the body. He closed the door behind him and joined Miriam in the courtyard. After a while Shmuel came out. "We had to make sure that the child was dead. Otherwise we can't bury her. That is the law."

Joseph was totally bewildered. He did not know which law the man meant, the Turkish or the Jewish law. He had never heard of it before. He grabbed Miriam. "Let's get the hell out of here."

Miriam followed him. "What was that all about?"

"You don't want to know. I'll tell you later. Not now." He kept quiet and breathed nervously. Then he turned to the wall and vomited. "Come, I want to forget this," he said when he had pulled himself together again.

When they were back in the hotel, Joseph gently explained what had happened. Miriam reflected for some time. "Maybe," she said, "maybe we should visit Yankele's family tomorrow. Rinse away this horrible experience. I don't want the panic to return. I am managing quite well now. I don't want to be left with this impression of Jerusalem."

"I just want to leave, now."

"I know, but the city deserves better than this memory."

"Perhaps you're right." He looked at her with grief. "You know, I pity them. Their poverty, their ignorance, their devotion. There are so many good people among them. Who am I to tell them what is good for them? I can't say to those people in Jerusalem, "You're totally wrong. Change!" Not only is it pointless, it also conveys contempt and arrogance."

But in the morning they wanted to go back to Moshe as soon as possible. On the way to Yafo, Joseph made himself as comfortable as he could in the carriage. He closed his eyes. Miriam laid her head on his shoulder. Despite the bad condition of the road, they both caught some sleep, and by the time they saw Yafo under the cloudless sky, their moods had lightened.

It soon became obvious that Rivka was not the only stumbling block. The entire concept of the school was a problem. Specifically, the subjects they wanted to teach – Arabic, English, mathematics. In a way Joseph was relieved. This made things easier as now he didn't have to think about his sister's involvement.

"Problem solved," he said. "We'll just do what we wanted to do all along. Let them figure it out there in Jerusalem. We'll start the Elsa Blumenreich School as we want it to be."

The *cherem* for the school was pronounced. Rav Yehuda described to Joseph what the scene must have been like in the synagogue in Jerusalem when it happened. The shofar was blown before the reading of the Torah and then the ban went into effect. Joseph had to laugh when he heard the account.

"I wonder if this is not the worst form of *lashon hara*. To proclaim in the open, with pomp and circumstance, that someone has misbehaved."

Rav Yehuda nodded. "I have never looked at it from that angle, I must admit. But you are in fine company. They even excommunicated Moses Montefiore."

"My faith is too precious to me to leave it to the fanatics," Joseph said. "I don't just want to view Judaism from a distance. I want to be inside, to deal with the changes, to speed things up and to be part of it all."

Involuntarily, Joseph thought of Max. Max had left the faith a long time ago and although he still watched from a safe distance, it did not affect him. He had placed himself outside, like thousands of others. What remained were the fanatics on one hand and the liberals on the other.

Rav Yehuda looked at him with concern. "I know you are having a hard time with all this. You should meet more like-minded people. They exist. They are trying to change things from within. I know a very fine man. Yehoshua Yellin. Still young, a bit an adventurer. His father came from Poland. Yehoshua started the *khan* on the main road, about ten kilometers from Jerusalem. It is called *Motza*. He was one of the founders of *Nachalat Shiv'a*, the new neighborhood outside the walls of Jerusalem. A deeply religious, but very open-minded man. You should visit him."

Motza was not far from where they had gotten lost after the earthquake. Where the sun had stood still. This time, Joseph went alone. A search for insight and understanding, as he called it.

Yehoshua Yellin wore Sephardic clothes and a large fez. His appearance was refined and his eyes had a slightly melancholy quality. His intelligent gaze made him look older than the mid-thirties that Joseph guessed him to be. The inn was modestly furnished with a few wooden tables and chairs, but it was certainly comfortable.

"Actually, I don't live here," Yellin started as some sort of apology. "I hired a manager to take care of things. I am still too much absorbed by other business affairs. Since my father's death, we have financial problems. He bought this place from the Arabs. I come here often, although not as often as I would like. You were lucky to find me here today. Eventually, God willing, I will settle here for good. That's why I won't sell it." He poured tea, as he sat down with Joseph. "Mint from our own garden," he said proudly. The tea was excellent. Yellin looked at Joseph with a cunning eye. "I have heard about you. A ban has been pronounced against you. They call you the provocateur of Yafo."

"Lovely title. I hope you don't think that I deserve it."

"No, no," he hastened to say and laughed. His warm, hearty voice convinced Joseph that the man did not support this scornful status.

Yellin invited Joseph to come outside. "Jerusalem can be a suffocating place for a man to shape grand ideas. I also started looking for fresher air myself. Literally." He sniffed the air. "Smell. This is wonderful. It is a blessing to live and work here."

"A blessing, indeed." Joseph's gaze went over the hills. It was beautiful. The experience with the runaway horses suddenly came back to him. The shady glade in which they had reposed. Was it the view or the smell that evoked the memories? The vividness of the vision faded but the recollection remained and it brought about a gentle mood. Miriam was the person par excellence to take off the sharp edges.

"I see that you also drift away at this panorama."

"I did indeed, briefly. Not in terms of place, but in terms of time. I have a fond memory of a place very nearby."

"I can look at the light on the mountains and valleys for hours. My wife Sarah usually brings me back to reality."

"For me, it is the other way around. I need my wife to look beyond. Despite my name, I am not a dreamer. At least not anymore."

Yellin gave Joseph a short tour of the building and the well-kept surrounding yard. "Look, these are the old Byzantine arches." He tapped the stones. "Robust. More than a thousand years old."

"Impressive."

"About three years ago.." he paused, as if counting the years in his head, "…1871 it was indeed, we started the inn. Particularly for the Arab merchants who go to the market in Jerusalem. We don't charge for the beds, only for the coffee," he added merrily.

When they were back inside, Yellin said, "I talk to a lot of people. Sooner or later everyone passes by. The Christians as well as the Muslims, and I have to say it all works out very well. Nearby is the village of *Qalunya* and the villagers and I are best friends. My father wanted to buy the land and they were willing to sell because they were poor. Now, they are happy and we are happy. We called the place *Motza* like in the book of Joshua. This is the real first new settlement outside the walls. We grow olives and vegetables of all kinds. And at *Sukkot* time, all of Jerusalem comes here to collect the willow branches."

"I will keep it in mind for next year," Joseph promised.

Turning to more serious matters, Yellin told him that Rav Jacobson and his community were still upset because Joseph had carried on with the school.

"They can't harm us in any way."

"I don't know. Don't underestimate them. They cannot tolerate being ignored."

"They are dinosaurs. Do you know what those are? An extinct species of gigantic reptiles that were recently discovered. Apparently, they walked the earth before the world was created. The ultra-Orthodox don't belong in this time, either."

"I'm afraid they won't easily become extinct. First of all, they are very committed, and second, they have a lot of children. You have to try to understand them. They protect their norms and values because they have experienced Christian persecution and after that, enlightenment corrupted their world. They believe that they have escaped. They fled to the holy city in the hope of finding protection and sanctity. They have given up everything, money, all their possessions, sometimes their families, only to have a safe place close to God. And then Westerners who think they know better come and threaten them with everything they have fled from. Try to understand them."

Joseph nodded. He wanted Yellin to see that he understood.

"But why interfere with people like me? In Yafo I am not a threat to their piety."

"They sometimes find it difficult to draw the line. Rabbis have built extra fences for centuries. Most of Jewish Law is extra safety. But they should also adapt to the people. It is like language. Language follows people, not the other way around. Language lives. All you need is grammar and scholars to adjust the rules from time to time. Not to make them. But funny enough, that is also why the reformers never will have it their way. Those rabbis only introduce modernism upon modernism. They all sit together, just like in a Christian synod." Yellin was pensive. "There is no point in changing the form," he said. "We have to reevaluate the content, and that has to be done from the bottom up."

"The rabbis," Joseph said, "have built dams to direct the streams, but they don't know that the land behind the dam has changed completely. Rivers must be able to flow. We have to restore the beds instead of building dams. They only hold back the water temporarily. At a certain moment the water frees itself with devastating force. Nature is unstoppable."

"I am afraid you are right," Yellin responded. "But which do you prefer? That, as you say, everything becomes flooded or that we deepen the river bed so that all the water stays nicely within the banks. Let me give you an example. What do you think I am? Sephardic or Ashkenaz?"

Joseph had to admit that he could not tell.

"I am Ashkenazi, but my wife is of Persian descent. A mixed marriage, one could say. We were married in 1856. 1856! Can you imagine the uproar? And I will tell you something else. A little too intimate maybe, but still. My wife's father forbade her to shave her hair before the wedding. That was unthinkable in our Ashkenazi community in those days. A lot of fuss of course, but in the end we managed to do as her father wanted. That's what I mean by change from within. Step by step."

"But I fear that the more the reformers insist, the more the Orthodox will dig in their heels. That is why I think this battle is lost in advance."

"Then, why don't you stop talking about it?" Yellin asked with a laugh.

"I believe in people. People in the image of God who have the task of improving the world. Who strive for justice. I think you have only to open any page in the Torah to see my case. I don't see the Messiah mentioned between all the sacrifices and admonitions. But justice and righteousness, yes. Dozens of times. Shouldn't we focus a little more on that? And then the long-awaited man on his donkey will have to come."

Yellin smiled. "Once I had the idea that God planned it that way. That the ultra religious are put here on purpose to slow things down. To put a healthy brake on everything. Otherwise, like a thundering train, progress would break everything down."

Joseph had a vision of the train that knocked down the old walls of the *Pantaleon* Gate in Cologne, heading towards the future.

"We have to think about the next generations," Yellin continued.

"They have to do better than we are. In them we place our hope. So what should we do? Simple. Education and more education."

"And why not a broad education?"

"When life gives you potatoes, you make latkes," said Yellin.

"Neither Moses nor Joshua invented the art of printing and yet isn't the whole library filled with printed books? Not everything that the *goyim* do is wrong. You know, the underlying principle is corrupt. They give an interpretation to something and no one can never deviate from that. They forbid any other explanation, even if you have the whole Talmud in your hand as proof. New is forbidden. *Chadash asur min ha Torah.* [(12)] It is all so short-sighted and hopeless."

Yellin shook his head. "After hundreds of years of oppression, humiliation, persecution, and murder, they suddenly should start trusting the non-Jews? Believe that their intentions are good? I think I understand their suspicion."

Joseph fell back into his chair. "Still, I feel like an uninvited guest. I am so tired; they call me a renegade, a heretic. Look, I am Jewish, I am religious, I live here, I know what I am doing. They don't have to tell me." He sighed. "I know. It doesn't sound very mature."

Yellin softly smiled.

Joseph told about the murder of Elsa. "And then I almost cursed the country. But I understand that the land cannot be blamed."

"You see," Yellin said, "*sinat chinam*, baseless hatred, was the reason why the second Temple was destroyed. People who supposedly did everything according to the law but hated each other. That's more or less the reason why my father was born in Latvia and not in Jerusalem. A lot of stories explain the reasons behind that final push. Let me tell you a story from the Talmud. A real eye opener."

Joseph nodded as Yellin continued. "Maybe you know it, but anyway... An apprentice sets his eyes on the wife of his master, a carpenter. The carpenter falls on hard times and needs to borrow money from his apprentice. The apprentice arranges it so that the master sends his wife to work for him as a housemaid. But the apprentice gives the master grounds to suspect his wife of infidelity and then suggests that he loans his master money to divorce his wife. The master accepts and reluctantly divorces his wife. To his surprise she now marries the apprentice. When the time for the loan is due and the carpenter does not have enough money to repay it, the apprentice says: "Come and work off your debt in my service." So the apprentice and the wife would be sitting, eating, and drinking, while the master stood and served them their drinks, and his tears would fall from his eyes into their cups. It was at that moment that the Divine decree was sealed: the Temple would fall."

Yellin sadly shook his head. "You see, no one in this story has actually done anything wrong against Jewish law, but it feels like the cruelest injustice. Makes you think, doesn't it?"

"It is sad, indeed. And I don't think we've learned anything since then. I'm not very forgiving either."

They fell silent for a moment.

"There are more people who think like us," Yellin continued. "But sometimes they don't dare to speak out. I will introduce you to some of them, if you want. Do you know Israel Dov Frumkin, the publisher of the *Havatzelet* magazine? You really should meet him. For me, he is perhaps a little too wild, but for you? Who knows? And then there's Stampfer, Gutman, Salomon, my friends with whom I started *Nachalat Shiv'a*. Five years ago, Stampfer walked here all the way from Hungary."

"Walked? You don't say! That's commitment."

"Yes, that alone makes him interesting. Although I heard the other day that he didn't walk the whole way. In Thessaloniki, he took the boat, but that doesn't make it any less impressive."

The conversation continued for a while. It comforted Joseph. Here was someone who understood him. And what he also understood was that he should be less upset; to worry less about everyday delusions. To enjoy life. That was the fundamental principle that he never should renounce. Choose life. Here he was where he belonged.

A few weeks later, Joseph heard pounding on the door while he was on the terrace with Richard. To his surprise, he opened it to find that some Turkish officers were standing outside.

"Would you please come with us to the office," asked one of them, a beefy man with a moustache that was far too big.

"What is going on, if I may ask?" He didn't want to sound aggressive. He had learned that the Turks summoned people for the smallest reason to accuse them in the hope of getting some money.

"We'll tell you at the office."

Richard offered to go along and the Turks didn't object.

"I'll tell my wife," said Joseph. Miriam decided to accompany them as well. She took his hand and said: "If they lock you up, they will have to lock me up as well."

Joseph was so pleased. "Thanks. Very different than in the past," he joked. "Then there was no one to defend me when the police came."

At the police station one of the officers told Joseph that he had been accused of inflammatory writing with the purpose of inciting riots.

"I'm not aware of any wrongdoing," he said, and he meant it.

The officer thrust a newspaper under his nose. He recognized the

Ottoman newspaper from Jerusalem. "Is this article yours?" the man asked.

"I apologize. I neither read nor write Turkish."

The man pointed to the name of the author, Joseph Shachar, at the top of the article.

"What is this about?" Joseph asked.

"It is a call to put the hypocritical Ottomans in their place and to revolt against these pernicious oppressors."

"I didn't write this. This must be some mistake."

"Whatever. We would like to take you to Jerusalem tomorrow for interrogation."

"Ho ho," Richard intervened. "This is all going a bit too fast. My friend is not going anywhere."

"Could those fanatics in Jerusalem sink so low," Joseph asked out loud.

Apparently, the Turk didn't quite understand what Joseph was talking about and said loud and clear. "Watch your words. We are in charge. You Jews have no business in Jerusalem."

"And why not?" Joseph willingly let himself be dragged into an argument.

"Because it is Turkish. It belongs to us. And it will never be yours."

"Then, maybe first the Turks should leave Byzantium then."

"What?"

"*Constantinopolis*. It is a Roman city. Your capital that you conquered and that isn't Turkish to begin with. The city in which you transformed a Christian church into the ultimate mosque."

He probably couldn't have insulted the Ottoman more.

The man wanted to attack Joseph on the spot, but Miriam positioned herself in front of him. A second officer pushed her away and she fell to the ground. With a scream Joseph knelt beside her. From a corner of his eye, he saw Richard push another Turk away. The latter wanted to grab him, but he underestimated the strength of the Englishman. As if he wanted to make up for something, Richard started fighting, but the Turk hit him on his head. That was the last thing Joseph saw before someone threw him behind the bars of a small cell. A minute later someone shoved Richard in as well.

"I owed you one." Richard said, carefully examining the bump on his head. "Don't feel badly. Tomorrow everything will be solved. I told Miriam to go to Amzalek immediately."

"I can't be too excited about it all."

"It is clear that someone snitched on you. Turks only care about Jews when other Jews betray them. The Ottomans are no good, but their indolence prevails over their malice. So they must have had a rat somewhere."

"I can't remember writing anything about the Turks," Joseph said, trying to find something that would explain the Turkish disconcert. "Certainly not for any newspaper in Jerusalem. The only thing I can think of is a draft that I wrote about the fanatics in Jerusalem. But that wasn't about the Turks. And I never sent it anywhere for publication." Slowly, the whole case became clearer. "You know what? That guy from Sarona, who was after Rivka. What was his name again? Schönfeld. He must have taken that article from the desk in my study when I stepped out. The text contained some chaotic thoughts about Jerusalem, not so nice, I guess. Of course, he gave it to Jacobson when he heard about the *cherem*. I'm sure of it. How I hate that Jacobson guy."

"Let's make ourselves comfortable," Richard said pragmatically. "I've been here before, although most occasions were a bit blurry," he said with a wink.

Joseph sat back against the barren, damp wall. The cell was dirty and it smelled. He knew the stench all too well. Their release would not take too long, he assumed, but the whole event triggered some bad memories. Nothing seemed to have changed, all in all. Here he was again in a cell. What would his son think of this? How pleasant it would be to live in a country where the police were Jewish. He looked at the outside wall.

"Don't you agree that in a prison they should always keep one stone a little loose?" he asked. "In order to give a prisoner the chance to escape. So he won't abandon hope altogether? Of course it shouldn't be immediately clear which stone it would be."

"I think that would seriously undermine the concept of prison, dear boy."

"Still..."

An hour later, Rachid came to report that they would be released immediately. They received a letter with an official apology from the Turkish authorities. It had all been a misunderstanding. Later they gathered that Amzalek had paid a rather high bail.

"I'm going to take revenge," Joseph promised Miriam and Rivka, when they were back home that evening. "Especially on Jacobson."

"There's no point in revenge," Miriam said. "You've said it yourself!"

"Take an example from Miriam's forgiving Richard," said Rivka.

"Apparently women are better at this," he murmured.

"Without forgiveness the world would be hard and unlivable," Miriam said. "It is one of the great things we have given the world. The second chance. You know who is the first to forgive, don't you?"

Joseph remained obnoxious. "Yeah, yeah. I know. My namesake. Well-known tale."

"Well. He had reason to be a lot angrier than you. Put in a pit, sold as a slave, then in prison for years. All done by his brothers. And yet he forgave them. Your ordeal was a joke compared to that."

Joseph wanted to be angry, but both Rivka and Miriam cracked up. Probably because of his sulking. If he remained angry now, he would be ridiculous. So he laughed along, at first against his will, but gradually he saw the humor of it all and felt better, although the feelings of revenge had not completely disappeared.

"I don't know what will come of this. Take the arrest. A few Turks, two Germans, an Englishman and some Arabs as audience. Quarreling and quarreling. What I do know is that we have to keep far away from those people. And from Jerusalem," he added, "although, it makes me sad to close my eyes to Jerusalem. It contradicts all of the principles, the axioms of Judaism. Everything we stand for. Do you remember the words we sang under the *chupa*, "*Im eshkachech Yerushalaim tishkach yemini.*"

"If I ever forget thee, Jerusalem, let my right hand forget its skill. No, I haven't forgotten," Miriam said with conviction. "But we must put our happiness first. We must think of our family. We are entitled to happiness."

"I don't know if one is entitled to that."

"I mean practically. For now, Jerusalem is just the center of money and power."

"I think that center is somewhere else. In Constantinople. In London, Paris. That is where the future will be defined, not in Jerusalem."

"I agree," said Miriam, "right now, Jerusalem is secondary."

"Jerusalem, secondary. Hear yourself talking, now."

6

(1876)

BONES

The great day had come; the first day of the *Elsa Blumenreich School*. The parents of eight children had agreed to send their sons. All Sephardic. Because of the ban from Jerusalem, it was clear that at least for the time being, there was no point in asking the Ashkenazi children. Rivka would be their teacher and Miriam would be responsible for all of the practical matters. Joseph was only indirectly involved. The three of them stood at the entrance, ready to welcome the children. Moshe nervously walked back and forth between his parents and his place in the classroom.

The classroom itself was beautifully decorated. Next to the name of the school above the blackboard, they had hung Richard's painting of Elsa. On the walls were maps of the world and plaques with the letters of the Latin and Hebrew alphabets. Moshe had made some nice drawings, which also had their place. If it had been up to him, he would have filled the whole room with his sketching but Miriam had tactically suggested that they leave room for the other children's work as well.

There were eight small desks, each waiting with pens and a notebook. Next to each notebook lay a *sidur* and a book of general knowledge. They had carefully removed the first page of these books, because it was marked with the stamp of the convent of the *Sisters of Zion*. As an extra, there was a cookie on each table.

School was to start at eight o'clock but by a quarter past eight no one but Moshe was there. Moshe was eager to get his cookie and Miriam reluctantly gave him permission to eat it.

"It's clear," Miriam said at half past nine. "Nobody's coming."

"Shall I ask around?" Rivka asked.

A little later she came back. "They're scared."

"Of what?"

"That they will get a ban. Just like the school itself."

"They could have thought of that before," Miriam said.

"I'm going to talk to the Rav," said Joseph. "Something must have happened."

"I will come with you," Rivka said. "Miriam, will you stay here with Moshe?"

The conversation with the rabbi of the Sephardic community was constructive and the man promised to urge the parents once more to send their children to school. "But I can't promise miracles."

At about eleven o'clock two parents brought their children. The boys joined Moshe and soon they were talking and playing.

"Please, keep it quiet that my boy is attending," said one of fathers at the end of the day.

"Yes, mine too," echoed the other parent. "But you are doing a great job. We hope it will work out."

In the weeks that followed, three more children signed up for the school. Rivka was satisfied. "For this situation and in this country, we can consider this a great success. Forget the problems and focus on the good."

Joseph mainly kept busy writing new articles, and once a week he visited the Turkish post office in Yafo to see whether his texts had been published. He collected the regular newspapers, and often found letters from Max. Joseph quietly read them in the coffee house at the harbor, while enjoying a scented hookah and a black coffee. The letters brightened his days.

This time, there was mail, but not from Max. He recognized his older brother's handwriting on the envelope. Aron wrote once every few months about the ups and downs in Frankfurt and about their father, no heavy subjects. Joseph always wrote back right away. It was their unspoken way to keep the family connection intact. But this time he had an immediate reason for responding. Their father had indicated that it would be a great honor and a mitzvah to spend the remaining days of his life in *Eretz Israel*. Aron had started thinking and weighing the possibilities. It was certainly a hassle. Hassle. That was the expression he used. And frankly Joseph had to agree with him. It was a hassle. His father coming here at his age. But then again, Elsa had done it.

Back home he asked Miriam what she thought of it. "I remember," Joseph said, "that at that reunion, when he turned sixty, he said that this was the place to die. No, how exactly did he put it? This was the place to stay forever. But when we told him that we were going, he looked as if he had serious doubts."

"That was, I think, more his stance towards you. Remember that Aron wrote that your father told everyone in shul he was so proud that you live here. And Rivka too."

Joseph grumbled. "Well, if Aron can arrange it there, we will of course do our best for him here." He picked up the letter and read it again. "Papa is evidently afraid that he will not belong to the resurrected. As you know, there are quite a few passages in the Talmud stating it is an honor to be buried in *Eretz Israel*." He looked more precisely and found what he was looking for on the second page. "Aron mentions tractate *Ketubot, Folio* 111a. Rabbi Eliezer says that the dead outside *Eretz Israel* will not rise again. There are those who say that the dead will then roll to this place through underground cavities." He laughed. "Papa never liked caves and enclosed spaces. Nor do I, for that matter. He may not have much confidence in the whole rolling procedure."

He dropped the letter again and looked at Miriam: "But that leaves us with quite a few practical problems."

"We came, didn't we? Why not your father?"

Joseph smiled. "Peculiar man. All his life he hardly comes out of the *Gasse*, you can't get him out of Frankfurt not even with a stick, and now he starts to travel." Joseph looked outside at the hills far away. "He often talked about it, about *Eretz Israel*. It always was, or is, one of the foundations of his faith." He turned to Miriam smiling. "I remember in the old shul at Shabbat *Mincha* he always said the words *Uva l'Zion Go'el*, A Redeemer Shall Come to Zion, with extra emphasis. He really is waiting for the Redemption."

"It would be nice if Aron could come along. Your father wouldn't have to travel alone and you will see each other again."

"Who knows? Maybe Aron has become more reasonable as he has gotten older."

"Maybe you have become more reasonable as you have gotten older."

Joseph directed Moshe to help him carry the wooden poles; it was the first time that he had involved his son in building the *sukkah*. The big poles were in the shed behind their house, but he remembered that last year they had run out of slats. Like all the previous years, he had no idea how he would do it. He would come up with something. Until now he had managed every year to build the *sukkah*, so why not now?

Moshe asked with caution: "Shouldn't we have a plan first?"

"We have a plan. We are building a *sukkah*."

"I mean how we are going to attach it."

"Making plans in too much detail is never right. Sometimes it is just better to start and feel your way toward your goal. You'll quickly figure out what doesn't work. If you want to plan everything in advance, sometimes you end up with nothing."

Moshe looked at him, a bit astonished, but picked up the wood without objecting.

"Just a few long pieces, for starters. In the meantime, I'll get the big planks from the attic," Joseph said.

He heard Moshe calling: "Shouldn't I help you, papa?"

"No need to, my boy. I can do this by myself."

Joseph walked inside and climbed the ladder to the attic. It was a mess. Everything had been piled up throughout the years. He realized that he could not do it on his own. But he could have a look, and maybe it wouldn't be as bad as it seemed. They hadn't cleaned the attic since moving in, seven years earlier. Fortunately, the planks he needed were on top. This meant that they had not added much stuff in the past year. He tugged at the largest and the slat moved, but it caused the rest to shift as well. Joseph looked again to see whether there was anything in the way and suddenly his eye fell on his trunk. He hadn't thought about it in years. He carefully eased it out of the surrounding piles, but decided not to take it downstairs. Hearing Moshe returning with the small poles, he asked him to take the planks, he would lower them down. Together they succeeded and Joseph climbed down the ladder and dusted himself off. Then he joined his son on the terrace and, in high spirits, the two set to work.

When they had finished building the structure, they put some large palm leaves on top of it. Then they sat on the ground in the middle and looked proudly at their achievement. Joseph noticed that he had forgotten to tie a corner, but it didn't bother him. He drew his son's attention to it and said, "A *sukkah* should not be too sturdy. That is the rule. And also, breaking it down and starting over again is not really an option. We will have to live with this structural defect."

Later that afternoon Miriam came home from her work at school and father and son proudly showed the *sukkah*, but Miriam's reaction threw cold water on their enthusiasm. "I only see sticks and slats. Don't you have any decorations to make it more cheerful? Where are the lemons, grapevines, and garlands?" And without waiting for a reaction, she walked into the house.

Joseph shrugged his shoulders. Moshe wanted to say something, but Joseph stopped him. "Let's wait and see."

Together they decorated the *sukkah*, and when Miriam entered, her reaction was entirely different. "Fabulous. What a beautiful *sukkah*. Thank you."

Joseph wanted to keep his promise to his friend Yellin; to go to *Motza* to get fresh willow branches. Moshe would skip school and come with him.

Just after noon, the coach dropped Joseph and Moshe off at Yellin's inn, and the proprietor welcomed them warmly.

"So, how's the provocateur of Yafo," Yellin said, teasing. "Still looking for justice?"

Joseph and Yellin sat under the old arches and enjoyed a pot of fresh tea. Joseph sucked on his pipe and their conversation continued until Yellin indicated that he had an appointment in Jerusalem.

"Come along. You can stay with me in my house near the Kotel. You didn't intend to return to Yafo tonight, did you?"

"No, it would be nice if we could spend the night."

"You can come to my meeting if you want to or walk around with your son and join me later. Jerusalem is always wholesome for the soul, especially this month."

"If you say so."

When they reached Jerusalem, Joseph was inclined to stay with Yellin, but maybe he should do something with Moshe? His son had been well behaved all day. But as they entered the city through the Yafo gate, he was distracted by a noisy parade of *chassidic* men dancing and drumming.

"What a lot of noise," said Joseph.

"It's a *chupa*," said Yellin. "They are picking up the groom to bring him to his bride."

The group consisted of young men who were carrying a still younger boy, almost a child, on their shoulders. The dancing was wild and before Joseph knew, one of the men from the parade grabbed him and started dancing with him. He looked around and saw Moshe. "Stay close to me," he yelled and saw to his relief that Moshe followed. Joseph danced clumsily with a forced smile, all the while keeping an eye on his son.

They were now swept into an alley so narrow that people could barely pass each other. The man dancing with Joseph, took Moshe's hand as well, closed his eyes, and sang his heart out. Soon Joseph had had enough and was ready to leave the parade. He looked for Yellin but couldn't find him in the crowd. Seeing a side passage, Joseph shouted in Moshe's ear, "Quickly, let's dive into this alley and get away." But Moshe stuck to the man.

"No, papa, this is fun. Let's stay."

Joseph sighed, shrugged his shoulders, and conceded. Now that he had decided to join in and go with the flow, he began to enjoy it. The only thing that worried him was how they would get in touch with Yellin again.

Eventually they arrived at a small square near the *Churva* Synagogue where a canopy had been erected. The tone of the festivities changed now. The singing became more dramatic. The men danced the young man to his place under the *chupa*. From a house on the other side came a veiled figure, surrounded by women who accompanied her to the *chupa* and left her standing next to the young man.

The drumming started again and a man with a violin started playing a soulful *chassidic* tune. However, someone immediately took the instrument from the musician's hands. Next to him Joseph heard the approving murmur of an older Orthodox man. "After the epidemic, no more musical instruments at weddings. That is the price we had to pay," the man explained in Yiddish.

"The price?" Joseph asked.

"They introduced this stricter law because of the plague of 1866. And the disease stopped as soon as they had declared it. The idea appeared to a wise man in a dream."

Joseph smiled sadly. "Perhaps the real reason was that they didn't want girls and boys to have fun together?"

"Who knows," said the man. "This is the holy city."

Joseph focused his attention again on the couple under the *chupa*.

"Something different, isn't it," he said to his son.

Moshe pulled Joseph's coat: "Look papa, that girl is not much older than I am."

"She is indeed young, very young, don't you think," he said. "Not even fourteen, I would say."

They stayed for a while watching but Joseph felt his heart saddened. Sometimes it seemed that everything here was done to speed up life and die early. Life as one big preparation for death. He remembered what Yellin had said about shaving the bride's hair before the wedding. How that practice had already made many a girl take desperate measures to avoid it. Conversion. Even suicide.

He felt a tap on his shoulder and to his delight he saw Yellin. "Speaking about the *Dybbuk*!" Joseph said cheerfully, glad indeed that his friend had found them.

When they were lying in their comfortable beds in Yellin's house that night, Joseph asked Moshe what he thought of Jerusalem.

"Very nice, papa. I could imagine living there. But I don't want to marry yet."

The evenings in the *sukkah* were cozy and Miriam outdid herself with her cooking. Joseph tried to share some thoughts with his son about the *Sukkot* festival. The fragility of the *sukkah* as a symbol of life. "You erect a flimsy shed in the hope that it will stand for seven days. But inside you create the most splendid atmosphere you can imagine. You feel at home and it is appealing." He lowered his voice to sound dramatic. "But then, one day, the wind starts blowing hard, rain pours down, and your beautiful interior is ruined. All you have left are some remnants of your *sukkah*. No more shelter, no safety. It has all been an illusion." In order to comfort his son who had started to look rather scared, he added. "But not today. Let's enjoy the holiday."

The trunk continued to loom large in Joseph's thoughts, so the next day he decided to take it down and have a look, telling himself that he was really just looking for the eulogy he had written for his mother.

"I still have a lot of things from Europe in the trunk in the attic. Will you help me?" he asked Moshe.

Moshe was fascinated.

"We will open it together," Joseph said. As far as he could remember, there was nothing that would distress the delicate soul of a child, and the presence of his son gave Joseph the hope that he would not fall too deeply into sentimental contemplation. Hadn't all of Europe become just a memory? Mostly vague, sometimes clearer, like the ridge in the distance. But always at a safe distance, not compellingly present.

"It was my parents' trunk. I took it when I left for Cologne," he told Moshe, adding in a sad undertone, "where it was plundered." He smiled at the memory. "It was a long time ago; when I wanted to start a new life. Here it is. My heritage of Europe. My legacy."

It seemed easy. The suitcase was balancing on the edge of the attic floor, just as he left it the previous week. Joseph grabbed for it too quickly and lost his balance. He slipped off the rungs, flailing, and fell more than two meters to the floor, landing flat on his back. He hadn't really hurt himself, he thought, but before he could move, the trunk came thundering down after him. Its sharp iron point drove into his right hand. Icy waves set his arm on fire. The throbbing matched the pulsing rhythm of his heartbeat. Until finally one and only one overwhelming sensation remained – pain. He screamed without sound, but it brought no relief. Standing up unsteadily, with Moshe at his side, he walked outside, opening his mouth as to create an exit for the pain. But it kept pounding. He saw Miriam rushing towards him. Vaguely he realized that she was wrapping his hand with a piece of cloth, while blood dripped from all sides.

The doctor came a quarter of an hour later and bandaged his hand properly.

"We have to wait and see whether there is any damage. I can't tell yet."

His hand pounded insanely when he woke the next day, but after breakfast, the pain lessened a bit. Because he had nothing better to do, Joseph decided to continue with his trunk project. He looked at his son with a smile. "Let's see what's inside."

Slowly he opened the lid.

On top was a sketch of the *Lorelei*, not Holstein's, but a similar one that he had bought later as a reminder; double nostalgia, a souvenir of a derivative. A weak extract of the powerful image of the original print. This was just an undressed woman on a mountain. He saw Moshe's suspicious look.

"Do you like this print? Is that allowed? Such a naked lady?"

Joseph laughed. "I don't know. It's art. Let's say, in art more is allowed." He took something more innocent out of the trunk.

"Look, papa. It's a drawing. It looks like a mystery map."

"That, my boy, that is a treasure map. And you never guess from whom. Edmond the Rothschild. The baron in Paris."

"How did you get it?"

"It's a long story. I will tell it before bedtime tonight. Come on, let's keep looking."

"Who is this, papa? That man has a big moustache."

"That's me. When I lived in Paris. It's a sketch for a portrait that was made then." He did not want to burden his son with the knowledge that he himself was the instigator of both the portrait and the moustache.

"I no longer have the painting. It did not come out well," he said with a faint smile.

He browsed through the pile with Moshe quietly standing at his side. Where was the page with the eulogy? Finally he found it. It was crumpled under a pile of notes and articles that he didn't recognize immediately. He read the words he had written at the death of his mother. At first they were rather commonplace, but further on they became more personal and emotional. Perhaps stylistically not a masterpiece, but he still found it very meaningful.

"Family is holy. A Mother's love is perhaps the loftiest thing that exists. It is the sacred source of our perseverance. It is spiritual and at the same time so earthly. Mama, you were goodness itself. You were a Tzaddeket. I want to be just like you. But I often stand in my own way. You are the greatest example of sacrifice and gratitude. You never judged. You were the best person in my life."

He saw that there was another sheet attached to it and now he remembered that he had written a second piece on the occasion of her *yahrzeit*, a year later.

"The last few years I saw you only occasionally. You were always pleasantly surprised when I showed up. I keep a drawing of you on the cabinet. Papa gave it to me last year. During the day my gaze often falls on your happy and cheerful image and for a moment I think that you are cheerful at home, as you always were. I imagine myself visiting you and telling you that I am doing well.

I know better. You are not with us anymore. And after a year, this reality is still hard. A conversation is no longer possible. But I am happy to believe that I don't need to tell you anything; you understand everything already, and have for a long time. You give us your blessings from above. You are happy to watch how our lives go on and then you boast to everyone who wants to hear it up there: 'These are my children; that is Joseph, my son.'

Mama, you were blessed in your contentment and I can only hope I can match you in gratitude.

May your blessing rest upon all of us forever."

He rubbed his eyes and looked at his son. "My mother was special. Like your mother."

There were no answers in the suitcase. No questions either. It was what it was.

But the upcoming arrival of his father had brought Europe closer. Old memories surfaced. As if a door had been opened, allowing in a draft that went right through his soul. Were there truly any reasons to be cheerful? Everything seemed so futile. Had he not just read this Shabbat in *Kohelet* that everything was *hevel*, vanity?

"I sometimes wonder what it's all for," Joseph asked Miriam. "All the hustle and bustle. All those busy people who want to be immortalized for posterity. But the ordinary folks, those who will be forgotten? They are all busy and what is their reward? At best, they stay alive. Maybe we should agree with the Arabs here. They hardly worry about anything and time just passes. Perhaps Yechezkiel had the wrong order in his vision. When I look around and I see all those well-meaning but wretched people lugging and plodding. Working themselves to the bone and not comprehending that there is only one outcome for them – to eventually end up on the big heap of dry bones."

"You are fun to have around."

It was a late October morning and the weather was beautiful. Joseph was still wearing his sling. According to the doctor, there was a possibility that he would never be able to use his hand properly again. But the doctor said to keep his hopes up.

The family went to the harbor together. As they walked to the port, Rivka took Joseph's arm.

"I still can't believe that they are coming," she said.

"Don't pinch me," Joseph said smiling, but he couldn't deny he also felt excited. He had been pacing back and forth nervously for days. What was he nervous about? His father? Aron? Miriam had told him repeatedly to calm down, but it hadn't helped.

"For me it has been much longer," Rivka said. "And there's so much to explain. When I was in my tiny cell in the monastery, memories, flashes of family life often surfaced. And I had to bury them. Now they will be part of the present again. For you it's different."

"I can imagine a bit. When I was in my cell, I also thought a lot about papa and mama."

"And you were there for only two weeks."

"Actually, sixteen days," he said, but immediately agreed that for Rivka it had been different.

"But I suppose that they don't care so much about all that has happened," he said.

"*I* am the one who cares. But we will see."

The port warden said that the ship from Marseille could arrive any moment. In every whitecap in the distance Moshe thought he could recognize a boat on which grandpapa was sitting. He waved a few tiny flags that he had received from Rachid to cheer up the arrival. Finally, after an hour the ship came into sight and Moshe was so thrilled that for a moment it looked as if he wanted to jump into the water with flags and all.

Soon Rivka saw Aron sitting in one of the sloops that were being rowed to shore. A rough beard covered his face. Where was their father?

"I hardly recognize him," said Rivka with excitement. She stood next to Miriam and held her hand.

"I don't see our father," said Joseph. "I had expected him to be eagerly looking forward to his first steps here."

"He must still be below deck," said Rivka.

They ran to the sloop as soon as it landed.

Aron looked pale, with large bags under his eyes. His shirt was torn.

"He was unable to complete the journey," Aron said softly. "Papa passed away soon after we left Alexandria." He embraced his brother and wept.

"*Baruch Dayan Emet*," [13] Joseph said and he tore his shirt. Miriam and Rivka now approached as well. Moshe stood timidly on the side.

"Where is grandpapa?" the boy asked with all the expectation a child could have.

Joseph looked at him. "Later, I will explain what happened," he said. "Grandfather is not coming."

With tears in his eyes, Aron told the story. "He was already weak when we embarked in Alexandria for the last stage but I thought he would have the strength to make it. But that evening he seemed to get even more frail. I sat by his bed the whole night. He didn't regain consciousness. In the morning he passed away. I stayed with him the rest of the journey."

Aron now looked at Rivka, "Rivka! What a moment to meet again." A bit clumsily, he embraced her. But the discomfort quickly disappeared when the real emotion overcame his shyness.

"More than twenty years," she said through her tears.

Only now did Aron see that Joseph's arm was in a sling. "What happened to your arm?"

"My hand, actually. Something heavy fell on it. The doctor fears I won't be able to use it anymore."

"Have you forgotten Jerusalem?"

"You are the umpteenth one to ask."

"I apologize. But can you no longer write?"

"Let's hope for the best."

"May we hear only good news."

They waited almost an hour for the deckhands to unload the temporary coffin from the boat. Everything happened with extreme caution. The funeral took place that same afternoon. They walked to the cemetery in Yafo, on the south side of the hill. The rabbi of Yafo led the group. Throughout the service, Joseph kept looking out over the sea in the distance. The sunlight above the water reflected brilliantly on the white stones of the graves. He had to squint, which made the image even more abstract. Framed in the green of the palms and olive trees and the azure blue of the sea in the distance, the white and light gray cubes of the graves formed a mosaic. The pieces, in a strange way, all fitted together. Next to him he saw Aron squinting as well. Were they having the same experience? He remembered the bravura of the Parisian painter Lirac, "I provide the light. Light is everything. And we, the seers, will bring the new light."

The body sank into the limestone. Despite the sadness of the moment, Joseph had the thought that his father would have been pleased with this stone, rather than the muddy soil of Frankfurt.

He had used the time before the funeral to prepare his eulogy. He had planned to say the words here, but it was very hot in the sun and the members of the *Chevra Kadisha* were already packing their things. Joseph thanked them from the bottom of his heart. They had fulfilled the noblest task. Joseph and Aron said *Kaddish* again, together. Then Miriam invited those in attendance to their home for *Mincha* and some refreshments.

After the prayers, Joseph stood and tapped his glass. "On October 25, 1877, 18 *Cheshvan* 5638, our father Ephraim Socher, Ephraim ben Avraham, Froyim, passed away and today we buried him here in Yafo." He looked at those present. "I would like to say something about my father. My father's name was Froyim, indeed Ephraim. I have often wondered lately, what inspired him to want to spend the last years of his life here? And in the question is the answer – the inspiration was his spirit, his soul."

He continued. "I never understood my father. At least I thought I didn't. Yet, I am coming to realize that I did understand him, I just didn't want to see. Maybe we weren't that different after all. He was a child of his time. I am his child." He looked up but nobody reacted. "His wife, my beloved mother, our beloved mother," he said looking at Rivka and Aron, "was taken from him far too early. And he found it difficult to make a new start. But in the end, he was at peace with his situation. And when he saw the end approaching, he decided to die in this land. Perhaps someone will say, 'but he didn't make it.' But my father found peace from the moment he knew he would reach this shore, that there would be no way back. He said farewell to the safe protection of his old world. He took a step forward and now we are here."

He coughed and then took the heavy book of the *Tanach*, which he had already opened to the right page. "Listen to the words of the prophet Yechezkiel." And softer he said to Aron, smiling: "The translation is perhaps a bit free. Don't be too critical."

1 The hand of the Lord was upon me, and the Lord carried me out in a spirit, and set me down in the midst of the valley, and it was full of bones;

2 and He caused me to pass by them and, look, there were many bones in the open valley; and they were very dry.

3 And He said to me, "Son of man, can these bones live?" And I answered, "O Lord God, Thou knowest."

4 Then He said to me, "Prophesy over these bones, and say to them, Dry bones, hear the word of the Lord.

5 So said the Lord God to these bones, Look, I will cause breath to enter into you, and you shall live.

6 And I will lay sinews upon you, and will bring up flesh upon you, and cover you with skin, and put breath in you, and you shall live; and you shall know that I am the Lord."

7 So I prophesied as I was commanded; and as I prophesied, there was a noise, and a commotion, and the bones came together, bone to its bone.

8 And I looked and there were sinews upon them, and flesh came up, and skin covered them; but there was no breath in them.

9 Then said He to me: "Prophesy to the breath, son of man, and say to the breath, So said the Lord God, Come from the four winds, breath, and breathe upon these slain, that they may live."

10 So I prophesied as He commanded me, and the breath came into them, and they lived, and stood up upon their feet, an exceeding great host.

11 Then He said to me, "Son of man, these bones are the whole house of Israel; behold, they say, Our bones are dried up, and our hope is lost; we are clean cut off.

12 Therefore prophesy, and say to them, So said the Lord God, Look, I will open your graves, and cause you to come up, out of your graves, My people; and I will bring you into the land of Israel.

13 And you shall know that I am the Lord, when I have opened your graves, and caused you to come up out of your graves, My people.

14 And I will put My spirit in you, and you shall live, and I will place you in your own land; and you shall know that I the Lord have spoken, and performed it, said the Lord."

Joseph cleared his throat and put the book down. "This raises some crucial questions. Whose bones are these? Can these bones live? What message does this passage convey?"

He continued, focusing intently. "The Talmud says that these bones are those of a portion of the descendants of Ephraim. They had not waited for the great exodus from Egypt, but had taken the initiative thirty years earlier to leave the exile and the slavery. Unfortunately, when they arrived in this land they were punished for their impatience; the Philistines slaughtered them immediately. The tribe of Ephraim came thirty years too early. But one day their bones – the bones from the vision of Yechezkiel – will come back to life."

"First attempts are often imperfect, half-hearted, doomed to fail. Perhaps a generation must die before anything new can begin.

"Why is Moshe the greatest prophet we will ever have? Because he saw the failure and smashed the Ten Commandments, right in front of our eyes! On purpose. But the new *Luchot HaBrit* were better because they came with *rachamim*, mercy. So, who knows, maybe this attempt by the children of Ephraim was necessary because it allowed the Exodus to happen."

He waited a moment.

"Are we unique in time and place or are we part of something much larger? A link in the big chain between past and future? In *Avot* it says, "It is not incumbent upon you to finish the task, but neither are you free to absolve yourself from it." Papa, we will do our best to continue the work."

He looked at Miriam, gratefully. "I already knew it was preferable – for better or worse – to live in this land. Now, in my father's name, I can wholeheartedly add, even in death it is better to be here than there."

$$\frac{7}{}$$

(1878)

GATES OF HOPE

The siblings spent quite some time together in the weeks after the funeral and they made some trips to Jerusalem and to the Galilee. Aron was taken by the land, and he admitted that Joseph had made a good choice. For himself though, he didn't think it would work. One rainy evening, Rivka gathered her courage and told Aron her complete story. He sat quietly for a while, then said that he appreciated her telling him. He didn't reproach her.

A few days later, Rivka and Joseph were sitting on the bench in front of Rivka's house. The evening sky was littered with stars.

"Yesterday I went to the *mikve*," Rivka said.

She waited for his reaction. At first, he didn't quite comprehend the import of what she was saying. "Did I miss something?" And then suddenly he understood. He got up and hugged her.

"Marvelous. Didn't I say we should de-baptise you?"

"Now I'm part of the tribe all over again," she smiled. "The whole kit and caboodle, with all the problems."

"Forget the problems. Think of the caboodle," he said enthusiastically. "What made you finally decide?"

"Everything actually. Obviously I wanted to. And it also will make working for the school easier. I'm not sure why I didn't do it earlier." She thought for a moment. "In a way, I guess, it was the admission that everything I have done since I married Rainier was a deviation. It's a bit like signing off your bankruptcy."

"You shouldn't say that. Your work with the school here is so great. And what you did in Jerusalem."

She looked at him with derision, "You have no idea what I did in Jerusalem. Have you ever seen a rosary?"

"No. Frankly, I have no idea what you are talking about."

Their conversation was interrupted by Aron who had gone for a walk along the sea.

"Family gathering?" he asked.

Rivka told him about the *mikve*.

Aron congratulated her. "Mazal tov! Now you are all Rivka again.

How happy papa would have been."

"I now feel one with the small family and one with the big family. And it doesn't matter how far away they are. Nathan in New York, you, Aron, in Frankfurt, us here. Mama and Papa somewhere up there." She waved vaguely towards the stars. "We are one. I don't want to be cut off." She thought for a moment if that word was too heavy. "I mean, I want to be part of it."

"Always," said Aron. "Don't worry about that. You are our sister."

"Does Miriam know?" Joseph asked.

"Of course. She was there with me."

"Ah," was all Joseph could say. "I wondered what you two were up to," he said and hugged her again.

"Miriam and I have often talked about it. She is the best, Joseph. You are really blessed with such a fantastic woman."

The next day, a terrible storm struck Yafo. It became clear that a ship had run aground, but that fortunately, everyone had come ashore in one piece. Amzalek had put all the passengers up in his official residence for the time being.

"One of the rescued men is a new immigrant from Russia," said Rivka. The storm had subsided and the sun was shining through the last shreds of clouds. Joseph was grateful that this kind of storm never lasted much longer than a day.

"He is from Odessa. A Jewish intellectual. Really something for you."

"What is his name?"

"Lupu, Alexander Lupu."

"Doesn't sound Russian, more Romanian."

"How would I know? Just go and visit him. Everyone calls him Sacha."

"I don't think every intellectual is interesting."

Rivka shrugged her shoulders.

But of course Joseph went to visit the newcomer, bringing Aron along. Lupu made a disheveled impression, but perhaps that was due to the hardships of the journey and the rescue. His long, wild hair fell in peaks over a face that was covered with the stubble of a few days. A large scar marred his cheek. He had round glasses, which gave him a intelligent look that contrasted with his tough appearance. His shirt hung open over wide leather trousers. The smell of seawater still surrounded him. More a pirate than a bookworm, Joseph thought, but his voice was clear and not unpleasant. "I was born in Romania," he said after they were introduced. He wore his heart on his sleeve and immediately started to tell his story. Joseph learned that his life had been nothing but flight and doom. "My father had a kosher shop but they set it on fire after he had been accused of stealing some candles from the church. Their thought was, pay according to your sin. Fire for candles. An eye for an eye. They had certainly read their Bible too well. We fled. I started wandering at the age of fifteen. From city to city. I had jobs everywhere. I didn't want to be forced into the Russian army, so I escaped to Odessa. I thought for the first time about a new beginning here."

Joseph was growing interested. The man really had something to say.

"The problem is that my ideas don't belong anywhere," said Lupu.

"But what are your ideas then?" asked Aron.

Lupu started. "We are outcasts and either people don't take us seriously, or they persecute us. I see only two options. One, we can dissolve completely. Like salt in water. The water will be a bit saltier, but that's all. Stop all the hassle. Maybe our Jewish identity once worked, but now it is outdated. Or, we can go to some new place," and he waved around him, "where we can constitute a majority, where we can determine our own destiny. Where we will never again have to ask for mercy and protection from the nations. Where we will no longer live at the whims of others." For a while he looked at his coffee as if it could inspire him. "Despite their good intentions, everything the Montefiores and the Rothschilds do is marginal."

"All the powerful people, nations, and countries are opposed," said Joseph. "But there's an even more serious problem. You will never convince the English, German or French Jews to leave their countries. They are happy there and to a certain extent I understand them. There they have opportunities, jobs, cities, universities. Here is nothing at all. Everything has to be built up. Look!" Joseph hit the ground with a stick. "See how hard this country is, *Eretz Chemda*! A pleasing country. No sensible person would want to drag stones here if he can quietly read a book in an easy chair somewhere else. I am afraid the only thing that could bring change is when the easy chair is kicked over, or worse. A few idealists won't do."

"The rise of states, socialism, the end of the oppression of the individual, that is what I am talking about." Lupu explained his views with a long discourse about equal opportunities and the end of poverty. Joseph looked at Aron who seemed completely taken aback by the man's insistent statements.

"What you are saying is all rather theoretical," Joseph responded. "I only see more problems. And I'm not even talking about the Arabs or the Turks. Look at us. I give good odds that within a few years, the Jews here will start quarreling among themselves to the extent that we will be thrown out again, in accordance with precedents. Just read the prophets."

"You are religious?" Lupu scoffed.

"Yes," Joseph replied.

"And what about Nietzsche?"

Joseph smiled. "He doesn't convince me." He probed Lupu. "Life, on the other hand, does convince me."

"Religion is not logical," Lupu said. "Atheism is the only right way. The rest is all stupidity." He made a grand gesture as if he would blow away all beliefs in one sigh. "Those who do not yet understand that are living in the Middle Ages. They are idiots."

"Thank you. By the way, I am afraid that most of the Jews you will meet here are that kind of idiot, even the enlightened ones. Would you call them enlightened idiots?"

Aron who until now hadn't said much, got up with a smile, "I'll leave you two at it. I'm going for a stroll in the garden." He nodded and left.

Lupu blushed. "What I mean is that we cannot build our future on faith or religion. We have to rely on knowledge and science. With those we can proceed. We are a people, and entitled to a country. Here or anywhere. The advantage of this land is that we can mobilize the religious. There are enough rabbis who see the advantages of a union with our nationalist initiatives. We have to make use of that. And we don't want to start a tribal struggle and exclude people a priori." After a short silence he added: "Although I don't see any benefit in their motivation per se."

"Do you want a country for Jews or a Jewish country?" Joseph asked.

"I do not see the difference."

"I do, and I think that difference is essential."

In the end, Aron had to go back to Germany. He had already left his wife and children alone there for a long time. They all said goodbye at the port. It was one of those rare gray days; low clouds drifted inland and the sea was dark with a frothy head here and there. The waves hit the coast unceasingly. It could start raining at any moment.

"Someone has to take care of the Jews in Europe," Aron tried cheerfully. "Do you realize that I am the last one of our family in Germany? Actually, in Europe, now Nathan has left for America. But we will continue. We will defend the fortress in Frankfurt. Our chances of survival there are better than they are here."

"I suppose so," answered Joseph, unconvinced.

"We will keep in touch," Rivka said. "Not like last time."

"Well. That wasn't completely my fault," Aron said, a bit defensively.

"I know. But you know what I mean. I missed you all the time."

They embraced for a long time and then Aron boarded the ship. The others went home, downcast, with the strong sense that they wouldn't see him again.

Joseph sat at his desk. Piles of paper were lying all over. He was aware that he hadn't produced a single article for his regular newspapers for a long time. With Elsa's inheritance, they had no financial worries, but still, he knew he had been idle for far too long.

Today he was trying to write for the first time since the accident. He forced himself to clasp the fountain pen in his damaged hand. When that was too painful, he tried it with his left hand. Pain-free but completely useless. He could not write a single legible letter. He wasn't really desperate yet, but he had to find a solution. Perhaps he could ask Moshe to write down his sentences? Or Rivka or Miriam? But they were already so busy with the school.

He was startled by a knock on the door. It was Rachid, coming to tell him that Amzalek had asked to see him. He had important matters to discuss.

A few men were just coming out of Amzalek's office. With their large beards and Eastern European clothing, they didn't exactly seem to belong in Yafo. Joseph was too curious to let it pass and he sent an amused but inquiring look toward Amzalek.

"Ah Joseph, please come in. They have been spending a few days with me. I am assisting them in finding and buying a piece of land to start a settlement. They are going to inspect an area near the *Yarkon*. The group is from Jerusalem. Hungarian Jews, I think. But not completely out of touch with the world. One even speaks Arabic. Stampfer or Salomon. I can't remember who."

"I have heard about Salomon," said Joseph. "He is an acquaintance of Yellin's. I've told you about Yehoshua Yellin before, haven't I? He runs an inn in *Motza*, on the route to Jerusalem. Not really standard business for a Jew either." They both laughed.

"This band tried to buy a piece of land near Jericho a few years ago. They wanted to call their project after something from the prophet Hosea. If you are interested, I will introduce you to them. From what I understand, only the men are going to set up camp. The families will be staying in Yafo."

"Splendid," said Joseph. "I mean it. I have great respect for these people. To exchange a totally passive existence for a life of effort."

"But I called you here for a prior matter," Amzalek sat down behind his desk and gave him an official document. The names of the three monsters stared at him from the paper, Riad Mahmoud, Abed Hassuna and Mohammed al-Kharoub. The three men who were hanged because of the murder of Esther Perachim and Mustafa Aqad, and the assault and rape of Saïda Kamal. Briefly, Joseph relived the horrible scene. Then, he had sworn he wouldn't rest until the perpetrators were brought to justice and sentenced to death. But now, the hanging of these three didn't change anything. It certainly didn't bring relief.

He talked about the settlers with Rachid. But his faithful companion had serious reservations. "That village by the river is called *Melabbes* or *Umlebbes*; it means "clothing" in Arabic. Something that looks better than it actually is. Every time, the place dresses up for new people. It is located near the marshes, on low ground. Not very good."

"But shouldn't they give it a try?" Joseph asked.

"I don't like to give advice."

Joseph insisted.

"There have been many hopeless attempts by Westerners," said Rachid. "I still remember the Dickson and Steinbeck families. They were all massacred. Then that strange group of Americans with their drunken leader, Adams. Failed. They all meant well, but they have no idea what to expect. I have to say that those Germans are doing better, but a lot of them, also children, have perished. I have little confidence in all these plans."

"But these people already live here, in Jerusalem. I suppose they know what they are doing."

"Surviving in the alleys of Jerusalem is something different than taking care of yourself among the Bedouins."

"What do the Arabs actually think about this?"

"The Arabs? They are mostly surprised by these crazy Europeans."

"But when they stop being surprised? What then? It's progress, isn't it?"

"I don't know whether they think it's progress at all."

"Clean streets, buildings that keep standing upright, fair justice. If you don't call that progress, then what is?"

"I wouldn't count on their experiencing it that way."

A while later news came that the group had indeed bought a piece of land near the *Yarkon*. David Meir Gutman, the oldest of the group, was put forward as the buyer. He was an Austrian, a smokescreen for the Turks. In the end their stretch was not by the river, but a bit further, on a hill. Apparently, the low-lying part had not been registered for sale to the Turks yet. The men from Jerusalem had reconciled themselves with the stretch belonging to an Arab merchant, Kasar. Rachid knew him well. He seemed reliable.

Joseph liked the group and he wished them luck.

"We are calling the settlement *Petach Tikva*," Gutman said. "We will leave next week. Put up the tents and first try to dig a well. Because we are up the hill, we don't have direct access to water."

"Maybe that's not so bad. Rachid didn't trust the location near that river," Joseph replied.

"We'll see," Gutman said. "In any case, the Ottomans don't have any problems with it. That piece of land is worthless in their eyes."

As planned, the women of the group found lodgings in Yafo. Sometime later, Miriam invited one of them for tea. Her name was Rachel Glick, a vivacious lady in her thirties. She was well dressed and spoke fluent English because her family had lived in London for many years. She had brought her daughter, Hannah, who immediately found a playmate in Moshe. Rachel Glick turned out to be a waterfall of words and it was not easy to keep up with her outpouring.

"I said to him, my husband, Ezra that is. I said to him, you'll be back within three days. That was when they went to check. To that plot of land they were going to buy. But, then they didn't know they were going to buy. In any case. Everyone called him crazy. Just a few men, all alone, among the Arabs, looking for a piece of land. And the rabbis cried out against it. Why couldn't he just do like the rest in Jerusalem. I said to him, it was insane to come to this disgraceful place and now you're going to leave me here too, I said. And he said he would just be away for three days. And he soothed me. He does that so well. It had the blessing of the rabbi. I still don't know which rabbi he meant, but anyway. He just told me to listen to him and that everything would be fine. Did he know? Is he *Ha Kodesh Baruch Hu* who knows everything? But he didn't come back after three days. And not after four or five. Thirteen, I tell you. After thirteen days he came back with a big smile on his face. As if nothing was wrong. Thirteen days. Well, I never. And I'm just stuck with the children, fearing for his life. I had already gone to the police, but those Turks said they couldn't do anything. I really thought he was dead." She held back and wiped a tear out of her eye. "For nights on end, I prayed and cried and then, he returns triumphantly as if nothing was wrong! And they had indeed bought a piece of land there." Suddenly she broke into a smile that lit up her whole face. "I am so happy. So proud of him. Now we can make our dream come true."

Miriam nodded with empathy and winked. She got up to get more tea.

"I will get it," Rivka said.

"Can I help?" Rachel Glick shouted after her.

"No. Everything is fine. Just relax."

Rivka came back with a fresh pot and Rachel picked up the story again.

"They are still living in the tents they took with them. The Turks do not allow anyone to build houses anyway. But if you put a roof on a structure very quickly, they are not allowed to demolish it, says Ezra. I hope he is right. Otherwise it will all be in vain and we have to tear down everything again. Oh dear! In any case, if the houses are there, then we, the women and children, will come. Of course, we visit them quite often. But first they have to dig the well. It's all about water. It is a pity that the river runs a little further but just too far away. It's no good. Ezra told me that they have already dug ten meters and still not found any water. I do feel it will work. It is blessed. But at the moment, we still have to bring them supplies. And it is a two and a half hour ride from Yafo, crossing the river. River!" She scorned. "There is not even water in that river, at all! Never mind. At any rate, it's not a problem but they say it will be more difficult in winter. Oh well, there are no real winters here, not like in Europe. So it will not be too bad."

"And the Arabs?" Miriam asked, when Rachel paused for a moment to sip her tea.

"As gentle as lambs. Really. Ezra said that they are mainly staring at those weird Jews." She nodded violently. "Yes, that's how he said it. Those weird Jews. But I think that if it turns out to be a success, they will be surprised. But first the well. They have already dug ten meters. Straight down and still nothing. Or did I already mention that? Anyway. Ezra and Yehoshua, that is Yehoshua Stampfer, have ordered plows. Modern European plows. The Arabs will not believe their eyes. And now there is also an expert. A real expert. His name is Raab. And he wants to bring in big oxen from Damascus for plowing."

Joseph was out of breath just listening to Rachel Glick.

"Perhaps we should go and have a look?" he proposed.

Rachel turned around and clapped her hands. "But that would be wonderful. And take the little one with you. He and my Hannah play so nicely together."

The same week, a new immigrant from Poland arrived in Yafo, a scholar and writer, Rav Yehiel Michael Pines. Joseph did not know exactly why, but he liked the man at first sight, although he was in no way distinguishable from the rabbis with whom he had had so many collisions in Jerusalem. It soon became apparent that he and Joseph had similar views on many issues. The man had clearly received a very broad secular education. Joseph invited him for Shabbat, but he politely declined. "I want to travel straight to Jerusalem. I need to talk to some important rabbis there. Maybe they think I'm a bit modern and certainly my ideas will make them frown, but it's a step that I have to take."

"I hope you will be more successful than I was. I also thought I should talk to them but those turned out to be short conversations. How is your Yiddish?"

"Excellent, thank you." He laughed. "I brought a big bag of money. That certainly will make them listen to me, I presume."

Joseph looked surprised, but was immediately ashamed that he had shown interest in the coffers he was bringing.

"It's from Moses Montefiore," Pines said. "There is a new project. The Moses Montefiore Testimonial Fund or *Mazkeret Moshe*. And the trustees have charged me, or to put it more kindly, asked me, to do meaningful things with it."

"We can write libraries about doing meaningful things here."

"The intention is to use the money mainly for economic enterprises. Specifically, to start agricultural colonies and build houses. My job is to find out how this can best be done. Therefore it's logical that I will settle in Jerusalem."

"Some people from Jerusalem have just started an agricultural settlement," said Joseph. "In the plain nearby, near *Umlebbes*."

"Petach Tikva. I have heard about it. I was planning to visit the settlers. We will see. Maybe I can help. Don't you want to go with me to Jerusalem, this first time?"

"I think it is wiser for you not to advertise your connection to me, there."

At first, the path was easy to follow. Their donkeys crossed the *Wadi Misrara*, where the family had headed years ago to see the raging flood. Now there was only a dry bed. Again, there were four of them, Miriam, Joseph, Moshe, and Rachid, who had thought it wise to accompany them. "It may seem like a friendly scenery, but there are swamps and also Arabs who are not always favorably disposed towards strangers. It is better that you not go alone." Because of work for school, Rivka had decided to stay in Yafo. They brought provisions for a few days, and two extra donkeys that were fully loaded with supplies for the settlement. "Maybe we can extend a helping hand to them," said Joseph in good spirits.

They were already half an hour ride from the *wadi* when they spotted a group of riders in the distance.

"Bedouins," Rachid said. "It's better to avoid them. They can be friendly, but for all we know they might prefer to slice our throats."

He saw something that looked like a path and they all immediately turned on to it, leaving the main track. The trail meandered through the vast fields of reeds. The plants reached far above them. Soon there was no longer any path to follow and they had no idea where they were. Apparently Rachid didn't know either. "I'm afraid we're a bit lost. It all looks the same. I apologize. I will make up for it." He rode to a low hill nearby and peered into the distance. "Still, I don't think it's that bad. Behind those reed fields, I think, lies *Antipatris*, the old crusader fort *Afek*. That would mean that we are a little too far to the east." He seemed more certain of himself now. "Then the *Yarkon* must lie there." He pointed in the distance. "If we run into that, all we have to do is follow it to the west."

They plowed further through the high reed fields. Occasionally they had to go through marshy stretches, swarming with mosquitoes, but the water never came higher than the legs of the pack animals. Joseph remembered the incident with Ferretti. He reminded Rachid of it.

Rachid laughed. "I don't think it's that bad here. This is firmer ground and it is also much later in the season. But," he added, "it's better to be very careful." A little further Joseph felt his donkey slip but the animal easily corrected its step. He breathed a sigh of relief. "Indeed, we had better pay attention," he said softly.

Soon they stumbled upon the river with some higher trees on its bank. Under the overhanging branches, there was some sort of a passageway. Rachid led the way. "I know where we are now. Come." They followed the winding path along the river. Joseph stopped for a moment. "Am I seeing this right? Is there a dead sheep floating in the water?" He pointed to the carcass of a sheep drifting with the current.

"You see that quite often. The river is used as a sewer. The people upstream throw in all their waste."

Joseph thought it was all pretty disgusting.

Rachid changed the subject. He shouted to Miriam and Moshe who were a bit behind. "We will soon reach a small lake with lilies. I remember it was very beautiful."

The small lake was indeed gorgeous. There were lilies all over the surface and the water was lined with tall cattails. The edges were steep, but they found a place where they could reach the water. The ground was too moist to sit on, so they ate their meal standing up. All around them were huge reed stems, through which a strange green light filtered.

The water between the huge lily leaves seemed brown.

"Is it deep?" Joseph asked.

"A few meters," Rachid said. "But I wouldn't like to plunge in. Apart from being dirty, you could get entangled in all the stems and roots." He had barely spoken the words, as Miriam yelled out. Joseph turned around and saw her slowly sliding into the water. She reached out to the muddy ground, but found no handhold. She slipped further and further into the water.

Joseph rushed to the waterfront, stretching out his hand while hanging on to a large, overhanging branch.

"Help! Joseph." Now only her head was still above the water.

"Rachid, do something. She can't swim and neither can I," he shouted desperately.

But Rachid had already taken the rope he always had with him. He had tied one end to his waist and the other to the branches of what looked like a sturdy bush. At the same place where Miriam had slipped into the water, he jumped in. Miriam was almost completely submerged. Rachid stretched out his hand and Miriam grabbed it. Her arm was all covered with leaves and lily tendrils. Rachid got a hold of her and slowly started to pull her out of the water.

"Sir, pull the rope."

Joseph, completely petrified, suddenly shot into action. He took the rope and pulled with all his might, ignoring the pain in his hand. Moshe helped as well. Perhaps it made a difference. Rachid backed onto drier ground, bringing Miriam out of the water. Now that the tension had passed, they all burst into laughter.

"Mamma, you look like a water plant."

Rachid was already busy sprinkling her clothes with water so that the dirt would come off.

"It dries quickly. In an hour you won't notice anything."

Despite the incident, they continued in good spirits, and not much later they came out of the reed fields and saw in front of them a few tents on a hill.

"That has to be it," said Joseph. "Petach Tikva. The Gate of Hope."

Someone must have spotted them, because two men were already walking proudly towards them. Joseph recognized Glick and he thought he also had seen the other man before.

"Welcome," said Glick. He introduced the other. "This is David Gutman. He is the actual owner."

Joseph introduced his family and Rachid, and they rode to the open area between the tents where work on the well was in full progress.

"Papa, you better not help them. Do you remember?" Joseph

looked slightly annoyed at his son's lack of trust, but Miriam laughed. "And maybe not mamma either." Now it was Miriam's turn to look indignant. "Moshe, keep quiet. What must these people think of us?" Moshe shrugged his shoulders and asked if he could play.

Joseph saw Miriam making a face, as if she had swallowed something filthy. "Are you all right?"

"I still have the taste of that water in my mouth. As if it had come straight out of the sewage system."

"Drink some clean water. Or even better, eat something as well." He gave her a few biscuits. He kept silent about the dead sheep he had seen.

"It keeps coming back." She sighed. "I hope it will disappear soon."

The men made space for them in one of the tents. Rachid looked at the primitive shelters, amused. Joseph saw this and said, "I know, Rachid. It's not the manner in which you are used to traveling, but at least it gives some shelter."

"I think I had better lie down," Miriam said. "I feel a bit feverish."

Joseph agreed. "Yes, take some rest."

The pioneers led them to the open space between the tents and proudly showed off the well.

"Twenty-five meters deep," said Glick. "We dug for two weeks. Raab would descend into the well and Stampfer and Salomon would hoist the buckets from above. But we found water. Isn't it fantastic? Of course it's still a pity that we're not right at the riverbank." He drank a sip. "Here, taste. Our water tastes so good. Even the Arabs of the neighboring villages come here to fetch water now."

They went to look at the work on the houses. In fact, nothing had been built yet. But the men had made plenty of mud bricks. Joseph saw Moshe playing with a few other children who were visiting. He was completely covered in mud, but he seemed to be having a good time. He also recognized the Glick's daughter.

"Papa, we should come and live here too."

"Who knows, my boy?"

"It's so fantastic here. Look, we turn mud and straw into blocks and let them dry in the sun. I've already made at least twenty of them."

"What, only twenty? I did at least thirty," Hannah, the daughter of the Glicks, shouted.

"Papa. I don't have time now. I have to catch up with Hannah." And he immediately plunged back into the mud.

"We have to delay the building process itself," Glick explained, "until we have enough blocks. The houses must have roofs at once, otherwise the Turks can order us to knock them down." Joseph nodded. He knew the rules.

"That's why, until now, we only have built barns and stables," Glick continued. "They don't object to shelters for the animals."

They had a tasty meal, sitting on the ground near the well. Miriam appeared, when they had almost finished.

"Have you left anything for me?" she asked hopefully. "I am feeling much better."

"Here you are," Stampfer gave her a loaf of bread and some eggs.

"If all goes well, our new tools and appliances will come before sundown," said Glick with excitement in his voice. "Raab ordered plows in Hungary and we heard that they arrived in Yafo yesterday. They should be here by now."

And indeed, half an hour later, some of the visiting children came reporting with anticipation that they had seen a group of people in the distance. A little later Yehuda Raab arrived triumphantly escorted by some young Arabs.

"The plows," he said with respect. "These and the oxen will ensure that we can cultivate the land like never before."

The men carefully removed the heavy plows from the cart and passed them along to everyone in the group. It reminded Joseph of *Simchat Torah*, the annual celebration of the renewal of the Torah. One by one the men kissed a plow and, while holding together the heavy devices above their heads, they started to dance.

The next morning Miriam was still not feeling well. She sweated and felt cold. Her eyes were burning. Joseph patted her forehead with a wet towel and felt her shivers.

"Shouldn't we go home?"

"We will see. If I still feel bad this afternoon, we will."

The group had put the oxen to one of the plows. The big moment was there. "For the first time in two thousand years we're going to work the land," Raab solemnly declared. He put the plow in the ground and spurred the oxen to pull. No movement. The oxen pulled, but nothing happened. It was as if the ground would only tolerate the plow being put into it, but no more.

Raab was slightly upset. "Maybe we should moisten the ground first." He stood still for a while. The others watched him with anticipation.

"Please, you focus your attention on the stalls. I need to think about this very thoroughly."

They didn't want to embarrass him, so in silence the others went back to the little square around the well.

"God will give us a solution for this too," said Salomon.

Stampfer quoted a text from Yechezkiel: *"But you, mountains of*

Israel, will produce branches and fruit for my people Israel, for they will soon come home. I am concerned for you and will look on you with favor; you will be plowed and sown."

In no time, everyone was as cheerful as before, and most of them went to work, dragging the mud bricks to the right place. A hard job in the burning sun. Joseph helped as best as he could with one hand.

That afternoon, Joseph and Rachid went to explore the area, leading their horses in the direction of the *Yarkon* river. After a short ride, they espied a collection of miserable huts near the river. "Come, Rachid, let's have a look."

"*Umlebbes,*" said Rachid. He dismounted and picked up a handful of soil. "This ground is black. Not the best. For a good grain harvest you need red soil. This is better for oranges. But that is probably not their biggest problem." He looked more closely to the huts. "This doesn't bode well."

Joseph asked him what he meant.

"Take a look at the villagers," said Rachid.

As Joseph drew nearer, he saw a few pale, emaciated men sitting in front of their huts, ailing, their faces yellowish. It was clear that there had been a terrible epidemic here.

"What could be the cause?" he asked Rachid.

Rachid shook his head, got back on his horse and climbed a small hill on the outskirts of the wretched village. For about five minutes he stayed there, and gazed in all directions. Occasionally he sniffed the air.

"I will tell you something. The air is not good here," he declared.

"What exactly do you mean?"

"Birds. There are no birds. Only mosquitoes. There is a lot of vegetation and it is teeming with insects, worms and more, but there are no birds. A bad sign. That means unhealthy air. Malaria. Birds immediately detect that."

Joseph nodded. It was obvious that Rachid knew what he was talking about.

"And what do you think we should do?"

"We," said Rachid, "we don't have to do anything. We have to get out of here as fast as we can, and get back to Yafo. And Mrs. Miriam has to see a doctor."

"And the Jewish settlers?"

"I think it's better on top of the hill where they are located. But here near the river I wouldn't want to live for all the gold in the world. People get sick and then get weaker and weaker. Sometimes it seems as if the disease has disappeared completely, and then suddenly it returns, more violently. Those who suffer from it also become more susceptible to other diseases. Two of my siblings had it. My youngest brother survived, but the older one, Moaz, didn't make it." He fell silent.

They left the cursed village and Joseph looked back. A feeling of doom took possession of him. Back in the settlement, he decided that they should leave straight away. He told Moshe who was very disappointed. Miriam also thought he was over-reacting.

"I really feel much better. Let's go tomorrow. And I promise that I will see a doctor when we are back home."

Joseph conceded. It would indeed be better to wait a day. It was already late and if they started now, they would have to make the last part of the trip in the dark.

The next day it seemed as if the gloomy clouds had disappeared. Miriam felt strong enough to ride the donkey and make the trip to Yafo. They said their farewell to the settlers and departed. But when they arrived, late in the afternoon, Miriam almost fell off her horse with fatigue.

"I need to lie down, if you don't mind. It will be better tomorrow. These were tough days," she added optimistically.

Miriam recovered quickly, but Joseph decided to heed Rachid's advice; it was always smart to listen to him. Miriam didn't want to hear it. "I have completely recovered. Really, it is not necessary. I don't need to see a doctor." But in the end Joseph convinced her.

The doctor took the matter more seriously than they had expected.

"I don't know what made her sick. Whether it was the swallowing of the water from that polluted river, the foul air, or the mosquitoes. Maybe she is more susceptible to this kind of disease. But the good news is that the fever has passed. To be on the safe side I will prescribe some medication."

With a worried face, he said goodbye.

In order to support the settlement, Joseph and Miriam often invited the families of the pioneers to their home. Miriam hadn't fallen ill all winter and one Shabbat, they entertained the Glicks again. This time Ezra was also present and they expanded the company with Richard and Lupu. Of course Rivka joined them as well. Moshe was happy to play with cheerful Hannah.

"Who knows," Joseph said joking to Miriam, "our flame also had been kindled during a Sabbath meal."

"Not so kosher, flames on Shabbat," she responded laughing.

Rachel Glick hadn't lost anything of her joie de vivre, although the content of her messages still had the occasional tinge of bitterness. "We suffer a lot from looters and robbers in the settlement. We can't shoot those bandits; then there's no end to it. They will start shooting back and then the Turks come and get involved. We try to become friends with the Arabs. They asked us the other day to choose sides when they had another dispute with some tribe. We helped them secretly. We gave them coffee. And potatoes. The last we had. Not really the last, but still. It couldn't be made public, but we are now friends forever with the sheikh of that tribe."

Joseph wanted to ask which tribe, but she had already embarked on a new story. "As I said, it's not all peaches and cream. Remember the farmhand we had hired?" She looked at her husband. "Who wanted to be a slave?" Ezra turned to Joseph and interrupted his wife. "He wanted to work for us; he was offered to us as a slave by the sheikh, but I don't want a slave, certainly not an Arab one. Then that man begged us to carve his name into his skin. In the end I wrote it with ink on his arm. Two weeks later he and his family left, taking with them two horses, one ox, and I don't know what else."

"But the Arabs always come to ask for water," Rachel brought forward.

"Right. We earned their respect by digging the well and by pumping up water. That's better than quarreling."

For some time Lupu had been shifting nervously on his chair. Apparently he had something on his mind, but Rachel offered him no chance to speak. When a silence finally fell in the conversation, he immediately seized the opportunity. "I have due respect for everything you are doing there, but I don't think it will help. The real progress will come from a completely different side."

Richard looked at him, amused. "What exactly do you mean?"

"It is no use. Next year those fanatics in Jerusalem will make you lay down the work for the *shmitta* year. That will be the end of Petach Tikva."

"We follow the law, and if it says that in the seventh year working the land is not allowed, then we will keep to that."

Lupu wanted to react, but Glick stopped him. "And I will say something else. We might be weird, but we are not crazy. The rabbis have always found clever ways to circumvent problems like this. I assume they will come up with something for the *shmitta* year as well. A solution everyone can agree upon."

Lupu shook his head. "I hope you're right, but not everyone is like you. They'll never agree to a leniency. I also understand that they are not at all charmed by your endeavors."

"There is a large group in Jerusalem that supports Petach Tikva," said Glick.

"I wonder how they will greet you when you have to return to Jerusalem with your tail between your legs. Because it is obvious to me that you will not succeed. No money, no knowledge, some odd European ideas. It is not based on a plan. Sowing some seeds is not cultivating the land."

"Normally I am not an advocate of the Orthodox community in Jerusalem," interrupted Joseph, "but there's progress there. They have already built a few neighborhoods outside the walls of Jerusalem and they continue."

"Would you like to live there?" Lupu asked in reply.

"That's something else. That's not what this is about."

"Those over-religious think that you have no connection with the Jewish people and no heart for the cause, if you don't follow their way. I suffered more because of my origins than they did, I can tell you."

"Stop it," Miriam said. "It's not a competition."

"I got to know them well when I lived there," Rivka said. "There are so many views within all those communities in Jerusalem. But they were so dependent on the charity. I felt sorry for them."

"I certainly don't want to be part of a group that evokes pity," Lupu said.

"Let's all be kind to each other to start with and eat," Miriam said. "We don't have to agree."

"They are the ones who hate," said Lupu. "You know," he added with a venomous undertone. "The strangest coalitions are emerging in Jerusalem. The *Mitnagdim* and the *Chassidim* have buried the hatchet among themselves in the great fight against the so-called unbelievers."

"Ah. Then unity is arising!" Richard exclaimed.

"But religion will lose anyway," concluded Lupu.

Joseph gave Lupu a dubious look. Would this be the new wind? Perhaps his first impression of the Romanian had been right after all – a lost pirate.

Pines told him that the settlers of Petach Tikva planned to go to Jerusalem on *Shavuot** to make the biblical contribution of the tenth part for the first time in two thousand years. The harvest had been good. Pines invited them to come to see the group's arrival in Jerusalem. Joseph, Miriam, Moshe and Rivka were lodged as Pines' guests in the new district that Rothschild had built around the hospital.

"You and your family can stay with me. Then at least, I will have some friends around me."

Joseph raised his eyebrows. "Is it so bad?"

"The mere address where I'm staying is suspicious. A man called Rivlin, who is also regarded as an enlightened danger. Meanwhile, they are considering proclaiming a ban on me."

"Welcome to the party."

Along the streets, crowds of people were waiting for the group from Petach Tikva. It seemed as if all of Jewish Jerusalem had come out to meet them. The end station was a specially vacated house in the new *Mea Shearim* area that would serve as the warehouse for the harvest. In the distance, just on the hilltop on the Yafo road, they saw a cloud of dust swirling and a few camels became visible.

"Mama," Moshe enthusiastically cried out. "I think there are a hundred camels."

"A hundred is perhaps a bit much. What do you think of thirty?" said Miriam smiling. Joseph looked at her admiringly; he hadn't seen her this radiant in years, as she stood there, her hair braided, wearing the white dress with the purple waistband and the pearls that she had worn on that memorable Shabbat in Cologne.

Indeed, a long caravan of camels appeared with the proud men of Petach Tikva at the reins. Their entrance was magnificent. Some of the men had brought their families and everyone had put on their most festive clothes. As the parade passed, they saw the enormous sacks of grain and other products on the camels' backs, and on each of them the name of the settlement was written in large Hebrew letters. No one could misunderstand this – Petach Tikva was an overwhelming success. People clapped and cheered. In the enthusiastic crowd stood a few people whom Joseph knew were against agricultural settlements. They watched quietly, perhaps thinking that whoever laughs last will laugh best. Next to him, someone said, "I said they were right. They proved it, our colonial brothers. *They* don't have to beg for food. And it is even safer there than in Jerusalem. This is the real way to live in the land. I'm going to sign up for the new plots that are going to be sold."

Joseph looked surprised at Pines; "Is that so? Will there be new building plots? Has that land already been bought?"

Pines nodded. "I have made a deal. We bought the whole stretch at the *Yarkon* and we will be selling the plots soon."

Joseph took him aside and gave him an detailed account of Rachid's assessment of the place. "The lowlands at the *Yarkon* are no good."

"We have taken it into account. There are very strict conditions. No water from the *Yarkon*, everything taken from the well. And much more. I've also heard of the bad air there. But let's party now." He smiled. "We will take care of these things later." But against his own recommendation, he continued. "It was quite easy to interest people.

The poor wretches all feel this is a miracle. The way to get food. But they are all laymen when it comes to agriculture and rural life. We will have to be very careful in reviewing the applications."

"The first settlers agree?"

"They know about the plan. This is one major propaganda stunt. First and foremost to prove that it is possible, to work the land and live from it, but also to win new souls."

The last words were lost to Joseph because at that moment, Miriam leaned against him.

"I feel a bit weak," she murmured, and fainted in his arms.

Joseph called Rivka and asked her to fetch a doctor. "Get one you know. One from your monastery or from the hospital." At the same time he asked Pines to take care of Moshe. He didn't want the boy to worry about his mother.

At Pines's house, they laid Miriam down on a sofa in the living room. Rivka had found a doctor in the hospital where she had often been as a nun. His name was Klotzinger and he seemed a real professional.

Miriam smiled weakly. "I just cause problems, don't I? Tomorrow will be better. Then we all can go home without worrying."

She turned on her side and in the candlelight it seemed that some color had indeed returned to her face.

"It must have been the sun. I didn't drink enough water. Nothing to worry about."

"Go to sleep now," said Joseph, and he kissed her forehead. The doctor looked concerned. He turned to Rivka. "Your sister-in-law has completely exhausted herself. The best cure is strict rest."

"Will she be all right?" Joseph asked.

"I would like to think that she will be." Klotzinger hesitated. "Probably. With malaria you never know. Some people recover completely."

"Can she travel?" Rivka asked.

"On a stretcher and then very carefully. The road is still pretty bad as you undoubtedly know. You'll have to go slowly."

Following the doctor's advice, they took their time on the trip back to Yafo. Once Miriam was settled at home, Joseph asked their family doctor if it would be better for her to travel to Cologne to be examined by a physician there. But Miriam was completely against the idea. "First of all, I feel much better. And I certainly don't want to worry my parents." There was nothing to discuss; she was staying here, with him and with her son. In the country she had chosen.

"My parents actually want to visit us," she said. "They sent a letter this week. I haven't told you with all the business in Jerusalem going on. They want to come for a few weeks."

"I hope they are not planning to pick you up and run off to Cologne," Joseph said.

"Don't make fun of it!"

Joseph apologized and they dropped the subject. In the following days, Miriam felt better and better, and after a week it seemed as if she were completely cured.

At the end of August, Avraham and Golde Ben Tov came on the steamer from Alexandria. Miriam's parents were the first to disembark. Miriam embraced them for a long time. Joseph deliberately greeted them warmly as well, despite his lingering resentment. Then the Ben Tovs turned their complete attention to their grandson, who chatted cheerfully and peppered them with questions.

"In the next sloop there is someone else you might want to see, Joseph," Avraham said with a strange smile. "Just look."

And to Joseph's surprise and boundless joy, he turned and saw Max disembarking. His friend was white as a sheet. He had been in his cabin for a week, too sick even to take a breath on deck. Max had grown old. He was gray around the temples and looked worn out. Joseph hugged him and told him he had experienced the same thing the first time.

"It passes. A little rest and everything will be fine. It is so good that you are here. It feels so right."

Rivka's house could accommodate the whole Ben Tov family. She had more than enough space and she enjoyed taking care of her guests. It did not matter to her how long they stayed.

Golde preferred to stay in the house, but Avraham wanted to see everything and asked Joseph and Miriam about the smallest details. As soon as possible he wanted to visit Jerusalem and Joseph asked Rachid to arrange the best transport and the best lodging for his in-laws.

They hardly mentioned Miriam's illness. The Ben Tovs were taken up too much by the exotic setting to be worried about something that was apparently no longer important to Miriam herself.

One day, Avraham asked Joseph to see him.

"I suppose Miriam has told you about what my wife tried to accomplish?"

Joseph wanted to wave it away, but Avraham continued. "I sincerely apologize."

"Accepted. Water under the bridge."

"I don't want anything to stand between us. I support you wholeheartedly and I have talked to Golde and she is really sorry about what she did. But she is a proud woman, so don't expect an apology from her immediately."

"I understand."

Avraham shook his hand firmly and thanked him.

"Glick has just returned from Petach Tikva," Rivka reported a few days later. "He has news. Everyone is eager to hear it."

But the news wasn't good. Ezra reported that things were going badly with the settlement. They had almost nothing left to eat, the *Yarkon* had overflown and inundated the whole area, causing the settlers to lose the entire harvest, and more and more people were getting sick. The water had polluted everything.

"There is now a group of Romanians who have settled in the lowlands near the *Yarkon* and they take water from the river." Glick said. "We have warned them so many times against it. The last month one after the other started getting sick. Five people of the new group have already died, including a four-year-old child. It was terrible."

He wiped his hand over his eyes. "And then there's the money. Everyone always wants money," he complained. "The Turks keep taxing, the Arabs overprice their products and our people quarrel about money among themselves. It's destroying us. Perhaps we made a mistake bringing new people in so soon. We sold plots of land too close to the river. When we were in Jerusalem, everything seemed to be going well."

Joseph had to think about the birds of Rachid. His confidant had assessed it well. The flats near the river were unsuitable for habitation.

"Now the new residents also want to live up on the hill and not near the river, where they bought the land. Nor do they accept the authority of the first group. Some have returned to Jerusalem, but they have not been welcomed there. Some there say, "you should have listened to us. It's hard enough already for us, we can't take care of you." The most wicked of them see it as a punishment for our irresponsible behavior. We can't expect any help from there."

"And now what?" Max asked.

"For the time being we will continue, but we need money and supplies. A couple of oxen have died and plowing has become practically impossible. Rav Pines also says that we should rather plant fruit trees instead of grain. The soil and climate are much more suitable for that." The man put on a brave face but Joseph saw that the misery was eating away at him. "I will bring my family back to Yafo. It is not healthy there."

Joseph wondered. Was this ultimately how things go in life? Just start in the hope that God approves and gives his blessing? And what if not? Would all this end with dry bones in a valley near *Umlebbes*?

"We'll wait until after *Sukkot*, in a few weeks," said Glick, "but then we might have to make drastic decisions."

At the end of September, just after the beginning of the Jewish New Year, Miriam's illness unexpectedly returned, now more severely. She felt very weak and lay in bed for days with a fever. Her eyes were completely inflamed and there were times when she could hardly see anything.

Not content with a single doctor, Joseph sent for everyone he could find. Each left the bedroom with a somber face. Miriam slept most of the time, and when she was awake, she was plagued with hallucinations and anxiety. Very occasionally, often in the morning when she had had a better night, she was lucid and Joseph could talk to her. But her optimism had disappeared.

"Joseph, I think it's not going well," she whispered weakly.

"Don't say that. The doctors don't know. And now and then your condition improves. Everything will be all right."

"That's only because of the medicine they give me."

She made a pained effort to sit up straight. Joseph shook out her pillow.

"You and Rivka have to take good care of Moshe."

"You shouldn't talk like this." Unable to cope, he turned away. "I promise. Of course. But you will be there for him as well."

"Do you really think so?"

"Yes, with God's help, it will all turn out right."

"I am tired, Joseph. I think I'm falling asleep again."

With tears in his eyes he left the room. He almost bumped into Moshe.

"It's going worse with mama? Please tell me."

"I don't think so. We must pray for her recovery and hope for the best." He stroked the boy's hair. "She is asleep now. You can see her later. Where is Aunt Rivka? Shouldn't you be with her?"

He tried to be cheerful with Moshe, but the boy understood perfectly that all the adults were on edge. Max supported Joseph as much as he could.

For Joseph, the Yom Kippur service was heavier than ever. In the small synagogue he sat next to his son, with Max and Avraham on his other side. The prayers didn't bring any consolation. The only thing Joseph could think of was Miriam's recovery. He would give up everything for that. The prayers asked who would die that year, who by fire, who by water. For a moment, Joseph cynically noted to himself that there was no choice – Miriam was being destroyed by both; the poisoned water burned her body and soul. The day did not bring solace and when it ended, that evening, he could not bring himself to help Avraham build the *sukkah*. Instead, Joseph spent the time sitting next to Miriam's bed, listening to Max and Avraham as they fixed and tied the poles. Rivka and Moshe were helping with enthusiasm, as far as he could tell.

Over the next days, Joseph did not leave Miriam's side for one moment. But she sank further and further away. Moshe tried to cheer him up every now and then, but Joseph saw the incomprehension and the sorrow in his son's eyes.

The day after *Sukkot*, there was still no change in her delirious condition, but by the beginning of the evening Miriam had fallen asleep. Like an angel in a white robe, she was lying on her bed. Joseph tried to shake the image; this looked too much like a shroud. For the first time in days, she breathed quietly. A glimmer of hope came to Joseph, but it faded when the doctor in attendance slowly shook his head.

Joseph kissed her gently on the forehead and took her hand in his. Miriam opened her eyes slightly. She had not been able to speak all day, but now she moistened her lips with difficulty. Still, she could hardly make a sound. Her eyes spoke. The fever had consumed them for days, but now they were clear. Joseph was relieved, although he feared it might be a sign of something really dreadful.

"Moshe went to the harbor with Max and Rivka, to look at the boats," he said, and without turning his eyes away from her for a second, he whispered to his in-laws, who had just entered the room, "No need. I'll stay with her this evening."

Quietly and reluctantly, Golde and Avraham left the small room. Joseph took a deep breath. So this was it. Death. Saying goodbye to life. To their life together.

Again Miriam opened her eyes. It seemed as if they were trying to convince Joseph, more insistently than ever, not to give up. The expression on her face was as delightful and lively as that late afternoon when they had to find their way through the wilderness after the earthquake. Then, time had come to a standstill. Joseph prayed that it would do the same now. If he could sit next to her for the rest of his life and see her eyes, it would be enough. That's all he could ask.

A faint smile appeared on her lips.

Joseph had to swallow: "I was thinking of that afternoon when time stood still. After the earthquake."

She nodded with effort.

"We never returned to that beautiful place," he said.

She moistened her lips and whispered. "It's in our hearts."

"Shall I tell the story of that wonderful day again?"

Again she nodded with difficulty. "And write it down."

Joseph started. "They were on their way from Yafo to Jerusalem. Rachid, their faithful helper, had arranged everything well." He saw her smile. He brought himself back to that day and he knew that Miriam followed him in the illusion.

"But of course, the evening finally fell," he said softly. "Their journey was the most beautiful that two people ever made. A miracle of love and hope. Of beauty and promise. God himself was on their side that day."

He closed his eyes and heard Miriam vaguely say something. He did not hear the words exactly, but he knew what they were.

He looked at her again. She did not move or breathe. The smile was still there. Through his tears he tried to see her clearly. To burn the image into his mind. He should never forget this. This cursed moment that he had tried to transform with his account and in which she had joined him and had followed him. He could no longer follow her now. It was over. Time had irrevocably gone further. He kissed her and saw his tears on her face.

GATES OF DESPAIR

The world did not stand still. Nor did it fall silent.

The funeral was austere. Afterwards Joseph could remember little of it. He knew who had been there, but he could not bring the event to mind. He remembered that he had held Moshe's hand throughout. Sometimes they had looked at each other through their tears. He vaguely remembered that Rivka had supported him. His parents-in-law on the other side. Max behind him. Richard was there. Vaguely Joseph remembered hearing him say how thankful he was that she had forgiven him. Her grave was next to that of his father. Then, he had spoken about the bones of Yechezkiel that had come to life. Now, there was no hope. Through his nightmare he had said *Kaddish*.

For the rest of the day he had sat in his chair staring gloomily. Nothing mattered anymore. Everything had changed, forever. He even thought about leaving. Maybe he could return to Monselice's garden house with Moshe and write. And abandon this world forever.

After the *shiva* he crawled completely into his shell. Miriam's death retroactively destroyed even the happiness of the past. After Elsa's death he had sought a justification for his presence here. Something to prove that he had made the right decision. Now he wanted nothing. He just endured. He did what he had to do – make sure Moshe went to school and that they had something to eat, but no more. And most of the time Rivka took care of these. He knew he should comfort his son but that required too much effort. Sometimes they looked at each other without saying anything. These glances were all the consolation they could offer each other.

Joseph spent most of his time in the never-dismantled *sukkah*. The beauty of the idyllic hut had lost its appeal to him, although all the plants and trees around it were in full bloom, the bougainvillea a whirling haze of pink and purple. But now the rickety *sukkah* represented his reality better than the beautifully furnished solid house. For nights he sat motionless in the barebones structure, of which only the wooden slats and a few withered palm leaves remained. When he buried his father, Joseph had tried to find something good in his passing. But that occasion had been less harrowing; arguably, it had been more of a theoretical exercise. Joseph had certainly felt emotion, but he had not suffered. And the sadness, although deep, had borne no resemblance to what he was experiencing now.

He thought back to the first Shabbat afternoon after Miriam had gone to visit her parents, when he had surrendered to the feeling of loneliness and desolation. But the source of that melancholy had been beauty. Now there was no beauty. Then it had been some sort of game. It had appeared in his head and he had been able to guide it. That thought-experiment seemed heavenly now. Then he could end it by taking up a book. Now there was no cure.

Generally Avraham and Golde moved softly around him, but one day their voices wafted toward him, Joseph realized that there was an argument going on.

"Do you want to stay here?" He heard his mother-in-law say. "Here, in this country that took away my daughter. Never. I was right all along."

Joseph felt uncomfortable. Eavesdropping was not nice and he really did not want to hear this. But it was too intriguing.

"It was my *Akeida*,"* Golde continued. "Only no angel who stopped it. Only the angel of death who came to fetch her. My daughter sacrificed for ... for what actually?"

"It almost seems as if you blame Joseph."

"I do blame him for taking my dearest child to this country. It had to end in a bad way. Sickness and poverty. She wasn't even forty." She stopped for a moment and said softly, "Maybe it happened because they did not want to wait until the time was right. You know how the spies were punished."

"Stop that nonsense. Joseph gave her everything. I don't want to hear any more about it. And you don't understand the story of the spies at all. They were punished precisely because they didn't want to come here."

Joseph was glad when they moved away. But in their wake, he felt an unreal sense of guilt.

The period of thirty days of mourning, the *shloshim*, passed. In an attempt to bring him back to life, Rivka asked Joseph to come and live with her for a while. "Then I can take better care of Moshe and I can also keep an eye on you." He said he would think about it.

There were days when he wandered aimlessly through the house. Every object evoked memories of her. They had bought each item together or had shared in its history.

"Are you in touch with anyone from Sarona," he asked Rivka.

"No, why?"

"Maybe they might want to buy the piano back. I can't bear it anymore. Seeing it makes me think of Miriam working on the Chopin preludes that she had studied for years.

"Maybe Moshe should learn to play?"

"Then we will get another one. One day. I will give the money from the sale to the community. Or even better, to those poor wretches of Petach Tikva."

He hadn't thought about the settlement for weeks. Was he unconsciously blaming them for Miriam's illness?

A week later, men came to pick up the piano. After they left, Joseph stood on the terrace looking out over the view that had once enchanted him. The sun was setting and the hills had melted into one undefined mass of humps, inhospitable and even frightening. The lovely invitation they had embodied was gone. Now he fought the urge to flee inside, to escape this view. He could hardly wait for it to turn completely dark so that there would no longer be any difference between heaven and earth.

"Yes, we will come and live with you," he told Rivka.

The next day Rachid came to speak to him. Since Miriam's death, his faithful friend had become distant and Joseph had a hunch as to why. But nevertheless he was shocked by what Rachid had to say.

"I can no longer stay here, sir. Every moment I feel guilt and shame about what happened."

"Rachid. Listen to me. You are not guilty. I am not guilty. Nobody is guilty. This kind of misery happens and God may know why. But you are certainly not responsible for it."

"Nevertheless my decision is final. I am going to my brother in Haifa. I can work there. My wife and children have already left. I didn't want to burden you with it."

"Rachid. I need you now, more than ever." But Joseph knew that he had to respect Rachid's decision. He shook his head. "If you think that's the best. I can't look into your soul. But please come and visit us."

They embraced and Joseph felt tears coming. "This farewell is too painful," he said, turning around and walking away. Would he be left by everyone? Was everyone dead, dying, or leaving? What was the plan behind this?

"I feel like a modern-day Job," he said to Rivka. "I don't understand. Is there a greater whole that I cannot see? Am I so limited?"

He found solace in Moshe's presence. The boy had a remarkable resilience.

"Papa," Moshe asked him one day, "do you still believe in God, after all that has happened?"

Joseph had known that the question would come eventually. But he still didn't have the right answer.

"I do, but it is difficult sometimes." He hesitated for a moment whether he should share his inner thoughts. "I do believe," he repeated. "But, it doesn't change anything. It is beyond us. Maybe what is important now is to focus on what we are supposed to do, rather than to think of God himself."

He realized this was hardly an answer. He had to address the boy's anxiety. "It is confusing, but I will try," he started. "Judaism is more a way of life than a belief. Man is split, God is one. You know that we say that twice a day. The rest is about how we should behave here and now. Honesty and modesty. Justice and righteousness. I don't think any of that changes because of mama's passing."

After a pause to collect his thoughts, Joseph continued. "The ancient Greeks believed that everything was predestined to end in drama. They thought that we have an unguided will that doesn't care about what is good, beautiful, or true." He smiled at his son. "But I won't go for that."

Moshe hugged him and said. "I want to believe there is something to believe."

"Do you know what one of our wise men once said? That every person should have two pockets with a note in each of them. One says that the whole world was created for him; the other that he is just dust and ashes."

Avraham and Golde left a week later. Joseph did not try to convince them to stay. The conversation he had heard was too explicit, but he did not blame Golde. There was no point in reproaches and arguments. She was who she was. And she was grieving.

Max stayed. "There's nothing for me to do over there," he said. "Germany is terrible. The atmosphere is poisonous. One article after another is published against us. As if nothing has been achieved in all these years. So why not stay here? You are family."

For the first time in weeks, Joseph felt something of joy. Was it conceivable that he could be happy again?

Occasionally he visited the coffee house in Yafo with Max. Sometimes, just sometimes, he forgot. Then only the present with his friends existed. They passed around the *nargilah* and discussed the situation in the world or simply chatted.

One day Sacha Lupu joined. Joseph had completely forgotten the man's existence.

"My decision is final. I'm going back," Lupu said. "To Odessa. I am more useful there than here. They founded a society, *Chovevei Zion*. To interest people in coming here."

"Odessa? It will be your death," said Max.

"Could be. So what? Better to look the enemy straight in the eye, to fight and perhaps to succumb than to die ingloriously of malaria in a swamp here." He realized too late whom he was talking to and he went out of his way to apologize. For the first time Joseph sensed that he was completely sincere. Then Lupu promised, "I will come back. With shiploads of new immigrants."

"Who knows," said Max ironically. "Who is braver? Those who persevere against their better judgment or those who honestly have the courage to face failure."

The question inspired Lupu to continue. "Who's talking about failure? Mark my words, I will bring more intellectuals like me. And against us, the old clique in Jerusalem will lose. They have the past, we have the future."

Joseph found it interesting to follow the discussion but he did not feel any urge to participate. It was nice to sense the sun on his body and to hear his friends converse. In the corner of his eye he saw Glick approaching. The man asked whether he could join them, and they found him a chair. Glick had a worried look in his eyes. He clearly had something of great importance to say.

"I'm going back to London. It's over here for the moment. I'll go as soon as I find suitable transportation. My family will stay here for now, in Yafo. If I may ask, could someone look out for them while I'm away?" Rivka immediately agreed to do so.

Then Glick looked at Joseph. "May I ask you something else? You are committed to our cause, aren't you?"

"Absolutely," said Joseph. "I feel very involved, although I might not have actually done much."

Glick dismissed the disclaimer. "You have done a lot." He now came to the point. "But perhaps now you can do something really important."

Glick explained that although most of the settlers had left Petach Tikva, the group didn't want to give up. "We want to make a new attempt. And for that, we need money. It's that simple. This is where you come into the picture."

"Money? Me? I want to give, but I don't have much."

"You misunderstand. I've heard – and forgive me for diving into your family affairs – that your brother is a successful businessman with offices in London and New York. When I'm in London, maybe I might talk to him. Especially if you give me a letter of recommendation.

Perhaps I could work for him?"

"A letter won't be a problem," said Joseph. "I'm happy to write one."

Glick was visibly relieved. Joseph continued. "But I can tell you that he's very no-nonsense. And he is probably not very dedicated to this cause either."

"Nevertheless, if you want to write a letter, I would be very grateful."

Joseph hesitated, wondering whether he should share his next thought, but in the end, he couldn't hold it back. "There might be another, better way."

Glick looked surprised.

"I know some people in Paris. Actually, not just some people. I know the baron. Edmond the Rothschild."

"You never said so!"

"Because there was no point in mentioning it. That would have seemed pretentious, no? I might still have direct access to him."

"You could send a letter!"

Joseph suddenly felt a spark of life. Paris. A completely different environment. He would take Moshe with him. A trip to Paris would be the perfect distraction. In Yafo, he only stared at the deserted mountain ridge in the distance. Joseph suddenly found the idea of walking through the streets of Paris again very appealing. He would certainly visit the baron, but that would probably be a formality. He had no reason to think that the man had any interest in colonization plans. On the other hand, one never knew. Maybe he could really achieve something? Rothschild had already given immense sums to the Alliance. What if Joseph could interest him in making an immediate financial injection into reviving Petach Tikva?

"I could visit him."

Max looked surprised. Glick jumped up, shook his hand and patted him on the shoulder.

"A thousand thanks, *Baruch Hashem*. You are our savior. Sir, you will do miracles," Glick said.

"I don't think I can do that."

"You are a *tzaddik*. We will pray for you and we will recite psalms."

"Hoho. First of all, I am only considering it. Blessed ideas and plans made in the evening often seem poor in the bright, harsh light of morning. Second, even if I do go, there is no guarantee that I will be successful. But he is a religious man; maybe he's not studying the Talmud all day, but that doesn't mean he wouldn't want a bigger share in mending the world."

The more he thought about it, the more realistic the plan became.

The next day he discussed it again with Max. Joseph thought he heard a slight disapproval in his friend's words.

"To Paris, who would have thought," said Max.

"Max, we're talking about twenty years ago, all right?" He laughed without joy. "What do you think? That I'm going to party again? I would certainly like to visit a museum or an exhibition again. Or go to the opera. And I would take Moshe with me. He will like Paris. It will be a good distraction for him."

"Miriam would have warned you not to go, I think," Max said.

"I don't know. Anyway, I can't ask her so I have to rely on my own judgment."

"Fair enough. Maybe you can even visit Cologne or Frankfurt?"

"It occurred to me, but I don't see the point. Do you want to come too?"

Max thought for a moment. "No. The idea of being there for a while sounds like fun, but I am not willing to make the sacrifice of weeks at sea. I'm still recovering from last time."

He returned to the subject. "Don't forget that if Rothschild gets involved it won't be gratuitous. I'm afraid it will put a big mortgage on the whole business."

"Frankly, I don't expect him to do anything."

The prospect of the journey served as a good distraction for Moshe. The boy was enthusiastic for the first time in weeks and spent days packing and asking questions.

Just before their departure, Rivka and Max came to see them off in the harbor. Joseph let his gaze wander over the water.

"You are sure you don't want to join us," Joseph asked Rivka.

"Are you mad. No way, Me going to Paris? Why would I go to that place? It was the worst period of my life."

"And you Max?"

"Me? No, no. You go. Then you will have something to be excited about when you return."

"I don't get it."

"To see me again. The world's upside down. You there, me here." He shook his head. "Just return quickly, will you?"

"You know that I have had the best time of my life here. If not for the recent misery, I would almost say that it was a happy time." With pain in their hearts, they said goodbye. The same boat was taking Ezra Glick and Alexander Lupu back to Europe.

Joseph and Moshe stood on the stern when the ship set sail. Joseph heard the constant crashing of the waves against the boat and the penetrating smell of the water suddenly reminded him of Venice.

But even the grimmest moments of his imprisonment were nothing compared to losing Miriam.

Glick joined them and kept looking back to the land. He had tears in his eyes.

"It is a disaster to leave my wife there," he said gloomily. "Oh, I apologize. I should have known better. How terrible, this remark." Ashamed, he looked to the ground.

"It doesn't matter," Joseph slowly said. "I know how it feels. There are different kinds of sadness. We all have our sorrow." His gaze was still focused on the coastline in the distance, trying to pinpoint Miriam's gravesite. When the coast disappeared, Glick turned away and did not look back. He admonished himself. "I will return. That's for sure."

Joseph nodded. He knew he would return too, but he didn't want to say it so categorically. He put his arm on Moshe's shoulders and kept staring at the water that became darker with the fall of night.

When they got off the train in Paris it was already dark.

"Papa, what huge buildings," his son exclaimed, as they walked towards *Rue de Rivoli*. It was the time of day when the offices were emptying and the cafes were getting busier. "It looks a bit like Jerusalem, but then chic and neat. And so much bigger. There's so much to see here."

Joseph smiled at Moshe's enthusiasm. "Indeed. So much to see here. I'm glad you'll have the chance to see it. Let's have a good look at it before we return."

"We are going back, aren't we?"

"Yes, Moshe. We will go back."

Joseph enjoyed the city, the cheerfulness and the hustle and bustle, the light and the spacious boulevards. It was even better than before, because now he saw it through his son's eyes. And these were not the eyes of Joseph as a young man. That boy had had to prove himself. Moshe was content with reacting to it. Joseph wasn't proud to think back to that time. But the cosmopolitanism of Paris grabbed him again. This was something completely different from the chaotic and dirty alleys of Yafo.

Had he advanced in life, had he changed? Was he the same person who had lived here? The one who, thirty years ago, had taken the bold step of leaving his parents' home? If he met that young Joseph, would he recognize him? Could they become friends? That person seemed completely different to him. Would he still understand the enthusiasm and ideals of a boy who hardly knew anything? When he read the writings of that young man now, it seemed as if a stranger were speaking, a random stranger. Time was a strange phenomenon. It moved forward, healing, giving direction, without regard for anything.

The next morning, it started to snow. Like a white sheet, a thin layer covered the world. When Joseph and Moshe came outside, small flakes were still whirling down onto the buildings and roads. Instead of concealing the shapes, it made them brighter, but at the same time, softer and kinder. It muffled all sounds. Moshe thought it was beautiful. Joseph could not remember ever seeing him so happy. He was grateful that the child still knew joy.

He had decided to take a long walk first, in order to let Moshe taste the atmosphere of the city. Rothschild could wait. They would probably have to come back in any case, as they would have to make an appointment.

"Do you know that Aunt Rivka also lived here?"

"Yes, she told me about the people and the theaters, the lamps and the mirrors."

They huddled close together under the umbrella and all morning father and son explored the city of lights that was living up to its name. They drank tea in *Café Riche*. The exterior of the stately building hadn't changed, but inside he saw that it had been substantially renovated. Nevertheless, the memories tumbled over each other. He had been drunk in every corner of this establishment. But that memory brought another, older one, when he and his brother had visited the café in Frankfurt; when they had seen Schopenhauer and had been thrown out. Then he had been unwelcome, now he didn't know if he wanted to stay.

Could that be the painter, Bleau, in the corner? It looked an awful lot like him. Not someone Joseph wanted to meet again. Further on, he saw another familiar face. It was the art collector, Georges de Bellio, an outsider, but interesting. Joseph had liked him. He was not predictable but he was probably a safe conversation partner. As far as Joseph knew, he had never wronged the man, although he had to admit that there had been many moments shrouded in alcoholic mists.

"Let's see whether Georges remembers me," he merrily told Moshe, who was staring at the lavish decoration.

De Bellio indeed recognized him. He looked at Joseph inquisitively. "But I haven't seen you for years. Where have you been?"

"I moved to Palestine. Rather far away."

"Palestine! Far away, indeed." De Bellio smiled. "I understand, however, why you came back," he continued. "The republic is great. The madness of the empire and the monarchy has passed. Paris is once again the center of the world, and rightly so." He looked at Joseph inquisitively. "I remember a conversation with Courbet. He was wondering who was more pompous, you or Napoleon the Third. It doesn't matter anymore, because the emperor has been gone for ten years."

They kept talking for a while and Joseph tried to steer the conversation away from awkward subjects that could upset Moshe.

"Please come and visit my gallery while you are here. You love the fine arts, don't you? I have a few paintings that will change the world. Believe me."

"Hush now. Here we are," Joseph said to Moshe. The *Pontalba* residence sat slightly back from the *Rue Faubourg*. Joseph thought that the huge building did not belong here; the neo-Renaissance façade would be more appropriate in Italy. He remembered the building from before the Rothschilds had bought it. Now Edmond and his family had lived there for years. The doorman ushered Joseph and Moshe into a waiting room, but not much later, returned to tell them that the baron had no time for an unannounced visit.

"And for that we came all the way to Paris? To hear that he has no time?" Moshe complained.

"Just wait. I still have a trump card to play." Joseph beckoned the man and gave him the treasure map of the then little Edmond. "Can you tell the baron that this map shows that we both know where the treasure is." He added, "Tell him, *Grüneburgpark*."

The doorman nodded and took the document. He returned a few minutes later. "Please follow me. The baron has had an unexpected cancellation of a meeting."

Moshe and Joseph looked at each other. Their eyes laughed but it seemed better not to say anything.

They entered into a large, richly decorated library. Edmond was sitting at a desk in a corner by the window. Joseph immediately recognized him, although the baron had aged considerably.

"*Monsieur* Shachar, *s'il vous plaît*." He offered a chair. "I didn't recognize the name. I believe you were once introduced to me as Lichtman?"

"You are absolutely right, but I have adopted a Hebrew name."

"That evening in Frankfurt is a long time ago. But I have not forgotten this." He held up the treasure map. "It was a beautiful evening. Although a bit sad. But you gave me courage then."

"Frankfurt is not only far away in time. I live in Palestine now."

"You live in Palestine? Very interesting. I hear many stories about it. Conflicting, I must say. My dedicated aid, *monsieur* Netter, reports to me here in France very frequently."

"Charles and I are friends. I have visited him in *Mikve Israel* a few times."

This broke the ice and as soon as it seemed appropriate, Joseph started to talk about the harsh reality of the people in the settlement of Petach Tikva.

"To make a long story short. They asked me if I could put in a good word for them."

Edmond looked out of the window for a while.

"*Monsieur* Shachar. You have to know," he started, "I dearly want to. But I fear it is a never-ending story. Now a few hundred thousand francs and then there will be another incident in a month and then another. Not to mention others who will come to beg when it becomes known that I am supporting this settlement."

"But you believe in it, don't you? I mean, in what those people envision."

Again, Edmond waited a while.

"Belief, *mon cher ami*, is a great good, but it may not be enough in this case." He stood up from his elegant arm chair and paced up and down in front of the large windows. "I have reservations. I am a realist. Wait, before you interrupt me. Indeed, sometimes we have to leave the harsh reality and go looking for the hidden treasure in good faith. But I am also a businessman. And what I see does not bode well. The Arabs own all of the good grounds. The rest are inhospitable, infertile slopes and deadly swamps. That is one argument. Another is also very practical – the Ottomans are opposed to it. It would trigger a fight with the *Porte* in Constantinople and I don't feel like it. Then another, perhaps not such a weighty argument at first sight." He looked at Joseph with piercing eyes. "I don't know how religious you are, but those settlers are for sure. They will implement all of the Biblical laws down to the last detail. And the *Shmitta* year is coming. I foresee serious problems."

"I assume there will be pragmatic rabbis who will make it workable. There are always ways out. Think of Pesach, think of the canceling of debts."

Edmond nodded. "Probably. But I would not underestimate the power of the Orthodox rabbis in Jerusalem in this respect. And they are the ones who decide in these matters there." He sighed. "Anyway, there is something else. Have you ever considered what would happen if things go wrong? What do you think these colonists would do? Stand in line for charity. So, I wouldn't be solving their plight, only making it worse." He sighed again. "But in the long run the biggest problem will be getting the two groups aligned – the religious, who see this as a biblical task, and the new movement with its nationalistic, secular motives. One group wants to be special, the other group specifically doesn't want that. For the time being, their goal is the same, but eventually they will clash."

"And on which side are you on, if I may ask?"

Rothschild smiled in a friendly manner, but did not answer the question. Joseph knew he had a point. More, it was clear that the baron had thoroughly considered this whole problem.

Rothschild continued: "If there is indeed such a thing as the Jewish problem, isn't going to America preferable? There are thousands of opportunities there. People are welcome, there is plenty of fertile land, and if an agricultural settlement doesn't succeed, there is employment in the cities." He sat down. "I don't see how this can work in Palestine, no matter how much money I put in it." He shook his head sadly. "I have told Charles, and I think by now, he agrees with me. *Mikve Israel* is not doing well. You probably know that. None of the Ashkenazim from Jerusalem come and only a handful of Sephardim. I'm afraid that you will have to return empty-handed."

He rose and Joseph assumed the conversation was over. But then Edmond turned to Moshe. "Do you like it there?"

Moshe blushed. "Very much. But mama has just passed away and it is hard now. Papa always says that we have to dream and pray and that God will then make sure that everything goes well."

"Moshe!"

Rothschild looked touched. "I'm so sorry to hear this. Was she from Frankfurt too?"

"From Cologne. Miriam Ben Tov. She was always optimistic, but as my son says; these are difficult times."

"My sincere condolences. But you will carry on there?"

Joseph knew that he would answer yes, but he also knew that he had felt doubts arising the last days. In a few months the winter would be over. Paris was beautiful in the spring.

"Yes. We have lost our hearts to *Eretz Israel*. We will stay there."

Edmond nodded. "If I can ever do something for you, don't be too shy to approach me."

The conversation had ended and the valet led them back to the large reception hall. They had to wait until he returned with their coats and hats. At that moment, a man whom Joseph thought he had seen before entered the room. An intellectual type with a well-kept beard and round glasses. The man was apparently a regular here, because while he nodded at them, he continued walking toward the baron's library.

"Sir, do I perhaps know you?" Joseph asked, out of pure curiosity.

The man stopped and looked at him. "Kahn. Rabbi Zadoc Kahn," he said as he extended his hand. "I do not believe we have had the pleasure of meeting before."

"I am a friend of Charles Netter. He mentioned you in our conversations."

"A friend of Charles? You don't say."

"We visited him in *Mikve Israel*. We live in Yafo."

"Interesting. What brings you here, to the Baron, if you don't mind my asking?"

Joseph took a bold step. It was probably not correct to talk about their conversation with others, but he knew the name of Rabbi Kahn. He was the baron's greatest confidant. "We were on a quest to find support for a new settlement called Petach Tikva. The situation is very worrying."

"And probably a rejection?"

Joseph nodded. "I completely understand the baron's concerns."

The rabbi smiled. "Sometimes a person needs patience." He looked cheerful. "I shouldn't really say this, but I think you probably are entitled to it. At the moment, *Monsieur* de Rothschild is reluctant about Palestine, but I know that he always weighs his decisions very seriously. I gather that there has been a change in his perceptions, but you should not expect an immediate result. He is also a businessman. Who knows what the future will bring."

Their conversation was interrupted by the servant who came with their coats. They said goodbye and Joseph was relieved. The baron had turned down his request but Rabbi Kahn's words ensured that he would not have to lie to the settlers when he would say that there was hope.

"Since we are here, we should enjoy Paris as much as possible. There is no point in spending weeks on a boat and then staying in a metropolis like this for just one day. What do you think, Moshe, shall we visit that Mr. De Bellio? He said that he would show us some beautiful paintings."

De Bellio welcomed them warmly and led them to a large back room – actually more of a hall. It was designed as a museum. In the ceiling were several windows installed so that a diffuse light fell into the entire room. The walls were covered with paintings, with even more leaning against the walls in the corners. Joseph stood for a long time looking at the first work that caught his attention – a painting of a train. Dark steam and puddles of light fought against the monster just entering the station. He was impressed and wanted to take a closer look, but when he drew nearer to the canvas, he saw nothing but stripes, dots, and splotches of paint. Chaos without significance. He took a few steps back and the image and the light reappeared. He was too excited to find this frustrating paradox worrisome.

"Monet," he heard De Bellio say. "One of the new masters. Most of the critics don't like him, but I think he's fantastic."

Joseph agreed. "Such light in the darkness here."

"Darkness? In Paris? You remain a weird guy after all." De Bellio shook his head and continued, "We're going to hear a lot from him. They even named this style after one of his works. Here."

Joseph now stepped to the next work, a bluish canvas with a rising sun in the same technique. A little quieter but the effect was the same. From a distance you could comprehend it, from close up it resulted in disorder.

"*Sunrise; an impression*, it's called."

"I would be happy to take one of these home," said Joseph.

"These are not for sale. For the time being they are too dear to me." He walked to the paintings that were placed against the wall. "These are for sale. Take your time."

Joseph studied a number of them and his eye fell on a landscape, a sun-drenched lane surrounded by fields of red flowers.

"That reminds me a bit of home. Galilee," he said to Moshe, who was sitting quietly on a chair and looking in amazement at the paintings, and especially at the welcoming man who had dedicated his life to them.

"What would be the price of this one?"

"Giving away prize." De Bellio mentioned the amount. Not unreasonable but still a lot, Joseph thought. He could find it. He felt an almost childlike desire to obtain something of beauty.

"Wait," said De Bellio. "If you are really interested, I have a few other acquisitions. From even more modern painters."

He preceded them to a next room, where paintings were displayed on easels.

"These might be for sale. With pain in my heart," he added, like a real merchant who praised his goods. He grabbed two paintings and put them next to each other in front of Joseph, well lit. Two landscapes. One of a field with trees, a random arrangement, it seemed. It was light and it was cheerful. The other presented a view down a road in a valley between some houses.

"What do you think?"

Joseph loved them both, but the second one charmed him the most. It was firmer, stronger. It was a small work, fifty centimeters by fifty, painted in pastel shades. But unlike the first painting, it seemed to be meticulously composed and constructed, without being obvious. This painting was based on an idea. The two paintings shared a technique; the painter had used large stripes and thick splotches of paint. And here too, both the image and the idea lost their meaning as soon as Joseph came closer.

"Cézanne. Paul Cézanne. One of the greatest geniuses in painting we will ever see, I predict," said De Bellio, full of adoration.

Moshe, who had not said anything until now, chipped in: "Papa, it's the road to Jerusalem!"

De Bellio and Joseph burst out in laughter. "That does it," said Joseph, who had already decided that he wanted this work at all costs. "If it is affordable."

Moshe now planted himself in front of the painting and said: "I also want us to have this one, papa."

"Easy, Moshe, we are in Europe here. You cannot just simply say those things."

"It was painted somewhere near Aix-en-Provence, his birthplace," said De Bellio.

But the boy was not easily redirected. "I really mean it. The road in the hills beyond Ramle."

Joseph smiled and stroked his son's head. He nodded at De Bellio but at the same time he had to acknowledge that Moshe had a point. Were these worlds then not so far apart after all?

"All right. We will call it "*A resting place on the way to Jerusalem*". Just among ourselves. I think the painter probably had different intentions."

They came to an agreement about the payment. A little later, when Joseph and Moshe were outside with the carefully wrapped package, he looked at his son with a grin. "Just for this it was worth coming to Paris."

"Where are we going to put it?"

"You know what," replied Joseph. "We will hang it over the chair where mama always sat."

(1881)

OVERTURE

On a morning in April, Max confided his future plans to Rivka. He wanted to discuss it with her before Joseph returned. His ideas needed a strategy, he said.

"I am getting old. I have long denied it, but there it is. This is not the place for me. I can do better work in Germany. Writing about this country, influencing people. My brother has asked me to help him collect funds and organize things. I have connections there. I could be useful still."

Rivka agreed.

"But, and it's a big but, Joseph will be devastated. So, when he returns I think I won't tell him right away. After a few weeks. When Moshe is in school again. He will be settled by then. That will be the time for the news. Do you agree?"

"You are probably right. It will be another blow. I am not happy that you are leaving either. I have gotten rather used to our witty conversations. Also, I don't believe that Europe is the place to be, with all the misery in Russia, now that the Tsar has been murdered."

"Yes, I know. They are blaming the Jews of course." Max tried to put optimism in his voice. "Maybe it will start a new exodus."

"I will stay, of course" Rivka said, "for better or for worse. Perhaps everything I went through was all for this purpose: To look after Joseph and Moshe. And be happy myself, of course," she added with a smile.

"You still have a lot of good work to do here," Max said. "You get along with all the groups, Jews, Christians, and Muslims. Even the Turks."

"Don't exaggerate."

On the last part of the journey home, some of Joseph's former energy returned. The thought that he had sailed here with Miriam in exactly the same way did not make him sad, but stronger. He wanted some kind of private vindication for everything. And especially on God. How could he advocate for the land when God himself left good people, who had sacrificed everything, in the lurch? Joseph would show

Him that he wouldn't be taken down. The only way to justify his return to the country that had caused him so much pain, was the conviction that it would be a success.

Moshe had given him immense delight over the course of the trip. He had seen Paris again through the eyes of a child and hoped that he could also rediscover *Eretz Israel* by imagining the world of his son.

On the quay Max and Rivka welcomed them. The reunion was cheerful.

"How are things over here," Joseph asked. "What about our settlers?"

Rivka shook her head. "It's all over. They are all gone. Except one, I hear. A man called Frumkin is refusing to give up and apparently still lives there. But there is no more agriculture. Some of the settlers moved to a village nearby so that they can keep an eye on things, but most of them went back to Jerusalem."

Joseph sighed. "What misery. I don't really have good news either. We can't expect anything at the moment."

He asked about Richard, but learned that he had taken a job at the English consulate in Cairo. An army function. He would try to visit soon.

"Who would have thought it? Richard in a British uniform. But that makes it even quieter here."

"By the way, I just had news that the cathedral in Cologne has been completed," said Max cheerfully. "I think you contributed to that as well."

A few weeks later a long-expected package arrived. One of the latest inventions – a typewriter. Joseph's first reaction was that it was too late. He hardly wrote anymore and he left the package unopened for a week. But then he got curious. He put the machine on his desk and examined it. Gradually he realized that this invention had come at exactly the right time. Just as his hand was failing, a solution offered itself. A new way.

There was a knock on the door. It was Max, who came in slowly. "I hardly dare to tell you, but I have decided to go back to Europe."

Joseph was devastated by the news. "Everyone is leaving." He made a grimace to hide his grief.

"Rivka is still here. And you have your son. Your place is here. I, however, am like a ball that is pushed under water. Somewhere else I bounce to the surface again."

Max explained what had brought him to the decision. "I am convinced that it is in the west that things have to happen. That is where the big changes are. You see improvements. Look at America. The slaves have gotten freedom and civil rights. Well, Lincoln was murdered and tens of thousands died, but suffering always accompanies change. It's the same here. In order to convince our people not to be in Europe, I need to go there. Ironic, isn't it? Do you remember that we once discussed this at the Rothschilds' estate?

"Yes, like only yesterday," said Joseph with a smile.

"As I said then, it was brilliant how I introduced you to everyone."

Joseph had to admit this.

"I remember talking about a country for our people," Max said. "And I remember that you were a little hesitant about that idea."

"I didn't understand then. Now I do."

"I do as well and of course I foresee huge problems."

For a while they sat silently, afraid to say goodbye.

Joseph broke the silence: "If you go back, maybe I should go back as well."

Max looked upset. "Why?"

"You have always been my mentor. You see things more clearly than I do. You have a more prophetic sense."

Max sadly shook his head. "I'm not a prophet. At best a third-rate Jeremiah. No, Joseph," he said with more strength. "You've managed without me all these years. Why should you suddenly follow me again?"

"Those were the years with Miriam. That was different. Now I am alone again. I am that loser of twenty years ago."

"You're certainly no loser." Max laughed. "Do you remember that we went to *Palais Grüneburg* and that you asked me how long it would take to walk there? In the old days, yes, then you were a bit of a strange chap. But now you have your future here. No matter how uncertain and vague it may be. As I said, I'm not a prophet, but things in the here and now I can discern pretty well. There is no place anymore for you in Germany. Who knows, maybe not even for me."

Joseph nodded. "You are right. I will stay here with Rivka and Moshe. My son can build a future."

"He is the future. I am the past. And I fear you will drift somewhere in between."

The boat had disappeared in the distance. Max had left and Joseph and Rivka assumed that they would never see him again. Joseph rubbed his eyes. These gloomy thoughts had to be dispelled. He looked at Moshe, realizing that he should not become a depressed model for his son. With a forced smile he said, "We have to be strong. Do you know what? Let's go to the beach. Breathe."

Moshe cheered up as if his father had pulled a magical switch.

Joseph turned to Rivka: "Will you come too?"

"No. I have work to do. I think the two of you should go."

"Moshe, what do you think, shall we first go to Mama's grave?"

"I..." said Moshe stammering, "I don't know." He looked guilty. "Maybe not? It makes me so sad. And she isn't there anyway."

Reaching the sea in the early afternoon, they went to Joseph's favorite part of the beach, the dune area just north of Yafo. He always came here when he wanted to breathe, to clear his head. Hardly anyone ever came here. No rocks interrupted the view of the endless water. The sea stretched continuously from north to south. They climbed the last dune and Moshe, who was ahead, shouted that he could see the sea. Now the whole panorama was in front of them. The sun stood high in the sky. For a moment, just for a second, no memories.

"Look, papa, the light on the water. It comes towards us."

Joseph nodded. "I am impressed, my boy. For more than one reason."

However, he himself looked more toward the northwest, where the emerald green of the water turned deep blue. Never before had he seen the sea so beautiful. Joseph had always looked at the brilliance of the light on the water, imagining that the light was there for him. But now, he saw the color, the beauty, that had always been there.

A little later, as they stood at the edge of the water, Joseph said, "I tried to write a book. 'See, this is my light' was the first sentence. But always something intervened. Or maybe I just didn't have it in me. I just couldn't do it. I think you should write it."

Moshe looked a bit shy. "All right, papa, I will write a book for you. With lots of pictures in it. About the land here."

While Joseph stared at the water, Moshe started to play in the sand. He placed a stick near a large hole he had dug, in the hope that the water would reach it. But the waves ran dead on each other, on counter currents.

"The water doesn't come to your pit," Joseph said.

"But it has been there," Moshe told him. "The sand is moist. It will come again. We will wait."

"It could take hours. But, all right, we can wait."

"Papa, can I say something?"

"Of course."

"Everything will be all right. It will be good to stay with Aunt Rivka."

Joseph hugged him. "Certainly. It's going to be fine."

"It is as if we were evicted from our old house before our new one was built."

"Very eloquent." He gave him a kiss. "Come, let's walk a little along the shore." The wind had gone down and it was pleasant in the sun.

As they strolled quietly, Joseph told his son about his dreams, his hopes, his ideals. His son would not understand every word he spoke, but he just wanted to have it said.

"It's not up to me," Joseph said. "Maybe not even to my generation. I am too limited. I can't see it. I might have meaning, but maybe I am just a lonely point in an otherwise empty universe. Without lines to the past or to the future. An anomaly. But I do not want to be a point. A point has no width, no length, no height, nothing at all. At least a line has direction. I am merely a stop on a long journey. You, Moshe, you will have more opportunities. You will be different. You grew up here. It's better. You will choose your own path."

Joseph told him he had made sure that the line of his parents and grandparents had taken a decisive turn, but that was all he could do. People were so limited. To live in the limitation of time. Only forward. But maybe in this lay a comforting salvation. Only be compelled to go further.

Joseph looked at Moshe splashing cheerfully through the water.

"Shall we go back to my hole?" Moshe asked.

As they walked back Joseph talked about freedom, about his journey to Cologne, about Europe, assimilation, then Palestine. Was it all an illusion?

"You know what your namesake says, 'I am a stranger in a strange land.' Here and there."

Moshe looked at him, as if he understood. "You are trying to bring your old things here. I don't think that's going to work."

Joseph thought about it and he nodded slowly. "Maybe you're right. You see it more clearly than I do. I'll tell you a nice story about the past." He told about how he walked into the canal in Venice when he visited a friend. "Up to my chin in the water," he exaggerated.

Moshe laughed. "Papa, you always have these crazy stories."

"I could try to walk into the water here, but it would be different." Joseph sighed deeply. "I have seen so many things pass by – nationalism, anarchism, socialism, romanticism. More than I could keep up with. And while there was something in each of them, as a whole they were all nothing. My motive was always personal, selfish if you like. Maybe I chose my own happiness too often, rather than the greater good. I haven't seen the greater good for a long time."

"I don't understand you all that well, papa."

"It doesn't matter, Moshe. That will come later." They walked a little further. "I showed you the trunk," Joseph continued. "I always carried that luggage with me. Not just literally. But I pass it on to you. You were born in Europe, whether you like it or not. And it has value, don't forget that. It's all a bit heavy." He laughed. "We are standing here on the coast of the Promised Land and I am still rambling on about old European art, however new it may be. But I can't help myself. I would like to go to London. I've never been to England. Perhaps I should have visited Nathan while we were in Europe. But it doesn't matter. I am here."

"I really don't understand what you are saying. What do you mean?"

"Mean? To give meaning to this life you need a lot of faith, because there is no meaning in reality or logic. Do you remember when we buried grandpa here in Yafo? What I said then? Maybe you can find comfort in the absurd idea that bones get flesh again and come to life. It is difficult to believe that. I know." He no longer knew whether he was talking to his son or to himself. "Do you remember the paintings we saw in Paris?" he asked. "And the painting that we hung over mama's chair? As in life, everything is fragmented into details that seem to have taken over everything. No one can interpret them, because we are in the middle of the picture. But as soon as you look from a distance, you see a beautiful image. I once stood in a painting. It was simple then. I played a role and that was it. I pretended to be a boy of your age. But you can't stand in a Monet painting. I can't see where I am now. What used to be here and what will be here in the future. Even here, on this beach."

Joseph looked around him. He saw the light everywhere. It had nothing to do with him. He pointed to the water. "Let's go into the water with blind confidence. A kind of ritual immersion. Let's start a new life. A second attempt."

Moshe heard his father talking, but he was saying strange things. The boy thought that he was behaving a bit oddly as well.

They took off their clothes.

"Papa, we have to be careful. This current is very strong. Rachid once told me that the water here is very treacherous."

His father smiled and walked into the water. Moshe waded towards him, thinking that they would be safer if they stayed together. Suddenly the sand seemed to be sucked away from under Joseph's feet. He felt it running away, as if there were a large hole, an hourglass, into which everything sank. Where the water a few seconds ago only had come up to his middle, it now came up to his chest. The current dragged him further from the shore. The beach was only a few meters away, so close and yet so far away.

"Papa come back."

"I can't swim," his father shouted. Moshe swam towards him with all his force. He knew he could save his father, would save him.

"I am coming, papa. Don't be afraid."

Moshe stretched out his hand and Joseph reached toward him. Their fingertips touched, their hands entwined, and they didn't let go.

Translation of Phrases

1. If I think of Germany in the night, I am jolted from my sleep.
2. In every generation, each person is obligated to consider themselves as if they personally had made the exodus from Egypt.
3. Behind the splendid view.
4. Calling up the sixth person for reading of the Torah.
5. I do not know what it means that I should feel so sad.
6. Forest solitude.
7. The combination of education and knowledge necessary to thrive in society.
8. Löwe is German for Lion.
9. Nimmer (never) + -lein, a fictional saint whose name day never comes. For example, when pigs fly.
10. Just wait, soon you will rest too.
11. A righteous person in a fur coat.
12. New is forbidden by the Torah.
13. Blessed be the one true Judge.

GLOSSARY

(Jewish terms used in Ephraim's Bones)

Acharonim – The leading rabbis and *poskim* (Jewish legal decisors) living from roughly the 16th century to the present, and more specifically since the writing of the *Shulchan Aruch*.

Akeida – The (almost) sacrifice of Isaac by Abraham.

Aliyah – Being called up to recite a blessing and / or read from a portion of the Torah.

Altglaubigen – German: Old believers – Orthodox Judaism

Amidah – Also called the *Shemoneh Esreh*, the central prayer of the Jewish liturgy. Observant Jews recite the Amidah at each of three prayer services in a typical weekday: morning, afternoon, and evening.

Aron HaKodesh – Often known as the ark, is the most important place inside all synagogues. The Aron Hakodesh is where the Torah scroll is kept.

Bar Mitzvah – The Jewish coming of age ritual for boys. When a Jewish boy turns 13 years old, he becomes obligated to observe the Torah mitzvot. (Jewish girls celebrate their Bat Mitzvah at age 12.)

Bima – An elevated platform in synagogues, it is used for Torah reading during services.

Bracha – A blessing or thanksgiving, recited in public or private, usually before the performance of a commandment, or the enjoyment of food or fragrance, and in praise on various occasions. The function of a bracha is to acknowledge God as the source of all blessings.

Brit Milah (covenant of circumcision) – A Jewish religious male circumcision ceremony.

Chanuka – Jewish festival commemorating the rededication of the Second Temple in Jerusalem at the time of the Maccabean Revolt against the Seleucid Empire. It is also known as the Festival of Lights. Chanuka is observed for eight nights and days, and may occur at any time from late November to late December.

Chassidim – A Jewish religious group. It arose as a spiritual revival movement in the territory of contemporary Western Ukraine during the 18th century, and spread rapidly throughout Eastern Europe. Israel Ben Eliezer, the "Baal Shem Tov", is regarded as its founding father.

Chevra Kadisha – An organization of Jewish men and women who see to it that the bodies of deceased Jews are prepared for burial according to Jewish tradition and are protected from desecration until burial. Two of the main requirements are the showing of proper respect for a corpse, and the ritual cleansing of the body and subsequent dressing for burial.

Eretz Israel – The Land of Israel is the traditional Jewish name for an area of indefinite geographical extension in what is now roughly modern day Israel.

Gan Eden – The Garden of Eden, also called Paradise, is the biblical "garden of God" described in the Book of Genesis and the Book of Ezekiel.

Gemara – The component of the Talmud comprising rabbinical analysis of and commentary on the Mishnah. After the Mishnah was published by Judah the Prince (c. 200 CE), the work was studied exhaustively by generation after generation of rabbis in Babylonia and the Land of Israel. Their discussions were written down in a series of books that became the Gemara, which when combined with the Mishnah constituted the Talmud.

Geonim – The presidents of the two great Babylonian Talmudic Academies. They were the generally accepted spiritual leaders of the Jewish community worldwide in the early medieval era.

Ghetto – A part of a city in which Jews were restricted to live and thus segregated from other peoples. The term was originally used for the Venetian Ghetto in Venice, Italy, as early as 1516.

Goyim – Goy is the standard Hebrew biblical term for a nation. Long before Roman times it had also acquired the meaning of someone who is not Jewish.

Ha Kadosh Baruch Hu – The Holy One, blessed be He, refers to God.

Haftara – The haftara is a publicly read portion selected from the books of Nevi'im (Prophets) in synagogue. This reading follows the Torah reading on each Sabbath and on Jewish festivals and fast days. Typically, the haftara is thematically linked to the weekly Torah portion that precedes it.

Hagaddah – The Jewish text that sets forth the order of the Pesach (Passover) Seder. Reading the Haggadah at the Seder table is a fulfillment of the mitzvah to each Jew to "tell your son" of the Jewish liberation from slavery in Egypt as described in the Book of Exodus in the Torah.

Halacha – The collective body of Jewish religious laws derived from the Written and Oral Torah. Halacha is based on biblical commandments (mitzvot), subsequent Talmudic and rabbinic law, and the customs and traditions compiled in the many books. Halacha is often translated as "Jewish Law", although a more literal translation might be "the way to behave" or "the way of walking".

Hallel – A Jewish prayer, a verbatim recitation from Psalms 113–118 which is recited by observant Jews on Jewish holidays as an act of praise and thanksgiving.

Hevel – The word Hevel in Hebrew has several meanings: One of them is breath. It is also the way to write and pronounce the name of Abel. However, in Kohelet (Ecclesiastes) it refers to vanity (Vanity of vanities; all is vanity).

Iyar – A spring month in the year on the Hebrew calendar. The name is Babylonian in origin. Iyar usually falls in April-June on the Gregorian calendar.

Kaddish – A hymn of praises to God in Jewish prayer services. The central theme of the Kaddish is the magnification and sanctification of God's name. The term "Kaddish" is often used to refer specifically to "The Mourner's Kaddish", said as part of the mourning rituals in Judaism. When mention is made of "saying Kaddish", this unambiguously refers to the rituals of mourning. Mourners say Kaddish to show that despite the loss, they still praise God.

Kiddush – Literally, "sanctification," kiddush is a blessing recited over wine or grape juice to sanctify the Shabbat and Jewish holidays. Reciting kiddush before the meal on the eve of Shabbat and Jewish holidays is a commandment from the Torah.

Kiddush Levanah – Kiddush Levanah is a Jewish ritual, performed outside at night, in which a series of prayers are recited to bless the new moon for the renewal of the month.

Kohelet – Ecclesiastes is one of 24 books of the Tanakh, where it is classified as one of the Writings (Ketuvim). In traditional Jewish texts, King Solomon is named as the author.

Kohen HaGadol (High Priest) – The title of the chief religious official of Judaism.

Lech Lecha – Literally "Go for you", this is the third weekly Torah portion (parashah) in the annual Jewish cycle of Torah reading. It tells the stories of God's calling of Abram to leave his native land and his father's house for a land that God would show him; to go into the land of Canaan.

Maariv – Also known as Arvit, is a Jewish prayer service held in the evening or night. It consists primarily of the evening Shema and Amidah.

Maror – The bitter herbs eaten at the Passover Seder, in keeping with the biblical commandment "with bitter herbs they shall eat it."

Mashiach ben Yosef / Mashiach ben David – Jewish tradition speaks of two redeemers, each one called Mashiach. Both are involved in ushering in the Messianic era. Mashiach ben David preceded by Mashiach ben Yosef.

The term mashiach, or "Messiah", refers specifically to a future Jewish king from the Davidic line, who is expected to save the Jewish nation, and will be anointed with holy anointing oil and rule the Jewish people during the Messianic Age.

Matzah – An unleavened flatbread that is part of Jewish cuisine and forms an integral element of the Passover festival, during which leavened bread (chametz) is forbidden. As the Torah recounts, God commanded the Jews to create this special unleavened bread.

Midrash – Midrash is biblical exegesis by ancient Judaic authorities, using a mode of interpretation prominent in the Talmud. The word itself means "textual interpretation" or "study".

Mikve – A bath used for the purpose of ritual immersion to achieve ritual purity.

Minyan – The quorum of ten Jewish adults required for certain religious obligations.

Mishna – The Mishnah is the first major written collection of the Jewish oral traditions known as the "Oral Torah". It is also the first major work of rabbinic literature. The Mishnah was redacted by Judah the Prince at the beginning of the third century CE.

Ne'ila – The concluding service, a special Jewish prayer service that is held only on Yom Kippur. It is the time when final prayers of repentance are recited at the closing of Yom Kippur.

Nisan – The first month of the ecclesiastical year in the Hebrew calendar. Passover (Pesach) falls on the 15th of Nisan.

Ostjuden – "Eastern Jews", in German, was the generic term for Yiddish speaking Jews from Eastern European countries that immigrated to Germany and Austria.

Parasha – The weekly Torah portion, a section of the Torah (Five Books of Moses) used in Jewish liturgy; to be read during Jewish prayer services on Saturdays, Mondays and Thursdays. There are 54 parashas and the full cycle is read over the course of one Jewish year, starting after Sukkot.

Pesach – Passover, a major Jewish holiday that occurs in the spring on the 15th day of the Hebrew month of Nisan. Pesach marks the Exodus of the Children of Israel from Egyptian slavery. To this day, the Passover ritual feast (seder) is one of the most widely observed rituals in Judaism.

Pirke Avot (Ethics of the Fathers) – A compilation of the ethical teachings and maxims from Rabbinic Jewish tradition. Avot is part of the Mishnah.

Psalms (Tehillim) – The Book of Psalms, commonly referred to simply as Psalms, the Psalter or "the Psalms", is a book of Tanach. The book is an anthology of 150 individual Hebrew religious hymns. They are used throughout traditional Jewish worship. The book is largely attributed to King David.

Responsa – Latin: plural of responsum, "answer" – a body of written decisions and rulings made by scholars in historic religious law, in response to questions addressed to them. The responsa literature covers a period of 1,700 years.

Rishonim – "The first ones" – The leading rabbis and *poskim* who lived approximately during the 11th to 15th centuries, in the era before the writing of the *Shulchan Aruch*. Famous Rishonim are Rashi, Rambam, Ramban, and Yehuda Halevi.

Rosh Chodesh – Literally "Head of the Month", this is the name for the first day of every month in the Hebrew calendar, marked by the birth of a new moon. It is considered a minor holiday.

Rosh Hashanah – Literally "Head of the Year", this is the Jewish New Year. Rosh Hashanah is a two-day celebration that begins on the first day of Tishrei. Rosh Hashanah customs include sounding the shofar.

Seder – Order. This a ritual feast that marks the beginning of the Jewish holiday of Pesach / Passover. The rituals and symbolic foods (matza and maror) evoke the twin themes of the evening: slavery and freedom. It is stated in the Hagaddah that *"B'chol dor vador chayav adam lirot et atzmo, kilu hu yatzah miMitzrayim* – In every generation everyone is obligated to see themselves as if they themselves came out of Egypt."

Selichot – Jewish penitential poems and prayers, especially those said in the period leading up to the High Holidays, and on fast days.

Shabbat – Judaism's day of rest on the seventh day of the week (Saturday). On this day, religious Jews remember the biblical story describing the creation of the heavens and the earth in six days. Since the Jewish religious calendar counts days from sunset to sunset, Shabbat begins in the evening of what on the secular calendar is Friday. Shabbat is ushered in by lighting candles and making Kiddush. Shabbat is a festive day when Jews exercise their freedom from the regular labors of everyday life.

Shabbat Chol Hamo'ed – A Sabbath that occurs during Chol HaMoed, the intermediate days of Passover and Sukkot.

Shacharit – The morning tefillah (prayer) of Judaism, one of the three daily prayers.

Shavuot – The Feast of Weeks, this is a Jewish holiday that occurs on the sixth day of the Hebrew month of Sivan (May/June). Shavuot marked the wheat harvest in the Land of Israel. In addition, Orthodox rabbinic traditions teach that the date also marks the revelation of the Torah to Moses and the Israelites at Mount Sinai.

Sh'ma (Shema) – Hebrew: "Hear", the Jewish confession of faith made up of three scriptural texts, which, together with appropriate prayers, forms an integral part of the evening and morning services. The name derives from the initial word of the scriptural verse "Hear, O Israel: The Lord our God is one Lord"

Shiva – The week-long mourning period in Judaism for first-degree relatives. The shiva period lasts for seven days following the burial. Following the initial period of despair and lamentation immediately after the death, shiva embraces a time when individuals discuss their loss and accept the comfort of others.

Shofar – Typically made of a ram's horn, it is used for Jewish religious purposes. The shofar is blown in synagogue services on Rosh Hashanah and at the end of Yom Kippur.

Shul – Yiddish: A term for synagogue, also meaning school.

Shulchan Aruch – The Shulchan Aruch, literally "Set Table", is the most widely consulted of the various legal codes in Judaism. It was authored in Safed (today in Israel) by Joseph Karo in 1563 and published in Venice two years later. Together with its commentaries, it is the most widely accepted compilation of Jewish law ever written.

Sukkah – A temporary hut constructed for use during the week-long Jewish festival of Sukkot. It is topped with branches and often well decorated with autumnal, harvest or Judaic themes. It is a symbolic wilderness shelter, commemorating the time God provided for the Israelites in the wilderness they inhabited after they were freed from slavery in Egypt. It is common for Jews to eat, sleep and otherwise spend time in the sukkah.

Sukkot – A Torah-commanded holiday celebrated for seven days from the 15th day of the month of Tishrei. It is one of the Three Pilgrimage Festivals (shalosh regalim) on which those Israelites who could, were commanded to make a pilgrimage to the Temple at Jerusalem.

Tallit – A fringed garment worn as a prayer shawl by religious Jews. The tallit has special twined and knotted fringes known as tzitzit attached to its four corners. In some communities, it is first worn from bar mitzvah. In many Ashkenazi communities, the large tallit is worn only from marriage, and in some communities, it is customarily presented to a groom before marriage as a wedding present.

Talmud – This refers to the collection of writings named specifically the Babylonian Talmud, although there is also an earlier collection known as the Jerusalem Talmud. The entire Talmud consists of 63 tractates. It contains the teachings and opinions of thousands of rabbis (dating from before the Common Era through to the fifth century) on a variety of subjects, including halakha, Jewish ethics, philosophy, customs, history, and folklore, and many other topics. The Talmud is the basis for all codes of Jewish law and is widely quoted in rabbinic literature.

Tanach – The Hebrew Bible or Tanach is the canonical collection of Hebrew scriptures. Tanakh is an acronym, made from the first Hebrew letter of each of the text's three traditional divisions: Torah, Nevi'im (Prophets), and Ketuvim (Writings).

Tefillin – Tefillin (sometimes called phylacteries) are a set of small black leather boxes with leather straps containing scrolls of parchment inscribed with verses from the Torah. Tefillin are worn by adult Jews during weekday morning prayers. The arm-tefillah is placed on the upper arm, and the strap wrapped around the forelimb, hand and middle finger; while the head-tefillah is placed between the eyes at the boundary of the forehead and hair.

Ten Commandments – In Hebrew: *Aseret ha'Dibrot*, these are a set of principles relating to ethics and worship that play a fundamental role in Judaism. The text of the Ten Commandments appears twice in the Hebrew Bible: at Exodus 20:2–17 and Deuteronomy 5:6–21. According to the book of Exodus in the Torah, the Ten Commandments were revealed to Moses at Mount Sinai and inscribed by the finger of God on two tablets of stone kept in the Ark of the Covenant.

Torah – The first five books of the Hebrew Bible, namely the books of Bereshit (Genesis), Shemot (Exodus), Vayikra (Leviticus), Bamidbar (Numbers) and Devarim (Deuteronomy). Torah means the same as the Five Books of Moses. If meant for liturgical purposes, it takes the form of a Torah scroll (Sefer Torah). If in bound book form, it is called Chumash. Reading the Torah publicly is one of the bases of Jewish communal life.

Tosafot – These are the medieval commentaries on the Talmud. They take the form of critical and explanatory glosses, printed in almost all Talmud editions on the outer margin and opposite Rashi's notes.

T'shuva – Repentance (Hebrew, literally "return") is one element of atoning for sin in Judaism. Judaism recognizes that everybody sins on occasion, but that people can stop or minimize those occasions in the future by repenting for past transgressions.

Tzedakah – A Hebrew word meaning "righteousness", but commonly used to signify charity. This concept of "charity" differs from the modern Western understanding of "charity." The latter is typically understood as a spontaneous act of goodwill and a marker of generosity; tzedakah is an ethical obligation.

Tzitzit – specially knotted ritual fringes, or tassels, worn in antiquity by Israelites and today by observant Jews. Tzitzit are usually attached to the four corners of the tallit. Wearing tzitzit reminds a daily practitioner to bring God's love into action by practicing all other mitzvot. Tzitzit are mentioned in the Torah and that part is included in daily prayer as the final paragraph of the Shema.

Yarmulke – Yiddish, the skullcap worn in public by Orthodox Jewish men or during prayer by other Jewish men. Also called "kipa" in Hebrew.

Yom Kippur – Day of Atonement, the holiest day of the year in Judaism. Its central themes are atonement and repentance. Jews traditionally observe this holy day with a day-long fast, confession, and intensive prayer, often spending most of the day in synagogue services. The High Holy Days comprise both Rosh Hashanah and Yom Kippur.

Historical People

(Mentioned or acting in Ephraim's Bones)

Abarbanel, Isaac ben Judah (1437-1508) – Portuguese Jewish statesman and Bible commentator.

Adams, George J. (1811-1880) – Leader of a schismatic Latter Day Saint sect who led an ill-fated effort to establish a colony of Americans near Yafo in Palestine.

Amzalek, Chaim (1828-1916) – Sephardi entrepreneur and British vice-consul for Palestine in Yafo.

de Bellio, Georges (1828-1894) – Art collector and homeopathic doctor in Paris, born in Bucharest. Specialized in Impressionism.

Boerne, Ludwig (1786-1837) – Born Loeb Baruch at Frankfurt am Main, was a German-Jewish political writer and satirist, who converted to Lutheran Protestantism.

Cremieux, Adolphe (1796-1880) – French Jewish lawyer and politician who served as Minister of Justice. He was a staunch defender of the rights of the Jews of France.

Dickson, Walter / Frederick Grossteinbeck – Their families moved to Palestine and lived in the American colony. In 1858 they were brutally attacked and murdered. The women of the family were raped.

Disraeli, Benjamin (1804-1881) – British politician of Jewish birth for the Conservative Party who twice served as Prime Minister of the United Kingdom.

Elisha ben Abuyah, Rabbi (1st century CE) – Rabbi and religious authority. After he adopted a heretical worldview, the rabbis of the Talmud referred to him as the Other One, Acher.

Eliezer ben Hyrcanus, Rabbi – One of the most prominent Sages (Tannaim) of the 1st and 2nd centuries in Judea.

Ezra (80-440 BCE) – Also called Ezra the Scribe. He returned from Babylonian exile and reintroduced the Torah in Jerusalem

Flaubert, Gustave (1821-1880) – French novelist. Leading exponent of literary realism. He is known especially for his debut novel Madame Bovary.

Frumkin, Israel Dov (1850-1914) – Pioneer of Hebrew journalism, author, and builder of Jerusalem. Born in the Russian Empire. He edited the Hebrew newspaper Havatzelet.

Gaon of Vilna (1720-1797) – Elijah ben Solomon Zalman, or by his Hebrew acronym HaGra, was a Talmudist, halakhist, kabbalist, and the foremost leader of misnagdic (non-hasidic) Jewry. He became one of the most familiar and influential figures in rabbinic study since the Middle Ages.

Geiger, Abraham (1810-1874) – German rabbi and scholar, considered the founding father of Reform Judaism.

Gutman, David Meir (1827-1894) – Participated in the acquisition of land to establish Petach Tikva in the Yarkon Plain, and went out with his wife among the first to settle the area.

Heine, Heinrich (1797-1856) – German poet, writer and literary critic of Jewish descent who converted to Christianity. His radical political views led to many of his works being banned by German authorities. He spent the last 25 years of his life as an expatriate in Paris.

Hess, Moses (1812-1875) – German-Jewish philosopher and proto-zionist. He published Rome and Jerusalem with the idea of Jewish national revival in 1862.

Hirsch, Rabbi Samson Raphael (1808-1888) – German Orthodox rabbi best known as the intellectual founder of the Torah im Derech Eretz school of contemporary Orthodox Judaism. From 1851 until his death, Hirsch led an Orthodox community in Frankfurt am Main.

Hoffmann, Christoph (1815-1885) – Leader of an independent Christian religious organization, known as the Templers. From 1868 the Templers started to create settlements in Palestine, first in Haifa, and later, in 1871, a colony in Sarona, near Yafo.

Kahn, Zadoc (1839-1905) – French rabbi, chief rabbi of Paris and later chief rabbi of France. Much of his time he gave to the work of the Alliance Israélite Universelle.

Lewald, Fanny (1811-1889) – German Jewish author. In 1843 she published the novel *Jenny*, which has been important for the emancipation of both women and Jews in Europe.

Manin, Daniele (1804-1857) – Italian patriot, statesman and leader of the Risorgimento in Venice.

Marx, Karl (1818-1883) – German economist, political theorist and socialist revolutionary. He became the most influential theorist of socialism and communism.

Meir, Rabbi – Jewish sage who lived in the time of the Mishna. He was considered one of the greatest of the Tannaim of the fourth generation; first a disciple of Elisha ben Abuyah and later of Rabbi Akiva.

Meiri, Rabbi (1249-1306) – Menachem ben Solomon Meiri was a famous Catalan rabbi and Talmudist.

Montefiore, Moses (1784-1885) – British banker and philanthropist from Italian-Jewish origin, he founded Mishkenot Sha'ananim in 1860, the first Jewish settlement outside Jerusalem. He visited Palestine seven times.

Mortara, Edgardo (1851-1940) – As six-year-old Jewish boy taken away from his parents in Bologna, and raised as a Catholic in Rome under the protection of the pope. He eventually became a priest.

Napoleon III (1808-1873) – The nephew of Napoleon I, he was the first President of France from 1848 to 1852, and the last French emperor from 1852 to 1870.

Netter, Charles (1826-1882) – Founding member of the Alliance Israélite Universelle. In 1870, Netter founded Mikve Israel, the first modern Jewish agricultural settlement in the Land of Israel.

Oppenheim, Moritz (1800-1882) – German painter, regarded as the first Jewish painter of the modern era. His work was informed by his cultural and religious roots.

Pius IX, Pope (1792-1878) – Pope from 1846 to his death. His 1864 Syllabus of Errors is a strong condemnation against liberalism and modernism. In his time the Papal States came to an end. He refused to recognize the new kingdom, Italy.

Pines, Yechiel Michael (1824-1913) – Russian-born religious Zionist rabbi, writer, and community leader. He received both a religious and secular Jewish education. He was elected to lead Mazkereth Moshe, a charitable institution. In 1878 he settled in Jerusalem.

Raab, Yehuda (1858-1948) – In 1875 eighteen-year-old Yehuda Raab and his family moved to Jerusalem from Hungary. One of the founders of Petach Tikva.

Rambam (1138-1204) – Moses ben Maimon, commonly known as Maimonides, was a medieval Sephardic Jewish philosopher one of the most prolific and influential Torah scholars of the Middle Ages.

Ramban (1194-1270) – Nachmanides or Moses ben Nahman was a leading Sephardic rabbi, philosopher and biblical commentator. Also an important figure in the re-establishment of the Jewish community in Jerusalem following its destruction by the Crusaders in 1099.

Rashi (1040-1105) – Shlomo Yitzchaki was a medieval French rabbi and author of a comprehensive commentary on the Talmud and the Tanakh. Rashi's commentary is the essential companion for any study of the Bible at any level.

Riesser, Gabriel (1806-1863) – German politician and lawyer. He became a leading advocate of Jewish emancipation.

de Rothschild, James Mayer (1792-1868) – German-French banker and the founder of the French branch of the Rothschild family; born in Frankfurt-am-Main. He amassed a fortune that made him one of the richest men in the world.

de Rothschild, Edmond (1845-1934) – Son of James Mayer; French member of the Rothschild banking family. A strong supporter of Zionism, his large donations lent significant support to the movement during its early years.

Rothschild, Mayer Amschel (1744-1812) – German Jewish banker and the founder of the Rothschild banking dynasty. Born in the Judengasse of Frankfurt am Main. His descendants furthered the family fortune across Europe.

Salomon, Yoel Moshe (1838-1913) – Religious Jewish pioneer. He bought a plot of land outside the walls of Jerusalem with six of his friends and built the neighborhood Nachalat Shiv'a. In 1878 he was one of the founders of Petach Tikva.

Schopenhauer, Arthur (1788-1860) – German philosopher. Best known for his work The World as Will and Representation, in which he characterizes the phenomenal world as the product of a blind and malignant metaphysical will. From 1831 he lived in Frankfurt am Main.

Shabtai Zvi (1626-1676) – Sephardic ordained rabbi from Smyrna. He was active throughout the Ottoman Empire; he claimed to be the long-awaited Jewish Messiah.

Shimon bar Yochai – Also known by his acronym Rashbi, he was a sage in ancient Judea, after the destruction of the Second Temple in 70 CE. According to the Talmud, Shimon and his son hid for twelve years in a cavern.

Smolenskin, Peretz (1842-1885) – Russian-born Zionist and Hebrew writer. He founded HaShachar (The Dawn), a literary platform for the Haskalah movement and early Jewish nationalism.

Stampfer, Yehoshua (1852-1908) – Zionist and one of the founders of Petach Tikva. He was a member of its first municipal council. When he was 17, he immigrated to the Land of Israel. With other pioneers he established new Jewish neighborhoods outside the Old City of Jerusalem.

Wagner, Richard (1813-1883) – German composer. His operas like Tristan und Isolde greatly influenced the development of classical music. His controversial writings express anti-Semitic sentiments.

Warren, Charles (1840-1927) – one of the earliest European archaeologists of the Biblical Holy Land, and particularly of the Temple Mount.

Yehuda HaLevi (1075 or 1086-1141) – Spanish Jewish physician, poet and philosopher. His greatest philosophical work was the Kuzari. He died shortly after arriving in the Holy Land.

Yellin, Yehoshua (1843-1924) – One of the founders of the Nachalat Shiv'a neighborhood in Jerusalem. On the outskirts of Jerusalem, at Motza, on land purchased from the Arabs of Qalunya in 1860, he built a khan (inn).

Zunz, Leopold (1794-1886) – Founder of academic Judaic Studies (Wissenschaft des Judentums). His investigations and contemporary writings had an important influence on contemporary Judaism.

ABOUT THE AUTHOR

David de Wolf was born in the Netherlands and studied Dutch Language and the History of Art at the University of Nijmegen. He graduated with a Master of Arts on the architecture of the Italian Renaissance. Since then he has worked as journalist, a tour guide in Italy, and, since 1995, as an independent communications manager. In 2011, he moved to Israel. He now lives with his family in Tel Mond, about 20 kilometers north of Tel Aviv. In 2013, he published his first literary novel *Solace of Stone*.

Made in the USA
Middletown, DE
18 May 2022

65868605R00248